dark heart of thuggery and murder. Finally, someone has taken on Saylor and Davis and brought us out of Rome at last!'

Robert Low, author of the Oathsworn series

'Alvey has combined the best features of a crime novel and a work of historical fiction. The result is **a pacy, exciting and intelligent story set in a rich world**. The plot is clever and solidly rooted in history, the characters vivid, sympathetic and lifelike and **the world of Athens is gloriously recreated**. Best of all, **while *Shadows of Athens* is taut and historically detailed, it also displays a quirky sense of humour** – [I] loved it'

Simon Turney, author of *Caligula*

'**Historical crime writing that virtually reinvents the genre**. Ancient Athens is recreated with a **masterly** touch, while the beleaguered Philocles is the perfect protagonist to lead us through this **vividly evoked** menacing world'

Barry Forshaw, *Financial Times* crime critic

'The historical detail is excellent, and the story and characters expertly spun out – a **very entertaining** and satisfying read'

Glyn Iliffe, author of The Adventures of Odysseus series

'There is a new star in the classical firmament. Philocles is engaging, inspiring and feels absolutely real. This is **historical writing at its best and crime writing worthy of prizes**. Riveting'

Manda Scott, author of the Boudica series

'If **you like C J Sansom's Tudor sleuth Matthew Shardlake, you'll love this** – a gripping murder mystery set in a fantastically fully-realised ancient Athens, which **will keep you guessing to the very end'**

James Wilde, author of *Pendragon*

'Intriguing . . . a **refreshingly different** setting portrayed with a convincing air of authenticity. **I hope it's the first of many'**

Andrew Taylor, author of *Ashes of London*

'**It's about time** someone did for ancient Athens what Lindsey Davis' Falco novels do for Ancient Rome. **Alvey sets the scene perfectly**, with easy brushstrokes and lightly worn learning. In Philocles we have an aspiring playwright, man of the people and reluctant detective. **I look forward to his next case . . .'**

Jack Grimwood, author of *Moskva*

'Historical sleuthing finally gets its grown-up colours. The book's got wit and knowledge and the amazing knack of immersing the reader in ancient Greece and the whole theatrical scene there. It shows a thorough understanding of time and place, and has **a**

Shadows
of Athens

JM Alvey

ORION

First published in Great Britain in 2019
by Orion Books,
an imprint of The Orion Publishing Group Ltd
Carmelite House, 50 Victoria Embankment
London EC4Y 0DZ

An Hachette UK Company

1 3 5 7 9 10 8 6 4 2

Copyright © JM Alvey 2019
Map copyright © Hemesh Alles 2019

The moral right of JM Alvey to be identified as
the author of this work has been asserted in accordance
with the Copyright, Designs and Patents Act of 1988.

A CIP catalogue record for this book is
available from the British Library.

ISBN (Mass Market Paperback) 978 1 4091 8063 0
ISBN (eBook) 978 1 4091 8064 7

Typeset by Input Data Services Ltd, Somerset

Printed and bound by CPI Group (UK) Ltd, Croydon, CR0 4YY

MIX
Paper from
responsible sources
FSC® C104740

www.orionbooks.co.uk

With gratitude

Maureen Hall

Doreen Innes
Barbara Levick
Kathy Wilkes

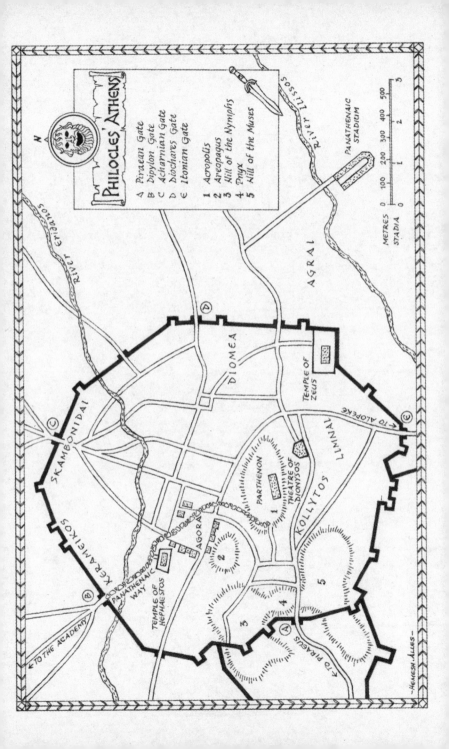

PHILOCLES' ATHENS

A Piraean Gate
B Dipylon Gate
C Acharnian Gate
D Diochares Gate
E Itonian Gate

1 Acropolis
2 Areopagus
3 Hill of the Nymphs
4 Pnyx
5 Hill of the Muses

N

METRES 0   100   200   300   400   500
STADIA 0   1   2   3

River Eridanos

KERAMEIKOS

SKAMBONIDAI

DIOMEA

Temple of Hephaestos

Panathenaic Way

AGORA

PARTHENON

THEATRE OF DIONYSOS

KOLLYTOS

LIMNAI

Temple of Zeus

River Ilissos

AGRAI

PANATHENAIC STADIUM

←TO THE ACADEMY

→TO PIRAEUS

←TO ALOPEKE

—HEMESH ALLES—

Chapter One

No one wants to find a corpse on the doorstep. Not on a
fine spring evening after walking home with the woman
you love. Not when your thoughts are wholly taken up
with the unparalleled honour and bowel-knotting terror
of seeing the play that you've written performed at the
greatest drama festival in the civilised world. Not when
you know that everyone who's anyone of influence in
Athens will see if the jokes you've spent days and months
crafting will make fourteen thousand people laugh.

Everyone else in the city was cheerfully preparing for
five days freed from work, ready to enjoy the spectacles
of the Dionysia processions and the drama competitions
at the theatre. There'd be feasting with family and friends
who'd travelled into Athens for the holiday, catching up
with all the news and gossip from every one-donkey
village in Attica. The streets were full of people hurrying
to and fro, with doors and gates opening and closing.

Today's rehearsal had gone well enough, thanks be to
Apollo. As we walked through the city's central market
place and took the road leading southwards, I drew
Zosime close within the shelter of my cloak, my arm
around her shoulders. Spring's equinox means the days

will soon be getting longer, but the evenings can still turn chilly.

Every household's high outer windows were bright with lamps. Excited voices floated through open shutters along with savoury scents that made my stomach rumble. I could picture the scenes within. Children would be scampering about and wheedling to stay up just a little longer, to greet Grandma and Grandpa from Prasiai or wherever. Slaves would be setting up bed frames and mattresses while wives put the final touches to some tempting meal. Newly arrived travellers would be eager to wash off their journey's dust, easing weary feet and backs. Here and there, torches on doorposts defied the twilight to welcome overdue guests.

Reaching the city walls, we waited our turn to leave through the Itonian Gate and take the road to Alopeke. Zosime and I walked more quickly now, both of us alert. It wouldn't just be honoured visitors from allied cities and country bumpkins from Attica's farms coming into the city for the festival. Cutpurses, cloak-snatchers and housebreakers would be idling in every alley and street corner within sight of the Acropolis for the next five or six days.

Hopefully that's where they would stay. Still, there was always the chance of one such scoundrel roaming further afield to prey on incautious citizens who thought these outlying districts on the edge of the countryside would be safe enough. More fool them. Three hundred Spartans may have held Thermopylae against the Persians but the best the Archons' three hundred Scythian slaves can hope for is keeping some measure of order within the city walls. Outside, we're on our own.

The further we got from the city proper, the more deserted the road became. It was full dark now. A few lamps glowed but it seemed that pretty much everyone had gone to bed early.

We reached the turn from the main road into our side street without incident. I breathed a prayer of thanks as we passed the pillar sacred to Hermes on the corner. Brushing a hand over his carved head, I felt the familiar stone worn smooth by years of others doing the same.

We passed our neighbours' homes, each one safe behind a high wall and the sturdy gate that protected the house and yard within. Some were two-storey dwellings though most were not in this district of modest households.

The lane was dark and silent but I wasn't overly concerned. The pattern of ruts and hollows was so familiar we barely had to think where to set our feet.

That made the shock of stumbling over a body a hundred times worse. A man was slumped against our gate, where the timber post met the solid brick wall. I fell headlong across his outstretched legs, sprawling on the trodden earth. Zosime yelped as I dragged her down with me.

'Shit!' I swore as she landed on top of me, her elbow digging deep into my gut.

'What—?' She scrambled to her feet.

I would have done the same but my shoes were tangled in cloth. Kicking out, my foot hit solid, senseless flesh. I was outraged. How dare some drunk sleep off his skinful

3

here? But as I kicked again, whoever it was didn't stir. There was no wine-sodden grunt of protest.

'Get Kadous, and a lamp.' On hands and knees, I groped through the darkness. I touched an ominously cool, clammy hand. Hoping against hope, I squeezed limp fingers, brutally hard. There was no response. As I was forced to admit that this man truly was dead, the body slid away from me, slumping to lie awkwardly twisted, face down on the ground.

Zosime was knocking on our gate, more puzzled than concerned and keeping her voice low out of consideration for the neighbours. 'Kadous? Hurry up! There's someone hurt—'

'Bring a light out here now!' I yelled.

'What's going on?' Kadous hauled the gate open as I got to my feet. The lamp my slave held cast a flickering golden glow. He didn't bother asking if the man was dead. Anyone who's been on a battlefield recognises that awful stillness when life has fled.

'Oh!' Zosime clapped a hand to her mouth, horrified.

Kadous took a step closer. The lamplight fell on the dead man's feet. He wore Persian shoes, so new that the nails in the soles were hardly scuffed, and with no more than a day's dust dulling expensive red leather.

'Who is he?' Kadous raised the lamp higher to reveal the rest of the corpse. 'How did he die?'

'Let's see his face,' I ordered.

Kadous stooped and pulled the man's shoulder, rolling him onto his back.

'Hades!' We both recoiled.

The dead man's throat was cut from ear to ear. A blade had ripped through his neck so deeply that pale bone glinted in the ferocious wound. His tunic was sodden with blood as far down as his belt. I forced myself to look at his face instead. No, I didn't know him. That wasn't much of a relief.

I looked up at Kadous. 'Did anyone come knocking earlier?'

'I didn't hear a thing.' The Phrygian shook his head, baffled. 'I've been reading in my room. But I wouldn't have opened up to a stranger, not after dark.'

I stared at the corpse. 'We must notify the Polemarch.' He was the magistrate responsible for visitors to the city.

'At this hour?' Kadous wasn't challenging me but he wanted to be sure that he understood my instruction. I took his point. We wouldn't find anyone manning the magistrate's office this late in the day.

'We can't leave the poor man in the lane like some stray dog crushed by a cart!' Zosime's shock veered into anger.

'I'm not bringing him inside our yard.' I was just as adamant. I wasn't having our little household tainted by this poor bastard's death, whoever he might be.

I looked at the corpse again. If the Fates insisted on cutting his life short, why couldn't some punch in a tavern brawl have killed him? I cleared my throat and forced myself to speak more calmly. 'Someone at the city prison will know what to do.'

That's where the Scythians would be taking anyone

they arrested during the festival, and I'd wager they would already be busy tonight.

Kadous handed the lamp to Zosime. 'I'll get my cloak and boots.'

'No.' I shook my head. 'It'll be better for everyone if a citizen reports this.' Unexpected corpses prompt serious questions. 'Go inside. Bolt the gate.'

Zosime looked at me, shaken. 'And make believe nothing has happened?'

Careful of the lamp she was holding, I drew her close and gave her a quick kiss. 'This has nothing to do with us.'

I looked up and down the lane again. I couldn't be certain that all our neighbours were home. If Sosistratos from four doors down stumbled across a dead man on his way back from his favourite drinking den, no one would have to notify the Polemarch. Citizens on the far side of the Acropolis would hear the uproar.

'Kadous, you keep watch out here until I bring the Scythians. We don't want anyone else tripping over him.'

The Phrygian nodded and I offered him a reassuring smile as Zosime closed the gate behind her. 'I'll be as quick as I can.'

Heading back to the city, I did my best not to curse the murdered man. He hardly deserved any more misfortune, but why did he have to die on my doorstep, tonight of all nights? I shivered in the night breeze and wrapped my cloak more tightly around myself. Had I offended some god or goddess? I honestly couldn't imagine how or who.

Perhaps these villains, whoever they were, had come

creeping down the lane intending to attack someone else. Only they had unexpectedly encountered this stranger in the darkness and all but cut off his head in their panic. Then the killers had fled into the night.

But who might have such murderous enemies? Mikos who lives opposite is a bore and a bully, beating his wife and her slave girl both, but bead selling's hardly a cut-throat business. Sosistratos and his sons can be noisy neighbours, but only at festival time and no one's going to spill blood over that. Besides, none of that would explain who the stranger was and what he was doing so far off the beaten track.

As I was waved back through the Itonian Gate, I got a grip on myself. It had been a long day with too little food and my imagination was running riot. I forbade myself any more pointless speculation and made my way as quickly as possible to the heart of the city.

There were still a fair few people in the agora, mostly gathered around the altar of the twelve gods. Honouring the deities with sloshed libations, they passed around quart jugs of wine and drank deep. I cut across the southern edge of the market place before turning down the road leading to the city's prison. To my inexpressible relief, a lamp burned beside the door. As I rapped my knuckles on the bronze-studded wood, a wave of exhaustion swept over me. I leaned my forehead against the cold stone wall and closed my eyes.

The door opened a crack. 'Yes?' a voice prompted.

I forced myself upright. 'I've come to report a dead body outside my house.'

7

'Do you know who it is?' The door opened a little more to show me a sharp-faced Hellene with an Athenian accent.

'No idea.'

'Is he really dead?' The public slave cocked his head, impatient. 'Or just dead drunk?'

'He really is dead,' I said curtly. 'His throat's been slashed open. Someone needs to come and take him away. I don't want to spend the festival stepping over a corpse to get in and out of my house. You'll need to notify the Polemarch in the morning.'

'All right,' the sharp-faced man said mildly. 'Kallinos!'

As he turned to call out to a colleague, I got a clearer view inside. Lamps in high niches lit an anteroom where a handful of men in plain, undyed tunics were playing dice around a table. Scythians in linen and leather body armour lounged on benches that lined the corridor flanked by the prison's cells. There were nowhere near three hundred of them, but still more than enough to give anyone fighting in the streets pause for thought.

Four were rising to their feet and reaching for their bows. They already had short swords sheathed at their sides. A fifth man was stretched out on the floor, his head pillowed on a rolled-up cloak, snoring softly. I didn't hold that against him. I'd learned to snatch sleep whenever I could during my own military training.

The tallest Scythian rolled his head from side to side to ease some stiffness in his neck. He kicked the sleeper's booted foot. 'Come on, Dados. Let's see what's what.'

'He must be a visitor to the city, the dead man,' I

explained as the sleeping Scythian got up and joined the rest of us at the door. He was still yawning and knuckling his eyes as one of his colleagues passed him a freshly lit torch.

'Never mind that now.' The tall man was already scanning the agora for potential trouble as the prison door closed behind us. At his shoulder, the man who'd been sleeping was more alert than I'd have expected. The other three were equally vigilant. I knew the Scythians weren't overly popular. I only hoped that no one tried settling some grudge tonight.

Kallinos, the tall one in command, shot me a sideways look. 'Where to?'

'Alopeke.' I could play laconic just as well as he could.

He nodded and lengthened his stride. Dados fell into step a few paces behind, carrying the torch. The others followed, matching their leader's rhythm. Out of habit, I did the same. Once trained to defend the city, an Athenian's a hoplite for life. And that was the sum total of our conversation until we turned in to the lane where I lived.

'Your house?' Kallinos gestured to the gateway where Kadous stood vigil with his lamp.

'That's it,' I confirmed.

'Your household?'

'Myself, my companion and one slave.' I hurried past the Scythians. 'Any trouble while I've been gone?'

Kadous shook his head. The Scythian gave my slave a searching look.

'You're sure this isn't your handiwork?'

'On my oath to any god you want.' Kadous spread his

9

hands, raising the lamp. We could all see there wasn't a drop of blood on him.

'Step back and let's see what we've got then.' Kallinos squatted down next to the body as Kadous retreated. Dados and another Scythian held their torches high to offer as much light as possible.

Kallinos said something to his men in their own tongue before looking at me with callous good humour. 'You're right. This unlucky fucker really is dead. Now, are you absolutely sure you don't know him?'

I studied the stranger's face once again. I guessed he was at least a handful of years older than my eldest brother though not as old as my father would have been had he lived, for all the silver frosting his beard. Whoever he was, he was used to hard work. His face was tanned dark from years in the fields and even in the slackness of death a lifetime of squinting in bright sun had scored deep lines between his bushy brows, and between his beak of a nose and his mouth.

'Quite certain.' I shook my head slowly. 'He must be a visitor—'

Kallinos silenced me with an upraised hand. 'Save it for the Polemarch, citizen. He'll send word when he wants to speak to you. After the festival, I'd say. Meantime, don't worry too much. This was a robbery, most likely.'

The Scythians like quick and easy answers.

'Then why didn't they steal his shoes? Persian shoes, and expensive ones at that.' I'd got a better look at his footwear in the bright torchlight. That was some truly fancy workmanship; deep-dyed red leather laced high up

10

his shins and tooled in swirling patterns.

'See his tunic?' Zosime stepped out from the shadows, opening our gate just wide enough to slip through. 'That brocaded panel down the front?'

We all looked at the stylised pattern of leaves below the disfiguring bloodstain.

'That's an Ionian style,' Zosime said firmly.

Her Cretan accent presumably convinced Kallinos that she would know, as well as explaining her readiness to speak to a stranger, unlike an Athenian girl.

He nodded. 'So he's a visitor who won't be going home.'

He said something else in Scythian to the others who'd still not spoken a word. One handed Kallinos his torch. He stooped and slid his hands beneath the dead man's shoulders to get a firm hold. Another took his feet.

As they lifted him up, the dead man's head lolled forward, hiding the ghastly wound. He might have been asleep, or senseless through drink. Those dark stains on his festival clothing could be spilled wine instead of blood.

'Do you collect so many dead bodies that this is all in a night's work?' I asked Kallinos bleakly.

'They're not so common, thank Hades.' He spared me an unreadable glance. 'Answers are rarer. Leave this sorry bastard to the gods of the dead, and thank Zeus that you and yours are all safe.'

He nodded to Dados and the sad little procession went on its way. I stood watching until the torches rounded the Hermes pillar and they disappeared into the night. Darkness rushed back with a vengeance, scarcely held at bay by the little lamp Kadous had left by the gatepost. I hadn't even noticed the Phrygian withdraw.

'Are you hungry?' Zosime bent down to retrieve the lamp. 'Kadous is cooking supper.'

In one breath I realised I was famished, and in the next that my throat was drier than a sun-baked hillside. Then I smelled herbs hitting hot oil and saliva flooded my mouth. I followed Zosime inside and bolted the gate. I wanted to shut everyone and everything out of our small courtyard tonight.

Kadous was frying sardines in a skillet over the cooking brazier, in the light of a lamp on the high windowsill behind him. 'Nearly ready.'

'Where did you get some charcoal?' I remembered him saying we had run out, only that morning. It seemed like half a year ago.

'Mikos's Alke gave me some. I fetched her water from the fountain by way of a trade.'

That prompted me to fetch a jug of water from our own big storage jar, along with a basin and a sponge. Stripping, I washed my arms and hands as thoroughly as I could before searching my tunic for stains. Once I was satisfied there was no trace of the dead man's blood soiling me or my clothing, I pulled my tunic back on.

Zosime was pouring watered wine from a mixing jug into three cups. Her hand was shaking. 'Who do we pray to tonight?'

'Erectheus.' Turning towards the distant Acropolis, I raised the wine to the earth-born god who shares that sanctuary with holy Athena. I silently commended the murdered Ionian to the mysteries that await the dead. Anger kindled beneath my breastbone. This was hardly the open-handed welcome that visiting Hellenes should expect from our city. Whoever had done this had insulted every Athenian, as well as Dionysos's sacred festival.

Zosime and Kadous echoed my prayer to the gods and we ate our belated dinner. The sardines were tasty, the barley bread was soft and the spring salad leaves were crisp and refreshing. Zosime had chosen a fragrant amber wine from my small stock of amphorae in our unused dining room. On any other night, it would have been a wonderful meal.

We ate sitting on stools around the brazier, glad of its warmth. As Kadous rose and cleared away our plates and cups, I stretched out a hand to Zosime. She laced her fingers through mine, looking mournful. 'That poor man. His poor family.'

I shook my head. 'Don't dwell on it. Didn't you hear the Scythians? They said it was most likely a robbery. Nothing to do with us.'

Zosime pulled her hand away. 'You don't believe that any more than I do.'

I sighed. 'No, but I don't know what else to think.'

Dumping our scraps into a bucket, Kadous paused. 'We never thought to check if he still had a purse.'

'I'd wager we'd have found one,' I said grimly. 'That wasn't a robbery. Any thief worth the name would have taken those shoes, even if his clothes were too bloody to steal.'

Not so long ago, my brother had mentioned a

neighbour's son who'd been robbed and left naked in some local alley. Such victims are rarely killed outright, because their families are far more inclined to track down a murderer than a mere thief.

'Cloak-snatchers don't often use knives,' I said thoughtfully. 'A club to the head does the job just as well and doesn't damage the plunder.'

'He wasn't rich. His cloak was homespun and his tunic was a cheap one.'

So Zosime had taken a good look at the dead man while I was fetching the Scythians. I suppose I should have expected that.

'That brocade panel of leaves though,' she persisted. 'That was old work, stitched onto newer cloth to make a good showing for the festival.'

I nodded. My mother had heirloom pieces of weaving laid aside in layers of linen with plenty of herbs to deter moths. Such fabrics were carefully resewn for each new head of the family and only ever worn on special occasions. But whoever the dead man's heir might be, he wouldn't be inheriting that finery.

I was more concerned with whatever legacy the murder might have left for this household. I glanced in the direction of the Areopagus where Orestes stood trial for murdering Clytaemnestra. That's when Athena persuaded the Furies to forgo their pursuit of bloody vengeance by promising them justice for the unjustly killed. I wondered uneasily what those divine goddesses of retribution were expecting me to do for this murdered man. I didn't relish facing their displeasure if I failed them.

14

'So he came from Ionia and had dealings with the Persians, or at least, with someone trading in Persian leather. What does that tell us?'

After six years without those wolves coming down from the hills, thanks to the peace Callias won for us with the Emperor Artaxerxes and his satraps, there's plenty of day-to-day trade between Ionia's coastal Greeks and the Imperial hinterland. Medes, Persians, call them what you like, they're one and the same. Every Athenian knows they're only waiting for some new excuse to march to the sea. Every ruler they've had since Cyrus the Great has been intent on seizing those Ionian cities, which Hellenes have held since before the fall of Troy. 'If he wasn't killed for his money or his fancy shoes, why slit his throat?' I looked at them both.

None of us had any answers.

I shook my head. 'We'll have to wait and see what the Polemarch finds out. Now we really must go to bed.'

Zosime nodded, though I could tell she was still un-happy. 'You've a busy day tomorrow.'

I couldn't think of anything to say to make this awful business any better, so we headed for our room in silence. Stripping off and falling into bed, I snuffed the lamp.

Chapter Two

Rosy-fingered dawn was barely plucking at the bedroom shutters when I woke up to lie staring at the ceiling. Zosime slept peacefully, curled up at my side with the blankets drawn up to her chin.

I let her sleep. She'd earned that over these past nine seemingly interminable months. Celebrating with me when I won my commission to write a play for the Dionysia. Enduring my initial, endless debates over which of my ideas to use. Tolerating my agonising as I shaped and reshaped the plot. Listening to me read snatches of dialogue as I shuffled the words around before mostly returning to where I'd started. Endlessly patient when I prompted her to tell me which were her favourite scenes, or to reassure me that my characters sounded like real people, that their schemes and concerns would truly engage an audience.

Today was our final rehearsal. Tomorrow, we'd show off our masks and costumes to the city's eager theatre-goers. The day after that, they'd see our play. The culmination of all my work, of all our work, would be a single performance for the Dionysia, judged against this year's other comedies. The drama competition was all or nothing, win or lose.

Yesterday I'd been fretting that I'd be remembered for a comedy that failed so spectacularly it was greeted with silence or groans or booing, fearful that the joke on me would spread from Lycia to Sicily as visitors travelled home. Every Hellene in the civilised world would learn my name. Philocles Hestaiou Alopekethen. The fool whose hubris in challenging the greatest comic playwrights of Athens had ended in greater tragedy than any blood-soaked tale of heroes felled by divine wrath.

This morning I remembered Zosime bringing me gently back down to earth whenever my fears reached such exaggerated heights. Life would go on, she pointed out with loving ruthlessness, however my play fared at the festival.

Meantime we'd stumbled across a real-life tragedy the night before. I wondered who the dead man was, and how he had come to die outside my door. What would the gods of the city and the dead expect me to do, to see his killers brought to justice?

A noise caught my ear. I rose onto one elbow and the rope-strung bed frame creaked. Was that someone knocking at our gate, turning up with answers just as I'd wished for them? That coincidence of timing would have theatre audiences throwing derisive nuts.

But no, I wasn't mistaken. There was definitely someone in the lane. I slid out of the bed, careful not to drag the blanket off Zosime. Shivering, I found my tunic on the stool, pulled it over my head and belted it tight.

Going out into the porch that shaded the width of our small house, I looked across the modest courtyard.

Our dining room stood to the left of the gate, the slave quarters on the right. Kadous's door was still closed and his window was shuttered. Looking up at a cloudless blue sky I felt the promise of the sun's warmth on my face. The pot herbs we grow were waking from their winter sleep and I breathed in the faint scent of spearmint, oregano and thyme. The reassuring perfumes of home. The knock came again. The chickens in the coop in the corner stirred and chucked to themselves, disturbed by the noise.

'I'm coming.' I didn't want the hens stirred into a frenzy and waking the neighbours. I opened the gate and found the last person I expected to see. 'Epikrates?'

The wiry slave stood there, anxiously wringing his hands. As one of three slaves who work leather for my family around the city, each with his own modest workshop, this morning he should have been taking my brothers our share of his last month's earnings. Then everyone could enjoy a well-earned rest as Athens' businesses closed up shop until after the festival.

I blinked. 'Is everything all right?'

'I've run out of hides,' Epikrates burst out. 'Dexios has been promising a delivery for three days but every morning it doesn't turn up. Every time I send my yard boy to ask, he just says that he's so sorry and swears by all the gods that his finest leather will be with me first thing tomorrow. But the delivery never comes!'

Watching Epikrates wretchedly twisting his hands around each other, most people wouldn't believe a word he was saying. We've all seen deceitful characters on stage shuffling their feet and looking here, there and everywhere except straight ahead. I've written them myself, discussing the best gestures to convey their dishonesty with actors and chorus masters alike. In this case, I knew better, having known Epikrates for years. Though we know nothing of his life before Father came across him in the slave market. He's a Hellene and his accent's Peloponnesian, but he's never spoken of his childhood. As my father told the story, he was a scrawny youth in filthy rags belted with a fine piece of leatherwork, which he swore he'd made himself. He assuredly had the bruises from fighting off anyone who tried to steal it.

I swallowed an impulse to ask what he thought I could do, today of all days.

'Do you want me to talk to Dexios?' I guessed Epikrates had been the first customer to go short. Dexios would have known the slave could be easily cowed, at least for a few days. But the tanner had to know my brothers wouldn't stand for this.

'I need to tell the masters.' Epikrates looked as if he expected to be whipped bloody. He always does whenever the slightest thing goes wrong, even though none of us have ever raised a hand to him. We've never had any cause. First, he proved himself in Father's workshop. Later, we set him up with his own premises in return for a share of his earnings. We've assured him he's free to marry and he need never fear losing his family to the slave traders, but after seventeen years in his own home, Epikrates still lives alone.

'What's amiss?' The door to our right opened and Kadous appeared, rubbing the sleep from his eyes.

'I need to go into the city, to see my brothers before I go to the rehearsal.' I went to find my cloak on the bench in the porch and sat down to lace up my shoes. 'Make sure you walk Zosime to her father's, whatever she says.'

'Of course.' Kadous might be a Phrygian but he's lived here long enough not to let a pretty girl walk Athens' streets without an escort with a forbidding scowl. Certainly not during a festival and especially not when Zosime lacks the legal protections of a citizen woman.

'Come on, then.' I fastened my cloak brooch on my shoulder and nodded to Epikrates. 'Watch your step . . .'

I broke off, puzzled. I'd been about to warn the scrawny slave to avoid the bloodstains in the lane, where our gatepost met the outer wall. None of us needed to risk that pollution, or to draw the attention of whatever vengeful Furies might be hovering to see that justice was served and ready to hound those who failed the dead.

'Master?' Halfway to the hen coop with the dinner scraps bucket, Kadous turned his head.

'Where's all the blood?' I pointed at the dusty, scuffed earth where the dead man had sprawled.

Kadous came over. There was no need for me to explain, now that we had the daylight. We had endured the carnage of Boeotia's battlefields together. When you've seen a spear point slash open a man's neck, you know that anyone within arm's length gets splattered from helmet to greaves.

The stranger's precious brocade tunic had been soaked with his blood. I remembered the leafy pattern on his chest obscured by that dark stain. His homespun cloak had soaked up a fair amount as well. But a dead man's blood doesn't flow as readily as it does when someone's still busy dying, frantically gasping as his heart beats its last.

I gestured to Kadous. 'Go and look up and down the lane for any sign of where he was murdered.' I suppose there was always the chance he'd dragged himself to our gate.

'Murder?' Epikrates whimpered.

'No one we know,' I reassured him.

We watched Kadous walk down the lane as far as the bend beyond Sosistratos's house. He returned and went in the other direction up to the Hermes pillar where the lane meets the road, studying the beaten earth all the while. He walked back to join us, shaking his head.

'No sign of blood. No signs of a fight.'

'So who brought his body here?' I wondered aloud. Why would the dead man's killer do such a thing? Or rather, the killer and his accomplices. Carrying corpses and wounded men during my military service had taught me the true meaning of 'dead weight'. No lone man had done this. So these killers had run the risk of being caught carrying a murdered man, even if they'd wrapped him up in his cloak to hide their crime. Though I had no idea how far the poor bastard had been carried from wherever he'd been killed. Each new discovery about this death brought me more questions I didn't have time for. Not with today's rehearsal to get to. Not with the problem of Epikrates' missing leather to tackle.

'Shall I go and tell the Scythians?' Kadous asked. 'In case they hear about some unexplained pool of blood?'

I shook my head. 'They'll find a hundred false scents down back alleys.'

Athenian citizens would soon be feasting on gifts of meat from the Dionysia's public sacrifices but resident foreigners and visitors have to throw their coins into a common pot and buy a sheep or a goat to slit its throat behind someone's house and celebrate their own rites.

'Master?' Epikrates quavered.

'Come on,' I said, trying to curb my exasperation. 'Let's see what Nymenios and Chairephanes make of Dexios's games.'

The walk would give me time to think of ways to persuade the Scythians to tell me the dead man's name when the Polemarch found out who he was. No one would come all the way from Ionia to the Dionysia alone, so someone would surely go looking for him when he didn't turn up for breakfast. The magistrate's office was the first place they'd go for help. Unless his travelling companions were the ones who'd cut his throat over some quarrel. Though that didn't explain why they'd dumped their carrion at my door.

We left our quiet side street, turning on to the broader road running northwards to the city. Birds tweeted and fluttered along the scrubby verges or hopped across the hard-packed gravel, pecking at seeds or insects.

As Epikrates and I went on our way, I guessed that most of the men I could see out this early were slaves. Their masters would want them reaching the agora as soon as the market's traders set up their stalls, ready to buy the freshest and finest provisions for their household's celebrations. Other slaves would be buying up bundles of firewood and sacks of charcoal, brought in from Attica by the cartload to feed the city's hearths and cooking braziers.

After reaching the city walls, we waited our turn to go through the gate, guarded by this year's contingent of young warriors called up for training. These lads would soon be kicking their heels on garrison duty somewhere on Attica's borders. I envied them. Better to be bored by days of drills than be thrown into battle barely used to the weight of your shield.

Things had been very different for me and my phalanx mates. There's scant chance of perfecting such skills when your shield wall's braced against roaring Boeotians all intent on ramming a spear point into your eye and out through the back of your skull.

'Good morning.' I greeted the youth approaching us and gestured at Epikrates cowering a few steps behind me. 'This is my slave.'

'Good day to you.' Hearing my Athenian accent, he waved us through the gate with a smile.

We still had a fair walk ahead of us. My family's home is overlooked by the Hill of the Nymphs, some way to the south-west of the agora and to the north of the Hill of the Pnyx, where the People's Assembly meets. We're registered outside the walls in the Alopeke district because that's where my great-grandfather lived, back when Cleisthenes established the voting tribes to secure popular rule. That's merely one of the ways our Athenian democracy ensures this city won't ever succumb to aristocratic tyrants again.

Anyway, as Grandfather's leather-working business

prospered, he moved inside the city to be closer to his customers. Father always reminded us to give thanks for that decision every Epitaphia festival when we commemorate Athens' honoured dead. Father remembered the fates of those people he'd known as a child, who'd still been living outside the walls when his family moved within the city. Those unfortunates had lost everything when the Persians invaded and devastated Attica with fire and sword.

When I knocked on that familiar gate, my eldest brother, Nymenios, opened up.

'Oh.' He looked at me, blank-faced with surprise.

'Who were you expecting?' I was equally startled. A slave usually manned the entrance.

He glanced over my shoulder at Epikrates. 'I should have guessed he'd go running to you.'

'What's going on?' We went into the courtyard. Broad, sloping roofs on either side sheltered piles of leather, baskets of off-cuts and racks of tools as well as wide work benches. This is where our household slaves turn out their share of the shoes, belts, purses and everything else that earns our family's bread. I could smell the familiar scents of oils and freshly cut leather and glimpsed two of the household's ferrets scampering around. With so many temptations to lure mice, my brothers need more than my mother's hens to hunt down all the vermin.

I glanced across at the front door, opposite the gate and sheltered by the wide porch where my mother's tall loom had been set up for as long as I can remember. A new striped blanket was wound around the uppermost beam, waiting for my mother or Nymenios's wife to return to it after the festival. There's always weaving to be done for a growing household.

As a small boy, I'd spent long afternoons in that porch with my brothers and sisters, playing with scraps of wool and leather while Mother deftly worked her patterns with warp and weft. As the family business prospered, more slaves arrived for Father to teach and then to supervise rather than work alongside. All too soon, Kleio and Ianthine had to learn the intricacies of running a household as well as the proper behaviour for an Athenian citizen maiden. Around the same time, Father decided Chairephanes and I were old enough to try our hand with some tools alongside Lysanias and Nymenios. Our sisters soon had their first lessons in tending our cuts and accidental gouges to our fingers.

Today the door to the house was firmly closed, and only the upper-storey window shutters were ajar to let in daylight and fresh air. I could hear the voices of Nymenios's children, indistinct above the purposeful murmur of conversation. The household's women were busy with their morning routines, completing whatever tasks needed doing before the festival.

'Syros never got the hides he was expecting yesterday.' Nymenios gestured to the newest of the slaves we'd set up with his own workshop, currently deep in conversation with Chairephanes.

'He's not the only one left empty-handed.' I explained Epikrates's problem.

Chairephanes came to join us. 'We've had late deliveries before.'

Nymenios snorted, sceptical. 'Never by more than a day, and Dexios always turns up in person to play the wide-eyed innocent, claiming some simple error.'

Though I hated to admit it, Nymenios was right. Five days of broken promises wasn't just the glib-tongued tanner mistaking one day for the next in his calendar.

'If he can't supply the hides he's promised, he's in breach of contract and he owes us reparations.' Nymenios thrust his jaw at me. 'You need to go to his yard and ask what he thinks he's playing at.'

I understood my brother's concern. Nymenios shoulders all the head of the family's responsibilities for this household and our workforce elsewhere in the city. We needed those raw materials.

'Dexios needs to know he's dealing directly with us. No more fobbing off slaves who daren't argue back.' Chairephanes looked at me, apologetic. 'And we need to know we'll be getting that leather as soon as the festival's over.'

'If we'll be getting *any* leather.' Nymenios clearly doubted it. 'Otherwise we need to make other arrangements, and fast.'

'I'm in the middle of final rehearsals for the most important play I've ever written,' I protested. 'I don't have time to traipse all the way out to a stinking tannery—'

'Dexios needs a boot up his arse today,' Nymenios insisted, 'and you need to remember where the money to feed and clothe you will come from when this festival's over.'

Nymenios could go kiss a piglet. I wouldn't starve in

a gutter without my share of our family's earnings. 'I pay my own way with my pen.' I scowled at him.

'True enough,' Chairephanes said quickly, 'which is why you'll be the one arguing our case in court, so you need to be asking the questions.'

'Not today.' I was adamant. 'Chances are Dexios won't even be in his yard. If I go to his house, his slaves will tell me he's out somewhere in the city. Oh, they'll be so sorry, but they won't know where he might be. It's the festival, after all. Even if I do manage to corner him, you know what he's like. He'll spin a yarn blaming somebody else. Someone I won't be able to find, or who won't have time to talk to me because they've got a house full of guests. I could waste the whole Dionysia trying to catch the slippery bastard in a lie.'

I raised a hand to forestall Nymenios's argument. 'If we wait until after the festival though, once the magistrates are sitting again, Dexios will know we can drag him straight into court if he doesn't explain himself.'

'Then he'll give us the leather he owes us,' Chaire-phanes said, ever optimistic, 'or we'll get supplies from somewhere else and everything will be fine. Don't fret so,' he urged Nymenios. 'Athens is never short of animal hides.'

He wasn't wrong. One or more festivals every month see herds of cows, sheep and goats led to the city's sacrificial altars. The gods take their sustenance from the smoke and steam of the burnt offerings while the free meat feeds the grateful populace. The sale of everything else, from the innards collected by sausage makers to the hides

27

sent to the tanneries, puts silver into the priests' personal strongboxes.

Nymenios glowered at us both for a long moment. 'All right.' He capitulated with ill grace before jabbing a finger at me. 'But I want you knocking on Dexios's gate first thing in the morning, the very first day after the festival.'

'Of course.' I nodded.

A thought struck Chairephanes. 'Did that man find you yesterday? I sent him to the agora to see if anyone knew where you were.'

I opened my mouth to say I hadn't seen anyone and to ask for more details, but Nymenios was already explaining. He does that a lot.

'He came here looking for you. He wanted to commission you to write him a speech.'

So far, so unremarkable. If I hadn't won the honour of writing a play for this Dionysia, I'd have been sitting in the agora yesterday, waiting for this stranger to find me. That's where I make my modest living offering a range of services to anyone who needs something writing. A soulful eulogy to honour a dead loved one. A joyful ode to celebrate a notable triumph. Speeches for the law courts. Whether a man's challenging another over some crime or answering an accusation, he needs a compelling argument to win the jury's votes. Most prefer someone well schooled in rhetoric to write it. That's business as usual in Athens.

'He was a Hellene, though I don't know where from,' Nymenios added. 'I've never heard an accent like his.'

28

'His shoes looked Persian,' Chairephanes observed. 'Fancy work.'

'Red leather?' As both of my brothers nodded, I felt sick. Having a potential customer dumped dead at my gate was very far from business as usual.

'What's going on?' Nymenios asked with sharp suspicion.

I explained what little I knew, leaving my brothers as much at a loss as I was.

'You have an entire chorus who can swear you were in the city until dusk.' Chairephanes scrubbed a hand through his dark curls. 'You couldn't have been the one to kill him. Why would you? You didn't even know him.'

'Just as long as Kadous doesn't fall under suspicion,' Nymenios said, belligerent in defence of our own. 'We'll all go to court as his character witnesses, if push comes to shove.'

'I don't imagine it will. The Scythians saw last night that Kadous had no more reason to kill the man than I did. He was a stranger to us all. Now, I must be going.' I held up my hands to ward off anything else they might say. 'I have to get to my rehearsal.'

Though, now that I knew this murdered stranger had been looking for me, I could ask a few other people some questions to try and find out who he might be and where he had lodged.

With a bit of divine blessing, that would tell us why he'd been killed. Then I could put all this behind me, content that the Furies were satisfied.

Chapter Three

The quickest route from one district to another in Athens is almost always through the agora. You can join the Panathenaic Way and cut right through the city instead of threading a winding path through the side streets.

There can't be a market in any other city to equal it: busier and noisier than visitors to Athens can ever imagine. Stallholders raise their voices over the morose protests of caged fowl awaiting their fate as somebody's dinner. Traders promise passers-by the finest fruits of the season fresh from Attica's farms, or brought in from Euboea. Garland sellers display their ingenuity with whatever flowers and foliage are currently flourishing, ready to crown wealthy guests at expensive banquets. Hot sausage vendors are on hand if anyone's hungry, and wine carts sell cooling cupfuls. Musicians and singers and all manner of entertainers ply their trades, hoping for half an obol tossed their way.

There's olive oil, raisins and herbs for sale, and spices ranging from humble garlic to seasonings as exotic as silphium from Cyrene. There are dates and almonds from Paphlagonia, more often than not. When the bells proclaim the day's fresh fish fetched up from the harbour at Piraeus, sometimes I honestly fear someone will get trampled in the rush.

People aren't only spending their silver. Some make offerings at the agora's many statues and shrines, honouring the gods and goddesses as well as the city's heroes. There are always plenty of citizens saluting Harmodios and Aristogeiton, who rid us of the tyrant Peisistratos and his sons. Others simply sit in the shade of the plane trees and swap news of family and friends with men they've served with on their district council, or fought alongside as hoplites, defending our democracy.

Even when the courts and the council aren't in session, details of cases to be tried and any bills proposing new laws are posted on large, whitewashed boards for all to read. Anyone volunteering for jury service or currently doing his duty in the People's Assembly has no excuse for not being well informed.

Every day is different. I always keep my ears open for some tale or some character I can work into a play. In between dealing with my own customers, I listen to the travelling tutors as they share their philosophies and histories. These teachers set up their schools surrounded by eager students in the shade of the Painted Colonnade, named for the paintings on its walls that celebrate Hellas's triumphs, from the fall of Troy to our miraculous victory at Marathon.

Today, though, I wanted to talk to my favourite wine seller and his wife, who were doing a brisk trade on their usual street corner. Anyone routinely spending their days in the agora soon learns which wine sellers rise early to fetch sweet water fresh from a spring to mix with their wine. The lazy ones dip their jugs in the murky streams that drain the Kerameikos district, and you'll risk losing half a day's income while you're emptying your guts into the public latrines.

I held up half an obol to get Elpis's attention. 'Half a pint of the black, if you please.'

'Right you are.' Elpis poured a measure from the jug standing ready on the cart's lowered tailgate. The strong dark wine was already mixed with water, and the sunlight struck red glints from the twisting flow.

I raised my eyes to Athena's temple as I offered her the first mouthful, tipped from the brim to vanish into the dry earth. Then I emptied it without pause for breath.

'Another?' he offered.

'Thank you, but no.' I tossed him another coin all the same. 'There is something else, though. Was anyone asking for me yesterday?'

'A Carian was looking for you, to ask you to write a speech for him.' Elpis filled a cup with scented golden wine for another customer.

'You're sure that's where he was from?'

'I'd know that accent anywhere,' the wine seller assured me. 'My mother was from Iasos.'

So Zosime had been right about the dead man's Ionian clothing. Carian meant he was from the southern end of that distant coast. 'And he was asking for me by name?'

Hermes only knew how this stranger had heard of me. I flatter myself that I do good work, but Caria's all the way over on the other side of the Aegean.

'He knew exactly who he wanted, so I gave him directions to your brothers' workshop.' Elpis paused before serving another customer. 'Is there a problem?'

'It seems the man turned up with his throat cut last night.' I decided not to say where.

'May the Furies drive his murderer mad!' Elpis was appalled. 'Killing a guest in Athena's own city, come all this way to honour her.'

'He was here to honour Athena? He wasn't just here for the festival?'

Elpis nodded, decisive. 'That's what he said.'

'Do you remember his name?' I pressed. 'His home town? Where he might be staying? You didn't see his travelling companions, by any chance?'

The wine seller could only offer a helpless shrug. 'Sorry, no.'

I sighed. 'Well, if you come across anyone looking for him, send them to the Polemarch. The Scythians took charge of the body.'

'Of course,' Elpis assured me.

I set down my cup on the wine cart and went on my way. My path was crowded with visitors but walking slowly gave me time to think.

So this stranger had come here to find me and been sent to my brothers' house. They'd sent him straight back to the agora. I wondered if he had gone asking around the other scriveners, looking for someone else to write his speech. Had he said the wrong thing to some hot-blooded Athenian, provoking sudden anger and an accidentally lethal swipe of a foolhardy knife? No, this killing looked personal. Had some enemy followed him across the Aegean, canny enough not to shit on his own doorstep? Perhaps, but that didn't explain how the dead man ended up at my gate.

I gazed around the agora, wondering where I might find some answers. Over in the Painted Colonnade, I spotted that historian from Halicarnassus who tells such wonderfully entertaining stories. The genial man had a lifelong traveller's weather-beaten complexion and flowing grey beard. He sat on a stool with his knees spread wide, his belly as expansive as his gestures. As he concluded some stirring tale, the audience applauded and showed their appreciation with a shower of coins into the folds of the cloak at his feet. As a boy brought him a well-earned cup of wine, I remembered his story about ants as big as foxes in India. Surely, they can't be real. At least, I hope they aren't. If they are, I fervently hope that they stay there.

I shook my head. I could waste all day here asking questions and learning nothing. I pressed on through the noisy crowds, heading for my rehearsal. Dionysos had as much call on my time as Athena and the Furies today.

The actors must be wondering where I'd got to. I ran through the hydra-headed list of things I needed to check. Had the masks arrived? What about the costumes? How much final fitting would be needed? Was my entire chorus taking advantage of my late arrival to get incapably drunk in some tavern? Were there any last-minute changes to the script I should be considering? But, this late in the day, that risked a missed cue when an actor said something new that a forgetful chorus-man wasn't expecting.

'Philocles! Philocles Hestaiou!'

I looked around, trying to work out who had called out my name. Then I saw a waving hand over on the steps at the far end of the Painted Colonnade, and recognised an amiable acquaintance.

Phrynichos is another writer who keeps himself clothed and fed by taking on day-to-day commissions while he pursues his true ambitions in the evenings and slack times. His heart's desire is a winner's garland for his poetry in competition at one of the pan-Hellenic games. Any of them will do: Olympic, Pythian, Nemean or Isthmian. He's not proud.

Today he was pointing me out to the young man standing beside him. Whoever this stranger was, he'd be worth a wager in a wrestling match at any of those games. Phrynichos is no short-arse, and this well-muscled lad was a full head taller than him.

The stranger hurried towards me, shoving through the crowds, either not caring or not noticing the angry looks it earned him. I stood and waited, wondering what this was about.

'You are Philocles Hestaiou Alopekethen?'

'I am.' And with that Ionian accent, this boy must be another Carian. My heart sank, even though I realised this was my chance to do my duty to the gods and to the dead man.

'Did he find you? Xandyberis?' He really was a big lad close up, with black hair curling in long locks though his beard was close-cropped like my own. He wore a homespun tunic and a faded grey cloak, the fabric taut across his broad shoulders.

'No, but—'

'We have the honour to serve the town council of Pargasa.' He seized my hands in a fervent grasp, dark eyes glittering with intensity.

'I have to tell you—'

He still wasn't listening. 'We must make our case before the Archons now that the tributes are under review. We are poor people in Pargasa. All Caria suffered so greatly under Persian rule. Even now that peace has come, we struggle to scrape the barest living from our harsh and stony fields. Please, I beseech you, we need a speech to convince men accustomed to Athenian riches that our hardships are real. Our town is small and we have no one to teach us such rhetoric, not when we must stand before your Council.'

'Wait, wait.' I pulled my hands free. 'What are you talking about?'

He stared at me, bemused. 'The tributes. We have brought our offering to Athena as agreed by treaty but we cannot raise the full sum demanded this year. Now that there is no need to raise armies and triremes to fight the Persians, we must get the levy reassessed—'

'Forgive me, but the Great Panathenaia isn't until *next* year,' I told him with growing unease. 'That's when the Delian League's business will be discussed, as it is every four years when all our allies assemble for that very purpose. This year's City Panathenaia is only for Athens and

Athenians. In any case, that festival isn't for another four months, at the start of the new year at midsummer—'

'There is to be a special reassessment at this year's Dionysia.' He shook his head, impatient. 'Now, you will need to know all about Pargasa to make our case. We can meet after we've presented our tribute to honour Athena. That will happen the day after tomorrow.'

'Yes, I know the ritual,' I said, irritated. I didn't need some Carian telling me how the Dionysia would proceed. 'But I must tell you—'

He brushed my words aside. 'You must convince the Archons to reduce this levy. We have barely recovered from the Persians' vengeance. Our fields and orchards were laid waste when Caria rebelled in my grandfather's day—'

I could believe that but it made no difference. I raised my voice to interrupt him. 'If there was going to be any reassessment of tributes at this festival, or any time this year, the Archons would have posted an announcement in the agora.' Even a blind man couldn't have missed that. It would have been the talk of the city.

The Carian shook his head in obstinate denial. 'You're lying. Who's paying you to silence our pleas?'

My sympathies for this lout evaporated like morning mist. If the dead man had been equally obnoxious, no wonder someone had cut his throat.

'You Athenians are all the same!' The young Carian clenched his fists. 'You want to pick our pockets of every last coin. You spend our silver on your shining new temples and filling your bellies as you gorge at your festivals!'

He flung out a hand. An instant too late, I realised he only meant to gesture towards the Acropolis, still crowned with half-built shrines. But I had already thrown up my own hand to ward off his fist, shoving him backwards for good measure. Caught unawares, he stumbled and fell down hard on his arse. Passers-by scattered, exclaiming. Some laughed, not knowing what was going on.

He stared up at me, scarlet with humiliation and completely taken aback. I wondered when he'd last lost a fight. Men used to throwing their weight around never expect to end up on the ground. Well, it was time he learned that lesson.

'Forgive me, I thought . . . Please, listen.' I offered my hand to help him to his feet. 'Your friend's name was Xandyberis? I'm so sorry. I have grievous news. He was found dead last night—'

'You lie!' Smacking my hand away, he spat copiously on my feet.

Bystanders oohed and aahed like a theatre audience. I could see several grinning in avid expectation of a fist fight. Fuck that. I had more important things to do. I took a step back and straightened my cloak, trying to ignore the foul slime oozing warm between my toes.

'Your companion was found dead last night,' I repeated crisply. 'The Archons' slaves took his body for safekeeping on the Polemarch's behalf. Address all your questions to them.'

As Athena was my witness, my duty to the dead man and to the Furies was done. The young lout was on his hands and knees now. I managed to lose myself in the

38

crowd before he stood up. As I edged away, I saw him looking around wildly. He looked younger than I'd first thought, standing there with his mouth open and his expression dismayed as he realised he'd lost me.

Forget him. I had a play rehearsal to get to, if the Fates didn't waylay me with any more problems this morning. Though, by the time I reached the road to take me out of the agora, I was having second thoughts. After stopping at a fountain to wash the disgusting slime from my foot and my sandal, I decided I had better make another stop first.

There was no telling if that arrogant young cock of a Carian knew where I lived. Kadous and Zosime needed to know not to open our gate if he turned up, keen to continue our quarrel.

Chapter Four

I doubled back across the agora and threaded my way through the narrow alleys of the Kerameikos district.

'Looking for a fun time, handsome?' A three-obol whore lounged against her curtained doorway.

'Not today, thanks all the same.' I spared her a smile regardless.

I'd sampled such delights hereabouts most nights after I'd come back from Boeotia. Drinking rough wine and fucking a sweet girl were fine ways to forget the stink and fear of battle. But, Athena be thanked, such sour memories fade. When I met Zosime I was more than ready to abandon brothels for a loving embrace in my own bed.

A few more turns and my destination lay ahead. The pottery's door stood ajar and sounds of purposeful activity spilled into the rutted lane.

As I entered, Zosime's father didn't raise his eyes from the pot he was carefully shaping. 'Philocles.'

'Good day to you.' I walked over, nodding to the other potters at their wheels and the vase painters working at their benches around the walls. Everyone was well used to me dropping in by now.

Menkaure lifted his hands away from his pot and let the wheel slow to a halt. Red clay was vivid on his fingers, his skin as dark as any I've ever seen from southern Egypt.

He and I had got chatting when I'd visited this workshop to buy kitchen pots for my mother. We'd emptied several jugs of wine as he satisfied my curiosity about his remote, sandy homeland. Not that I was looking for some setting for a play: I wanted to know whatever he could tell me about the blood-soaked island in Egypt's northern marshes where my brother Lysanias had died.

It was only when Menkaure shared his own grief at the loss of his beloved wife that I realised his daughter was one of the girls painting pots in the back of the workshop. I don't think he had been seeking a protector for her, in case some ill fate befell him, but when Zosime and I exchanged our first shy smiles, he'd made no objection.

'That's a fine piece.' I nodded at the wine-mixing bowl he was shaping.

'It will be, as long as Disculos doesn't screw up when he decorates it.' Menkaure raised his voice to make sure his fellow craftsman heard.

The painter replied with a cheerfully obscene gesture without looking up from the olive garland he was drawing around a long-necked jug.

'She told me what happened.' Menkaure's dark eyes fixed on me, unblinking, as he cleaned his fingers with an ochre-stained rag. 'She said you were as restless as a pistachio on a griddle all last night.'

'Are you surprised?' I said with feeling.

41

'Hardly,' he assured me, 'but if you don't know who the dead man was, can you be so sure you have seen the end of this, just because the Scythians took the body away?'

'It seems our dead man was a Carian looking for a speech writer. He just happened to hear my name. I met one of his travelling companions in the agora and I told him to claim the body from the Polemarch.' I shrugged.

'Good to know.' Menkaure tossed the rag into an old chipped pot by his feet. 'I'm glad you called by. Thallos says he wants to lock up early today. I was planning to leave at noon anyway. Some old friends are here from Memphis for the Festival, but Zosime isn't interested in coming with me. Can you get word to Kadous to collect her earlier than we arranged?'

I could see the sense in that. Official festivities might not start till tomorrow but this part of the city was already heaving with visitors looking for fun, trouble or both. 'I'll make sure she gets home safely.'

Menkaure set his wheel spinning again as I walked to the back of the workshop. 'I'm looking forward to finally seeing your chorus all dressed up,' he called after me.

'Just remember that masks and costumes aren't everything,' I said over my shoulder.

'Shouldn't you be supervising your rehearsal?' Zosime looked up from the white oil flask she was decorating. 'And what took you into the city so early?'

I pulled up a stool and explained about Dexios and the leather deliveries. Then I shared what I'd just learned about our Carian corpse. 'So his friends can claim his body from the Polemarch and if they come knocking on our gate, we ignore them. We've no idea who killed the poor bastard and I won't risk getting dragged into some stranger's quarrels. Now, your dad just told me everyone is leaving here early today.'

She nodded. 'Thallos has a horde of relatives coming in from the country. If he doesn't get back to help his wife, she swears she'll shut him out of her bedroom till midwinter.'

She'd do it, too. She was a formidable woman, like so many I knew. People hear such exaggerated tales of women's lives in Athens: how we shut our citizen-born wives and daughters away so that the only females ever seen on our streets will be slaves and whores. A few household tyrants might live like that, but I've never known a woman who would put up with it.

That meant today's work was as good as done. Thallos made these decisions as the most senior artisan in this workshop. It wasn't a family business like the one bequeathed to me and my brothers. Resident foreigners share these premises with citizens from the lowest class; the men who row Athens' triremes. They all work alongside each other, splitting the costs and profits.

'If you're nearly finished with that, you could come to the rehearsal with me?' I suggested. 'There'll be someone there who can walk you home.'

'Or I can wait until you've finished rehearsing and we can walk back together. I'm sure someone can take a message, to save Kadous a wasted trip into the city.'

She laid down her brush and I admired the portrait she was painting. A youth reclined at the feet of a muse as she sat in a chair playing a lyre. 'That's beautiful.'

'He loved music, so his father says.' Zosime's smile faded as she recalled the man's sorrow.

These slender white, black-footed flasks are only ever used for pouring gifts of oil or wine onto graves, to honour the gods below. They are Zosime's speciality, so she's always crafting some remembrance of a family's loss. But she still prefers painting these personal, intimate pictures, instead of time-worn mythological scenes in black and red with their endlessly familiar cast of characters.

She put the flask carefully at the back of her work bench. 'Let me tidy up and I'll come with you.'

I looked idly around the workshop while she rinsed her brushes and gathered up the shards of broken vases she uses to practise a likeness, until the family paying for her skills are satisfied with the depiction of their loved one.

Most of the other artisans were finishing up, too. They all had families eager for the festivities. The only man here for the next few days would be the aged Thessalian with hands too twisted with arthritis to do anything more than feed the kiln's stoke hole and threaten would-be burglars with his hefty olivewood club. He had no one to go home to, so Zosime told me. The Persians had killed all his family in the wars.

'Let me wash my hands.' She went over to the ewers, which the Thessalian filled every morning, and poured a little into a basin. She'd spent enough of her childhood carrying water not to waste a drop.

Satisfied she was free of paint, she smoothed her draped

dress over the curve of her hips and turned to smile at me. 'Ready?'

'Did you wear a shawl this morning?' Another layer of cloth between Zosime's charms and some lecher's groping hands wouldn't go amiss in these crowds.

'I did.' She fetched her brown woollen wrap from a peg and swung it around her shoulders. 'Shall we go?'

I took her hand as we walked down the lane. 'Your father said he was seeing some friends. If you join him, you won't have to spend the day listening to me fretting.' I tried to make a joke of it and failed.

Zosime freed her hand from mine and slipped it through the crook of my arm to pull me close. 'I'll find a way to distract you. And, no, thanks all the same. Dad and his cronies will be drinking and talking about people and places I don't even remember.'

She had been barely ten years old when Menkaure and his wife had fled from Egypt to Crete to seek shelter with her mother's family. He was wise enough to see which way the wind was blowing before the full might of the Persian army arrived to crush the Egyptians' rebellion. A rebellion that Athens had been foolish enough to support, at the cost of so many deaths, including my lost brother and the firstborn son of my play's patron.

We were on our way to his house. The man whose substantial wealth was financing my comedy is called Aristarchos. He lives in that favoured district of Athens to the north of the Acropolis and to the east of the agora. This means his spacious and elegant residence is within easy walking distance of the courts and the Council

Chamber as they flank the market place. It's only a short stroll further to the People's Assembly up on the Pnyx, or to the Areopagus for a murder trial in the court there. After all, wealthy men like him spend a great deal of their time on the people's business, safeguarding the city's interests.

They safeguard their own wealth and households with tall walls and narrow, barred windows high enough to stop passers-by peering in or sneak thieves slipping through. It's a world away from the neighbourhood I grew up in, with constant comings and goings amid bustling workshops and storehouses, with families living cheek by jowl.

As Zosime and I made our way through the quiet streets, I could hear light lyre music floating through open shutters above my head. Women who marry men like Aristarchos have the leisure to enjoy artistic pastimes and to share such skills with their daughters. I'd grown up with the sound of women's laughter in the room overlooking the courtyard and my father's workshop, punctuated by the muted thud of spindles dropping on floorboards as my mother and her slaves turned combed wool into yarn.

When we turned the last corner, I saw somebody standing outside Aristarchos's gate. I walked faster, dreading bad news from the mask maker. Perhaps some disaster had befallen our costumes. Messengers on the stage seldom herald anything good.

Had my most hated rival discovered who would be performing my music? We'd done our best to keep that particular secret throughout our months of rehearsals, but there was always the risk that one of the chorus had let something slip while sharing a jug of wine. Had Euxenos sent his scene shifters to snap Hyanthidas's double pipes over his head? No, that was a ridiculous notion.

We drew closer as a young man came out through the gate, his back to us as he spoke to the first youth, who was kneeling to retie his shoe.

'You know they want to see your father embarrassed. Why else foist an untried poet on him?'

'He won a prize at the Lenaia last year,' countered the lad having trouble with his laces. I realised it was Aristarchos's son, Hipparchos.

'*Second* prize,' the disdainful one spat. 'His first attempt at a play wasn't even placed. They didn't award him a chorus the year after that.'

'My father—'

'Regardless, the Lenaia is not the Dionysia,' the arrogant prick continued. 'Those plays merely brighten up winter's gloom with a few cheap laughs for our own citizens. It doesn't matter how feeble Philocles's jokes are there. But the Dionysia's great tradition of drama is as valuable as our city's coin, honoured far and wide. These performances influence how all Hellas sees our city. This great festival's reputation should not be tarnished by debased doggerel.'

Now I recognised Hipparchos's friend Nikandros. I wondered who he was mimicking, as brainless as a tame jackdaw. From what I'd seen, he wasn't the type to study rhetoric and come up with phrases like that.

Nikandros snorted, contemptuous. 'You saw the crowd's reaction yesterday when this year's plays were announced. What sort of title is that? *The Builders*? And how much of your father's money is he squandering? You can never trust that sort of scrounger. Their judgement is as flawed as their morals.'

As I braced myself, I felt Zosime do the same. This pair would see us as soon as they turned around. With every gate shut and guarded hereabouts, there was nowhere for us to hide.

The kneeling lad stood up. 'Let's get a drink. As long as you're paying.'

Nikandros laughed. 'Why not?'

The pair strolled away down the street. I don't think they even realised we were there.

Zosime's hand tightened on my arm. 'Who are they?'

I struggled to keep my voice level. 'The one unused to tying his own shoes is Aristarchos's youngest son, Hipparchos. The one who knows everything about anything is his friend Nikandros Kerykes. They both think their fathers' wealth makes them untouchable.'

And as far as people like me were concerned, those cocky young swine were right. Third of Aristarchos's surviving sons, Hipparchos, was seven or so years younger than me and I was willing to bet he hadn't done a day's work since he'd come home from his military training last year. Noble born and rich, he'd served out those two years sitting on his arse on a horse, safe enough even if war returned. Cavalrymen never fight as hoplites and they're rarely asked to risk their precious necks and expensive steeds in battle.

Aristarchos's gate guard Mus grinned as we arrived. He'd heard every word those two young arseholes had said, and more besides, most likely. 'Here for the rehearsal?'

His smothered laugh rumbled like distant thunder. Mus is one of the biggest slaves I've ever met, muscled like a statue of Heracles. A statue whose sculptor roughly shaped the marble but forgot to finish smoothing the stone. I think he's from some mountainous land far beyond the Black Sea; one of those places where ancient Argives went voyaging when Homer's granddad was still a boy. I pity any gang of housebreakers fool enough to come hammering on this door hoping to overwhelm an unwary porter with yells and clubs before rushing in to steal what they can.

'Is Aristarchos at home?' Hearing Hipparchos and Nikandros outside in the lane had given me pause for thought. 'I'd appreciate a quick word if he can spare me the time.'

'He is, and you're always welcome to speak to him, you know that.' Mus ushered us through the gate into the outer courtyard.

Thanks to Aristarchos' ancient lineage and wealth, this outer courtyard alone was twice the size of any home I could ever hope for, with a full upper storey of luxurious rooms above the household slaves' quarters below. All four sides of the paved expanse offered porches furnished with comfortable seats and tables. There was no need to

49

keep such space clear for mundane tasks like setting up a loom, or a cooking brazier. This courtyard's pale stones would never be sullied by ash or charcoal or chickens. Households like this have kitchens where day-to-day food is cooked whenever it's called for and sumptuous banquets can be planned and prepared.

My actors and most of the chorus had already arrived. Apollonides, Menekles and Lysicrates were discussing something in a corner while Chrysion the chorus master was pacing out a transition some of the chorus were still finding tricky.

'Zosime! Darling!' Lysicrates bustled over to embrace her.

I relinquished her with a kiss. 'I just need a moment with Aristarchos.'

An arch admitted favoured visitors into more private family accommodation set around a smaller courtyard. Aristarchos sat in the shade in the south-east corner, relaxing in a cushioned chair of glossy black wood. He's much the same age as my father had been when he died, though he looks ten years younger. Aristarchos's hair is barely touched with grey and the only lines on his face are crow's feet from narrowing his eyes as he studies letters, ledgers and scrolls of history or philosophy.

My father got his exercise fetching and carrying in his workshop and walking the city's streets to visit customers and suppliers. His shoulders were irrevocably rounded from years hunched over a workbench. Aristarchos still regularly visits the gymnasium to run and wrestle and hone his skills with discus and javelin.

The greenery around him wasn't pot herbs. Wonderfully lifelike fig saplings were painted on the plastered walls, commemorating Demeter's gift of the first fig to his revered ancestor Phytalos. He is one of those men with no need to identify himself with his father's name and his voting district. Athens' most ancient families command instant awe with their clan name alone. That lineage means every son of this family rides a finely harnessed horse into war as befits the nobly born. My ancestors have all marched stolidly into battle carrying shields and spears. Though the gods aren't impressed by such distinctions. Aristarchos's eldest son's blood soaked into Egypt's black earth just like my brother's. If we ever recovered their bones, there'd be no telling them apart.

He looked up from the letter in his hand and gestured to a stool. 'Please.'

'Thank you.' I shrugged off my cloak and sat down.

'Can I offer you something?' He gestured to a dish of olives and pine nuts on the little table to his right. Another table to his left held a further stack of documents.

I took the dish. 'Thank you.'

Aristarchos looked quizzically at me. 'Shouldn't you be overseeing your rehearsal? I expected you rather sooner.'

'I had some unexpected delays.' I tried to cover my hesitation by selecting a particularly plump olive.

'He's probably right,' Aristarchos observed. 'Nikandros.'

I looked up, shocked, to see him smiling.

'I take it he was still favouring anyone within earshot with his theories on his way out? He seems to think if he keeps repeating himself, everyone will eventually be forced to agree.'

Then I saw the glint in my patron's dark eyes.

'Nikandros and his cronies are probably right to say that my rivals are smirking into their wine cups at the prospect of the play that I'm sponsoring coming last in this year's comedy competition. But they're wrong to think you only won a chorus to make sure that the Phytalid name is humiliated. Patrons and playwrights are matched by lottery, and Praxiteles is an honest man. There wasn't a voice raised against him when his fitness for office was reviewed and there won't be any corruption uncovered when his year as Chief Archon is audited.' Aristarchos was certain of that.

I chewed on a pine nut. 'No one knows what to make of a play called *The Builders*. I should have called it something else.'

'They don't know what to make of the title, so they'll be nicely curious by the time your chorus takes the stage.' Aristarchos sipped from his cup. 'I saw both your plays at the Lenaia. You made people laugh. More than that, you learned from the jokes that failed in your first attempt. You listened to your lead actor's suggestions before staging a second play.'

I wanted to protest that my first play would have gone much better if that chorus leader had listened to me, to my suggestions for gesture and emphasis to enhance the words I'd written. But he had been old and set in his ways and I had been young and tactless. But that was all washed away downstream now, so there was no point in saying so.

Aristarchos continued. 'You deserved to be called to read for Praxiteles, to compete for a chance at the Dionysia. You beat those other playwrights fair and square. Whoever's spreading this slander is simply trying to undermine me, hoping to gain some advantage if we ever oppose each other in the courts or before the People's Assembly.'

I supposed that could be true. While even the humblest citizen can spend a year as Ruling Archon, if the gods decree his name comes up in the annual lottery for magistrates, it's still men like Aristarchos who take the lead in bringing cases before the law courts or proposing new legislation in the public interest. They have the leisure to pursue such concerns, thanks to income from their estates outside the city, or their interests in craftsmen's workshops within the walls. Then there's the return on their investments in the merchant ships that leave the docks at Piraeus full of olive oil amphorae, before filling their empty holds with luxuries from Egypt or the Hellespont for the journey back. They never know when they might need some advantage over each other, and are always on the lookout for an opportunity to secure one.

From time to time these wealthy men are chosen to put their silver to other uses for the general good, like paying for one of the triremes that helped secure the present peace. Or financing a play for the Dionysia. Aristarchos had been awarded that honour back at the start of this year, so he was paying for everything from the piper who'd accompanied my comedy's first rehearsals to the wine and nuts the audience would enjoy at the performance.

'Do you have some important case coming up?' I asked. 'Or a particularly contentious law to propose to the Assembly?'

'Perhaps our rivals are simply worried that you'll win,' Aristarchos mused. 'You've hired three very fine actors and your chorus master is one of the best. You saw how interested the crowd was to see Apollonides and Menekles walk out to join your chorus yesterday. Perhaps the naysayers hope to cast a shadow over your chances, if their spiteful whispers reach potential judges' ears.'

I nodded but still couldn't help myself. 'Euxenos got the best piper. You saw how Diagoras was cheered.'

'Euxenos got the best pipe player he *knew of*,' Aristarchos corrected me. 'He got the piper everyone was expecting, whom they've heard tootling year in and year out. You're bringing them someone new.'

'True enough.' I smiled at that thought. I don't suppose it would even occur to Euxenos to discuss such matters with his own paymaster. Would Xanthippus have been so ready to help him, as Aristarchos had done for me? I have no idea if other rich men take any notice of the entertainers who arrive when their banquet tables are cleared so the evening's wine and songs can begin.

Who knows? Who cares? What matters is, barely a day after I'd been awarded my chorus, Aristarchos had sent me the name of a Corinthian piper who'd impressed him at a recent symposium. Back then, Hyanthidas had only just arrived in the city. In the months since, so Aristarchos said, the Corinthian garnered quite a following among the wealthy men who host such lavish dinners.

'Was there something particular you wanted?' Aristarchos prompted. 'Or are you just wishing me good day?'

'There is something.' I took a deep breath and explained about the dead Carian and this morning's encounter in the agora. I hadn't intended saying anything, but Nikandros's casual insults had given me second thoughts. Anyone out to make trouble for Aristarchos could spread slanderous hints about some sort of scandal if word of a dead man on my doorstep got around.

He was shocked. 'How thoroughly unpleasant. But there can be no question of you being suspected, or your slave?'

'I don't believe so, but if we can find out more about the dead man, perhaps that will explain who killed him. That'll put the question beyond doubt. His name was Xandyberis and he was part of the delegation bringing the annual tribute from Pargasa, one of our allied cities in Caria.'

'A robbery?' Aristarchos looked dubious. 'Some thief followed him out from the city all the way to your door?'

I grimaced, still unconvinced. 'I don't think he was a rich man, even if he was dressed in the finest he could afford. Perhaps his companions can shed some light on his fate. Is there any way that you could find out where this particular delegation is lodging?'

Presenting those tributes from the Delian League was as much an integral part of the Dionysia's formalities as the procession Aristarchos would take part in when he was honoured as my play's patron. The same officials would be organising both events.

'I can certainly ask those who will know.' Aristarchos's eyes grew distant, thoughtful.

I hoped the rest of the Pargasarene delegation proved more reasonable than the lad I'd met in the agora. I thought Aristarchos was about to say something more but he shook his head. 'Leave it with me.'

A flourish of pipe music in the outer courtyard told us both that the final rehearsals were about to begin.

Chapter Five

By noon I was ready to head for Piraeus and jump on the first ship going anywhere. The further the better. The rehearsal was a disaster.

'All right, all right, simmer down!' Lysicrates got everyone's attention. 'Let's try that again.'

Menekles, who was playing Meriones, and Apollonides as Thersites, took centre stage. Two Homeric heroes, playing for laughs.

Meriones turned to Thersites with an expansive sweep of his spear. 'This is to be our new home!'

Thersites cocked his masked head. 'So you say, but where are we? I swear, Meriones, Odysseus will get home before we do. I knew you were lousy at driving a chariot but you're just as hopeless at navigating a ship!'

Meriones spurned such criticism with an extravagant toss of his helmet's horsehair crest. 'This is a land of opportunity, Thersites! A realm of fertile slopes where olive trees look down on fine soil for planting vines! Where fertile pastures will nourish sheep and horses! Where tall timber grows fit for building us a whole new fleet of ships! Where—'

'Where *are* we?' Laying his shield down, Thersites

57

squared up to Meriones, hands on hips.

Meriones looked from side to side. Now his gestures were nervous. 'We're—'

'You don't know, do you?' Thersites challenged him before turning to the audience. Or at least, where the audience would be sitting when we were performing this comedy in the theatre. 'Well, isn't that just lovely? We're lost!'

'An Achaean is never lost,' Meriones objected hotly. 'He's just . . . on his way from one place to another.'

'So this isn't our new home? We're only stopping off here? Oh my aching arse!' Thersites squatted and groaned, heart-rending, as he kneaded his well-padded buttocks.

A slight smile tugged at the corner of my mouth.

'No,' protested Meriones. 'We're staying here, truly. We've anchored the ship—'

'Aha!' Thersites sprang acrobatically into the air. 'Gotcha. So where are we?'

That was Chrysion's cue to lead the chorus into the first of their song and dance routines. Twenty-four well-drilled men should have celebrated the virtues of this unknown land.

At least six started singing several words behind the rest. Four went right when they should have gone left and one tripped up the man beside him. He fell over and took down the next in line. The song dissolved into protests and recrimination. In the colonnade opposite me, Hyanthidas lowered his reed-tipped pipes. At his side Lysicrates, who'd been poised to make his

58

own entrance, shook his head, exasperated.

'Oh, come on!' Menekles dragged off his helmet to glare at Chrysion.

Apollonides was using an old mask until Thersites's costume arrived. He shoved the painted and plastered linen up onto his forehead and rounded on the chorus. 'What do you think you're playing at? We get one chance to get this right on the day!'

I clapped my hands so hard that they stung. I didn't care. I was furious.

'Listen to me! This is no laughing matter! You've been hand-picked to present this play at the greatest drama festival in the civilized world. The great and the good of Athens will be sitting on those marble seats of honour. Leading citizens among our allies will be honoured for their loyalty, to reaffirm the ties that bind Hellenes together; our common blood and language, our shared gods and customs—'

'Tell us something we don't know!'

I don't know who shouted from the back of the chorus as they all stood shuffling their feet. I couldn't see anyone's expression behind the motley collection of battered masks they were wearing to rehearse. I don't know what I'd have done next if someone hadn't hammered on the house's outer gate.

I turned and stalked towards the entrance. Mus had just opened the grille in the door to see who had knocked.

'It's Sosimenes.' He opened the door to reveal the mask maker along with his skinny slave pushing a handcart.

'We were expecting you earlier.' As soon as the curt

words were out of my mouth, I regretted them. Sosimenes is one of the best mask makers in the city and I was lucky to have his personal attention. I wouldn't have got through the door of his workshop without Aristarchos's fortune backing me.

'You don't think I'm busy today?' he snapped. 'You don't think everyone wants their masks delivered?'

I raised apologetic hands. 'Of course.'

There'd never been a realistic chance that Sosimenes would only make the masks for my play. The Dionysia's five comedies alone demand one hundred and twenty masks and that's just for the choruses, never mind the individual character roles. Add three tragedians each writing a trilogy and a satyr play besides, and it's no wonder that the finest mask makers have the heaviest strongboxes in whichever temple banks their silver.

Sosimenes glared at me as he pulled back the cloth covering the handcart to reveal a stack of gurning faces.

I looked at him, aghast. All thoughts of apology vanished. 'Where are my masks?'

These weren't the hilarious, exaggerated caricatures that we'd so painstakingly devised. These masks had scarlet wigs. Mine had black hair.

The slave clapped horrified hands to his face. 'I brought the wrong cart!'

'Where are mine? Are they under cover? If it rains ...' The briefest shower could reduce those carefully shaped and painted layers of linen and gypsum to a useless, soggy mess.

'You see clouds?' Sosimenes flung a hand to the un-sullied spring sky. Any actor would be proud to convey such incredulity.

'I don't see the masks Aristarchos has paid for,' I retorted.

'What's the problem?' Lysicrates appeared at my elbow and looked into the handcart. 'Oh.' He reached for one of the red-haired wigs. 'Who's got a chorus of Thracians?'

Sosimenes slapped the actor's hand away. 'Leave off!'

Were these for Euxenos? But his comedy was called *The Butterflies*. None of the competing titles announced yesterday had anything to do with Thrace. How could Euxenos get laughs out of barbarians and butterflies? I couldn't think of a way but he'd been an actor for a decade before he became a playwright. He never failed to tell me that he knew more than I could ever hope to about what made people laugh.

'Where are my masks?' My voice rose to a shout.

'They'll be back in the yard.' Sosimenes scowled at his slave. 'Won't they?'

Before I could decide which one to grab first and shake until his teeth rattled, Lysicrates laid a firm hand on my forearm. 'How soon can you get our masks to us?'

'We'll get these to—' Sosimenes caught himself just in time '—to their destination and go straight back to fetch yours.'

'That's all we ask.' Lysicrates's grip tightened to make sure I stayed silent. 'Now, let's all get on. None of us have time to waste today.'

Sosimenes cuffed his slave around the head, so hard that he sent the skinny old man sprawling. 'Get a move on!'

As they hurried off, I stood there trembling with anger, unable to string five coherent words together.

Lysicrates patted my arm. 'We all need a lunch break. You and Zosime go and eat somewhere nice in peace and quiet. The masks and costumes will be here by the time you get back.'

I drew a deep, shuddering breath. 'All right.'

I'll never say so to Apollonides or Menekles but Lysicrates was the first actor I spoke to after winning the right to stage a play at this Dionysia. Not just because he's the best at playing women's roles that Athens has seen for over a decade. When my first play at the Lenaia festival had been such a dismal failure, Lysicrates had come to find me afterwards, sitting with me while I tried to drown my humiliation in cheap wine. He'd encouraged me not to give up, but to learn from my mistakes. I will always be grateful for that.

Zosime appeared. 'Why don't we go home for lunch? Then Kadous will know he needn't come to fetch me later.'

I wanted to argue. I wanted to strangle half the chorus. So it was probably best for everyone if I walked those urges off.

We bought olives and cheese in the agora and walked through the cheerfully noisy crowds to the Itonian Gate. Outside the city, the road was less busy and the tensions that had racked me like some traveller on Procrustes' infamous bed began to ease.

Unfortunately, when we got home the last thing we found was peace and quiet. Mikos, who owns the house opposite, was squaring up to Kadous in the middle of the lane. He brandished a vicious-looking vine stave. 'I'll thrash you like a dog, you Black Sea bastard!'

'You lay a hand on my property and you'll answer to me!' I advanced on the pair.

'I caught him sniffing around my doorstep.' Mikos gestured menacingly at Kadous. 'You weren't expecting me back till tomorrow. Thought you'd set my wife squealing!'

'Put that stick down,' I said sharply, 'before I take it off you.'

Doing that would be easy enough. At least twenty years older than me, Mikos had grown fat and lazy now that Athens was at peace. In theory he was still young enough to be called up for military service but any district official in charge of a muster would be a fool to think any general would take him on.

Mikos dropped the stave but only so he could stride over and poke a pudgy finger into my chest. 'I'll see your slave executed for screwing my wife!'

'What?' I stared at him, incredulous. For one thing, the woman grizzling in the gateway opposite wasn't Onesime, Mikos's wretched wife. It was her sad little handmaid Alke.

He shook a fist at Kadous. 'He sneaks in to spread my wife's thighs when I travel to Corinth to buy beads. This

63

was my first trip of the year, so I hurried back to catch them—'

'Did you? No,' I retorted, 'he's no such fool!'

I knew Kadous wouldn't risk the hazards for any slave dragged into a citizen's adultery. Though it was possible the Phrygian had been tickling little Alke's fancy. As soon as we got a moment alone, I'd get the truth from him. For the moment I could only gesture for Kadous to get behind me.

'Where's your proof?' I demanded.

I couldn't let Mikos's accusation go unchallenged. Not with gates opening up and down the lane. I didn't want spiteful rumours taking wing around the neighbourhood. Once a slave gets a bad reputation, he gets blamed for everything and anything that goes awry.

It's not as if slaves can defend themselves. In any mire of claim and counter-claim in court, slave evidence must be tested by the public torturer. Most admit guilt or simply flee before risking such agonies.

'I caught that slut letting him in,' Mikos snarled.

Alke, the thin-faced slave girl, buried her face in her hands. I noticed vicious marks from that vine stave on her bare arms, freshly red and starting to bruise.

I stood toe to toe with the fat jeweller, raising my voice to make sure that all those flapping ears along the lane could hear me. 'She gave Kadous some charcoal yesterday when we had run short. He was carrying water from the fountain for her by way of thanks.'

Mikos sneered. 'A likely story.'

With a silent breath of thanks to Poseidon, I pointed

to a bucket I recognised sitting in a puddle of slopped water. 'Why else was my man carrying that? If that's your case, I'll happily see you in court.'

Mikos wasn't about to back down. 'If he sets foot in my house again, I'll gut him like a fish!'

'You won't get the chance,' I assured the bead seller.

Not that I imagined he'd try. Kadous was big and strong enough to beat the fool to a bloody pulp with his bare hands. I was thankful he'd had the sense not to respond to this provocation.

'Send your own slaves to fetch water in future, or your wife, if you dare. Meantime, if you lay a finger on my property outside your own walls, I'll see you answer to the magistrates.'

'Backed by your new noble friends?'

Before I could ask what he meant by that, Mikos stormed into his own house, dragging Alke with him. As the gate slammed, I winced. We all heard her rising wail cut short by a brutal slap.

I picked up the vine stave and handed it to Kadous who was standing in our gateway, scowling. 'Let's get some lunch.'

He nodded, his expression thunderous, turning away and muttering something in his mother tongue.

I looked at Zosime as I closed our own gate behind us. 'Do you think he could have killed that Carian?'

She grimaced. 'A stranger knocking on the wrong gate during a festival? Surely Mikos would have asked his business before butchering him?'

I wasn't so sure. 'He must have had some reason to

think he'd find Onesime with a lover. Are there rumours around the fountains?'

Zosime nodded. 'She's as false as that coloured glass that Mikos swears is garnets. She's been spreading her legs for Pyrrias since last summer, so the whispers say.' She didn't hide her contempt.

'She must have a taste for fat old men.' Pyrrias was much the same age as Mikos. He traded in spices from a warehouse down in Piraeus.

'She has a taste for their fat purses,' Zosime said curtly. 'Besides, Mikos married her to get some sons with citizen rights to inherit his business. That was nearly two years ago and I imagine he ploughs her furrow often enough. If he can't plant a seed to swell her belly, she has to find someone who can. If she's divorced for being barren she'll be sent back to her father's house and stuck there for life.'

That made distasteful sense. Pyrrias has eight or ten children thanks to his exhausted wife. 'There'll be trouble if they're caught.'

'Maybe this uproar will warn Pyrrias off.' Zosime shrugged.

I nodded. 'Let's hope so.'

Though who knew what tale Onesime might tell, especially if Mikos tried to beat the truth out of her. After this morning's farce, he'd be the laughing stock of the neighbourhood unless he could salvage his pride by proving he was right.

Whatever Onesime or Alke said, I'd defend Kadous to the hilt. The distance between slave and master closes up

66

after you've been in battle together. Even so, Kadous and I are closer than most. My father had bought him as a young slave when my brother Lysanias reached his eighteenth year and went off for his military training. When the phalanxes were called up for that disastrous Egyptian campaign, the Phrygian was at my brother's side. They were both trapped on Prosopitis, that thrice-cursed isle that the Persians encircled for a year and a half. When the Mede's army finally overran the mud banks, Kadous saw Lysanias die.

I don't know if the Phrygian ever told my father how he escaped the slaughter, or why he came back to Athens to tell us how Lysanias had fallen. He could so easily have vanished in such confusion. As long as he stayed clear of Attica, there'd have been little enough chance of meeting anyone who would know his face and could condemn him as a runaway slave. But he'd come back and he had seen Chairephanes and me through our own hoplite training, fetching and carrying our gear and advising us how to sleep comfortably camped out on a mountainside. He'd taught us when to move quickly and quietly to avoid a commander's wrath. I'd never asked why he had come home. It was enough for me that Kadous could tell us Lysanias hadn't died alone.

He came out into the porch from the storeroom to the left of the central chamber where Zosime and I sleep. The room on the right houses Zosime's loom and wools, and a spare bed for Menkaure or my brothers on nights when they've stayed too late to walk back to the city after dinner.

'There are some sardines left from last night. I bought

fresh bread before I fetched Alke's water.'

'We've brought olives and cheese.' I handed them over.

'I'll fetch some plates.' Zosime headed for the storeroom.

We all ate in thoughtful silence. I took care not to drip oil onto my clean tunic. Zosime gathered up our scraps for the hens. With any luck they'd soon be laying eggs again now that they were over their autumn moults and winter sulks.

I looked at the unfinished dining room to the left-hand side of our gate, opposite Kadous's quarters. At the moment, it housed an old, scarred table, my scrolls and papyrus scraps, pens and ink, together with a couple of stools, and my modest store of wine. When I got rich, it would have plastered and painted walls, with sumptuously cushioned couches and a mosaic floor. If I ever got rich. I couldn't imagine wealthy men would shower me with commissions after they'd seen the shambles of my play at the festival.

I wanted to run out to prostrate myself before the ancient statue of Dionysus Eleutherios in the little shrine overshadowed by the Acropolis. It wasn't too late to beg for his favour or, failing that, his pity. Alas, his most revered icon had been carried out of the city to the Academy's grove. It wouldn't be brought back to the theatre until this evening, and I had to be there to see it. There was no getting out of such duties.

I heaved a sigh. 'I'd better get back to the rehearsal.'

Zosime leaned over to kiss me. 'We'll see you at the theatre later, to honour Dionysos's return.'

Chapter Six

When I reached Aristarchos's gate, Mus opened up. Lysi-crates hurried towards me, grinning from ear to ear.

'Your masks are here and the costumes have just arrived.'

I didn't give Mikos or the dead Carian another thought. Better yet, the difference between the morning's pandemonium and that afternoon's rehearsals was like comparing a bawdy satyr play with the finest high tragedy. All three actors were perfect in word and gesture while the chorus danced and sang as though the muses performed among them. We ran through the market scene several times, and if their costume changes left Apollonides and Lysicrates breathless, that only added to the overall effect.

Menekles nodded approvingly as Hyanthidas saw the chorus off stage with a last flourish of his reed pipes. 'Euxenos is a fool to think he'll have the best music.'

As everyone murmured agreement, I wondered idly where my old pipe might be. As a boy I'd wanted to be a theatre player and my favourite uncle found me a battered instrument from somewhere. I'd practised and practised and practised until my brothers threatened to shove that pipe up my nose – or my arse – if I didn't stop.

Naturally I defied them until Father made his own disapproval clear. Making a living writing was one thing. That offered opportunities for respectable fame. But scratching around for chances to play music at private parties, in temple processions or at drama competitions? I might as well go begging for scraps at rich men's doors. After that I only played for my own amusement, and at family gatherings so my sisters could dance, until I had no sisters left at home.

Apollonides looked up at the gathering dusk. 'I think we should call it a day.'

'Thank you, all of you,' I said fervently. 'Take things easy tonight. You've earned your rest – but not too much wine, I beg you. Tomorrow we dedicate our performance to Dionysos, then we'll set Athens laughing loud enough to be heard in Delphi!'

That won me a rousing cheer.

'Let's have your masks and costumes, please.' Chrysion dragged three big baskets out from the shelter of the colonnade.

Aristarchos appeared in the archway from the inner courtyard. His personal slave Lydis was behind him, nimble and quick-witted, with a shock of unruly black hair. 'We should probably make our way to the theatre, Philocles.'

'Of course.' I ducked my head obediently.

A burly slave escorted us as we followed the road around the eastern end of the Acropolis. I contemplated the scaffolding framing the new shrines rising from the ashes and rubble on the heights. Whatever you say about Pericles, and safely behind closed doors my family says a lot, he's brought peace to our city. Peace and prosperity, enabling us to finally restore the temples burned by Persian barbarians ten years before I was born. Peace had secured the silver to refurbish the theatre where we were headed.

How dare that Carian lout accuse us of greed? Our forefathers had left those blackened ruins untouched to remind us every day that we must defeat the Persians. We saw them from first light to dusk, whenever we turned a street corner to glimpse the Acropolis high above us. That boy thought we didn't know suffering? We had seen Attica's farms and olive groves burned as well as our sacred city sacked. Regardless, Athens defied Darius at Marathon with only the Plataeans to help us. We cut down those invaders for the sake of all Hellenes. We defeated them at Salamis and Mycale and Eurymedon. Three generations of Athenians shed their blood in that once-endless war.

How quickly our ungrateful neighbours forgot how much they owed us. After he returned from Egypt, Kadous marched behind me when my contingent from Alopeke followed General Tolmides as he led Athens' soldiers to quell dissent in Boeotia. We'd celebrated the capture of Chaeronea with captured wine and women. Then we'd retreated shoulder to shoulder, step by dogged step, from the bloody battlefield at Coronea, leaving Tolmides lying dead behind us.

The price of our army's safe passage home had been Boeotia's release from the Delian League that had once sworn such fervent unity against Persia. They'd been happy to hand over their coin, while Athenian armies spent their lives saving all Hellas from slavery. Once we had peace though, they bickered and moaned at every turn.

'I've been thinking about our conversation this afternoon,' Aristarchos remarked as we took the path leading to the theatre. 'About these Carians and this story about the Delian League's tributes being reassessed at this festival. How likely is it that they've confused the Dionysia with the Panathenaia?'

'Unlikely,' I conceded. Every Hellene from Sicily to the Black Sea knows when it's a Great Panathenaic Year, just like everyone knows when to head for the Olympics or the Pythian or Nemean Games.

Aristarchos stopped walking. 'Our allies know exactly when they must pay tribute. No one wants to risk defaulting.'

'And no one would come all the way across the Acgean to plead poverty without good reason to believe they'd be heard.' I recalled the young Carian's conviction when he'd accosted me in the agora. 'So who persuaded this Xandyberis that the Archons would listen?'

I was beginning to think whoever was stirring up trouble had miscalculated, not imagining that the Carian would enlist an Athenian to write a rousing speech for him. That risked the lie becoming the talk of the agora and a lot of people asking awkward questions. The first thing the authorities would want to know was who had started this rumour.

'Why do you suppose your dead man's throat was cut, if not to silence him?' Aristarchos asked with an edge to his voice as he started walking again.

'I think we had better find out,' I said grimly.

But that would have to wait. By the time we reached the theatre, the approaches were thronged. The marble seats for the great and good had long since been claimed by keen folk who'd come prepared with cushions, along with the slaves sent even earlier to reserve places for the likes of Aristarchos. Lydis waved to a skinny youth in a dark tunic whom I thought I recognised from my patron's household.

'I'll see you after the procession and we'll make our own private libations.' Aristarchos dismissed me with a courteous smile.

I hurried to the theatre's western entrance where I'd arranged to meet Zosime and Kadous. They were already waiting for me. Distant brass pipes and cymbals heralded the approach of the torch-lit procession as Kadous forced a path for us through the jostling crowd. We managed to cram ourselves onto the end of a bench, high up on the hillside.

The procession soon arrived. The well-born youths escorting the god's statue answered cheers from the packed seats with raucous shouts. Their ribaldry was enough to make the bawdiest poet blush. Alongside those honoured to carry baskets holding more decorous offerings for the rituals, young men brandished oversized stuffed-cloth

73

phalluses, to remind us how Dionysos's displeasure could strike men down with sores and boils on our tenderest parts.

That was a warning of the risks of straying from the sanctified marital bed, so my mother told me and my brothers when we were still young enough for such mysteries to lie well ahead of us. Father was more inclined to joke quietly about being reminded not to drink too much wine. Either way, the god always has the last laugh at some over-cocky lad's expense.

As the procession reached the theatre, some of the devotees' gestures were comical, others merely obscene as they spilled across the dancing floor where the festival choruses would soon be performing. These young men had just been released from their teachers' and trainers' supervision at the gymnasium, or they were returning from garrison duty as newly minted soldiers. No wonder they were feeling a rush of blood at the prospect of a few days' freedom amid the city's entertainments and temptations.

While I clapped and cheered along with the crowd, all my attention was fixed on the battered wooden effigy on its slowly rolling carriage. It is so shapeless that it barely resembles a man except for the mask it wears, but that revered and ancient icon has epitomised Dionysos since the days when gods and heroes mingled with mortals. As a focus for my prayers to implore his divine favour, it was second to none.

The effigy was approaching the central plinth. The rites unfolded with pious prayers and generous libations as the sacred image was reverently manhandled into place.

I didn't take my eyes off it, silently beseeching Dionysos's favour in return for all our dedication to the play. I was so lost in my thoughts that Zosime had to shake me to let me know that the crowd was starting to leave.

'Sorry, yes.' I shivered. The night was growing cold as the stars twinkled overhead. Recollection abruptly hollowed my stomach. 'I'm supposed to meet Aristarchos. He said we'd pour a libation together.'

'He's down by the statue.' Zosime pointed at a group silhouetted against the festival torches.

I stifled a sigh of relief as we made our way down to the dancing floor. I was less thrilled to recognise the two young men standing with Aristarchos, now released from their processional duties.

'Who is this lovely lady?' Hipparchos smiled lopsidedly and nearly dropped the festival phallus he held carelessly sloped over one shoulder like a spear. As he laughed uproariously I smelled the wine on his breath.

'This is my companion, Zosime. My devoted companion,' I said meaningfully. I didn't want to insult Aristarchos by slapping down his son, but I didn't want these young pricks thinking Zosime was fair game just because she wasn't a citizen's Athenian-born wife.

Nikandros laughed a little too loudly, holding up his hands in mock surrender and nearly dropping his own festival phallus. 'Oops!'

Hipparchos giggled so convulsively that I thought he was going to throw up. Now I could guess what prompted my patron's distaste for drunken young men carousing through the city.

'It's a pleasure to meet you.' Aristarchos bowed courteously to Zosime before turning to the two youths. 'If you'll excuse us, we would like to make our own offering for our play's success.'

Hipparchos might be stupidly drunk, but he understood that this was a command not a request. He managed to offer his father an unbalanced bow. 'Then we'll bid you good night.'

'Good night.' Nikandros ignored the rest of us as he bowed to Aristarchos with perfunctory respect. 'I'll see you – whenever.'

Hipparchos sketched a wave in the air and the pair of them headed unsteadily towards a knot of laughing youths loitering by the entrance. The gaggle greeted their friends, all gilded by the torchlight.

Aristarchos turned his back on them. 'Lydis?'

The slave stepped out of the shadows. He held a jug of wine and a pouring cup. Dionysos only knows where he'd got them from.

The young men headed off for some fresh revelry. We were left surrounded by darkness only relieved by the pine-resin torch held by Aristarchos's burly bodyguard. I felt a curious sense of isolation. Sounds of festivities down in the city seemed no more than the noise of the sea. It was as though we stood on the shore of a steep and rocky island, with the cliffs of the Acropolis rising behind us. The night air was fragrant with woodland scents rolling down from the thickets high on its slope.

Aristarchos stood silent, contemplative. Then he shook

off his preoccupation. 'You should do the honours, Philocles.'

I took the cup from Lydis and fought to still my trembling hands as the slave poured the wine. I dared not make a mess of this, overlooked by the city's most sacred shrines. But what should I say? There are times when making my living from words is absolutely no help at all. I could only summon a heartfelt plea.

'Master of comedy, look favourably on our efforts tomorrow. Everything we do is in tribute to you.'

As I spoke, I fervently hoped that everybody else, from Apollonides to Hyanthidas, was offering Dionysos the first taste of their wine this evening. I tipped the cupful over the statue's plinth.

Aristarchos took the cup and made his own libation. 'We can ask no more and we will do no less than our best. We swear it by all the gods and goddesses above and below.'

I looked up as I heard an owl's faint call. The bird floated overhead on silent wings as it returned to its roost in the shadowy crags. An omen of good luck, but was it meant for us?

Aristarchos had heard it too. He gazed up at the star-strewn night sky. Then he looked at me and smiled. 'We have a busy few days ahead of us. I think an early night would be wise.'

'Indeed,' I agreed.

We left the theatre and walked together in amiable silence along the path skirting the southern flank of the Acropolis, through the haphazard rebuilding by Athenians who'd reclaimed their looted homes as soon as the Persians retreated after we defeated their navy at Salamis.

Reaching the junction of the roads that led up towards the agora on the one hand and southwards out of the city on the other, we all halted.

'Until tomorrow. Have a good evening.' Aristarchos bade us both a courteous farewell before heading for home, flanked by his watchful slaves.

Chapter Seven

The first day of the Dionysia started very nicely for me. The bed frame creaked as Zosime rolled over and slipped her arms around my neck. Lithe and naked, she drew me close to kiss me long and hard. That wasn't the only thing growing long and hard as I stroked her burnished copper skin, her firm buttock, her soft breast. She pressed herself against me as I teased her nipple with my thumb. As her hand slid down between us to encourage my arousal, I murmured my appreciation.

She pulled away and sat up. Opening the small chest beside the bed, she anointed a scrap of sponge and tucked it deep inside herself. Olive oil. Blessed Athena's gift to our ancestors, which secures our eternal devotion. It's the foundation of every meal, it heals and cleans our bodies and lights our homes after sunset. It's the highest prize at the games held in our goddess's honour and a man can be put to death for felling an olive tree. Finally, when the dregs of an amphora sour, Athena offers women one last boon. That oil can stop a man's seed taking root in a fertile womb.

Neither of us wants a baby. We discovered we had that in common when I came back to the pottery to buy a white flask for funeral rites. Her first and longed-for pregnancy had been the death of my younger sister. While Zosime sketched a likeness of Ianthine with her brush, she told me her mother had died in childbirth, labouring after a string of miscarriages in her determination to give Menkaure a son. I'll leave raising the next generation of Athenian citizens to my brothers. Besides, any sons or daughters Zosime gave me would be bastards by Athenian law, with precious few rights or privileges. I won't burden a child with that, any more than I'll give up the woman I love.

Zosime straddled me. A few strokes of her oil-slick hand and she guided me inside her. As she leaned forward, I cupped and kissed her breasts and we lost ourselves in that bliss which the finest poets can't hope to describe. A comedy scribbler like me shouldn't even try.

No wonder I dozed off again. I only stirred when Zosime got out of bed and poured water into a wash-basin.

'So what did Aristarchos have to say about the dead man, Xandyberis, last night?'

I recognised that tone. This wasn't just some passing remark. I opened my eyes. 'How do you mean?'

'Did you tell him what the boy in the agora said? Surely you want to know why these Carians are so convinced that the Delian League's levy will be reassessed?' she challenged me.

I gazed at the ceiling. I did. I also wanted to know who'd killed Xandyberis, because I'd been thinking some more about why his corpse had been dumped at my gate.

If his killers thought we'd already met, and that I'd accepted his commission, it would have been an emphatic warning for me to mind my own business.

I hoped that satisfied whoever was lurking in the shadows. Unless someone decided the benefits of shutting my mouth outweighed the risks of killing an Athenian citizen. I had better take care not to walk back from the city on my own after dark.

That wasn't the only thing darkening my mood. 'Our allies offer a tribute to Athena,' I said curtly. 'They're not paying a levy.'

'It might have been a tribute to Apollo when the League's treasury was still in Delos,' Zosime retorted as she washed herself briskly, 'but that's not how people outside Athens see it these days.'

I rolled onto my side, raised myself up on one elbow, and stared at her. 'What do you mean?'

She emptied the basin into the slop pail. 'Ten years ago Pericles moved the League treasury to Athens. Then the city started building all these new temples even though that money's supposed to be for ships.'

'The people debated all the new building plans and voted to approve them,' I protested.

'The *Athenian* Assembly voted for Pericles's plans,' she countered, opening her clothes chest. 'What about anyone in Naxos, or Thasos? When did the Samians agree?'

'It was agreed when Callias made peace with Emperor Artaxerxes,' I insisted.

'Not according to everyone.' Zosime shook out a length of pale blue wool. 'Besides, how is that free and clear agreement? A man in the Miletus market place would have agreed to anything to end the war with Persia.'

'It's in everyone's interests to honour Athena,' I asserted. 'Without her aid, the Persians would have conquered us all.'

'Who can doubt it? But isn't it still better to ask than just to take?' Zosime changed her mind about the blue and pulled out a vivid red that my sisters would envy. With only herself and her father to spin and weave for, she can buy the costly dyed wools that my mother calls unnecessary extravagance.

'Besides, it's not only these new temples and the theatre and the Council Chamber, and whatever else Pericles has planned.' She shook out the cloth. 'People come here for the festivals and hear how ordinary Athenians are paid to serve in the Assembly and to sit on a jury. Where does all that money come from?'

'From Attica's silver mines in Laurium. Everybody knows that.'

'Are you sure everyone believes it?' Zosime cocked her head. 'You don't think that man in the Miletus market place wonders if the Archons are helping themselves to the Delian League's money?'

You know that expression 'lying like a Cretan'? Ever since meeting Zosime I've wondered who coined it and why, because she never spares me the most brutal truths.

'All sorts of unfounded nonsense must slosh up and down the Ionian coast,' I said crossly. 'Who knows what garbled rumours get passed from ship to ship and from island to island?'

'What's that got to do with the price of fish?' She folded over the top quarter of the red rectangle with a deft twist of her wrists. 'This Xandyberis risked coming all the way here at the very start of the sailing season. He was ready to pay you to write him a speech, most likely out of his own pocket. Someone must have convinced him that the journey would be worth it.'

'He had to come to the Dionysia regardless, to bring his town's tribute and the armour they owe to Athena.' I was still brooding over the notion that Ionians might suspect Athens of double-dealing. Surely everyone knows that anyone holding public office here faces a merciless audit at the end of their year's service. No magistrate would dare to misappropriate funds, still less risk divine wrath by embezzling coin from Athena's own temple.

'Someone had to bring their tribute, but I'll wager good money it didn't have to be Xandyberis. A man of influence who could afford Persian shoes could have sent somebody else.' Zosime wrapped the cloth around herself, trapping the fold loosely under her arms. 'He came because he was certain he could ease the burden of the levy for his people. He risked his life on that voyage, Philocles. You've never been further than Boeotia. I still remember sailing here from Crete. The ship nearly foundered twice, and the captain said we only met summer squalls.'

I sat up, hugging my knees. 'But who would tell such a lie and why?'

I could only think of reasons that might make a

comedy plot. To get a stern father away from home so a feckless son could do something stupid. So everyone might believe the head of a household had drowned, until he returned to cause endless confusion. An old man might go on a journey to fake his own death before returning in disguise, to see if he was truly mourned. Instead, he'd find everyone celebrating. I should write those ideas down.

Zosime tugged up the fold of cloth to pin it on each shoulder with matching silver brooches. Now the loose fabric hung down to cloak her gorgeous breasts with a decorous double layer. 'Maybe that boy you met in the agora has some answers.'

I doubted it. He looked the type to fight first and not bother with any questions later. Let's hope he had some companions with cooler heads.

'I wonder how many people are here from Pargasa. If Aristarchos can find out where the delegation is lodging, I'll go and see them and ask a few questions. After the festival, though.' I threw back the blankets.

Zosime made sure the unsewn cloth overlapped at her side and secured her dress with one of Epikrates's best belts. It never ceases to impress me how quickly a woman can transform a simple length of cloth into an elegantly draped garment.

'You know, there's more to the Delian League than just fighting the Persians,' I reminded her as I got up. 'Settlers from Attica founded every town in Ionia, back in the days of the heroes. They all acknowledge Athens as their mother city. That's why they begged us to lead the struggle against the Persian Emperor. Those new temples on the Acropolis honour that ancestral relationship. That's why the first portion of their tribute goes to Athena and that's acknowledged in the public record for all to see.'

'Tell me something I don't know.' She cocked her head, sardonic, as she donned the gold filigree earrings I'd bought her from a Carthaginian trader to celebrate my success at the Lenaia.

'But don't you see how many people are drawn here now we have peace?' I refilled the wash-basin. 'From all over Hellas. Not just masons and architects to build the new temples but all manner of craftsmen; sculptors, bronze-casters, goldsmiths—'

'Potters and painters?' Zosime raised her eyebrows. 'What does my father's decision to come here mean to some poor Carian struggling to feed his children on the other side of the Aegean?'

'The harbours at Piraeus sees more ships come and go every year,' I said with irritation as I washed. 'That trade sends at least as much silver east as we see coming westwards. That's not all Ionia gets from us. This Carian boy mentioned his town council? They make their own laws and manage their own affairs and they can thank Athens for that. Otherwise that young fool and his family would be crushed by some local tyrant ruling by whim and decree. Either that or an Imperial satrap would screw them for every last grain of their harvests, sending bushel baskets to feed Persia's armies while their children starve.'

I warmed to my argument as I went to my own clothes chest to find the sage-green tunic my mother had woven and sewn, to be sure I looked respectable in front of the whole city today. 'Do you suppose they'd have any right of appeal? Anyone who raises a hand under Persian oppression gets it chopped off. If he's lucky. Otherwise it's his head on the block. Those satraps keep order through fear, brutality and blood. But Athens is every Ionian's mother city. They can all appeal to our courts if they feel local judgement is lacking. The humblest can stand before the Assembly and speak without fear or favour, to make their case when their tribute's reviewed.'

'Only if they can afford to travel to Athens!'

Zosime seemed determined to argue. I hate it when that happens. It's not like quarrelling with my sisters or anyone else born and raised in Athens. I can read them like a freshly written scroll. Zosime though, she can be as impossible to understand as Egyptian hieroglyphs.

Thanks be to Athena, Kadous called us for breakfast. He'd already been out to buy honeycakes. As we sat and ate, I heard passers-by in the lane.

'Is everyone hereabouts going to the festival?' I felt uneasy about leaving our little house unprotected.

Kadous shook his head. 'Pyrrias's mother is too feeble this year.'

'Sosistratos's daughter-in-law is staying home with her new baby,' Zosime added.

'Good to know.' Both women would be attended by slaves and most likely would have visitors as well. Plenty of witnesses to raise an alarm if anything untoward happened.

Even so, when we walked up the main road after

86

breakfast, it seemed as if Alopeke's whole population was heading for the city. The crowds grew even thicker inside the walls, pungent with sweat and perfume.

Taking the southern path skirting the Acropolis, I glanced upwards but, even in the daylight, I couldn't see the building work from this angle. Instead I took a fresh look at the ramshackle houses and workshops thrown up amid the remnants of the Persian destruction.

Doubtless those first returning Athenians had sworn this was only temporary shelter. They'd soon rebuild their homes, they'd told each other, more elegant, more substantial. I pictured the scene, though I couldn't see any way to make a comedy out of this. Soon winter had come, and the burden of keeping their families clothed and fed while the city struggled to rise from the ashes took its toll. Not many laughs in that.

It was easy to see how plans for proper rebuilding had yielded to making running repairs, knocking through walls and adding rooms, piecemeal, as time and money allowed. By now, even the most loyal Athenian had to admit this district was a mess.

Pericles planned to sort it all out. The theatre wasn't his only project hereabouts. I'd heard Apollonides and Menekles discussing rumours of a grand new hall for play rehearsals and concerts.

Disgruntled Ionians would hardly be thrilled to see yet more facilities for Athenian festivals paid for out of public funds. I remembered what Zosime had said earlier. It's all very well saying that the great celebrations like the Dionysia and the Panathenaia are open to all but there's no denying those of us in Attica benefit most, having the least distance to travel.

Though, at the moment, it seemed that every Hellene from Sicily to the Black Sea had come here. We were jostled from every direction, deafened by citizens and visitors alike shouting joyful greetings. I kept my arm around Zosime's shoulders and Kadous walked on her other side, warding off the crush.

'Can you see Nymenios or Chairephanes?' I called over Zosime's head. We had a long-standing agreement to meet at the theatre's western entrance, but it looked as if half of Athens had made the same arrangement.

The Phrygian scanned the crowd, shading squinting eyes with a leathery hand. He pointed. 'Over there.'

As the flood of humanity threatened to sweep us past my family entirely, Kadous forced a path towards them. I tucked Zosime close behind him and brought up the rear, watchful for any thieves ready to snatch her earrings or my purse from my belt.

My brothers flanked Melina, Nymenios's wife, and our married sister, Kleio. Her husband, Kalliphon, was deep in conversation with my brothers' neighbour Pamphilos, presumably discussing woodwork since they're both carpenters. I noted that Chairephanes was escorting Pamphilos's daughter, Glykera, today.

'Philocles!' Melina waved a gleeful hand. She wore a crisply pleated saffron gown and her hair had been curled with hot irons and swept up with an embroidered ribbon. She was ready to make the most of five days setting aside her daily routine of childcare, cooking, cleaning, laundry, spinning and weaving. Foreigners who believe all those tales about Athenians locking their wives and daughters away should consider all the chores that keep women busy, certainly in families like ours that can't afford a phalanx of domestic slaves.

'Mother's not here?' I looked at Nymenios as Zosime joined the other women to share embraces and admiration for each other's dresses and jewellery.

'She said she'd rather look after the children.' Nymenios lowered his voice. 'That way she can supervise the cooking. You know she won't believe the girls will do everything right unless someone is watching.'

'She'll be here to see your play tomorrow,' Chairephanes assured me.

Kalliphon interrupted everyone with a brisk clap of his hands. 'We'd better find some seats. The procession will soon be here.'

'We'll see you later.' Zosime gave me a quick hug and kiss.

I watched them climb up the rocky slope. Kadous followed close behind until Nymenios claimed an empty bench scant moments before some other family reached it. The Phrygian continued on to the very topmost seats where other slaves with permission to enjoy the holiday were already gathering.

I skirted the stage and its buildings, heading for the rehearsal ground on the theatre's eastern side. Whatever Pericles might have in mind to replace it, for the moment temporary wooden walls and awnings divided up the space. Officially this was to stop rival choruses distracting one another. This close to the competition, with everyone's nerves as ragged as a barbarian's beard, the flimsy barriers mostly stopped actors, dancers and singers coming to blows.

A lanky youth trod on my foot, recoiling without looking behind him when he realised he was about to walk into the wrong enclosure.

'Watch where you're going!' I snapped.

As he turned, I saw he barely had a bristle on his chin. Too young to be singing in any play's chorus, he must be here for the youth choir competition between the ten voting tribes. I took pity on him. 'Who are you looking for?'

'Cecropis,' he quavered, his accent fresh from the slopes of Hymettos.

'Over that way.' I took hold of his shoulders and turned him around.

'Philocles!' a voice trilled. A plump matron in a vivid yellow gown flapped eager hands to attract my attention, blocking the entrance to a sailcloth gateway.

'Is everyone here?' I tried to swallow my apprehension.

Lysicrates wagged a disapproving finger. 'Tell me if you like my new dress,' he chided in a breathy falsetto.

He turned and preened, tossing his close-cropped head as though he was already wearing the ludicrously bewigged mask he held in his other hand.

I grinned. 'Darling, you look fabulous.'

'Don't I just?' he chuckled in his usual tone: resonant and masculine and invariably startling for anyone who'd only ever heard him on the stage.

Anyone who thinks any actor can play a woman's role is a fool. There's so much more to a convincing performance than hiding a man's beard behind a mask and cloaking his muscles in draperies. An array of subtle hints persuades an audience that they're watching a woman: the way a character walks; her manner as she stands; how she reacts to the men around her. Onlookers might never notice, or rather, they won't realise that they're noticing such details, but without these unobtrusive tricks an audience really has to force themselves to forget that they're watching a man in a dress.

Then there's the voice. Even experienced actors can all too easily sound like they're mimicking their mother after too many cups of wine. Lysicrates could find the right tones for any woman from a slender, soulful nymph to a bawdy brothel madam with bosom and buttocks so fat with padding she's as broad as she is tall.

As soon as I'd had his promise to play his part I knew that Zosime, Melina and Kleio wouldn't be scorning the women in my play as foolish caricatures.

'Why are you standing sentry?'

Lysicrates grinned. 'The other choruses are all trying to see our costumes. No one knows what to make of *The Builders* as a title for a play.'

'Really?' So Aristarchos was right. I hoped that was a good omen.

'Not that there's much to see,' Lysicrates chuckled.

I surveyed the assembled men helping each other secure their masks. They all wore the customary body-stockings from the neck down, and Aristarchos's coin had paid for tightly woven cloth. No seams or folds sagged or drooped to embarrass this chorus with catcalls from the audience. Over those stage skins, each man wore a plain tunic, some of them smudged with paint, others powdered with plaster and stone dust, a few stained with clay.

'Good day to you!' Chrysion appeared.

I glanced meaningfully at his groin. 'There hasn't been anything to see, I hope?'

'Everyone knows to be discreet,' he assured me. 'No one will suspect a thing until the performance.'

I could only hope so. 'Have you seen Euxenos's costumes?'

'His Butterflies?' Chrysion snorted. 'Very gaudy but hardly practical. If that chorus gets through their first dance without treading on each other's wings, I will eat Lysicrates's wig.'

'Really?' My spirits rose. 'Have you drawn the lots to see who goes first? Where are we in the procession?'

'Third. Now—' he shooed me away '—we've got everything in hand. Go and see our patron arrive. Say a prayer to Dionysus Eleutherios.'

Menekles snapped urgent fingers from the far side of the chorus to attract my attention. 'Go and find out who the judges will be!'

'Of course.' I hurried to the eastern side of the stage. Every head in the crowd was turning westwards, hearing the dulcet song of the double flutes. The patrons' procession was approaching.

Chapter Eight

Today's rites had none of last night's ribaldry. The Dionysia's patrons were to be honoured for pouring out their silver like wine in tribute to the gods, bringing glory to our city. Ten of Athens' wealthiest men had financed the men's choirs from each voting tribe and ten more had financed the boys'. Comedy was picking the pockets of five others, one for each play, while Tragedy gravely accepted tribute from a further three.

Now all those well-born men could breathe easier knowing this public service meant their fortunes were safe from the Archons for this year and the next. Better yet, they wouldn't be called on to finance a trireme; a public honour incurring considerably greater cost than staging a play, and winning far less widespread acclaim.

Well-born youths and girls carried offerings of oil and wine. Others held baskets of bread and grain. They led the procession across the dancing floor to Dionysos's statue. The masked effigy stood there, inscrutable.

Aristarchos and the other noble patrons were entering the theatre. He walked with calm composure, as though having thousands of citizens stare at him was of no particular consequence.

His white tunic of pristine, pleated linen was sumptuously embroidered with tiny flowers and leaves in vivid blues and greens. I wondered if that was his wife's or daughters' work, to show the city their pride and devotion. More likely, I suspected, some talented slave had spent her last few months bent over that cloth with needle and thread. Gold plaques adorned his broad leather belt, doubtless embossed with mythological scenes to impress those who got close enough to see. The tunic's hem brushed his equally expensive shoes, the sunlight catching their bronze-tipped laces. A formal cloak with generous folds was elegantly draped around his broad shoulders, deep-dyed the colour of a dusky sea. Phytalids need never skimp on fabric out of consideration for the cost. Crowned with the golden diadem that a festival patron's generosity earns from the grateful city, Aristarchos carried his finery with enviable poise. I suspect he'd practised. Some of those other influential men had doubtless looked very fine standing before their admiring households, but after processing across the city they mostly arrived at the theatre looking like an unmade bed, clutching at slipping swathes.

What would such an untidy display do for their standing, the next time jurors of modest means listened to them prosecute a case in the law courts? What would traders and craftsmen remember, when these men argued for some new law proposed in the People's Assembly? This chance to impress Athens' citizens, to convince us that men of substance should be heeded and obeyed, was the unspoken repayment for their coin.

For the moment, these patrons were courteously ushered to their marble seats of honour, already softened with cushions. Now everyone heard the clacking hooves and sedate murmurs of the cattle brought for sacrifice before Dionysos's shrine. The consecrated beasts, their horns decorated with spring flowers and trailing ribbons, were carefully guided through the theatre and past the god's statue. The audience nudged each other, eyes bright as they anticipated the feasting to come. These were fine, plump beasts, reared in peace and plenty now the strife of recent years with Euboea, Boeotia and the Spartans was over.

Eagle-eyed theatre hands darted out with shovels and brushes to remove unseemly traces left by the cattle as the Archon for Religious Affairs rose from his own seat of honour and climbed the steps at the side of the stage. 'We will now select the judges for this year's competition!' His words were lost in cheers from the audience, all the way up to the slaves on the topmost benches.

Down in the front few rows, I could see some individuals acknowledging applause around them with nods and smiles. These must be the candidates put forward by each voting tribe. Not as richly dressed as Aristarchos and his fellow patrons, they were still men with well-filled strongboxes, and clearly flattered at being the centre of attention.

A voting tribe's officials always listen whenever a play's patron suggests they propose a particular man as a potential judge. That's why the final choice rests with the lottery guided by the gods and goddesses. Even then, only five of the ten judges' votes will count towards winning a victory, making any attempt at swaying the competitions' results futile. Mortal men must work hard to secure divine favour.

A stagehand carried the first tall, narrow-necked urn onto the stage. He knelt before the Archon and offered it up.

'The judge from Acamantis will be . . .' The magistrate reached in, ostentatiously looking away even though the urn's mouth was barely wide enough for his clenched fist to withdraw a potsherd. He opened his fingers and looked at the name scratched on the broken pottery. 'Agathokles Apollodorou.'

The man made his way to the end of the row where he'd been sitting and was escorted to the very front seats. He was trying to look suitably modest at being selected by Dionysos but he couldn't restrain his smile of delight once his backside hit the cushioned marble.

I waited, tense, for the name to be drawn from the next urn. Would the judge for Hippothontis be one of the men who'd so openly sneered at my play for the Lenaia? What if it was someone with political reasons to vote against any victory honouring Aristarchos?

'Timon Pamphilou.'

No, I didn't know him either. That was a relief. By the time the last seat was filled, only one of the men now enjoying the best view of the stage gave me any concern.

Apollonides insisted that Dracontides, son of Euathlos, held a grudge against him. The influential landowner from Aiantis had been mercilessly mocked in Morsimos's last play, *The Ploughmen*. Apollonides had played the lead role of the country farmer whose savagely cutting lines had been directed at a thinly disguised caricature of Dracontides. Naturally the audience had greeted such ridicule with howls of laughter, even the ones who hadn't set foot outside the city since the walls to Piraeus were built.

It was hard to believe a judge would punish a completely different performance because of words another playwright once put in a hired actor's mouth. Well, there was nothing we could do if he was so petty. We'd just have to pray that tainted vote wasn't one of the five that counted. I glanced at Dionysos's masked effigy with a silent appeal.

As the stagehand retreated with the last of the urns, the religious Archon raised his hands high, first to the crowd and then turning to the god's ancient statue. 'The city of Athens dedicates this festival to Dionysos!'

As the magistrate left the stage, the crowd shuffled and murmured, eager to get their first look at the choruses and actors who'd be entertaining them for the next few days.

My time had come. The moment was finally here. I was about to take the stage in front of the largest audience I had ever known. My stomach felt so hollow, I might not have eaten for days. Not that I could have swallowed anything. My throat had a lump in it like the stone that tricked Kronos, out to devour the infant Zeus.

This was a hundred times worse than the Lenaia. There were thousands more people out there. If they didn't like my play, I'd be humiliated to the end of my days. My legs

97

were as stiff as carved marble. I couldn't take a single step.

'Mind your back, Philodemos!' Euxenos shoved me aside as he led his Butterflies out. The chorus scurried after him, flapping wings of painted cloth sewn to the side seams of their costumes and tied to wrist and ankle. His actors were a trio of men dressed for travel, escorted by Diagoras. Their musician raised his double pipes with a flourish of familiar notes that won a ripple of happy recognition from the crowd.

Bastard. Anger burned through my nausea. If I could have reached Euxenos, I'd have punched him for calling me Philodemos. He knew what my name was and as Zeus was my witness, he'd better fear it. Now this competition really was underway.

As I clenched my fists, Pittalos walked past, alongside a suave man about town, a frivolous nymph and a stooped old countryman. His chorus of Sheep trailed after their leader, whose mask was complete with leather collar and bell. Their pipe player was making an excellent job of mimicking plaintive bleating, already prompting laughter from the upper benches.

'Ready?' Lysicrates appeared at my side, masked and wigged. 'Any disasters among the judges?'

'I don't think so. All right, let's go.' Discreetly wiping my sweating palms on the sides of my tunic, I walked out onto the circular dancing floor with Lysicrates on my arm throwing flirtatious nods and gestures in all directions.

Apollonides and Menekles marched on either side of us, bold heroes in breastplates and helmets. Chrysion followed, leading our gang of workmen who could have strolled off any building site in Athens. Almost as plainly dressed, in contrast to the other musicians' fancy tunics, Hyanthidas brought up the rear. He was playing a jaunty medley of the tunes such labourers favoured. We'd agreed he'd keep his original compositions for the performance itself.

I fixed a smile on my face, as immoveable as the one on a comedy mask. Acknowledging the massive crowd with a wave, I tried to look as though I didn't have a care in the world. Inside, I was quaking. I could already see this vast audience weren't interested in us. Most were looking over our heads in hopes of some more impressive spectacle.

They got it in Strato's Brigands, who swaggered on wearing those red-headed Thracian masks, with swirling barbarian tattoos painted all over their body-stockings. The trio of actors dressed as Athenian travellers, mother, father and youthful son, all cringed with appropriate terror as this chorus capered to raucous northern rhythms.

While the audience clapped and murmured, I stole a discreet sideways glance at Chrysion's men. I could see the end of a cheeky red leather phallus poking out below the hem of a couple of tunics but there was nothing more obvious to see than any of the other traditional comedy cocks worn by every other actor in male garb. So far, so good.

Last, and after the Brigands, clearly least in the eyes of the audience, Trygaeos led on his chorus of Philosophers, all wrapped up in faded cloaks with flowing white beards and wigs. Seeing his actors were two callow youths and a stern father, muttering suggested the crowd had already worked out that play's plot for themselves.

As the comedy companies followed each other around the dancing floor, I saw Chrysion was right about Euxenos's Butterflies. Those gaudily painted wings trailed tantalisingly on the ground whenever a chorus member let his arms hang down, just waiting for someone to step on that painted cloth and tear it loose. If I'd been a little closer, I might even have done so myself. That's probably why Lysicrates's firm hold on my arm held me back to a stately, measured pace.

Coming full circle, we slowed to allow Pittalos's Sheep to leave the theatre ahead of us. Menekles gave me a long, slow wink through his mask's eyehole. I could hear him smiling with satisfaction as he spoke.

'We're going to give them all a good run for our patron's money.'

'Oh yes.' Apollonides had no doubt. 'Oh, sorry, please excuse us.'

We stepped aside to allow the first of the tragedy choruses to go past. They were ominously costumed as Odysseus's men gaunt with hunger on the Isle of Helios. I was looking forward to Zoilos's tragedies and seeing what new twists he'd found amid Homer's canny hero's misadventures.

Once we returned to our designated enclosure, Lysicrates knelt down to allow one of the chorus to unpin his colossal wig. 'So what are your plans for the rest of the day?' he asked me.

'Come and watch the choir competition with us,'

urged Menekles. 'We should look for some up-and-coming talent.'

Chrysion nodded as he removed his own mask. 'It's never too early to approach good singers for next year's Lenaia.'

'They'll all be singing because they've chosen to,' said Menekles with mingled relief and satisfaction. 'Not just to get the military deferment.'

'Have you had any thoughts?' Apollonides looked expectantly at me. 'For your next play?'

I blinked. 'We don't even know who'll be called to read for the Archons at New Year.'

All three actors laughed. Lysicrates grinned. 'I don't think you need worry.'

'Really?' I didn't know whether to be flattered or terrified by their confidence in me.

'Right, you lot!' With an ear-splitting shout, Chrysion turned to the chorus. They were busy undressing and stowing their masks and costumes in vast wicker baskets. Stagehands were waiting to get everything safely stowed under lock and key in the theatre buildings.

'Enjoy the choir competition. Go home and feast with your families. Do not get so drunk you can't get out of bed bright and early,' he said with emphasis. 'I want you all here in good time tomorrow, in case we draw first place in the order.'

Hyanthidas raised his hand. 'Would that be to our advantage or not?'

He was endlessly curious about the ins and outs of Athens' drama competitions. Music and poetry contests at Corinth's Isthmian Games were very different, from what he'd told me.

'You can argue that coming and going,' Chrysion told the pipe player. 'Go first and everyone who comes after has to measure up to you.'

Menekles shrugged. 'Go later and your performance is fresher in the judges' minds.'

Apollonides would have said something but the first full-throated verses in praise of Dionysos drowned him out. The choir competition had started. All the actors' heads turned and I swear if their ears could prick like a dog's they would have.

If this was any indication, the standard of singing this year would be higher than ever. I reckoned Menekles was right. None of these choirs had been lumbered with tone-deaf croakers forced into their ranks to please a patron and his cronies by securing their sons' exemption if the hoplite phalanxes were mustered to fight.

I clapped Chrysion on the shoulder. 'I'm going to go and sit with my family.'

I waved a brief farewell to the chorus, who surprised me with a discreetly muted cheer. None of them wanted to interrupt the singers. These men had first proved their own talents in such choirs, volunteering to represent the districts that acknowledged them as citizens.

Circling round the back of the theatre building, I saw Euxenos hissing at the stagehands hefting his chorus's baskets through a storage-room door. He shot me a filthy look, as baleful as Hephaistos with a hangover. I couldn't think why, though it raised my spirits to see him so agitated.

Further down the slope the broad stone altar outside the ancient shrine to Dionysos had been swept clean of old ashes and freshly whitened with chalk. Bundles of firewood were stacked ready beside it while the robed and garlanded priests sharpened their sacrificial knives. Muscular acolytes stood ready to subdue any beribboned bullock inclined to change his mind about participating in the forthcoming ritual.

Reaching the theatre's western entrance, I waited until the boys' choir from the Acamantis tribe filed out, to be quickly replaced by fifty beardless youths from Pandionis.

I climbed up the hillside before cutting across to join my family, stooping low and whispering apologies as I edged between the benches. Nymenios shuffled along to make room for me beside Zosime. As I sat down, she slipped her hand into mine and squeezed, loving, reassuring.

'Your costumes look . . . interesting,' Nymenios murmured mischievously.

I shot him a warning glance. He grinned at me, unrepentant. Thankfully a stout man in the bench below turned around to glare at us both. I guessed he must have a son or nephew singing his heart out down below and was determined to hear every note.

Chairephanes passed along a wineskin and Kleio produced twists of cloth holding spiced pastries from the basket at her feet. I eased my arm around Zosime's shoulders and drew her close. There was nothing I could do about the play now, so I might as well enjoy the choir contest.

I didn't sit there taking note of particularly fine voices or graceful movers as the choirs came and went. I wasn't about to tempt Dionysos or Athena or any other deity to slap me down for arrogantly assuming I'd be awarded another chorus by the freshly appointed Archons at the new year.

Instead I drank wine and ate treats with my family and enjoyed the spring sunshine's warmth on my face and arms. Melina, Kleio and Glykera all covered their heads with lightly woven shawls though, and their long gowns had loose, flowing sleeves. They weren't about to risk the darkly tanned skin that marks out the poorer women who work in the marketplaces. Zosime had no such concerns. Her father's blood had bronzed her complexion and her Cretan accent ensured nobody cared.

Not everyone stayed for the entire competition. People discreetly took their leave in the brief intervals as one choir made way for the next. After three more performances, Nymenios nudged me in the ribs and leaned close to whisper, 'Shall we go down to the sacrifices now?'

'Good idea,' I mouthed. It was already nearing noon.

Nymenios looked along the bench, catching Chairephanes' eye. He nodded and nudged Pamphilos and Kalliphon, who gathered up their cloaks.

'We're going to the shrine,' I murmured to Zosime, and she nodded her understanding.

As soon as the singing stopped again, we made our way

quickly to the end of the benches and headed down the hill. That did leave all four women under Chairephanes's sole protection but nothing untoward could happen in broad daylight in the middle of the theatre.

Besides, nothing short of Pegasus could have carried Melina away from her entertainment. She and Kleio and Glykera would be sitting there until the judges' votes were counted and the winners announced.

The sacrifices were already well underway at the Shrine of Dionysos. The whitened altar was liberally splashed with blood, and ashes were piling up around its base as fresh wood was heaped on to keep the flames burning fiercely for each new offering. A soot-smudged priest slapped down the next portion of bones wrapped in fat. The altar fire hissed and flared and savoury smoke surged upwards for the gods' delectation.

The smell set my mouth watering and I realised I was ravenous. Fortunately, with so many beasts being sacrificed, the priests were happy to share out the treats that were usually their sole privilege after the omens had been read. Youthful acolytes were cooking strips of liver on skewers over the altar fires, handing them to slaves to be distributed among the crowds. I beckoned one of the slaves over and relished the succulent offal.

'We'll meet you back here.' Pamphilos and Kalliphon headed off to join another group of men who were watching shrine slaves haul a freshly gutted bullock away for butchering. As well as both being carpenters, they're men of the Kollytos voting district and I recognised one of their councillors over there.

'Aischylos!' Nymenios waved to one of Alopeke's officials.

The thin, balding man greeted us with flattering enthusiasm. 'So good to see you both. Philocles! We're all looking forward to your play.'

'Thank you, sir.' I hastily swallowed a mouthful of hot liver, meek as a schoolboy.

I first met Aischylos as a wide-eyed three-year-old at the Spring Anthesteria festival, clutching my little jug. Aischylos was the man who had filled it with the wine pressed the autumn before. That's when I'd poured my first libation and first tasted Dionysos's great gift, suitably well watered.

Along with all the other boys born in the same year, I'd been presented to the brotherhood that my father and grandfather and all our forefathers had belonged to since time out of mind. District brotherhoods may not boast noble names like the Phytalids, but our roots go just as deep. Every man who'd stood witness when my father swore my brothers and I were his true-born sons would vouch for our citizens' rights life-long, just as we would vouch for their sons.

For the moment, everyone was catching up with everyone else's news of family doings, joys and calamities since the last festival had brought us together. Friends asked Nymenios about his children's health and sent good wishes from their wives to Melina and our mother. Some took the opportunity to do a little business here and there.

Meantime, Aischylos, along with the treasurer and

the other brotherhood officials, was scanning the crowd for unfamiliar faces. With so many visitors in the city, there are always some slinking around, trying to claim a fraudulent share in the sacrificed meat. Then there are the men who've been convicted in the courts and lost their citizen privileges as a consequence. Woe betide anyone here today who was challenged and couldn't call witnesses to confirm his rights. Hauling slaughtered bullocks about gives temple slaves the muscles to inflict painful chastisement for such impiety.

I felt a familiar pang at the thought of Zosime missing out on this bounty, but there was no point trying to bring her to a family festival meal. She wouldn't agree to come, for one thing. My relatives were happy to spend time with her out and about in the city and no one had any concerns about us living together. But she wasn't my wife and she wasn't a citizen, so asking her to cross an Athenian threshold while we honoured the city's gods simply wasn't appropriate. She would be as uncomfortable at our family table as my mother would be to see her there.

As we watched some slaves expertly skinning a beast, Nymenios nudged me. 'I've been asking around, to see who could supply us with leather if Dexios lets us down.'

'And?' I really wished we could leave this until after the festival but I knew Nymenios wouldn't shut up until he'd had his say.

Nymenios scowled. 'Pataikos has precious few hides not already spoken for, and none of his finest quality, though we're welcome to the pick of the rest. He's having his own troubles getting fresh skins.'

'Really?' That got my attention. This was bizarre.

Nymenios nodded. 'He's been dealing with the Sanctuary of Castor and Pollux for years now, but the priests said they'd had a better offer for raw hides, and he needed to go elsewhere. He's negotiating with the Sanctuary of Heracles out at Acharnai.'

'He can't find anyone closer?' Acharnai is as far out of the city as a man can walk and return in a day and still have time to do some brisk business there.

But before we could discuss it further, Aischylos called for our attention. A junior priest was hacking up a sacrifice and, unlike some, he wasn't keeping the choicest cuts for his own friends and family. We each got solid, meaty chunks of haunch and loin. I decided to take that for a good omen. Dividing a bullock into equal portions is all very well in theory but some shares are definitely more worth having than others.

We carried our spoils back to the theatre, so Chairephanes could carry the meat home to be cooked long and slow into tender succulence for the evening. I took particular care not to get any bloodstains on my smart new tunic. As we arrived, one choir was making way for the next and people were quitting or reclaiming their seats. As Nymenios waved to attract our brother's attention, insistent fingers plucked at my elbow. Startled, I turned to see Lydis, Aristarchos's personal slave.

'My master's compliments.' He smiled and handed me

a letter. Before I could ask what it was about, he slipped away through the crowd.

'What's that?' Nymenios demanded as I passed him the beef I was carrying.

'How about you let me read it?' I cracked the wax seals and found Aristarchos's neat script, concise and to the point.

I'm told that the Pargasarenes are at a travellers' hostel owned by Proclus of Miletus in Heliotrope Lane, in Kollytos. The head of their delegation is called Azamis.

As far as I can establish, no one has informed them of their companion's fate. If you are the first to tell them, make note of how they react. That may tell us something significant.

Don't delay. Once you have spoken to them, come to my house. Don't mention my name at their hostel, and be careful where you share your own.

There was no signature. Had Aristarchos heard something to give him cause for concern or was he simply being cautious?

Never mind. I could ask him when I told him how these Pargasarenes took the bad news. After that, I could head for my father's house and eat sacrificial beef along with fish and fowl and cakes and whatever other festival dishes Melina's slaves had prepared, with or without Mother's help.

I waved the papyrus at Nymenios. 'I have an errand to run. Tell Zosime I won't be long.'

Chapter Nine

I left the theatre and headed for the Kollytos district. Thankfully it wasn't too far, between the agora and the city's southern Itonian Gate. Once I left the main roads I was familiar with, I began looking for someone I could ask for more detailed directions. That took longer than I expected. These side streets were deserted. Everyone who wasn't at the theatre was evidently enjoying their leisure with relatives and friends. Here and there I heard snatches of laughter and conversations carried on the breeze.

I quickened my pace, eager to get this done and get back to my own family feast. A few more twists and turns and I saw an elderly man sweeping wilted petals from festival garlands out of a gateway. Most likely he was a slave but it's never wise to assume, so I greeted him as politely as I would speak to any citizen.

'Good day to you. I wonder if you could help me. I'm looking for Heliotrope Lane.'

He obliged with a toothless smile. 'Take the first left down there and then the third on your right. You can't miss it.'

He wasn't wrong. Heliotrope plants flourished along

both sides of the hard-packed earth, and someone had crowned the Hermes pillar on the corner with a garland of the dark green foliage. Someone, or perhaps the same person, had wound another spray around the pillar's jutting stone cock.

Gates stood wide on either side of the lane, showing me broad courtyards enclosed by pillared porches. I heard a handful of different languages as I passed by. Travellers and their coin were warmly welcomed here.

A dark-skinned man with Phoenician features was walking towards me. I waved a hand. 'Good day. Can you tell me where to find Proclus of Miletus's house?'

Incurious, he barely slowed as he pointed and answered in heavily accented Greek. 'That one.'

'Thank you.' The open gate revealed paving crowded with tables and stools. I knocked on the doorpost. 'Hello within! I'm looking for Azamis of Pargasa.'

A slave boy in a grimy tunic big enough for him and a friend to share appeared from a dark doorway.

'Who shall I say wants him?' He was barely as tall as my elbow, but he knew to be cautious when strangers asked for paying customers.

I remembered Aristarchos had told me to be discreet and decided not to give my name. The courtyard's porches were crammed with pallets offering festival visitors a temporary bed. A good few were still occupied by men who must have drunk deeply and unwisely last night. They might not all be asleep and there was no knowing who could overhear me.

'Tell him I have news about his friend Xandyberis.'

I could see the lad recognised that name, so I was in the right place. Good.

'Please, have a seat.'

As the slave vanished into the house I went into the courtyard to take a stool, trying to compose suitable condolences. It's not often that I wish I write tragedy, but that would surely have made this task easier.

The boy reappeared with a venerable old man. Ice-grey hair flowed to his shoulders in the eastern fashion and his beard reached almost to his belt.

'Good day to you. I am Azamis of Pargasa.' Carian-accented, his Greek was nevertheless fluent. He looked at me anxiously.

I swallowed a surge of acid burning my throat. 'Is there somewhere more private we could talk?'

The wrinkles on his face crumpled deeper and for one horrifying moment I thought he would start weeping. He had clearly been fearing the worst. Well, he'd have to be a fool not to, two days after his friend had disappeared.

He clenched his fists, breathed deep and nodded. 'Follow me, please.'

He led me into the house and up the narrow stairs. I discovered Pargasa's supposedly meagre funds had hired their men an airy room, spacious even, with four beds in it, one set against each wall.

Two men were sitting down. They looked up as soon as we entered, as apprehensive as their elder. The younger one was the Carian who'd insulted me in the agora, but this wasn't the time to air that grievance.

He sprang to his feet, as hotheaded as before. 'What are you doing here?'

I ignored him, addressing myself to Azamis and to the other man whom I guessed was the greybeard's son. He looked about the same age as the dead man.

'My sincerest condolences. I regret I bring you grievous news.' There was no stirring honey into this bitterest of cups. 'Your companion, Xandyberis, was found dead just before the festival. The Archons' slaves took his body for safekeeping, on the Polemarch's behalf.'

Was it truly only the day before yesterday? It felt as though half a lifetime had passed since I'd tripped over the poor bastard's corpse.

The oldest man sought for some explanation to soften this awful blow. 'Seized by some sudden illness? An apoplexy?'

His son's face twisted with grief. 'Struck down by some thief?'

The youth broke into loud protests in his mother tongue. They might be Hellenes but Ionians speak their own incomprehensible dialects as well as civilised Greek. Though I could make no sense of his words, his denial was clear enough.

Before his father or grandfather could answer, he took a long stride across the room to challenge me. 'What proof do you have that he is dead? What do you know of his misfortune? Did you have any hand in it?'

I folded my hands behind my back, curbing an impulse to slap some courtesy into him. 'Your friend was wearing fine red shoes in a Persian style and a tunic with a central panel brocaded with olive leaves. He had a beak of a nose that any eagle would envy and a life of hard work had carved him a permanent frown.' I traced the deep creases I'd seen on the dead man with a finger on my own face. 'He was dark-haired in his youth but in recent years he'd been growing grey, his beard most of all.'

The young buck shook his head, obstinate. 'I don't believe you.'

'Then where is he?' I demanded, exasperated. 'Do you think he's been dallying with wine and whores for the last two days?'

The youth had no answer. I thought he was going to try hitting me instead. As I glared a warning his father barked a swift rebuke. One or the other convinced the young fool to step back.

The oldest man, Azamis, sat down heavily on the bed behind him. As he buried his face in his hands, his muffled sobs broke the oppressive silence. The youth sat down and put a muscular arm around his grandfather's shaking shoulders. My opinion of him improved a little.

The man in his prime got his own emotions in hand, square-cut beard jutting. 'Please forgive any discourtesy that my son has shown you. My name is Sarkuk. Azamis of Pargasa is my father and my son is called Tur.'

Then he fixed me with a steely look. 'May I know your name and how you come to bring us such tidings?'

Fair questions and he deserved some answers. This man, Sarkuk, didn't look likely to give way to grief like his father, or be overtaken by foolish anger like the lad. Add to that, I was already convinced he'd had no hand in Xandyberis's murder, and nor had either of the others. After spending the last nine months with Athens' finest comedians, I was confident I could spot play-acting. No one here was trying to hide a guilty conscience. This news had come as a genuine shock.

'My name is Philocles Hestaiou Alopekethen,' I said formally. 'I gather your friend was seeking me out, hoping to commission me to write him a speech—'

'And you turned him down!' The lad Tur sprang up. 'Don't deny it! You insulted him—'

'No,' I said sharply. 'We never met, as Hermes is my witness.'

Sarkuk said something cutting in the Carian tongue and Tur subsided to sit on the bed, embarrassment darkening his tanned cheeks. Sarkuk turned back to me.

'Then how did you learn Xandyberis was dead and why are you the one who has come to tell us?' He wasn't going to be distracted until he got his answers.

'His body was found outside my house,' I explained. 'I reported the death to the Scythians who keep order in the city, to make sure that his body was treated with respect. When I met your son, and he told me you were from Pargasa, here to pay your town's tribute, I asked the festival authorities where you might be lodged. I wanted to make sure you got the full story of your friend's fate. I wanted to be certain that the Polemarch knew who he was and where he had come from.'

Sarkuk gave me a measuring look. 'Why was he at your house?'

'I honestly have no idea.' I hoped they could see this

was the truth. 'Did he say he was going to see me? Do you know anyone who could have told him where I lived?'

'Not at all.' Sarkuk shook his head slowly, pensive. 'Besides, you told my son that this has all been some mistake. That we will see no relief from the levy at this festival or even this year.'

'There was no mistake,' snarled Tur, rising to his feet yet again. 'We have been deceived. How do we know we're not still being lied to? You could have killed him yourself before playing the good citizen to cover up your crime!'

'Why would I kill a man I don't even know?' I'd make allowance for the boy's grief but I wasn't going to be accused.

Tur hesitated but he was still determined to find someone to blame. 'You could have—'

'Enough!' Sarkuk snapped. 'You insult our visitor and make a fool of yourself. Forgive my son,' he said stiffly. 'He is very young.'

'So were we all, in our day.' I forced a thin smile to take some of the sting out of my words.

The old man, Azamis, looked up, dark streaks of tears in his beard. 'He said he was going to see Archilochos when he left here that night.'

'Who's that?' I looked hopefully around the three of them.

'A trader,' Sarkuk said thoughtfully. 'A regular visitor to Pargasa. He brings our town council the news from Athens several times a year.'

'Did he tell Xandyberis that the tribute would be reassessed?' My pulse quickened. Aristarchos would want to know about this. 'At this year's Dionysia, not at the Panathenaia?'

'Perhaps.' Sarkuk looked uncertain.

'Do you know where to find this Archilochos in Athens?' I tried to hide my urgency.

Sarkuk shook his head. 'Xandyberis always dealt with him.'

'Xandyberis believed that knowledge is power.' Azamis surprised us all with a humourless laugh. 'He wasn't inclined to share either.'

I looked at Sarkuk. 'You should tell the Polemarch about this man, this Archilochos. It may help the magistrates find out who killed your friend.'

He nodded, grim-faced. 'And we must recover his body.'

'Let me show you the way to the city prison,' I offered. 'The Scythians there will be able to tell you what to do.'

I wasn't only being helpful. I wanted to hear everything that Sarkuk might have to say about this mysterious trader. I also wanted to learn whatever the Scythians might have discovered about Xandyberis's death in the past few days. Then I could hand all this new information over to Aristarchos and head off for dinner with my family. It was still early enough in the afternoon. I'd get home in plenty of time to find some honeycakes left.

Then, with Athena's blessing, I could put all this unholy mess safely behind me. Then all I would have to worry about was my play's performance tomorrow.

Chapter Ten

I wanted to take Sarkuk to see the Scythians alone, but the youth Tur insisted on coming.

'You're not walking these streets without me at your side,' he said forcefully to his father.

I caught the lad's sideways glance. I could see he still didn't believe I wasn't involved in Xandyberis's murder. He was just longing to find some excuse to confront me. I didn't react. I grew up with three brothers.

The greybeard Azamis didn't help. 'I will be quite safe,' he assured his son. 'I won't open the door to anyone.'

'Make sure you don't.' Sarkuk slung a cloak around his shoulders and looked at me. 'Shall we go?'

I led the way. The far end of Heliotrope Lane joined a road leading out of Kollytos towards the Hill of the Pnyx. We soon reached the tangle of streets inside the Piraeus Gate and headed north to cut between the Hill of the Areopagus and the Acropolis.

'You didn't say how Xandyberis died,' Sarkuk said abruptly. 'You can tell me, though I'd be grateful if you didn't distress my father by . . .'

He fell silent, not wanting to yield to his worst imaginings.

'His throat was cut.' I offered what little comfort I could. 'It looked as if he fell to a single blow. He wouldn't have suffered.'

'Xandyberis taken unawares?' Tur shook his head. 'I don't believe it.'

I wasn't sure if his scorn was for the dead man or for my implausible tale. I let that go because I'd just realised something.

Unless a foe strikes very lucky, it's vanishingly rare for a first thrust to kill. Mortal wounds usually follow any number of lesser slashes and gashes. Those few times when I've seen some poor fool injured in a tavern fight or attacked in the street, it's the unexpected attacks that prevail. Attacks from a man the victim was drinking with or talking to mere moments before.

I wondered if the killer was someone Xandyberis was willing to walk beside or to sit next to, never expecting such a companion would turn a blade on him. Someone he trusted like this trader Archilochos.

I'd have to be absolutely certain, with witnesses or evidence to back me, before I dared lay any such accusation before the Athenian courts. The penalties for malicious prosecution would beggar me if no more than one in five of the jury agreed that I'd proven my case.

'So, Archilochos,' I said as casually as I could, 'what does he trade in? What does Pargasa buy and sell?'

'Precious little,' Sarkuk said frankly. 'We grow olives and almonds and raise sheep and goats but there's scant land with enough water to grow grain. There are seldom years when we can harvest more than we need to feed ourselves.'

'Fewer still when we can sell any surplus for our own profit. All our hard work goes into hoarding silver to pay Athens' so-called tribute.' Tur glowered as though I was personally responsible for the Delian League's finances.

Sarkuk said something quelling in Carian. Tur replied with spirited defiance, refusing to back down when his father grew volubly annoyed.

I was beginning to wish I knew something of these incomprehensible eastern languages. Not that there's a school in this city that teaches them, when the whole civilised world speaks Greek.

When they had finished quarrelling, I tried again. 'What do your townsmen buy from Archilochos?'

Sarkuk's answer surprised me. 'Scrolls, mostly. Poems and plays. Odes and epics.' He offered me a strained smile. 'When we find him, you should discuss what terms he might offer for selling copies of your plays in Ionia.'

Tur muttered something under his breath and I didn't need to understand Carian to know it was insulting. Thankfully his father refused to rise to the bait.

'Just poetry and lyrics?' I asked. 'Not histories or rhetoric?'

Sarkuk took a moment to consider this. 'No, just poetry.'

'Does he only bring work from Athens?' If so, it might be worthwhile Aristarchos sending a slave to ask around the copyists to see if they knew anyone who specialised in that trade in Caria. Not that I believed for a moment this man was truly called Archilochos. If his business was trading in verse, I guessed he'd adopted the name of Paros's most famous poet to garner reflected glory.

Sarkuk's answer dashed my hopes. 'No, he offers us scrolls from Thebes and Corinth as well as from Lesbos and Ceos and other islands.'

'He trades his wares all through Caria.' Tur scowled. 'There's nothing special to bring him to Pargasa.'

Did that stone in his shoe explain his bad temper? Had coming to Athens shown this boy just how insignificant his parched little town really was? I had more serious concerns. By now I suspected Xandyberis had been killed to stop him identifying the source of any rumours about the Delian League tribute being reassessed. If this Archilochos saw me out and about with the dead man's colleagues, he'd guess that particular piglet was out of its sack and running away down the street. I'd better watch my back. Though I still had no idea what this poetry peddler hoped to gain by spreading such a pointless lie.

We joined the Panathenaic Way and soon reached the south-eastern corner of the agora. There weren't many stalls set up today. Vegetable sellers, fishmongers and olive merchants enjoy their festivals as much as anyone else.

'The city prison is down that road.' I pointed to the far side. 'We'll call there, to find out where the Scythians have taken Xandyberis's body. He may have already been buried,' I warned, 'just as a temporary measure.'

Even this early in the year, the days were sunny and warm. Still, the last few nights had been chilly and the Carian had barely been dead for two days, so corruption shouldn't have set in too fast. Hopefully the Scythians had him somewhere under cover on a cold stone slab.

Movement caught my eye. A man stood by the

monument dedicated to the ten heroes of Athens. As he spoke, he gestured with the flourishes favoured by the more old-fashioned rhetoric teachers. He was gathering quite an audience.

That was odd at the start of the festival. Neither the People's Assembly nor the courts were sitting, so there was no official business for a speaker to influence. Half the city would be sitting in the theatre for the next five days, eating nuts and drinking wine, laughing at my jokes tomorrow and then watching three days of tragedies full of bloodshed and betrayal. No one would remember speeches made here today by the time Athens' normal routine resumed.

Since our path took us over that way, I paused on the edge of the crowd to listen. The speaker was stirring himself into quite a fury.

'Are we to stomach this outrage? Not just an affront to the city's populace but so gravely dishonouring our goddess who is denied her rightful share of the tribute! Haven't you heard? Those ungrateful Ionians wish to short-change divine Athena. Not content with that, they offer unforgivable insult to Dionysos at his very own festival! They will have the impudence to parade their contemptible offerings in the god's own theatre, before his most ancient and sacred icon! Showing no shame, they offer no apology. What do they expect us to do? Meekly accept the pittance they deign to give us while they hoard their silver back home?'

'That's not right.' Tur was scowling.

'He doesn't know what he's talking about.' Sarkuk was

glowering as darkly as his son, strengthening their family resemblance.

I was grateful they were at least speaking Greek. 'What's going on?'

Sarkuk bit back his indignation to answer me. 'This past year, some of our neighbours have been even more hard-pressed than Pargasa. They're simply unable to raise the coin for the levy. They have sent all that they can,' he assured me, 'and their delegates have brought their town councils' proposals for paying the balance over the course of the year, if Tarhunzas sends us rain and good harvests.'

I guessed that must be some Carian god. I held back from suggesting they'd do better to entreat Demeter and Zeus.

'We are the ones who are insulted.' Tur clenched his fists as he glared at the speaker.

'But how does this man know?' Sarkuk looked at me, concerned. 'We are to present our tributes tomorrow. That's when all these details will be entered into the city's records.'

'That's a very good question.' I turned my attention back to the orator. I also noted uneasily that the crowd listening to him was growing bigger.

'What are they doing with their silver, these Ionians, while they deny it to Athena? Spending it on luxuries for themselves, no doubt,' he sneered. 'But they'll still expect the sweat of your brow and the toil that bends your backs day after day to pay for the triremes that they will assuredly beg for when the Persians threaten to march, to steal this hoarded wealth.'

He gestured eastwards. 'Our so-called allies will call on your sons to fight and to die on that far-distant shore to save their own treacherous skins. The dead will include those noble heirs to heroes who've already shed their lifeblood to uphold Athenian honour. Those sons of fallen fathers, those brave boys whom our beloved city will arm and armour, thanks to the taxes you loyally pay. Is that right? Is that just? Is that loyalty?'

'You lie, you dog!'

Tur's bellow caught me wholly unprepared. With Sarkuk between us, I couldn't even grab the idiot boy's arm as he strode forward to challenge the man by the monument.

'You lie! You dog, you lie!'

Was that all the bull-headed youth had to say? My heart sank as I realised it was. No wonder the Pargasarenes didn't buy scrolls of famous speeches; there couldn't be a rhetoric teacher in the place. Whereas this Athenian orator proved he'd had plenty of practice dealing with hecklers.

'So you say,' he scoffed at Tur, 'with your Persian hair and your empty Ionian promises. So, tell us! Where have you been spending your silver? Paying for a satrap's favours? Are you one of those cravens who'd rather kneel at the steps of Artaxerxes's throne than stand shoulder to shoulder with free Hellenes?'

Tur choked on his indignation. 'Who are you to call me a coward?'

The speaker turned to the wide-eyed crowd with a sarcastic laugh. 'They say that Darius's queen urged him to invade to find her some Greek handmaidens. Is his grandson now looking to Ionia to find pretty boys like this? I bet he'd give a satrap a hand-job for the sake of a quiet life.'

Now I did grab Tur's arm, doing my best to hold him back. I didn't have much luck. The young fool was built like an ox. Then a voice from the crowd stopped him in his tracks.

'Why shouldn't we spend our silver how we wish? Better to guarantee our peace by feeding Persian lions than see them prowling outside our gates. That's a better use for our coin than handing it over to you. We see how you build yourselves fine new temples and gorge unrestrained at your festivals!'

Outrage spread across the agora like ripples from a rock dropped in a pond. Men idly standing near this new speaker recoiled. No one would risk being mistaken for his ally. Such ingratitude verged on blasphemy. Even if Zeus's thunderbolts didn't strike him down, such insolence was rank provocation, here in the heart of Athenian democracy.

That meant we got a good look at him as the crowd parted. He was another Ionian, his accent unmistakeable. He wore a tunic brocaded with purple seashells and his hair trailed to his shoulders in long locks. Even his beard was curled like a Persian's.

Sarkuk yelled something in his native tongue. The man didn't reply even though everyone else immediately turned towards us. The man in purple still didn't react, staring intently at the orator standing by the heroes' monument.

Following his gaze, I saw that the orator seemed genuinely bemused. He glanced from the Persian-bearded

Ionian to Tur and back again. In the next breath, as Athena is my witness, I saw the man in purple nod to the orator. That jerk of the Ionian's head urged the Athenian on.

The orator rounded on Tur and Sarkuk. 'You dare to come here, you filthy Mede lovers, and spit your rebellion in our faces? When you should be crawling on your wretched bellies to beg our forgiveness for your dereliction? When you should be raising monuments in your own dung-strewn market places, to show your gratitude for Athenian blood spilt on your behalf for three generations!'

I saw faces all around us turn hostile. Some shouted their own insults at the Carians, father and son. The orator had to raise his voice as he challenged me, standing beside them.

'You there, Athenian! Why do you let these traitors drip their poison in your ear? Have you no shame? Have you no honour? Have you no pride? You stand there with men thrice damned for betraying their sacred oaths to Apollo, to Athena and to their allies!'

Whatever else he said was lost as yells and scuffles broke out around the man in the seashell tunic. Violence spread through the entire crowd with frightening speed. I looked around for the clearest path out of this chaos. We needed to get away.

'We have betrayed no one!' Tur strode forward, shoving some hapless bystander aside. 'It's Athens who betrays us, murdering our—'

A punch in the face cut his wrath short, from some bloke with a stonemason's calloused hands and the muscles to match.

126

Tur rocked back a step. Only a step and only for a moment. He really would make an excellent wrestler. Surging forward with a furious roar, he was ready to retaliate and not just with his fists. His right hand held a gleaming curve of steel as long as my forearm, with a wicked, needle-sharp point.

I hadn't realised the young fool had a blade. I couldn't let him use it. If he skewered some citizen in this spreading mêlée, Sarkuk and Azamis would see him buried alongside Xandyberis. Every witness here would condemn him at a trial, and Tur would swiftly be delivered to the public executioner.

I kicked the idiot boy hard in the side of one ankle. As he staggered, I punched him in the kidneys. That dropped him to his knees. I wound my hand in his hair, wrenching his head back. 'Give me that fucking knife!'

He tried to stab me instead. Expecting exactly that, I seized his hand, twisting so hard I felt his wrist bones grate together. He let go of the knife with a furious yell.

I tried to put my foot on the hilt, to stop him or anyone else grabbing the blade. But the stonemason had decided that he and I were clearly allies. He aimed a punch at the side of Tur's head as the boy knelt, still captive in my grip.

If that blow connected, it could kill the young fool. I jerked his head out of the way before tearing my hand free along with some of his curls. As Tur scrambled to his feet, I stepped into the stonemason's path.

'Leave him to Dionysos, citizen. He's an idiot and he's drunk.'

It took the man a breath to realise I wasn't going to let

him have Tur. His face twisted with contempt. 'So you *do* suck Persian cock!'

I didn't debate the point. As the mason threw a punch, I sidestepped so quickly that his knuckles barely grazed me. As I moved, I shoved his other shoulder, hard. Hooking my heel behind his forward knee knocked him off balance completely. He landed hard on his back, left gasping, winded by the impact.

I made sure he stayed down by stamping on his belly. Noble families' sons learn the niceties of Olympic competition. The old wrestler who taught me and my brothers reckoned Athenian lads like us needed to know how to fight dirty.

Where was Tur? What about Sarkuk? I looked swiftly around, all the while alert for anyone keen to take up the stonemason's cause.

The older Pargasarene was holding his own with no need for a knife. Sarkuk used his fists like a man who'd fought his way out of a fair share of trouble. He blocked a wild blow with his forearm and drove his other fist straight into an attacker's eye.

Reeling backwards, the Athenian tried to flee. He didn't find that easy. Men were fighting on all sides now. Some had been stirred up by the orator. Others were just caught up in the fracas.

It wouldn't be long before the Scythians arrived and they don't carry those bows for show. Anyone running away from a brawl in the agora risked an arrow in the leg or the shoulder. Let the Carians try denying their role in this riot after that. The best they could hope for was being thrown out of the city and then we'd never learn the truth of all this.

I grabbed Sarkuk's shoulder. 'We have to get out of here!'

He spun around, his clenched fist pulled back. Recognising me, he abandoned the blow. 'Which way?'

'Head for the Temple of Hephaistos!' I jabbed a finger at the shining new temple half-built up on Kolonos Hill.

That was our quickest route out of the agora to somewhere with enough people for us to lose ourselves in a crowd. Given the choice, I'd have run straight for Aristarchos's house, but trying to fight all the way across the market place would be madness.

I still had to rescue Tur. The lad wasn't faring nearly as well as his father. He'd been surrounded before he'd recovered his balance and five men were attacking him now. Too many to fight all at once. Trying to do that was the boy's first mistake. He was still on his feet but barely. They'd have him on the ground any minute and then he'd be kicked to death.

I threw a punch at the closest man's head. He must have glimpsed me in the corner of his eye and blocked my fist with an upraised elbow. So I grabbed his arm and hauled him sideways. As he staggered I drove my knuckles into his midriff. He decided that beating the shit out of some Persian sympathiser wasn't worth any more bruises and scurried away.

One of the others surrounding Tur tried to punch me in the side. I barely managed to twist away to save myself from broken ribs. Even so his fist landed hard enough to force me backwards. He followed up with a jab to my belly.

I met his knuckles with my outspread palm, drawing the force from the blow. I tried for a curving punch to his ear with my other hand but he knocked my fist aside with a bruising sweep of his forearm. Doing that spun him around. As he took a step to keep his balance, his feet spread wide. I kicked him hard in the balls and he collapsed, retching.

Now he was facing better odds, Tur was holding his own against the other three. I winced at the crack of a man's jaw breaking. One of the others recoiled. Not fast enough. Tur dropped him with a kick in the gut. The last one seized his chance to flee.

'Tur!' I bellowed. 'Tur!'

He stood swaying like a pine tree in a gale. Perhaps he couldn't hear me. The din all around us was deafening. Some men shouted insults while others protested this was none of their business. The rest just howled wordless abuse.

No, it wasn't the noise. The young Carian might still be on his feet, but he was barely conscious. One eye was swelling red while blood streamed from brutal cuts on both his cheekbones and across one thick eyebrow. Another blow had split the corner of his mouth and his nose was surely broken.

'It's me, Philocles!' I hesitated before trying to grab him. He might be half stunned but I didn't want to risk taking one of his punches.

'Tur!' Sarkuk shouted something in their mother tongue.

The boy's open eye focused blearily on his father. Sarkuk shouted again, pointing up at the temple.

'Grab him and follow me!' I started to force a path through the fray. That won me a whole new collection of scrapes and bruises before we reached the Council Chamber at the side of the agora. That's what happens when you're more concerned with getting away from a fight than defending yourself.

Someone grabbed hold of my tunic. I tore myself free with savage threats and ripping cloth. Behind me, I heard Sarkuk cursing. As long as I could hear him, I didn't bother looking back, shoving and shouldering my way through the crowd.

Finally we slid into the narrow space between the Temple of the Mother of the Gods and the Council Chamber. I paused, leaning forward, hands braced on my thighs and wondering if I had a cracked rib. My side was viciously sore. It took me a few moments to catch my breath. At least that eased the pain a little.

'Where are we going?' Sarkuk demanded.

I forced myself upright. 'There, to begin with.' I gestured up the slope towards the gleaming white temple.

I wasn't going anywhere near the prison today. Not with the three of us so obviously fleeing from this brawl. It was a fair bet the Scythians would take whoever they collared straight to the lock-up. Anyone fool enough to offer themselves up would get thrown in a cell. Most likely they'd be stuck there until the end of the Dionysia, when the magistrates reopened the courts.

'Give your son your cloak,' I told Sarkuk. 'Keep the hood up, boy.'

A man going hooded in such fine weather would draw curious glances but that would be better than letting people see Tur's battered face. He looked grim enough to set dogs barking.

Now we needed to get somewhere safe, and as quickly as possible. I gritted my teeth against the stabbing pain in my side as we scrambled up the scrub-covered slope towards Hephaistos's new temple. It was still lacking a roof, its western pediment and most of its carved decoration, but it would be splendid when it was finished.

Was it being paid for with Carian coin? I saw Sarkuk's lip curl as he gazed up at the Parian marble columns. Well, we could debate that later. As we reached the temple precinct I hurried onwards. Now we could lose ourselves in this crowd of people looking down, aghast, at the chaos in the agora.

I ushered Sarkuk and Tur through the temple and out the other side. Then I swiftly worked out a route to skirt around the agora to reach Aristarchos's house. He'd told me to report back to him, once I'd spoken to the Carians, though I don't suppose he imagined we'd turn up in quite such a battered state.

Mus answered my knock on the gate. The slave stared at my bloodied companions, appalled. 'You can't bring them in here.'

Chapter Eleven

'This house is full of guests and the master's family. The mistress won't stand for admitting you and two strangers beaten bloody.' Mus stood blocking our path, as immovable as Mount Olympos.

I looked down at my torn tunic, streaked with dirt where I'd slipped and fallen on the slope leading up from the agora to the Hephaisteon. I saw gory smears from my badly grazed knuckles and probably from people I'd punched. My hands ached as villainously as all my other bruises.

'Then where can we go?' I pleaded. 'Ask Lydis. We have to get off the streets and we need water and rags.'

The slave was staring past me at Sarkuk and Tur, who were barely managing to hold each other up.

'Mus!' I said sharply. 'Do you want the neighbours' slaves gossiping about this when they're filling tomorrow's water jars? Leave us standing out here and it'll be the talk of the neighbourhood fountain. Believe me, your master will want to help us. These men are Carians and loyal allies to Athens. They've been victims of deliberate malice and your master is trying to uncover who's behind it.'

That goaded the granite-faced slave into action. 'Come inside, but don't leave the porch.' He summoned a passing slave with a snap of his fingers. 'You, watch the gate.'

'Thank you.' I hurried over the threshold. Then I realised the Carians were hesitating and had to turn around and pretty much drag them inside. Sarkuk looked horribly uneasy about intruding into such a wealthy Athenian household. It was hard to see any expression on Tur's battered face.

Mus strode off as we sank onto the stone ledges that served as seats just inside the entrance. I heard music and laughter from the inner courtyard, and saw a bevy of slaves busy carrying food and wine to the feast within. My stomach growled as I realised I was ravenously hungry. This far into a Dionysia afternoon, I should be half-drunk and sprawled on a cushioned couch talking nonsense with my brothers, all of us stuffed like festival fowl.

Before I could decide how I was going to explain my absence, my bruises and my wrecked tunic to my mother, we heard voices outside in the street. As Mus's deputy opened the gate, Aristarchos's son Hipparchos sauntered in. He looked at us, bright-eyed with curiosity.

'Good day to you all. Hermes!' He took a step backwards as Tur lowered his hood. 'What's happened?'

'We were attacked by street robbers,' I said quickly, to forestall some angry response from the young Carian. Though I couldn't have blamed Tur. It was a bloody stupid question, when the answer was as obvious as the smashed nose on the boy's face.

'Dear me.' Hipparchos's sympathy was no more than conventional courtesy. He went on his way, whistling loudly to attract a slave's attention. When no one appeared, he called out, irritated. 'Thraitta!'

Three girls appeared from different doorways, all dressed alike in clean white tunics.

'You'll do.' Hipparchus pointed to one. 'Bring me something to eat in my chamber.' Dismissing her with a nod, he disappeared through a door on the far side of the courtyard.

As the other slaves returned to whatever they had been doing, Sarkuk looked at me, curious. 'There are three girls here called Thraitta? Doesn't that cause confusion?'

'That's what he calls them all,' I explained awkwardly. 'It's his mother's family's custom, to save time apparently. They call all the male slaves Illyrios.'

As Sarkuk and his father exchanged a glance, I could see they found this as peculiar as I had when Mus had first explained. On subsequent visits I couldn't help noticing that Aristarchos allowed his slaves the dignity of their own names, whatever his wife might do.

A moment later Mus came back with Lydis. The little slave was appalled at the state of us.

'There was trouble in the agora,' I explained. 'It was none of our making, I swear it, but we need to get cleaned up. Your master won't want them falling foul of the Scythians on the way back to their lodging.' I jerked my head towards the Pargasarenes.

'No indeed. Follow me.' Lydis ushered us all out onto the street. 'This way.'

Tur was staggering and Sarkuk looked fit to drop. I grabbed the young fool's hand and draped his arm over my shoulder. Relieved of his burden, Sarkuk fared better and we hurried after the slave.

A few twists and turns took us into the narrower alleys tucked behind this district's fine houses. Lydis used a latch lifter to open the gate into a small courtyard ringed by separate rooms. A cluster of stools surrounded a central brazier. I guessed this was accommodation for Aristarchos's most favoured slaves.

'Please, tell your master I am sorry for bringing such trouble to his door,' I said to Lydis.

'We will be on our way as soon as possible,' Sarkuk assured him, painfully anxious.

The gate opened behind us. I was halfway to my feet before I realised the newcomers were a handful of slaves looking to Lydis for instructions. One girl carried a heavy jug and another had a bundle of well-worn linen rags. Two men had brought kindling and charcoal, along with some embers in a hollow fennel stalk. They quickly lit a fire in the brazier and one of the girls set a pot on the flames to heat up some water.

The last slave was an older woman with a basket of small pots and vials. As she opened one, I caught the aroma of familiar herbs. It smelled like my mother's salve for everyday cuts and scratches, made with the leaves she harvests on her forays outside the city walls, and pounded into the lanolin from her brothers' sheep. The scent was unexpectedly comforting.

Lydis was giving further instructions to the men who'd

brought the firewood. 'Keep a lookout for strangers. Tell the maids to keep their ears open for anyone asking nosy questions. Watch for some stranger hanging around with no real reason to be in this neighbourhood.' He turned to one of the girls, gesturing at my ripped, filthy tunic. 'Find them some clean clothes.'

Sarkuk stood up, tense. 'I must get back to my father, at our lodging. He will be wondering what has become of us.'

'Aristarchos will make certain he's safe.' I looked expectantly at Lydis. 'Your master will want to hear what he has to say, I am sure of it.'

'I will see that he's brought here.' The slave nodded as he ushered the other slaves out and left us in the courtyard with one remaining girl and the older woman.

'Clean yourself up before your father arrives.' I dampened a clean scrap of soft linen and handed it to Sarkuk. 'The more normal you look, the less distressed he will be.'

Scrubbing the blood and dirt from my hands stung ferociously but the slave woman's salve worked wonders. There wasn't anything to be done for my bruises, but a clean tunic would cover the worst. I drew a cautious breath and was relieved to feel only a dull ache in my side, not the stabbing pain of a broken rib.

Sarkuk hissed with pain as he cleaned a deep gash between his knuckles. His hands had suffered badly. Thankfully his face was unmarked. Hide those swollen, bruised fists inside a cloak and no one outside on the street should look at him twice.

Tur was another matter entirely. He sat dumbly on a stool as the slave woman tended his hurts, with the younger girl standing ready to swap soiled rags for clean ones. She threw the gory scraps onto the brazier, where they hissed on the coals.

Blood matted the young Carian's hair and beard, and his broken nose was as bad as any injury I'd seen among wrestlers at the gymnasium. Both of his eyes were closed tight. One was so nastily swollen that I feared for his sight, though I didn't ask the nurse what she thought. There would be time enough for such worries later.

Sarkuk murmured something fond and reassuring in their Carian tongue. Tur managed a nod, clenching his jaw against the pain. I saw his lips were quivering like Nymenios's little son Hestaios after he's taken a bruising tumble. The nurse stroked the young man's dirty hair and he leaned his forehead against her comforting belly, broad shoulders shaking.

Sarkuk heaved a sigh. 'Whose house is this? What are we doing here?'

'This property, these people, they belong to Aristarchos Phytalid.'

Sarkuk's eyes narrowed. 'Why are Pargasa's affairs this rich man's concern?'

'He was concerned when I told him you expected your tribute to be reassessed at this festival. He knows that you have been lied to. If someone's out to make trouble by convincing our allies they'll see some relief when, truly, there's no chance of that happening this year, it concerns all honest Athenians. Aristarchos Phytalid is

138

a man with the authority to convince the magistrates that you have been duped by this Archilochos. The city's authorities will definitely want to know what he has to say for himself.'

Tur managed to squint at me now that the nurse had wiped away the blood sticking his less-injured eye shut. 'Will we see justice for Xandyberis?' he mumbled indistinctly.

'Let's all ask the gods for that,' I said grimly.

Judging by the boy's grunt, he'd prefer more direct action to prayer.

'I've brought some honeyed wine.' Lydis returned with a jug, which he set on the brazier as a young boy followed with a bundle of clothing.

The older slave woman was examining the gash in Tur's eyebrow. 'This needs to be closed with a stitch,' she said briskly. 'Wait here while I fetch—'

'We must get back to Grandfather.' Tur stood up and swayed.

'Sit down.' The slave woman was easily able to force him back onto his stool before she bustled off through the gate where a thick-necked man stood watch. I recognised him as Aristarchos's personal bodyguard.

'Tur?' I looked at the lad, wondering uneasily just how hard he'd been hit on the head. 'Your grandfather's coming here. Don't you remember us saying that?'

He stared at me, bleary-eyed. 'What?'

'Tunics and a cloak with a hood for the boy.' Lydis gestured at the bundle the lad had put down on an empty stool. He bowed politely to Sarkuk. 'Once you've had something to eat and drink, and your father has arrived, my master has a house nearby where you can stay. He will escort you.' He nodded to the burly slave by the gate.

I assumed Mus and Lydis had sent someone equally brawny to fetch the old man. I hoped Azamis would get here soon. I wanted to get to my family's house as quickly as possible and not just in hopes of honeycakes. It wasn't only the cool in the shadowy courtyard raising gooseflesh on my arms.

Xandyberis had been asking around the agora where he might find me, and Elpis had sent him to my brothers' house. I was worried that whoever lurked behind all this would send brutes to my family home, to harass my brothers into telling them where I was. They would surely want to beat me into telling them what I'd learned from the Carians. Then they'd want to discover where these three had gone.

Sarkuk and I stripped and dressed in fresh clothes. It was strange to see the Carian in an Athenian tunic. Between us, we managed to get Tur out of his filthy garb and into something clean.

'Please offer my sincerest thanks to your master,' Sarkuk said stiffly to Lydis.

'The gods bless those who help strangers in need.' The slave gathered up our discards.

The motherly slave woman returned with a box of medical equipment. She clucked with disapproval when she saw what we'd done with Tur. 'You couldn't wait till I'd stitched him up? Oh well, just hold his hands down.'

She tucked more clean rags into the neck of the boy's

tunic and got to work. There wasn't much blood, and he bore the pain like a hero though, to be fair, he was in no condition to fight back. He couldn't have fended off a garland girl from the market.

By the time she was done, he was shaking like a bay tree in a winter gale. There was an old hoplite cloak in the bundle of clothes and I wrapped that around his shoulders. Sarkuk poured a cup of honeyed wine from the jug on the brazier. He held it to his son's lips, coaxing the boy to drink.

The slave guarding the gate peered through the grille to see who was knocking. As he opened up I was relieved to see the old Carian, Azamis, flanked by two muscular escorts.

'Did anyone come looking for us?' Sarkuk demanded. 'Has anyone sent word of the riot in the agora?'

'No.' The old man was mystified. Then he saw Tur and gasped. 'Oh, my poor boy!'

The young Carian's bruises were starting to colour, and his cut and swollen face looked truly frightful. At the same time, he was unhealthily pale beneath those gruesome injuries and his uninjured eyelid was drooping ominously.

Sarkuk ushered his father to a stool, forcing him to sit. He said something in their own tongue.

'Here, drink this.' I reached for the jug of warm wine and poured a generous cupful. We should have thought to warn the old man how shocking his grandson looked. The last thing we needed was Azamis keeling over from some spasm of the head or heart.

Thankfully a couple of swallows brought a flush of colour to Azamis's sunken cheeks. I took a cup of wine for myself and offered the first taste to Apollo and his healer son, Asclepios.

The gate opened yet again and Aristarchos appeared in the archway. He took the scene that greeted him in his stride, though even he raised his eyebrows when he saw the extent of Tur's injuries.

'Good day to you all.' He turned to his slave. 'Lydis, send word to the Academy. I'd be grateful if Spintharos could call here as soon as he finds it convenient.'

How nice, I reflected, to be able to summon your chosen doctor when you needed him, instead of carrying or cajoling a patient to one of Apollo's shrines, where you could only hope that whoever you found on duty was a halfway competent physician.

'If you please,' Sarkuk said, strained, 'we cannot afford—'

'If your son has been injured in Athens, it is Athens' duty to see him cared for.' Aristarchos's courteous manner nevertheless made it clear that particular discussion was closed. 'Philocles, what do you have to tell me?'

I'd been organising my thoughts while we waited, and gave him a succinct summary of everything that had happened in the agora. While I was speaking, two slaves appeared with refreshments, two more carrying trestles and a table top. They set out wine, olives and pine nuts, together with fresh sliced cheese and wheat breads.

Aristarchos poured a polite libation to Hermes, for

the sake of all messengers and travellers. 'And your conclusions?'

Before I could answer, Azamis raised his hand like a student at a lecture. 'If you please, honoured sir, do not believe what that other Ionian in the agora claimed. I swear that Pargasarenes have no wish to be ruled by Artaxerxes. We know how harsh any satrap's rule would be. The Medes still remember how Ionia rebelled against them in my grandfather's day. They bear us a mortal grudge.'

He shook his head, his grey beard flowing. 'We wish to stay in the Delian League and not just for fear of the Persians. As long as we look to Athens, this city's author-ity helps to uphold our own small council, our people's assembly and our town's law court. Cleisthenes's reforms, which guarantee your own freedoms, are what inspired so many of our towns to throw off Darius's rule, so we might govern ourselves in the Athenian way.'

That wasn't how my father told that story. According to him, Ionia's revolt was the bright idea of a couple of Milesians who'd been Darius's vassals to begin with and got ambitious on their own account. Athens had been dragged into Ionia's wars for the sake of our shared Hellene blood and to uphold the rights of free men and popular rule against tyranny. What we got in return was the Persians marching into Attica to plunder and burn, and the bloodshed of Marathon and all the battles that followed.

This was neither the time nor the place for that debate, so I held my tongue, drank my wine and ate some food. Now Azamis was saying something much more interesting.

'If we break our ties with Athens, even if we stay free of the Persian yoke, there are Hellenes in Pargasa who claim ancient blood rights to rule.' The old man's voice grew harsh with emotion. 'Foreign tyranny or home-grown oligarchy? What choice is that? To be devoured by Scylla or by Charybdis!'

'No one on the council wants to see a favoured few putting their boot on our necks.' Sarkuk took up the tale as Azamis reached for his cup to wash the bitterness from his mouth. 'But those citizens who think they can seize power are always the first to complain, and the loudest, whenever the council and the assembly discuss gathering the levy payment each year. This is why Xandyberis was determined to stand before the Archons and have his say, to make our case to have this burden eased.'

'Only we find that we have been lied to, and our friend has been killed.' Azamis could barely restrain his fury. I was starting to see where Tur got his temper.

'Then we must find out who has lied and why,' Aristarchos said crisply.

'I've been thinking about that.' I spoke quickly. 'Sarkuk, did you recognise that Ionian's—'

'What?' Tur interrupted, startling us all. 'You think we must all know each other?'

'No,' I shot back, 'and if you'll keep quiet, I'll explain why I don't think he was an Ionian at all.' I asked Sarkuk again. 'Did you recognise his accent as Carian, or Lydian, Mytilenean or Hellespontine?'

He considered this for a moment. 'No. I'd have said he was a man who'd left his home town or island many years ago. Still Ionian in his speech but anything distinctive to mark out his birthplace has been smoothed away by years of travelling and speaking only Greek.'

'You called out to him, in the agora. What did you say?'

'That he had no right to speak for the rest of us,' Sarkuk said robustly.

'I don't think he even realised you were talking to him. I don't think he understood a word you said.' I turned from the Carian to Aristarchos. 'I think he was in league with the man who was making that speech condemning the Ionians. I saw the two of them swap a glance when the rabble-rouser was so surprised to see Tur step forward. They made use of the interruption quickly enough, though.'

Sarkuk frowned as he considered this. 'I believe you are right.'

'Someone's conspiring to stir up trouble, turning Athenian citizens against Ionians in the streets.' Aristarchos looked grim.

'And we were unlucky enough to walk right into it.' All the same, I had some good news. 'But I believe we have a scent to follow. I reckon that man who was playing the Ionian is an actor. I'd say he's a professional who specialises in regional characters.'

'I suppose that's possible.' Aristarchos sounded dubious all the same.

I pressed on. 'I think that orator's an actor as well. He made a joke about Greek handmaids giving Persian satraps hand-jobs.'

Aristarchos pursed his lips with distaste. 'Hardly high-flown rhetoric.'

I nodded. 'Quite so, but I've heard that joke before.'

'Where?' Aristarchos leaned forward. 'When?'

'When I was called to read for the Archon the year before last, in hopes of a chorus for the Lenaia. A playwright called Timodemos used that exact line for an Athenian oarsman at Salamis.'

More fool him, thinking he could make a comedy out of that crucial battle. The Archon's distaste had been clear before any announcements were made.

Aristarchos took my meaning. 'So these conspirators have most likely hired an Athenian writer as well as at least one actor.'

'How will you find them?' Sarkuk asked.

I grinned. 'At the theatre, where else? Keep your eyes open when you come to watch my play tomorrow.'

Tur was still determined to be contrary even though he was swaying on his stool and every word he spoke was an effort. 'You think you'll recognise two men among however many thousand . . . ?'

'Maybe,' I retorted, 'and regardless, you'll all be safer there than anywhere else in the city. No one's going to try knifing you or beating you up with an audience that size to witness it.' I looked at Aristarchos. 'But I think we'll have better luck if I ask Lysicrates which actors have a particular talent for playing foreigners, and who among them might be persuaded to do something like this.'

'Persuaded or merely paid. That's a sound notion, Philocles.' Aristarchos turned to Azamis. 'Forgive me, but

I don't think it's wise for you to return to your hostel. I have property nearby where you can stay as my guests and we can ensure no enemies know where to find you.'

I could see that Azamis was reluctant, but equally he could see that Aristarchos was a man used to being obeyed. The old man exchanged a glance with his son and Sarkuk nodded.

'We are honoured by your hospitality,' he said formally.

'It's little enough restitution for all that you have suffered. Lydis, send to the hostel for their belongings and pay any outstanding bill. Meantime, I will send word to the Polemarch's office, so you may claim your friend's body.'

When the Pargasarenes had finished interrupting each other, thanking him profusely, Aristarchos turned to me.

'I really have to get to my brothers' house,' I said quickly. 'My mother's going to have my balls for loom weights as it is.'

'Of course.' Aristarchos set aside whatever he intended to say.

When I arrived at my family home, I was relieved to find that all was peaceful, or as peaceful as any festival day can be, with laughter and music and feasting all along the street. Of course, there was a harsher note here and there. With too many people sharing cramped quarters, indulging in late nights, too much wine and rich food, family rows often break out. Drama's never limited to the theatre during the Dionysia.

No strangers had come asking after me. They hadn't

even heard about the riot in the agora. My fears receded as I considered how quickly Pamphilos and the other neighbours would come to the household's aid if trouble-makers turned up.

The best of the festival food had already been eaten, so I was glad Aristarchos's slaves had fed me. Not that I said anything about visiting his house. I just hinted that nerves over tomorrow's performance had dulled my appetite.

My mother saw my hands were bruised. There was no hiding such details from her eagle eye. I made light of it, insisting I'd just run into some drunks on the Panathen-aic Way. Mother was ready to believe that. As far as she's concerned, Athens is a city of lawless brutes, so unlike the peaceful countryside she'd known as a girl.

Mother was born out in Kolonai. Her family have lived thereabouts since the time of the Titans. There's every chance she'd have stayed within half a day's walk for the rest of her life, happily married to a local boy. But when the Persians invaded, everyone in their path came scurrying into Athens for safety.

Nymenios was fawning over Melina. Wine always makes him amorous. Chairephanes was happily playing with our young nephews and our little niece. I man-aged to turn Mother's thoughts to the prospects of him marrying Glykera and blessing the family with more grandchildren. That put an end to any awkward questions.

I was glad of it. The less anyone hereabouts knew of my dealings with the Carians, the safer everybody would be. I didn't want doorstep chit-chat carrying gossip to the neighbours. Rumours could float away on the breeze until word reached whoever was behind this business. I couldn't swear the kitchen girls or the workshop slaves to secrecy. Nymenios is head of this household, not me.

I made my excuses as soon as I decently could, walking home fast through the fading daylight, eager to see Zosime. Now that Aristarchos had taken charge of the Pargasarenes, my only concern was my play. I could put everything behind me and look forward to seeing my comedy performed in the world's greatest city's theatre.

My good mood lasted as far as my own door. Even in the swiftly fading daylight, I could see that someone had painted a foul accusation along our outside wall in bold, black letters as big as my hand.

Philocles spreads his arse cheeks for any Persian who wants to bugger him.

Chapter Twelve

For the benefit of anyone passing who couldn't read Greek, whoever had come all this way to insult me had also painted a crude rear view of a man leaning forward. His hands were clasping his buttocks, all the better to show the world his gaping arsehole, with cock and balls dangling below.

I stood there for a long moment, struggling to believe my own eyes. Then I managed to swallow the rage choking me long enough to hammer on the gate. Kadous opened up with a cudgel in his fist, scowling like an avenging Titan.

Lowering the weapon, the slave looked stricken. 'Philocles—'

'When was this done?' I snarled.

'The paint was nearly dry when I got back here.' Kadous gripped his olive-wood club so hard that his knuckles showed white. 'Zosime—'

I pushed past him. 'Where is she?'

'I'm all right.' She came out of the house. 'It was done before Dad and I got back.'

Speechless, I wrapped my arms around her. Despite her calm words, I felt her trembling. Acid fury burned my throat. 'We'll find the bastards who did this.'

Fine words, but if this were a comic play, some character would promptly tap on my shoulder to ask, 'And how will you do that exactly? What will you do to him then?'

I had no idea. Real life doesn't have helpful answers turning up just when you need them.

A voice called out in the street. 'Hallo within!'

'Menkaure.' As I greeted him, my heart was sinking. We'd arranged to meet at the theatre after the choir competition, but I'd been nowhere to be found. Chairephanes had assured me he'd seen Zosime into her father's care but, if the Egyptian didn't think I could keep his beloved daughter safe from vile insults or worse, I hated to think what he would do. I could hardly protest if he insisted she went back to his lodgings.

As he entered the courtyard, Menkaure held up an oil jar he'd got from somewhere. I caught a powerful aroma, reminiscent of the resin that seals the insides of wine amphorae.

'Terebinth. This'll shift it.'

'Thank you. Kadous! Find some scrubbing brushes!'

'Let me.' Zosime pulled free of my arms and headed for the storeroom.

I looked at her father, apprehensive.

He cocked his head. 'You don't think I believe this nonsense?'

'What? No.' That wasn't bothering me. Not that he'd think I was a Persian sympathiser, or that he'd have any concerns if he thought I'd ever had a male lover. Egyptians are as sensible as Hellenes, not inclined to the peculiar outrage you hear of among northern barbarians. They know it's no one else's business if young men training together become lovers or those on a military campaign share some comfort beneath their blankets.

If that proves to be a man's lifelong preference, so be it. Most will still meet their obligations to their families by taking a wife to bear children. A man's choices to satisfy his appetites only become an issue if self-indulgence sees him neglect his duties as a citizen.

That was the point of this insult of course. Likening me to the wretched boy whores in their one-room hovels in the Kerameikos District. The wastrels renting out their bodies after they've squandered their inheritance, disgraced themselves through cowardice in battle, or been thrown onto the streets by their family for some other shameful deed. How dare they, whoever had done this?

Zosime reappeared with some old brushes and her father soaked them with the pungent liquid. Heading out into the lane, I scrubbed that obscene picture so hard that my bruised arms ached. To help me ignore the terebinth's vicious sting on my grazed knuckles, I imagined I was scouring the flesh off the face of whoever had painted it.

My anger faded along with the daylight and I was forced to consider who might be responsible. Someone had been stirring up Persian prejudice in the agora, after all. If they thought I was an ally of those Carians, they might well attempt to discredit me. How much further would they go?

'Scrub any harder and you'll be shifting bricks.'

Menkaure worked steadily beside me, obliterating the raggedly daubed letters. Kadous attacked the obscenities further along.

'You had better take Zosime home with you tonight,' I said through gritted teeth.

'Why?' The Egyptian stepped back to assess his progress.

'No.' She was standing in the gateway.

'I have to know you're safe.' I looked at her father, expecting his agreement.

'It's better for me to stay here tonight,' Menkaure countered. 'If whoever did this comes back, there'll be three of us to tackle them. You, me and Kadous. Not that I think they will,' he assured Zosime.

'Then I'll be perfectly safe.' She folded her arms. 'And tomorrow, we'll all be going to see your play. There's nothing to fret about.'

True enough. What I'd said was as true for Zosime, Menkaure and Kadous as it was for the Pargasarenes. No one would attack them in the theatre.

She narrowed her eyes at me. 'What's going on?'

Menkaure saved me from having to answer. 'I wonder when this happened.' He turned to Kadous. 'You said the paint was nearly dry? Was it tacky to the touch or still wet enough to coat a fingertip?'

The Phrygian gave it some thought. 'Wet enough for me to draw a line in it.'

'Painted not long before we got here then.' Menkaure shrugged. 'For whatever that might be worth.'

So this had happened after the fracas in the agora.

Kadous stepped back from his labours. 'I reckon we could try washing this down now.'

'I'll get some buckets.' Zosime disappeared into the courtyard.

As she headed for the fountain, flanked by Kadous and Menkaure, I looked up and down the lane, wondering which of our neighbours had already seen the insult. At least we lived on an out-of-the-way street, well away from the city's thoroughfares. But Sosistratos's sons would think it was a fine joke if they'd wandered past before I got home. They'd share it with their loose-lipped drinking friends before the night was over. It could be all over the city before the end of the festival. It might even reach the ears of the judges who'd be giving their verdict on my play tomorrow. Once Rumour takes wing there's no calling her back.

What about after the Dionysia? People wanting a speech or a eulogy have plenty of other scriveners and poets to choose from, all sitting hopefully in the Painted Colonnade. My livelihood would be hit hard if murmurs about my supposed Persian sympathies spread. There's not a family in the city, or beyond the walls out in Attica, who doesn't have good cause to fear and hate them. The same is true for all the islands overrun by the Medes in the past fifty or sixty years.

Even if we haven't clashed in battle since my father carried his spear as a hoplite, Persian intrigue has stirred more recent strife between ourselves and Sparta. Even those born since Callias secured the peace are being raised like Nymenios's children. His sons and little daughter hear their grandmother's tales of being driven from her home by invaders. She warns them not to stray outside the gate in case some treacherous Mede steals them away.

Movement caught my eye even though the dusk was thickening fast. Turning, I saw a shadow quickly vanish from a barred window high in Mikos's wall. Not quickly enough. I'd caught a glimpse of Onesime's face as she cupped her hand around a lamp flame.

I didn't know if she was waiting for Mikos or Pyrrias and I didn't care. Either way the faithless bitch was risking more than a painful fall perching so precariously on a stool or a table to see what was happening outside their walls. If he saw her, Mikos would surely accuse her of waiting for some lover, however loudly she claimed to be standing vigil for him.

I wanted to know if she'd seen anything that might tell me who had defaced my wall. Finding out would be a challenge though. With Mikos so sure she was unfaithful, he'd be guarding her closer than the Hesperides's golden apples.

Come to that, I didn't imagine she'd have recognised who it was. An Alopeke housewife would hardly cross paths with lowlifes for hire around the theatre, or mysterious conspirators spreading lies in towns on the far side of the Aegean.

Menkaure, Kadous and Zosime returned, carrying dripping buckets. We sloshed water all over the wall. I took a few paces back to judge the success of our efforts. The brickwork now looked thoroughly unsightly, dappled with paint stains and streaked with damp, but that foul insult had been obliterated.

Maybe it would look better when it dried, though that made little enough difference to me. I'd be seeing those words every time I walked down the lane, even if no one else could see a trace remaining.

I washed my hands clean as best I could in the last of the water. 'Let's have some wine.'

Menkaure raised his eyebrows. 'Don't you want an early night before your big day?'

'I won't sleep till I've got the stink of that stuff you brought out of my nostrils.' That was the simple truth, if not the whole truth. I managed to grin at him. 'Don't get me wrong, I'm very grateful. Trust a potter to know how to shift paint.'

'Does anyone want something to eat?' Zosime looked at us all. 'There's spiced barley porridge left from yesterday.'

Kadous went to fetch yet more water while I found a mixing jug and chose an amphora from my small stock in the dining room. Menkaure lit a lamp and set it on the bench in the porch while I diluted the blood-dark wine once the Phrygian returned.

'All praise to Dionysos.' Once everyone was sitting down, we offered the first taste to the god.

'Kadous,' I said casually. 'When you get a chance, ask Alke if she saw any strangers hanging around this afternoon.'

I could always hope the gaunt little slave had been standing guard for her mistress. She might have seen something useful.

'Anyone carrying a paintpot, you mean?' The Phrygian scowled. I was about to reassure him, saying I didn't blame him for not catching whoever defaced our wall, when Zosime asked him something else entirely.

'How badly do you think Mikos will punish her if he catches Onesime with another man?'

'Bad enough, but he knows if he thrashes her too hard he'll have no one to cook his meals and sweep his floors.' The Phrygian looked even grimmer.

I decided to change the subject. 'So what did you do after the choir competitions?'

Kadous refilled his cup. 'I went to Elaios the cobbler's workshop, over by the Diochares Gate.'

'Ah, of course.' Elaios is well known for opening his doors to folk from the Troad and the Hellespont. Ever since the age of heroes, Hellenic cities have founded colonies to the west of the Halys River, which marks the boundary of Persia's Phrygian satrapy. Kadous could always be sure of finding some of his countrymen there. 'Did you enjoy some good company?'

'Yes, and no. It's usually the same crowd,' my slave continued thoughtfully, 'even if we only see some of the traders once or twice a year, when they come for the Dionysia or the Panathenaia. But there were a handful of strangers there today, all with fire in their bellies. They were claiming that paying the Delian League's levy to the Athenians is as bad as paying taxes to the Persians, maybe even worse.'

I didn't like the sound of that. 'Surely they were just full of wine?'

157

Kadous shook his head. 'I reckon they were set on strife.'

'Did they get any fish to bite?' Menkaure asked.

Kadous nodded darkly. 'That's why I left. Fists and cups were about to start flying.'

So there hadn't only been trouble in the agora today. 'Does Elaios's crowd honestly think that the League tribute is so unfair?'

'Not normally. Not beyond grumbling into their third or fourth cup.' Kadous shrugged. 'Everyone does, when they've racked up some trading loss, or heard of a bad harvest at home. But these strangers were up in arms, condemning the levy as vile injustice.'

'Drink fuels a lot of folly,' Zosime remarked. 'I doubt they'll remember much when they wake up wine-sick tomorrow.'

Menkaure shook his head. 'Words like that are like arrows. You can't call them back and they stick in the mind of whoever might hear them.'

I shared his concern. 'Is the whole of Ionia nursing this grievance?'

Whoever these unhappy men might be, they lived a long way from Pargasa. The Troad and Caria are at the very top and the very bottom of the Ionian coast respectively. If you're heading for the Hellespont from Athens, you sail a northerly course across the Aegean by way of Lemos and Samothrace. Or you travel by land through Thessaly, Macedonia and the coastal cities overlooked by Thrace. The only sensible routes to Caria lie southwards, taking ship from island to island, by way of Delos and Mykonos, or Paros and Naxos, to Cos before making landfall at Halicarnassos.

'If they are, Athens needs to take heed.' Kadous looked me in the eye.

I knew what he meant. Rumours of Boeotian discontent had rumbled like distant thunder for several years before their revolt broke out. But the Archons had still seemed as amazed by the uprising as a man struck by lightning from a clear blue sky.

When we'd been camped out and waiting for battle at Charonea, every hoplite in my phalanx had agreed that if the great and good of Athens' fine families had only kept their ears open in the agora, maybe all that bloody trouble could have been nipped in the bud. If so, perhaps the Megarans and the Euboeans would have thought better of taking up arms as well and we'd be safely back at home. I hated to think the peace we enjoyed now was so fragile. Before I could pursue that cheerless notion, Menkaure spoke up, unconcerned.

'They'll all calm down once they know there's to be a fresh assessment of the levy at this year's Panathenaia.'

'Who told you that?' exclaimed Zosime.

'That's the word from Crete.' Menkaure's brow furrowed. 'I'm not sure who mentioned it first. Maybe Zokyros? But a good few others had heard the news too.' He looked quizzically at his daughter. 'What's it to us?'

'Remember the dead man dumped at our gate?' she retorted. 'He said there would be a reassessment at this Dionysia.'

'There's been no notice of any such thing posted in the agora,' I pointed out.

159

Menkaure shrugged. 'Your dead man got the wrong festival. Everyone knows League business is debated at the Panathenaia.'

'Only at the Great Panathenaia and that's not until next year,' I insisted.

'No, Zokyros said there'll be a special assessment this year.' Menkaure had no doubt about it. 'There'll be some declaration posted beforehand, you'll see.'

'Perhaps, perhaps not.' Meantime, I'd better learn as much as possible about these rumours, and warn Aristarchos. 'Will you do me a favour? Can you ask around and find out exactly who's heard this? Can you ask who first told them? I'd like to know who's particularly upset about having to pay the tribute.'

Menkaure looked more closely at me. 'Why are you so interested?'

I gestured towards Kadous. 'He says there's discontent in the Troad. That dead man at our gate was from Caria, and he was saying the same. Now you bring this supposed news from your Cretan friends. Doesn't that seem strange to you, all coming at once?'

'Once is happenstance, twice is coincidence, thrice is a hint from the Fates.' Menkaure had spent enough time among Hellenes to know that. 'Fair enough. I'll see what I can find out.'

'Not tonight,' Zosime said firmly. 'It's already late and we need to be up early to get good seats in the theatre. Let's go to bed.'

Kadous obediently rose and began tidying away the wine cups and jug.

Menkaure stayed sitting where he was, looking at me. 'What will you do with whatever I might find out? Who will you tell? I don't want my friends accused of sedition if this is some honest mistake.'

'The only person I'll take this to is Aristarchos. I'll make sure he understands no one's out to make trouble. If there really will be a reassessment at this year's Panathenaia, then no one need worry.' I managed a grin. 'I'll be asking your friends from Crete if they want to hire me to write their speeches.'

Menkaure pursed his lips. Clearly, he still had reservations. 'Let's see what I turn up. Then we can discuss what to do.'

'Agreed.' I got to my feet.

As I made sure the gate was solidly bolted, Menkaure stood stools and empty cooking pots along the base of the wall inside the courtyard. They would make plenty of noise if anyone climbed over under cover of darkness. At my nod of dismissal, Kadous went to bed, closing his own door. As Menkaure headed for the end room, Zosime took the lamp from the bench into our bedroom.

I followed to find her stripping off. She got under the blankets, purposeful rather than seductive. She didn't snuff the lamp but looked at me, expectant, until I dragged my borrowed tunic over my head.

Seeing her study my bruises in the flickering golden light, I stood silently until she nodded as though she had come to some conclusion.

'I could tell from your hands that you'd been in a fight.

Tell me everything. I want to know exactly what's going on.'

I considered trying to tell her that she need not concern herself with such troubles. That I would soon have everything resolved. But that would be a lie. A whole series of lies. She was involved now that our home had been defiled. Besides, I still had no idea how this particular drama would play out.

There is also one thing that I'm certain of. If I ever lie to Zosime, if I ever forfeit her trust, then I will lose her for good before the sun sets on that ill-fated day.

'Can I get into bed first?'

'All right.'

As I got in beside her, she licked two fingers and quenched the lamp wick. I kissed her hair as she lifted my arm and slid into my embrace.

She rested her head on my shoulder and laid a hand on my chest. 'Tell me.'

I moved her hand to my belly, to take the weight of her arm off my bruises. Somehow the darkness made things easier. I told Zosime what had happened in the agora, what I suspected about that rabble-rouser and his fake Ionian, and how I hoped to track them down for Aristarchos. She didn't ask many questions, only prompting me to continue when I trailed off into silence.

'Then I got back here and saw that filth painted on our wall.' I racked my brains for anything else that I should tell her. No, I had nothing more.

'I see,' Zosime said after a long moment. 'Then we had better find some answers and put an end to this.'

She stretched up and kissed me. Then, to my guilty relief, she curled up and settled down to sleep. Much as I adored her, body and soul, after the day I'd had, I didn't think I could possibly do her justice if she had wanted a night of passionate lovemaking.

Chapter Thirteen

Perhaps it was relief after unburdening myself to Zosime. Possibly it was pure exhaustion after that seemingly endless day. Either way, I slept deep and dreamlessly, and woke up refreshed the following morning. So refreshed that I rolled over to face my beloved and ran a gentle hand down her flank beneath our cosy blanket.

As she smiled, eyes closed, I shifted closer and kissed her forehead. With a fond murmur, she tilted her face so I could kiss her lips. I slipped my hand behind her back to draw her tighter to me. She reached around and took my wrist, draping my fingers over her breast instead. I felt her nipple tighten beneath my fingertips. She reached down to caress my own stiffening flesh. I propped myself up on my elbow, lowering my mouth to tease her breast with my tongue. Then we both heard a knock at the door.

Zosime opened her eyes. Her gaze met mine. Neither of us spoke.

'Philocles!' Kadous's voice was quiet but urgent. 'You need to hear this.'

I let my head hang, stifling my frustration.

Zosime ran her fingers through my hair, gripped and

lifted my face so she could kiss me with brisk dismissal. 'Go on.'

We both knew that Kadous wouldn't intrude without good reason.

As I got out of bed, Zosime swung her feet to the floor. I grabbed a respectable tunic from my chest. By the time Zosime was decently dressed, my erection had subsided and I could open the door without embarrassing myself.

'Please, come to the gate.' Kadous beckoned us across the courtyard. Alke was standing in the lane with a cloaked and hooded companion.

'Onesime?' Zosime looked at the second woman.

Mikos' wife pushed back the edge of her hood to look up and down the lane, to be certain that no one saw us talking. Heavy water jars stood by Mikos's gate, their excuse for going outside without his permission.

'You saw who defiled our wall?' I didn't care if she'd been on watch for her lover or merely bored by her confinement.

Onesime nodded.

'Did you know them?'

She shook her head. 'No, I'm sorry.'

'Never mind.' I tried to swallow my disappointment. A woman couldn't give evidence in court anyway.

'But I've seen them before,' she insisted, her low voice at odds with her urgency. 'They dumped that dead man at your gate. The one the Scythians took away. What's going on? This is a respectable neighbourhood!'

Respectable? With her on the lookout for her chance

to commit adultery with Pyrrias? I managed not to say that.

'We are trying to find out. What else can you tell us? Did you hear them speak?'

'They were Athenians, no question.' Her gaze slid to Zosime. 'With a poor opinion of foreigners. I'm so glad that you weren't home. If you had been, if you'd opened your gate, I would have driven Mikos out to help you. I'd have stuck my distaff up his backside if I had to.' She was desperate to be believed.

I forced myself not to ask what these men had been saying. The obscenities I could imagine were bad enough as I pictured them salivating at the idea of getting their filthy hands on Zosime. 'Did you see anything that might mark them out as slave or free?' Though that was a vain hope in Athens.

Onesime was rightly dismissive. 'Hardly.'

Alke jumped like a startled rabbit. 'We have to go.'

I braced myself for confrontation with Mikos. Then I realised the noise was the rattle of a chain over at Sosistratos's house. The thought that our neighbours had started chaining up their gates sickened me, though I could hardly blame them after a dead body had been dumped here.

Both women snatched up their water jars, spilling half the contents in their haste. I reached out to detain Onesime, hastily withdrawing my hand as she recoiled.

'Would you know them again?'

'I would.' At least she didn't hesitate about that.

I considered this new information as we retreated

to our own courtyard and Kadous closed the gate. It might be helpful to have someone identify these ruffians, though I couldn't think how to get Onesime to wherever we might find them. Mikos would never agree to me or anyone else escorting her through the city.

Besides, there was still no proof that the men who'd painted the wall had murdered Xandyberis. All we could be sure of was that they'd dumped his body. Zeus only knew who had told them to do that.

Still, now we knew that yesterday's insults hadn't just been spite from a rival playwright or someone who'd seen me accused of Persian sympathies in the agora. I was being deliberately targeted by this conspiracy. I needed to tell Aristarchos about it. If we could put an end to this plotting, all these disturbances should stop. Ideally before my neighbours started dropping hints that I was no longer a favoured friend. I didn't want to have to move away. I liked our little house. I wanted to decorate my dining room with painted fruit trees and swooping swallows.

But all that would have to wait. I had more important things to do. This was the day my comedy would be performed.

'How about getting breakfast in the city?' I suggested to Zosime and Kadous.

We reached the theatre so early that my family hadn't even arrived. Even so, we weren't the first there. As soon as he saw us, Chrysion came running across the dancing floor, stage-naked in his pale body-stocking.

'Where've you been? Never mind,' he said breathlessly.

'Come on, you need to draw your lot for our place in the competition!'

'Good luck.' Zosime grabbed me to snatch a fervent kiss.

'Come *on*!' Chrysion seized my elbow and forced me across the sandy circle like a herder with a recalcitrant goat.

As we approached the rehearsal ground, I could see the Archon for Religious Affairs, along with a stagehand holding a small urn. The other comic playwrights were waiting with their own chorus masters already dressed in their under-costumes. I could hear the hum and bustle of preparation from the comic actors, choruses and musicians behind the wood and sailcloth walls.

'Good of you to join us.' Euxenos looked down his long nose.

Strato didn't say anything, shifting from foot to foot like a man with a radish up his arse. Pittalos seemed unconcerned and Trygaeos even offered me a smile.

'We've time in hand,' the old playwright assured me.

The Archon thought otherwise. 'I need everyone to know the order of the day before I attend to other matters,' he said testily.

'Forgive me.' I bowed a deep apology to him, and then to Dionysos's statue, just for good measure.

The Archon pressed thin lips together and nodded to the slave. I don't know if Euxenos had arrived earliest this morning, but he was the first to be offered the urn. He reached in and removed his hand, keeping his fist tight closed.

My turn came last, possibly a rebuke for being late. I grinned cheerily at Euxenos as the other three drew their lots. I had no reason to do that, I just wanted him to think I had some secret he didn't know. To my satisfaction, he narrowed his eyes suspiciously.

When I took the final broken piece of pottery I gripped it so tightly that I had to force myself to relax before the sharp edges cut into my palm.

The Archon looked around the circle. 'If you please?'

As we all opened our hands, I saw the letter alpha clearly scratched into the black glaze on mine. Euxenos would follow us, then Trygaeos and Strato, with Pittalos and his Sheep bringing up the rear.

'Excellent,' Chrysion breathed with deep satisfaction.

'Proceed.' The Archon nodded to us all and departed in a bustle of self-importance.

'Really?' I asked under my breath as the chorus master and I hurried towards our enclosure.

'Any troublemakers in the audience haven't had time to get drunk.' Chrysion's grin came and went. 'As for the judges, who knows? Still, look cheerful. That might put one of the other choruses off their stride, if their leader thinks we got what we wanted.'

I swallowed a laugh. 'If you say so.'

When we pushed the sailcloth gate aside, I saw Hyan-thidas sucking his twin pipes' reeds, ensuring they were precisely moistened for the performance. He waved a greeting.

Our three actors and the rest of the chorus were already wearing their under-costumes. As one man, they turned,

169

expectant. If they were that well synchronised out on the dancing floor, we had nothing to worry about.

'We're first up,' Chrysion said briskly.

That impressive coordination broke up into what looked very much like disarray. Some pulled on their tunics. Others hurried to the basket holding the custom leatherwork which my brothers and our slaves had toiled over. Lysicrates started laying out masks while Apollonides and Menekles helped each other into their heroic armour.

I watched the chorus all adjusting the belts and straps that secured the comedy cocks hanging just below the hem of their tunics. I felt like a spare prick at a wedding.

Lysicrates came over, yellow skirts swishing. 'Go and find somewhere to sit and watch. There's nothing more for you to do. It's up to us now, win or lose. You've offered the god everything you can and he knows it.'

It was strange. Whenever I'd imagined this moment, I'd expected to be racked with nerves. Now it came to it, I felt oddly numb.

'Good luck.' I shook Lysicrates's hand and waved to the others as I left them for the short walk to the theatre.

There's no official place for playwrights to sit. Not so long ago, they were in the midst of the action, as an actor or chorus leader, maybe even in the singers' ranks. It still hasn't occurred to the Archons to accommodate writers like me who merely supply the words. We don't get any rewards for winning, not even an ivy leaf garland. It's the patrons who get all the honours, on the day of competition and thereafter. They customarily set up a monument to their victory to honour Dionysos, which is still more expense for them of course, so I'm happy enough to be spared that.

As for the actors, the finest performance in a tragedy wins a prize, but there's not even that much recognition for comedy. Not from mortal men anyway. I found my way to the end of the first row of wooden benches and gazed at the god's ancient statue. His approval was what really counted.

The theatre was growing noisier. The drama competition's patrons and their closest associates were arriving to take their marble seats in good time. They were all dressed in their festival finery but there was nothing of yesterday's formality. The city's most influential men laughed and joked like schoolboys as they congratulated those who'd sponsored yesterday's winning choirs. Hangers-on commiserated with the unfortunates whose silver had been spent in vain, and wished good luck to those who had opened their purses to ensure the city enjoyed all the new plays over the next four days.

Aristarchos was yet to take his seat. For the moment, he was exchanging courteous smiles and greetings with the wealthy and well-born. Lydis stood a pace behind him at his right side. The slave was covertly scanning the throng for anyone his master would be ill advised to snub, even by accident.

Higher up the hillside, the wooden benches were rapidly filling with ordinary Athenians. Frantically flapping hands caught my eye and I waved to my family. I was pleased they had got good seats and hoped my mother couldn't see that I wasn't wearing my new sage-green tunic. I didn't want to have to explain it had been ruined in that fight in the agora.

I searched the seats higher still. Zosime would be sitting somewhere up there with Menkaure and most likely Thallos, the old Thessalian, and everyone else from the pottery. I guessed Kadous would be with the other slaves from our family workshops right at the top of the slope. I hadn't a hope of picking him out at this distance.

Nymenios stood up, beckoning to me. I turned away, pretending I hadn't noticed him. There was no way I was going to sit with them all. I couldn't face hearing my family's unguarded comments as the play I'd spent so much time and passion on unfolded before us.

Before Nymenios could bully Chairephanes into coming to get me, a flourish of pipes announced the Archons' arrival. Everybody hurried to sit down. The sooner the city's business was done with, the sooner the comedies could start.

The Dionysia is the ideal time to honour those who've done Athens some great service. A succession of men from within the city and across Attica each received a diadem as the crowd cheered. As the last grateful and appropriately humble citizen returned to his seat, a further fanfare announced the display of tributes to Athena from our allies in the Delian League.

I leaned forward to get a better view as each successive city was named and its representatives carried the coffers that held their silver around the dancing floor. These contained a sixtieth part of their tribute to the Delian

League, token payment at the festival. I wondered how many caskets were lighter than they should be, how many towns were short of the full tally of coin owed to Athena.

It wasn't easy to match each new contingent to the names being sonorously proclaimed from the stage. The list seemed endless as the Archon of Record announced every dusty town in Ionia, from the Hellespont and the Thraceward districts, which apparently went on forever.

Finally he reached some place names I recognised as Carian. The list scrolled on and on: Madnasa, Lepsimandius . . . The delegates all looked as poor as Aesop's country mice. At long last, I heard Pargasa called out.

Azamis shuffled forward. His grey head was bowed and his shoulders were stooped beneath the burden of his years and their town's coffer. Sarkuk walked beside him, straight-backed, with his face impassive. They both wore their finest clothes but neither one could boast shoes or a tunic as impressive as those Xandyberis had worn.

There was no sign of Tur. I was relieved to think the young fool wouldn't be here causing trouble with his volatile temper, or prompting gossip as people saw his cut and bruised face. On the other hand, I'd be relieved to know he'd made it through the night after taking such a vicious beating. I'd seen more than one man go to sleep after a thrashing, never to wake again.

Now that they'd completed their circuit, the Ionian delegates were leaving by the theatre's western entrance. I was on the eastern side. So near and yet so far. I was itching with frustration. I could hardly run down there and chase the procession to ask them my questions and share my news about the rumours Kadous and Menkaure had heard. I'd have to find them later, or maybe try and catch Lydis, to give him a message for Aristarchos. For the moment, I could only watch as Azamis and Sarkuk walked away, and the Ionians were replaced by nervously smiling delegates from the Chersonese and the countless islands strewn across the Aegean.

At last, when the procession was over, the allied delegates were escorted to seats reserved for them. Shading my eyes with one hand, I was able to pick out where the Pargasarenes were sitting. No one with evil intent would be able to reach them there.

Now the penetrating clamour of brass trumpets announced the arrival of young men who'd just completed their military training. These weren't all of their year's contingent though; only the ones whose fathers had died in battle fighting for Athens.

Some of their fathers had been men in my phalanx who'd perished, I shouldn't wonder. I owed so much to those older soldiers who'd offered their help and advice on the punishing march to Boeotia. They had bolstered us when we were as green and untested as these young men on the dancing floor, when we stood shoulder to shoulder and defied our city's screaming foes.

Under the solemn gaze of the city's generals, Pericles prominent among them, these young warriors were presented with their hoplite armour by a grateful city. There were a lot of such deserving young men this year. More than could be rewarded with the sets of warrior's gear donated by Athens' allies at the last Panathenaia.

That extra equipment would have been paid for from the public treasury. Families who've lost so much will never face the humiliation of seeing a hero's son demoted to the ranks of the rowers because they cannot meet the costs of equipping him.

That's another reason why I've no wish to father citizen sons. It's why I set some of my earnings aside for the day when I can repay Nymenios for my share of the family business's profits. I'll honour my father's memory by helping to educate and equip young Hestaios and little Kalliphon, along with any other boys born to Melina, and to Glykera and Chairephanes if that match gets made.

Public money might maintain the gymnasiums' wrestling grounds, running tracks and the teachers holding classes among the Lyceum's groves or the Academy's colonnades, but there will be further fees to pay if my nephews are to benefit from the best trainers and tutors. Lectures by visiting philosophers, sharing their latest thoughts on history, mathematics or whatever else the boys show a talent for will cost still more silver.

Sombrely watching this parade of those bereaved by war, I remembered my father relating his struggles to see all four of us properly trained and equipped. Though every sacrifice was worth it, he swore after a few cups of Chian, sloshing his wine for emphasis. No son of his would sweat at a trireme's oar with some lentil-muncher on the benches above him farting in his face.

I never asked if he felt the same after Lysanias died in Egypt. Glancing at the seats of honour, I saw Aristarchos sitting with his hands knotted in his lap. I couldn't see his expression at this distance. Was he remembering his own slain son, who was now wandering the shadowy asphodel fields in the realm of the dead?

As I commended Lysanias to the care of the gods below, I wondered if it would have been better or worse if my lost brother had left a son to be honoured at a Dionysia. Would that have tempered my father's heartbreak, or leavened my mother's grief? I've never been able to decide.

There was a pause as the generals left the stage and Athens' newest soldiers marched off in well-drilled formation. Slaves were ready and waiting to receive their gleaming armour so they could come back to enjoy the comedies. I hoped a few of my jokes would ease the ache of their loss. That, and a few swallows of the wine provided at Aristarchos's expense.

A cohort of slaves began carrying amphorae and cups up and down the theatre's aisles. It was good-quality wine, Lydis had assured me. As people took this opportunity to stretch their legs or have a word with friends and family, I noticed Aristarchos summon his secretary with a snap of his fingers. As I made my own way towards them, Lydis came quickly around the edge of the dancing floor, beckoning to me. We met halfway.

'The master begs the favour of a quick word.'

'Of course.' I hurried down the slope with the slave. 'The boy, Tur, how is he? Has a doctor seen him?'

Lydis nodded. 'Spintharos advises that he rests completely, for several days. He is concerned about the blows he took to the head.'

'Understandable.' I only hoped the young idiot would take the doctor's advice, or his father and grandfather could convince him. Either that or tie him to his bed.

We reached the marble seats ringing the dancing floor and Aristarchos turned to greet us.

I wasted no time. 'I've been hearing more strange rumours. There's talk of widespread discontent with the tribute. More men have been saying there'll be a reassessment this year, maybe even at this Dionysia.'

Aristarchos narrowed his eyes. 'Other Carians are spreading this nonsense?'

I shook my head. 'I don't think so. My slave heard it from men fresh from the Hellespont, and a potter I know said that visitors from Crete believed the same.'

A resonant chord from a mighty concert lyre prompted everyone around us to hurry back to their seats.

'There's more,' I said hastily. 'My home, our wall was painted with insults last night, accusing me of Persian sympathies. It could be just some rival—'

The great concert lyre's music rang through the theatre again. Everyone was settling down, expectant.

'We'll have to continue this later.' Aristarchos grimaced. Then he surprised me with a conspiratorial smile. 'I hear that our play will be seen first. That'll give everyone a few new notions to debate.'

'Let's hope so.' I scurried back to my vantage point. As a slave with a tray passed by, I grabbed a cup of Aristarchos's wine and downed it in one swallow. Fine vintage or not, I didn't even taste it.

A theatre slave walked up the steps to the stage. A lean

man with a deep, ringing voice, he made the announcement that brought everyone who knew me to the edge of their seats.

'Let your play commence, Philocles!

Chapter Fourteen

Menekles strode onto the stage with his head held high. A fine Homeric hero, he cradled his helmet in the crook of one arm and sloped a spear over his other shoulder. He gazed around with satisfaction before addressing the audience in ringing tones.

'Have you heard the glorious news? Troy's topless towers have fallen! Who among us ever thought this great victory would come? Yet truly the day has finally dawned. We have prevailed after so much tribulation, lamentation and bloodshed. After ten long years of struggle, sacrifice and dedication, the menace in the east is no more. Now we can look forward with hope. Now we can plan with ambition. Now we can build anew!'

Apollonides ambled into view, bow-legged and with his wig carefully teased so that tufts of hair stuck out in all directions. He dragged his shield along the ground with one hand and was rubbing his cloth-covered arse with the other.

'Where have we washed up now? Can we at least stay here until the blisters on my backside have healed? Rowing's harder work than you think,' he confided to the audience.

That won the play's first cheer from the upper benches and I breathed a little easier. Hopefully acknowledging the city's lowest ranks this early on should save our chorus from being showered with nuts and insults by those assuming a play about heroes had nothing to say about their humble lives.

Though I was still apprehensive about the ten men in those marble seats, five of whose votes would decide my fate. Would the well-born of Athens think I was mocking them? Add to that the fact that Homeric heroes like Meriones and Thersites are the stock-in-trade of tragedy. Would the judges look askance at me meddling with tradition?

As the two of them came to the end of their bickering, I held my breath as I waited for Chrysion's cue. The chorus appeared on the dancing floor accompanied by Hyanthidas playing a bold new tune.

The Corinthian's appearance prompted a surge of murmurs from the audience for several reasons. Firstly the talented musician was playing two interlacing melodies, with a different dance of his fingers on each of the twin reed-tipped pipes in his mouth. That's not something you see every day. I'd never seen Euxenos's tootler try it, however skilled he might be at swift and swooping dances.

Secondly, Hyanthidas wasn't wearing a pipe halter and that was taking quite a risk. As anyone who's ever played a pipe will tell you, using two instruments together is a very different challenge to only playing one. Keeping your lips tight around two reeds as well as sustaining taut, puffed cheeks quickly makes your face ache. If your cheeks and lips cramp or quiver, you'll shred your tune with sudden squeaks and silences.

Sustaining a single song or dance tune on twin pipes is one thing, but accompanying an entire play is a real challenge. No wonder some long-forgotten musician devised a solution, more interested in getting paid than worrying about looking a fool. All the other plays' pipers would wear leather halters with straps running across their mouths, pierced for their twin pipes' reeds. But Hyanthidas had sworn he didn't need such assistance.

Thirdly, he was playing Etruscan music, and there were plenty of citizens and visitors in this audience who'd travelled westwards to Italy's Hellenic cities. They recognised those characteristic lilts and rhythms, and eagerly nudged their neighbours. As Chrysion led the chorus in extolling the virtues of this unknown land, I watched the whole crowd sitting up straighter as whispers spread. Soon everyone was wondering where the jokes might be in stranding Homeric heroes in that wolf-ridden wilderness.

Keen interest wasn't only kindled on the wooden benches. Down below on the marble seats, I noticed several of the great and the good sneak sideways glances at Aristarchos. All they saw was polite interest on his face. None of them would be able to guess that he'd been the one to insist my play should look westwards.

I'd originally set this story in the Chersonese, far away on the Black Sea's northern shore. I'd written a particularly fine speech for Apollonides's character, Thersites, speculating with calculated obscenity on the unlikelihood of

Meriones ever fathering sons, if he couldn't even guide his trireme's jutting prow into the Hellespont's moist and inviting opening.

But Aristarchos was adamant and, since he was paying the piper, the actors, the chorus and the writer, he got his way. Apart from losing that particular joke for Thersites, I hadn't been overly bothered. My characters could say what I wanted when they were standing on an Etruscan shore as easily as they could on some Euxine beach.

Though after seeing Strato's Thracians yesterday, I'd been wondering if Aristarchos had picked up some hint from their play's patron. Had Lamachos said something indiscreet over a fourth or fifth serving of some choice vintage at an aristocratic banquet? If so, I was grateful Aristarchos had been there to hear it.

Even before a few cups of wine, a festival audience wouldn't have seen much difference between a chorus of red-headed barbarians from Thrace and my Achaeans meeting copper-topped characters in Taurica. When a play offers the upper benches something they've already seen, a shower of nuts or worse is pretty much guaranteed. The competition's judges aren't overly impressed either, to many a hapless playwright's discredit.

As the chorus's first song drew to a close, with everyone note-perfect and precisely in step, I knotted my hands together. Now for Lysicrates's entrance.

Here she came. Egeria, sensuous, seductive and, as far as Thersites was concerned, completely terrifying. He stood there quaking as she greeted the astonished Achaeans in the name of all Etruscans. Then she explained, in precise and provocative detail, exactly what bedroom talents the local women expected from these prospective husbands who had just washed up on their shore.

Not that I believe for a moment the overblown tales you hear about the western barbarians. Their women train in gymnasiums alongside their men, all of them unashamedly naked? Husbands and wives alike see nothing wrong in taking lovers to their beds in full view of anyone passing by?

But such nonsense makes for a good bawdy story and that's what a Dionysia audience likes. Even the ones who pretend to prefer Pindar and mourn the loss of his high-flown odes. Everyone was laughing now, from highest seats to lowest and even though I knew every punchline, I found myself grinning.

As Egeria chased Thersites off stage, Meriones turned to his loyal crew, aghast. 'We had better decide for ourselves how our new city is to be ruled, and quickly, if we don't want to find ourselves under the thumb of a woman like that!'

'They sound as scary as the Spartans,' Chrysion said with a shudder.

'Perhaps we should fall into step with the Spartans!' Inspired, Meriones brandished his spear. 'Let's conquer these tribes and make serfs of them all! What do you say to that, lads?'

But the chorus was all standing still with their arms folded, emphatically shaking their heads.

'Lads?' he pleaded.

'You want to start more fighting? When we've finally

arrived in a place where we can enjoy some peace and quiet?'

Chrysion led the chorus in loud disapproval of all Meriones's arguments in favour of returning to war, not to mention scorning the Spartans' unrelenting regime of discipline and drill with precious little sex.

'Then I must rule you myself.' Admitting defeat for his initial proposal, Meriones struck a heroic pose that could have come off any pot in Menkaure's workshop. He stood with his spear drawn back for throwing and his other arm outstretched. 'Thereafter my sons will rule over your sons, and their sons will govern after them, down through the endless generations!'

Thersites scurried back on stage. 'What about my sons?'

'What about them?' Meriones demanded, affronted.

'Who's to say they won't be brighter than yours?' Thersites challenged him.

'I don't think there's much danger of that.' Meriones looked in the direction Egeria had gone. 'Not if I find them a mother like that one.'

'Oh, you think you could handle a wife like that?' Thersites mocked.

'After ten years sitting in a tent outside Troy with Achilles sulking because he didn't get all the pretty girls for himself? I'd like to handle her often as possible.' Meriones cupped his hands lewdly in front of his chest. 'I like a strong-willed woman.'

'So did Agamemnon,' Thersites pointed out. 'That didn't turn out so well for him. I hear Clytemnestra cut him down to size with an axe.'

The audience laughed as the actors bickered for a while about the merits and drawbacks of hereditary leadership. I hadn't intended to make this a particular theme, but Aristarchos had encouraged me to draw out this scene for longer and longer until, once again, Meriones found all his arguments had been undermined.

'Never mind that,' he said testily. 'If we're debating who's best suited to rule here, then who's led this expedition from the very first? Who slew Phereclos, son of Tecton, with this very spear on the plains of Troy?'

'Not with that very spear,' Thersites countered. 'You left your first one sticking in Deiphobus's shield and had to go back to your tent for another one.'

'Never mind that,' Meriones said testily. 'I still killed Phereclos.'

'Yes, but—'

'And Adamas, son of Asios.'

'Yes, but—'

'And Harpalion, son of Pylaemenes.'

'Yes, but—'

'And Laogonos, son of Onetor.'

'Yes, but—'

'Who won the archery competition at Patroclos's funeral games?' Meriones preened.

'Yes, but how good are you at keeping men alive?' Thersites squared up to him, truculent.

'A very good question while we're stranded here on this barren shore,' Chrysion confided to the audience before turning to his fellow Achaeans. 'Here's another one for you. How soon will we see these noble heroes come to blows if one or both of them assume some divine right to lead us? No city can stand, divided against itself. We need unity, not tyranny!'

Now Hyanthidas's glorious music drew on the marching songs that every hoplite knows, while the chorus remembered how fighting in a phalanx had saved them in the battles for Troy.

They decided to stick with that winning strategy now that they had found peace. They all wanted votes in a People's Assembly and equality for all men under the law. As their song concluded with a triumphant shout, the chorus all wheeled round to look up at Meriones and Thersites, every stance expectant.

Those heroes looked at each other and made a show of counting up the heads of the chorus men, before adding the audience beyond. Turn by turn, they picked well-known faces out of the throng, or at least they pretended to, since I'd had no way of knowing who would actually be in the audience when I wrote this particular satire.

Claiming to recognise their shipmates in the audience, they praised these men for their supposed gallantry outside Troy, all the while slyly alluding to recent scandals and humiliations that had been the talk of Athens' taverns through this winter just past. The crowd loved it.

Then our heroes counted themselves, to discover with comic dismay that their side amounted to the two of them up on there on the stage. The audience chuckled as the actors ran to and fro, looking in vain for someone, anyone else to add to their number.

Eventually, grudgingly accepting democracy soon provoked a lively squabble over which of them would do better in a popular vote. Finally the two men shrugged and nobly wished each other good luck, before walking to opposite ends of the stage and each confiding in the audience exactly how they intended to court popular goodwill with bribes and gifts.

Chrysion promptly led the chorus in mocking them both. The gods themselves would appoint this new city's leaders in a properly conducted ballot for magistrates and council members. The only time these heroes would see a popular vote was if the people chose to expel one or other of them, for the sake of peace and quiet hereabouts.

Thersites grovelled, swearing he hadn't intended to cause any strife.

Meriones agreed with fulsome apologies. Then he clapped his hands.

'If we're to build a new city, we'd better start building. If you want an assembly and the rule of law, we'll need a council chamber and courts.'

Apollonides interrupted. 'First and foremost, we should build a temple, high and bright on that sacred hill. After all, the gods help those who help themselves.'

When I'd written those words, I'd been confident that everyone agreed on the merits of Pericles's building plans. I thought I was happily reflecting Athenian pleasure in the rewards of the peace we now enjoyed for the first time since our grandfathers' day. This morning I couldn't help wondering what the Pargasarenes and the other Ionians made of this notion. I looked down but all I could see was the backs of the allied delegates' heads.

'Who should we dedicate this new temple to?' wondered Thersites.

'Athena! Who else?' Meriones indicated the imaginary landscape with that same sweeping gesture. 'We're surrounded by olive trees! How can we doubt her blessing in sending us here?'

'What tools do we have for building this city you've got planned?' Thersites looked around.

Meriones heaved an exaggerated sigh and offered his spear. 'It's a bit narrow for a shovel, but I suppose it's the best we've got.'

Thersites went to retrieve his shield. 'We can use this for carrying things.'

Meriones considered his helmet. 'A bucket?'

Thersites nodded before suddenly clapping a hand to his head in a florid gesture of despair. 'But how can we build if we can't measure anything?'

'Oh, that's no problem,' Meriones laughed, confident. He reached under the front of his tunic. 'There you are. That's a foot long.'

It worked, thanks to Nymenios's expert knowledge of how to cut and sew leather. As Menekles tugged on what I sincerely hoped everyone in the audience had just assumed was the usual comedy phallus, the jaunty red cock tripled in length.

Judging by the roar of astonished hilarity from the entire theatre, we'd successfully kept this trick up our sleeves. Well, not our sleeves exactly.

Apollonides had to wait for the noise to die down to

have any hope of his next line being heard. 'A foot? I don't think so. I think you'll find *this* is a foot!'

With a jerk and a suggestive thrust of his hips, he produced a cock twice the length. That got an even louder and longer reception. People probably heard the laughter in Sparta.

Apollonides and Menekles had to stand there waiting for the roars to subside, waving those ludicrous phalluses around before they could appeal to their loyal Achaeans to decide which standard measure they were going to adopt.

Naturally the chorus responded by displaying their own suddenly impressive appendages. I saw the riotous mirth sweep all around the theatre with private satisfaction. Follow that with your pretty Butterflies, Euxenos. Whatever else they might think of my play, those judges in the front row would have no trouble remembering it, no matter what the Brigands, the Sheep or the Philosophers might get up to.

Best of all, the audience loved it. I'd promised Aristarchos they would, because he'd looked extremely dubious when I outlined this particular part of my plan. As I'd explained, it's all well and good having comedies that promote civic virtues and honour the city's democracy by means of elegant satire, but when an Attic farmer comes to the city after a year of seeing the same faces, the same houses and trees, and the same mule's arse day in and day out, what he really wants is a play with plenty of belly laughs and lots of cock jokes.

Lysicrates timed his entrance superbly, ostentatiously

creeping along the stage just in front of the scenery with a finger held to his mask's lips to hush the audience.

'Well, that's an interesting tool!' He stepped up close, so the rapacious Egeria could peer over Thersites's shoulder. 'This new city of yours will be full of marvellous erections!'

Thersites shrieked and ran off the stage, high-stepping like a startled satyr. Egeria scampered after him, hitching handfuls of skirts indecently high.

Once the laughter had died down, the audience got a chance to catch their breath as the chorus sang in a more reflective mood. They painted a lyrical picture of the fine buildings that would adorn their new city. This would be the Builders' legacy for their sons.

With my words and Hyanthidas's music, it was a very fine song. But was it long enough? I knew what was coming next and wiped apprehensively sweating hands on my second-best tunic. Lysicrates and Apollonides had rehearsed this next series of swift-moving scenes time and again but there were so many ways that things could go horribly wrong.

'Nice new city you've got here. Wanna buy some amber?' Lysicrates was unrecognisable, dressed as a northern barbarian from the snowy slopes of the Alps as he sidled up to Menekles. Even his voice was completely different as he extolled the mysterious virtues of electrum.

'How about some nuts?' Apollonides was a hoarse-voiced Sardinian approaching from the opposite direction. 'Got to have nuts in a market place.'

'I've never known a market that wasn't full of nutters,' Menekles agreed.

The jokes came as thick and as fast as the costume changes as Apollonides and Lysicrates dashed on and off the stage only to reappear as different merchants with something new to offer each time.

Menekles did a splendid job of portraying Meriones's heroic disdain for bartering like a common trader, before he realised the fun and profit to be had by playing these merchants against each other.

I think the audience was as breathless as the actors by the time our erstwhile hero was left alone on the stage once more, contemplating all the goods he'd amassed.

'Mine. All mine,' he gloated, hugging himself.

'Really?' Chrysion stepped forward from the chorus to challenge him. 'When we're the ones building the city that these merchants are flocking to? You don't think you should show a little gratitude by sharing some of that out?'

'What? Oh, oh, yes, of course,' Meriones said unconvincingly.

The chorus began planning the fine meals they would cook, congratulating each other on the comforts that would furnish their homes.

'Oh! Meriones! You shouldn't have!' As the music wound down, Thersites returned to the stage with Egeria on his arm. 'A wedding feast for us? How generous. Truly, a noble gesture!' he told the audience.

'What? Wait! No—' But Meriones's protests were drowned out as Hyanthidas's music led the chorus in

191

a triumphal marriage hymn. Chrysion predicted great things for the sons of Thersites as the music changed to a traditional wedding-night ballad and the happy couple were escorted off to bed.

The nuptial song ended with an intricate flourish as the last man in the chorus passed by the end of the stage, leaving the theatre. Applause for the actors and singers swiftly changed into loud conversation and people hurried to and fro along the benches. A festival audience knows when to seize their chance to change places or find refreshments or to head for a public latrine before the next performance.

I sat on the end of that wooden bench, looking at the empty stage and dancing floor. My first play at the Dionysia. It was all over. Nine months of work, endless rehearsing, so much effort and skill put into those costumes, into the masks and that glorious, unexpected and original music. Everything was done with.

I heaved a sigh as I sat there alone amid the festival hubbub.

Chapter Fifteen

We didn't win. That honour went to Trygaeos and his Philosophers. The sly old comedian astounded us all as he breathed new life into his tale of fatherly wisdom challenged by youthful presumption. Dazzling wordplay impressed the city's intellectuals while ever-accelerating action entertained the rest.

After scorning their old man's reliance on the hoary sayings of Hellas's Seven Sages, the play's two sons belatedly realised that he still knew a thing or two about the best ways to charm pretty girls. More importantly, he knew the secrets of impressing the watchful mothers and wealthy fathers of potential brides. So the hapless lads came begging for help after their own comically scant success. One had tried showing off the latest mathematical and rhetorical theories, only to discover that bored the girls rigid. His brother fared no better despite flexing well-honed muscles and boasting of his discus and javelin victories. He learned that girls aren't very interested in a man who's most interested in himself.

The play's underlying message was that ancient Hellenic wisdom, hallowed at Delphi and echoed by Athens' favourite sage, Solon: nothing to excess. The music was solidly traditional and skilfully played so I've no doubt that impressed the judges as well.

Trygaeos was ecstatic as his patron Simylos was awarded the winner's ivy-leaf crown. Even with disappointment gnawing at my guts, I couldn't help but smile at the old man's delight. I watched him thanking his actors and the chorus who came crowding around. Meantime Simylos accepted congratulations from his wealthy and well-born friends, along with the ornamental bronze tripod. He'd soon be setting it up as a public monument, to remind everyone that he'd won this honour for eternity. Meantime, Trygaeos's actors and chorus would dedicate their victorious masks to hang in Dionysos's shrine.

Besides, *The Builders* came second, and that was some salve for my wounded pride. Even if second place doesn't win any prizes, I reckoned that should keep my name in people's minds when they needed a man skilled at turning a phrase. It should certainly help me compete for a chorus for the next Dionysia.

I got up, dusted off my backside and walked down the slope to offer my own congratulations to the winners. As I caught a glimpse of Aristarchos in the well-born crowd around Simylos, I wondered how my patron was taking this result. His smiling face gave nothing away.

I noticed his son Hipparchos had appeared from somewhere. He stood close by his father, accepting jovial commiserations and compliments on the play which his father's money had financed and my imagination had created. He clearly had no qualms about taking credit for other men's hard work.

Mind you, a few paces away, his friend Nikandros looked as sour as an unripe apple. I sincerely hoped the arrogant prick realised how stupid he looked, now that his predictions for my play's abject failure had come to nothing.

'Well done, my young hero!' Pittalos nearly spilled his cup of wine down my tunic. 'Well done indeed!'

'You do realise I didn't win?' Was he really that drunk? 'First prize is the one that counts.'

'True enough, but after that, what matters most is not coming last,' he said cheerily. 'As long as a poet avoids that humiliation, we're all equal before the gods. No one will even remember who came second, third or fourth by the end of the festival.'

He certainly wouldn't, if he kept on drinking at that rate.

'True enough.' I smiled and went on my way.

Truth be told, Pittalos and his Sheep could just as easily have taken second place. The country visitors in the audience had been especially taken with his tale of a humble farmer duped by a quick-talking conman. The crook swore the farmer could breed sheep with blue or scarlet wool if he paid for rare and miraculous herbs. The old fool had only been saved from ruin by the loyal sheep themselves, fearing their flock would be stolen or slaughtered by rival shepherds.

They'd persuaded a mischievous nymph to lead the conman astray, promising him untold erotic delights. The crowd had particularly liked the scene where the nymph duped the conman into eating goat shit, imagining the pellets were grapes. Jokes about dung are nearly as popular as ones about pricks. Then the nymph and the sheep set about convincing the old man that, if something looks too good to be true, that's what it'll prove to be.

I headed for the rehearsal ground in search of Apollonides, Menekles and Lysicrates. As I reached our enclosure, Chrysion and every man of our chorus greeted my arrival with heart-warming cheers.

I bowed to them all, smiling. 'Thank you, thank you all for your hard work and dedication. This is as much your not-quite-victory as it is mine.' That got a laugh.

The three actors were talking to Sosimenes while the costumes and masks were being packed away.

'Betting on the outcome?' I wondered who'd won and who'd lost.

The mask maker chuckled. 'You think we'll let all that good cloth go to waste?'

Apollonides grinned. 'This year's under-costumes will lay the foundation of the next festival's masks.'

'Whichever plays win or lose, Sosimenes always come out on top,' Lysicrates said wryly.

'Good to know.' I nodded at the basket. 'Is there any money in second-hand wigs?'

'Oh, I'll take those off your hands.' Though Sosimenes raised a cautionary finger. 'I won't be in a hurry to get rid of them though, in case you need them for the Country Dionysia season. You'll be getting an offer from more than one rural theatre, if I'm any judge.'

'Really?' I looked at the actors, trying to decide if the

mask maker was serious or having one last joke at my expense.

Menekles nodded. 'I'd wager on it, but it would be unfair to take your money on a sure thing.'

'Just hope the best offer comes from somewhere closer than Thorikos.' Apollonides grimaced. 'I don't fancy that journey again.'

'We'll show you how to shepherd a chorus of country bumpkins around,' Lysicrates assured me, 'without them tripping over each other.'

I hadn't really thought about the possibility of the three actors and me being hired to reprise our play at one of the district festivals out in Attica around the winter solstice. If that happened, I'd be the one leading a chorus of local volunteers. That was a daunting prospect. I'd sung in a few plays in my time, in tragedy choruses for the Lenaia, but taking the lead in a comedy was a very different challenge.

'Don't shake hands on any agreement without discussing it with these three first,' Sosimenes advised. 'You want the best possible price for your time and trouble.'

On the other hand, being paid a second time for work I'd already done definitely appealed, even if that meant putting on a chorus mask and costume myself.

A moment later, voices passing our enclosure entrance caught everyone's ear.

'Some judges can always be swayed by showy tricks over subtle performance. And of course, Trygaeos won sympathy votes because no one expects another play from him. He'll be dead by next year.'

197

Euxenos was sneering as he passed by with his patron, Lamachos. The comedy writer looked as cheery as a man with an eagle chewing his liver. The wealthy gentleman was clearly none too pleased that all his coin had seen his play come last.

Lysicrates made a farting noise and our chorus all jeered. Euxenos didn't betray any obvious reaction but I saw the back of his neck go red.

'He's got no time for showy tricks?' mocked Menekles. 'I can't remember when I last saw the stage crane get that much use in a comedy.'

The chorus leader's butterfly costume had assuredly looked very fine, swooping to and fro as the theatre slaves hauled on the ropes that swung the machinery holding him up in his harness. As for the rest down on the dancing floor, only one man had trodden on another's trailing drapery, as far as I could tell. But their dazzling colours had been the most memorable thing about Euxenos's play. That and the impatient shouts to get on with it and give everyone a few laughs. Heckling from the upper benches had come thick and fast, whenever the chorus embarked on yet another soulful song extolling the muses' gifts to humanity.

I was more surprised to get a filthy look from Strato as he stalked past a moment later. His *Brigands* had been well received and rightly so. That family's misadventures had been highly entertaining as they followed the road from Athens to a citizens' settlement up in Macedonia. No matter how bad things got, the deluded hero continually consoled his family with the promise of their handsome allotment of land, so different to their cramped hovel in a burned-out slum. His faith had been rewarded, and if different judges had been selected, there was every chance such a heart-warming play could have come second.

Well, if Strato was going to sulk that was his problem, not mine.

Apollonides clapped his hands. 'Where are we drinking tonight?'

As the chorus all clamoured for their preferred wine sellers, insistent fingers plucked at my tunic. I turned to see Lydis, Aristarchos's slave.

'My master's compliments, and can you spare him a moment?'

'Of course. Excuse me.' I waved a hand at the actors. 'Our patron wants a word. I should see my family as well before they leave the theatre. Where shall I meet up with you?'

'Soterides's place, by the Itonian Gate?' suggested Menekles.

That won general approval.

'I'll see you there,' I assured them before following Lydis over to join Aristarchos.

Standing by his marble seat, our patron was deep in conversation with another well-bred Athenian whom I didn't recognise.

'You think we should seriously consider looking westwards?' the other man queried thoughtfully. 'For corn as well?'

'We already know that Sicily can rival Egypt as a bread

basket,' Aristarchos pointed out. 'Surely it's better to fill our granaries from an island where we can trade in peace and profit instead of risking treading on some Persian satrap's toes?'

'Isn't it wiser for us to buy up the corn which some overly ambitious satrap would need to feed his armies?' the other man countered.

'Why not send out our own citizens to plough fertile land we already know lies fallow,' another man inter-jected, unasked, 'to grow our own crops without being beholden to anyone?'

I recognised him. Pheidestratos had been Strato's patron, and he was looking as disgruntled as the playwright.

'Another valid strategy,' Aristarchos agreed, 'and surely it's better to look westwards into wilderness lands for such opportunities rather than along the already crowded shores to the east?'

Pheidestratos looked ready to argue that point but the unknown man had noticed Lydis and me, and politely indicated our arrival to Aristarchos.

'Ah, excuse me.' He smiled and ushered me away to-wards the theatre's western entrance where we could talk without being overheard.

'I didn't mean to intrude. Lydis did say you wanted to see me.' I may have spoken a little sharply. It had been a long and stress-filled day.

Aristarchos smiled, though I saw that calculating glint in his dark eyes. 'You think I should have introduced you? Wouldn't you rather they dismissed you as some scribbler whose face they need not even remember by tomorrow?'

'Forgive me, but I don't follow you.' I was too tired for riddles.

Aristarchos rubbed a thoughtful hand over his beard. 'Pheidestratos said something curious when we discussed his play. He seems quite certain that, sooner rather than later, Athens will have good cause to send out settlers to start farming good land sequestered from our allies in Ionia.'

'Sequestrations?' I didn't like the sound of that. The Athenian Assembly handing over plots of confiscated land to our own citizens had been one of the grievances prompting rebellion in Euboea.

Aristarchos looked at me. 'What might persuade the People's Assembly to take such action, to secure the commerce and resources that our city so assuredly needs? Do you think that our fellow citizens could be convinced by a surge of dissatisfaction from our allies, and ill-tempered disputes over tribute payments?'

'Surely it would take more than that?' I fervently hoped so.

'Probably,' Aristarchos allowed, 'but who's to say this discontent you've been hearing about won't lead to something more, to something worse? How would the Athenian people react to outright defiance in Caria perhaps, or refusals to pay the Delian League tribute owed by towns in the Troad or Crete?'

I recalled Tur's anger when we'd first met, when I'd told him there was no chance of the tribute being reassessed this year. I remembered the tavern talk that Menkaure and Kadous had related.

'Do you think Pheidestratos asked Strato to write a play about citizens setting out for a distant land allotment because he's seen these straws in the wind?'

'Or because Pheidestratos is friends with men who'd like to set a few stones rolling down that particular hill,' Aristarchos said crisply. 'Men who seem very keen to get that particular notion into potential Assemblymen's heads.'

I stared at him, bemused. 'You can't imagine Strato will invite me to go drinking with him and helpfully spill some ripe secrets?'

'Hardly.' Aristarchos allowed himself a moment's sardonic amusement. 'But it's plain that something is going on and we have a duty to the city to find out more. I can make discreet enquiries among the great and the good, to learn what's prompted Pheidestratos's current thinking. Your talents and contacts are much more suited to discovering who's goading our visiting allies and seeing where such rabble-rousers might lead you.' He glanced sideways. 'It will be interesting to see if they come knocking on Pheidestratos's gate. Wouldn't you rather he had no idea who you are, if your enquiries take you to his household?'

'Trying to provoke an allied city to default on its tribute would a bold undertaking for one man.' I'd have to be incredibly careful, as well as certain that I had proof, before I breathed a word of such suspicions. I didn't have Aristarchos's resources if I was hauled into court, charged with slander.

'We must uncover who's behind this, and quickly,

before such contagion spreads.' Aristarchos looked grim. 'We've barely got used to peace. Do you want to see the hoplites mustered again, sent to enforce Athenian will overseas, while we wait for urns of ash and bones to come home?'

'Of course not,' I said fervently.

Aristarchos shook his head. 'Defence is one thing. Provoking a fight's quite another. My father taught me that when I was five years old, on the night before he marched to fight at Marathon.'

Aristarchos must have seen my surprise. His noble father would have trained as a horseman. I bit back my question but he answered it anyway.

'Yes, he marched with the hoplites. Even though the cavalry hadn't been called up, he was determined to fight for the city. Barely ten years later, I hadn't even done my military training when he gave me a spear to escort my mother and brothers and sisters to safety in Salamis when the Persians invaded again. Like him, like you, I would give my life to defend Athens and her people, but I won't see another of my sons, or anyone else's child, lost to serve some selfish fool's ambitions.'

'Master,' Lydis warned, low-voiced. 'People are starting to look this way.'

I looked at Aristarchos, troubled. 'Do you really think there's some conspiracy to stir up trouble among our allies?'

'It might all be some misunderstanding.' He shrugged. 'But mistakes can be just as lethal as malicious intent. A man carelessly walking into a javelin's path on a gymnasium field is as dead as one run through with a spear in battle.'

Was this the final answer to the puzzle of the dead man being dumped on my doorstep? Xandyberis's killers could well have hoped to ruin my play's chances by getting me accused of murder, at the same time as stirring up Carian outrage when they learned their envoy had been killed. If Strato had won the competition, then everyone would be talking about his play while annoyance with ungrateful Ionians swirled around the city. On the other hand, this could all be as far-fetched as any notion a dramatist might concoct.

Aristarchos continued, brisk. 'Let's see if we can gather a few more facts. There should be at least one of the tribute commissioners at the banquet I'm attending tonight. Meantime—' he surprised me by clasping my hands in his own and smiling broadly '—let's pretend we've been discussing *The Builders*. I'm assuring you that I thought your actors and your chorus did superbly well. Second place at your first Dionysia is absolutely no disgrace. Well done, to all of you.'

The warmth in his voice and the strength of his grip convinced me these congratulations were genuine. 'Thank you.'

'Better still, I don't have to pay out yet more money on a plinth for the victor's tripod. Go and celebrate with your players, and here's some of the coin you've saved me.'

He turned to Lydis and the lithe slave reached inside the low-cut armhole of his sleeveless tunic. He produced a bulging leather pouch that had been concealed by the fullness of the cloth bunched up by his bronze-embossed belt.

Aristarchos dropped the purse into my hands. 'This should keep the wine flowing.'

'Thank you.' Feeling the weight, I reckoned that much silver would quench every thirst in Soterides's tavern.

'Now, you must excuse me.' Aristarchos shook my hand in farewell.

'Of course.' That was a relief. I could see my family waiting impatiently by Dionysos's statue, along with Kadous and our other slaves. Menkaure and Zosime stood a few paces away.

Nymenios and Chairephanes greeted me with loud satisfaction over how well their leatherwork had performed. As I had anticipated, Mother and Melina had been tremendously entertained by Egeria, the lascivious Etruscan. Naturally, they were also scandalised, as was right and proper for respectable citizen women.

Kadous and the other slaves merely grinned broadly. I could see they were holding their tongues out of respect for my mother and my brother's wife. There'd be plenty of ribald speculation the next time I visited the workshop, discussing where exactly I'd found inspiration for men exaggerating the length of their cocks.

'I still don't see why you didn't win first prize,' Mother complained.

Everyone echoed her with loyal and loud indignation.

'As Dionysos is my judge,' I assured them all, 'it was a fine and fair result. Maybe I'll do better next time.'

I noticed Melina hold out her hand to Nymenios. As he put a supporting arm round her waist, she leaned against him, closing her eyes.

'It has been a very long day,' I said. 'Thank you so much for waiting to see me but you must be ready to get home and have something to eat.'

'You're dining with your actors, I take it?' Nymenios looked mildly envious.

'Dining and drinking,' Chairephanes chuckled. He'd drunk more than his share of the day's free wine.

'Come and see us tomorrow.' Mother embraced me in swathes of rosemary-scented pleated wool.

'I will,' I promised.

'After the tragedy and the satyr play,' Melina reminded me. 'We'll be coming to watch those.'

'Of course.' I watched them walk away before turning to Menkaure and Zosime.

The Egyptian grinned. 'It was a very good play.'

Zosime threw her arms around my neck and kissed me long and deep. 'I told you so,' she said when she was forced to take a breath. 'I'm so proud of you, my love.'

I kissed her back, just as fervently. 'I couldn't have done it without you.' That was the simple truth.

She kissed the tip of my nose before taking a pace back and looking at the fat purse I was clutching. 'What's that?'

'Silver to reward the chorus and actors, to pay for an evening's revelry at Aristarchos's expense.' I looked at Menkaure. 'Care to join us?'

He shook his head, amused. 'I'll see Zosime to Alopeke.'

'Take Kadous, then he can bring you safely home,' she said firmly.

'There's no need for that,' I objected.

'There could be,' the Phrygian slave said darkly, 'if you're going to be spending coin like some sailor fresh off a boat in Piraeus. Someone could follow you down a dark alley to see if you've got anything left worth taking.'

'We still don't know who killed that Carian.' The fear in Zosime's eyes stifled my protest.

'Very well.' I capitulated.

Besides, if Kadous came with me, he could keep his ears open for anyone stirring up discontent around the taverns. That would put some of Aristarchos's silver to good use.

Well, that was my intention. I can't actually remember what anyone discussed that night. My chorus and the actors were intent on honouring Dionysos by drinking all the wine they could lay their hands on. I've no idea if I walked home or if Kadous had to carry me.

Chapter Sixteen

Zeus roused me the next morning with a thunderbolt that split my head in two. The thunder came again. And a third time. After that, I was forced to realise that my brains weren't actually leaking onto my pillow. There was no hope of the Underworld's shadowy peace. The worst had happened. I was alive, and I was awake. Fuck.

Next, I discovered I was lying face down, sprawled corner to corner across my bed. My empty bed. I guessed I hadn't moved since they'd dumped me here to sleep off my folly. I was still wearing yesterday's tunic. At least someone had taken off my shoes.

I also found out I'd been drooling because my face was stuck to the pillow. As I licked repellently sticky lips, my mouth tasted as sour as wine dregs left in a jug overnight. Fuck.

I wondered if I could lift up my head without my skull shattering like a cracked pot put on a hot hearth. Before I could decide, that fucking thunder rolled across the heavens again. Though an unbiased observer would probably say someone was knocking gently on the bedroom door. 'Yes,' I croaked.

The door opened. Daylight struck, blinding as a

lightning bolt. I buried my face in the blanket with a groan. 'Fuck.'

'Good morning,' Zosime said crisply.

'Where'd you sleep?' I mumbled, guilt-stricken.

'In the spare bed. Kadous made up a pallet on the floor for my father.'

'Fuck.' So Menkaure had seen me as drunk as a hedgehog gorging on fallen, fermented grapes. Roaring drunk? Soppy drunk?

'Is he still here?' I rolled onto my side and squinted up at her. The sun was still dazzling, even with the pillared porch shading the doorway.

'No, he's already gone to the theatre.' She shrugged with apparent unconcern.

Even wine-sick as I was, I could see that she was less than pleased about something. Belatedly I realised why. 'How late is it?'

'Late enough that you need to get up now,' she said meaningfully, 'if we're to see today's plays.' Sitting on the edge of the bed, she offered me a cup.

I hadn't thought I could feel any worse. Now I realised I could. I'd promised Zosime we'd see all the tragedies in this year's competition. I knew she was really looking forward to seeing some drama that would be completely new to her. She knew every line of my comedy by heart, after all. If she missed her chance to see today's trilogy, that promise was dead and gone. Unless some rural theatre hired those particular actors for their country festival. Would I be able to find that out? Maybe we could travel . . .

209

Such desperately scrambling thoughts were no match for my thumping headache. I shifted and reached for the cup. 'Just give me a moment. I'll get up, I promise.'

'Yes, you will,' she agreed. 'And then you can read the letter that's just arrived from Aristarchos.'

'A letter? Let me have it.' I tried to sit up. That was a serious mistake. The room rocked like a ship's deck in a storm. I slumped back onto the blanket with my eyes tight shut and waited until it stopped. 'Fuck.'

Zosime's hands closed around mine, to save me from spilling the cup and soaking the mattress. 'You need to drink this.'

I wanted to tell her there was no chance of that, but I didn't think I could open my mouth without spewing bile all over the bed. It took a few long, uncertain moments before I felt the odds shifting in my favour. I sat up again, very, very slowly. After some deep, deliberate breaths, and still painfully cautious, I took a sip from the cup. The well-watered amber wine had already been sweetly aromatic before Zosime added honey and a few choice herbs. I could definitely taste fennel, but the rest was anyone's guess.

Whatever was in it did help. I opened one eye to offer Zosime a crooked smile.

'Eat this.' She handed me a heel of plain barley bread.

That was a much greater challenge. I managed a couple of bites before the thought of chewing and swallowing any more made my stomach lurch. Once again, it was a few moments before I thought I could talk without heaving what little I'd eaten back up.

I held out my hand. 'Please may I have my letter now?'

Zosime had it tucked into her belt. She handed it over and took the empty cup in exchange. 'What does he say?'

I snapped the seals and winced as I unfolded the aggressively crackling papyrus. The next challenge was forcing my bleary eyes to read the damn thing. As before, Aristarchos came straight to the point.

What light could Lysicrates shed on those performers in the agora?

'Fuck.' That had completely slipped my mind. I hadn't asked any of the actors who they thought could impersonate Ionians well enough to fool an Athenian crowd.

'For a man who makes his living with words, you're getting tediously repetitive.' Zosime stood up. 'Come on, get out of your sty and turn yourself back into a man fit for decent company.'

'Yes, Circe,' I muttered as she went out through the door.

She wasn't wrong though. I smelled as bad as any drunken swine, reeking of stale wine sweat. I eased my legs over the side of the bed. So far, so good. Then I realised my tunic was pungent with fatty smoke from a tavern's griddle cooking sausages and skewered gobbets of fowl.

I managed to wrench it over my head before the stink made me vomit. Throwing the garment into a far corner I swallowed hard, barely managing to quell my nausea.

Then I tried calling out through the open door. 'Kadous? I need hot water for washing.'

Chairephanes swears by a Spartan steam bath after too much wine, but even if I'd had the time I couldn't have faced the Lyceum today. The gymnasium would be full of hearty athletes who had no taste for tragedy. They would be spending their Dionysia roaring at each other as they raced to a sprint's finish line or cheering on each other's long jumps and discus throws. Such uproar would rival any torment Odysseus had seen in the Underworld, as far as I was concerned.

The Phrygian appeared with a grin. 'A pot's already steaming.'

I managed a rueful smile. 'I assume I can thank Zosime for that?'

He came into the room. 'You should make sure she knows you're properly grateful.'

I considered asking Kadous about last night's debauchery. No, I decided, there was nothing to be gained by hearing how badly I'd embarrassed myself. Besides, I was pretty sure Lysicrates would tell me every last hideous detail the next time we met.

'Is she very cross with me?' I asked, apprehensive.

'Cross enough,' he said drily. 'Better not keep her waiting. I'll find you some oil.'

As he left, I rose slowly to my feet. I trod on my belt buckle. 'Fuck.'

Looking down I saw a leather pouch on the floor. The purse Aristarchos had given me. Empty. Discarding the notion of bending over to reach for anything, I settled for kicking the purse out of sight, under the bed.

Outside, the sunshine was still painfully bright. I barely opened my eyes while I rubbed myself down with olive oil and scraped every last trace of grime and stink off my skin. After sluicing myself from head to toe with warm water, I took a long drink from the jug Kadous brought fresh from the fountain, and another one after that.

That felt better. I was still very far from recovered but I should at least be able to take Zosime to the theatre. If I did that, as well as remembering to ask Lysicrates about actors who were good at playing Ionians, the day wouldn't be a total loss.

I was about to head back to our bedroom and find some clean clothes when Zosime surprised me, appearing from the not-yet dining room. She held out a papyrus sheet.

'I've been thinking about the men Onesime saw painting that filth on our wall. Maybe you could find someone who saw Xandyberis with some strangers. If you knew where and when he met them, perhaps that would help you learn who they are. Maybe seeing this will jog a few memories.' She handed me a portrait of the dead man. Her artistic skills brought him vividly back to life with deft strokes of a pen.

The ink was still glistening. I waved it in the hot sun to dry. 'You're a marvel. I don't deserve you.'

'Just as long as you remember that.'

Even though she smiled at me, I felt a chill in the warm sun.

Every coin has two sides. As no more than my lover and as a resident foreigner besides, Zosime has none of an Athenian citizen's rights. That also means she has none of the ties that bind women like Melina to their hearths and homes: love for their children, and with Aphrodite's blessing, for their husbands as well.

My mother, my sisters, my brother's wife, they spend their whole lives within sight of the Acropolis, under watchful Athena's grey gaze. They share every passing year's joys and sorrows with family, friends and neighbours. Leaving their homes and friendships would be like cutting off a limb.

Menkaure and Zosime could take a ship from Piraeus tomorrow and not look back. They'd already lived for years in three different places. Another new start would hardly be a great challenge. With their skills as potter and painter, they could make a good living in any Hellenic city.

Zosime must have seen something in my face. 'Stop moping,' she chided. 'You earned that headache.'

'True enough.' I hid my apprehensive thoughts with a repentant smile. 'Give me a moment to get dressed and we'll get to the theatre.'

I threw a silent prayer to Dionysos that we'd still be able to get decent seats.

'We'll see today's plays then find somewhere to eat in the city,' I suggested. 'If we have an early night, we can be up and at the theatre tomorrow first thing.'

'You said you'd see your mother today,' Zosime reminded me.

'Okay, but that'll just be a quick detour.' I scrubbed a hand through my wet curls to try and quell the thumping in my head. 'Let me get dressed.'

I found a plain brown tunic in my clothes chest. That would do. I carefully rolled up the portrait Zosime had drawn and tucked it through my belt for safe keeping.

'I should stay here today,' Kadous said glumly as I went back into the courtyard. 'Better not leave the house unguarded again.' He managed a wry grin. 'If I see anyone creeping up with a paint pot, I promise the fucker will end up drinking it.'

I considered that for a long moment, looking around our little house. I assessed what someone might find, breaking in here to smash and steal. The chickens. Zosime's jewellery. My precious library of scrolls. Whatever treasures Kadous might have stowed under his bed.

All were things we'd grieve to lose. There was nothing that couldn't be replaced though, given time, money and effort. Nothing was as valuable as Kadous's life. The men who'd dumped Xandyberis's body had already come back here to try and intimidate me a second time with their painted slanders. I wouldn't bet against these bastards cutting my slave's throat if they found him here alone, to make sure I got their message for the third time of telling. Whatever their message might be.

It was humiliating to admit I didn't feel safe in my own city, in my own home. I didn't like the idea of yielding to an enemy either, but I'd learned the difference between a rout and prudent retreat in Boeotia.

'You're not staying here on your own,' I said firmly. 'Until we know who our enemies are, we watch each other's back.'

'If you're sure.' Kadous didn't protest too much. Either

he'd thought this through like me, or he really wanted to see today's tragedies.

Setting out, I wasn't sure if the walk to the city would kill me or cure me. Thankfully a fresh breeze was blowing. By the time we were approaching the Itonian Gate, my headache had subsided and my stomach no longer felt as if I'd swallowed something dredged from the River Styx.

Just before we reached the gate I was surprised to see Mus striding down the road. He saw me and waved a broad hand, clearly relieved. 'The master sent me to make sure that all was well with you.'

'Is Aristarchos at the theatre?'

Mus nodded. 'With the Pargasarenes.'

'Let's not keep them waiting,' Zosime suggested.

'Of course.' Mus turned around and set a punishing pace back into the city. I was hard pressed to keep up with him. For all that I'm more of a runner than a wrestler as the sculptors classify a man's physique, I was evidently still suffering the after-effects of that fight in the agora, as well as last night's drinking. Just to rub salt in my wounds, Zosime had no trouble keeping up with the big slave, lithe and limber as always.

When we arrived at the theatre, I saw Aristarchos on the edge of the dancing floor, chatting to Azamis and Sarkuk. It wasn't Lydis standing with him today but the broad-shouldered slave who'd carried a torch on the eve of the festival. Anyone menacing Aristarchos would have to go through that bruiser, so I wouldn't bet a mouldy olive on their chances.

'Go on.' Zosime had seen me looking. 'It's all right, I

can see my father.' She pointed and Menkaure waved at us both. Thank all the gods he'd got here early enough to claim a well-placed bench.

I kissed her quickly. 'I won't be long.'

'I'll see you later.' Kadous looked further up the slope to the slave seats.

I hesitated. I'd much rather he sat with us. It wasn't as if anyone who didn't know us could tell he was a slave. The city is full of all manner of accents, even more so at festival time. But we knew that someone was out to make trouble for me, for all of us. Someone who knew where I lived, and I guessed they knew my household. If Kadous sat with us, someone could accuse me of encouraging my slave to claim a citizen's rights. They couldn't make a case that would hold up before the courts, not out of one transgression in the theatre, but they could make a lot of noise around the agora. Like thrown mud, some slander always sticks.

I nodded. 'But we don't leave the theatre without each other.'

'Of course.' Kadous looked grim.

I made my way towards the Pargasarenes. Sarkuk waved as he saw me coming.

Aristarchos turned to greet me. 'Good morning.'

'Good day to you all.' I looked at the Carians. 'Tur has no taste for tragedy?'

Though I wasn't sorry not to see the boy. His appalling bruises must be an even more shocking sight today. Add to that, I still didn't trust him to control his temper if some unknown enemy sidled up to taunt him.

217

'The doctor set the bone in his nose straight, first thing this morning.' Sarkuk grimaced. 'He has no interest in going anywhere today.'

'I can imagine.' I winced with genuine sympathy. I once broke a bone in my foot and that had been agony until it healed.

Azamis was looking a lot brighter today. 'Let us join our fellow delegates.' The old man nodded towards the seats reserved for Athens' allies.

Those distant towns' and islands' representatives were settling down for the day's entertainment. I noticed a good few clusters of three or four sitting with their heads close in conversation. I recalled the way these visitors had been looking around before yesterday's comedy competition. They'd been gazing out across the theatre, admiring the city, or twisting in their seats and craning their necks to look up at the Acropolis behind them. They'd been eager to take in all the sights of our grey-eyed goddess's city. Today though, whatever they were discussing was evidently more important.

Sarkuk glanced at his father. 'Let's see what someone may let slip about whoever's urging us to defy the levy.'

'We'll see what they say when they learn that someone thinks that we're just foolish monkeys to be led into trouble so that foxes can profit.' The shrewd glint in Azamis's eye suggested that the people of Pargasa had good reason to keep him on their council.

I pulled Zosime's portrait of Xandyberis from my belt. 'See if anyone remembers seeing your friend on the day he died. Show them this. If we can learn where he went, and when, that might help us find his killers.'

'Is this your delightful companion's work?' Aristarchos pursed his lips, admiring. 'She is very talented.'

Sarkuk's hand shook as he took it, making the papyrus rattle. 'It's him, to the life.'

'Let's meet at the end of the day and share what we've learned,' Aristarchos suggested.

'Are you sure you want to be seen in public with the three of us?' I asked him bluntly.

This conversation might still be taken for a passing encounter. Whoever was behind the riot in the agora already knew that I was linked to the Carians but perhaps they still thought that Aristarchos was no more than my play's patron. Seeing us meet up again risked confirming that we had ongoing common interests.

'Oh, I think so.' He smiled without humour. 'Let's see what these rabble-rousers make of our alliance. What they do next may give us a hint as to who they are.'

'If you think that's best.' I glanced towards the actors' entrance onto the stage. People were already milling about in costume, though not yet masked. 'If you'll excuse me, I'll go and see if I can find Lysicrates before the plays get underway.'

'Good idea,' Aristarchos nodded.

Chapter Seventeen

I got a few odd looks as I arrived at the rehearsal ground. Today's chorus men remembered seeing me in all the bustle of parading their masks and costumes on the festival's first day. They knew I'd written a comedy. I had no business here now that tragedy had taken over the theatre. No playwright ever composes both.

As it happens, I'd have liked to try my hand at tragedy, but committing to writing three full dramas and the satyr play that follows would have taken more time than I could ever spare from keeping my household fed with my other commissions.

Add to that, Thalia, muse of comedy, has claimed me for her own while Melpomene has resolutely withheld her gift of tragedy. No matter how serious my theme, whenever I try my hand at penning solemn drama, jokes always edge their way in.

I smiled at the curious chorus men and went on my way. Thankfully I couldn't see any sign of Oloros, whose *Theseid* was to be performed today. The few times we had spoken, he'd struck me as a remarkably humourless man. Taut with festival nerves, he'd be perfectly capable of telling the nearest stagehand to throw me out.

Inside the actors' enclosure, there was plenty of elbow room without five comedy choruses and their leading characters all crammed in together. As was customary, actors who weren't involved in this year's competition had come to hang around with their fellow professionals, as had the comic actors whose work was now done.

I spotted Apollonides. He laughed as I approached.

'You've recovered from last night? Did you wake up with your head in a bucket?'

'You don't want to know,' I said ruefully. 'Have you seen Lysicrates?'

Apollonides thought for a moment. 'I saw him by the Shrine of Dionysos a little while ago.'

'Thanks.' I waved farewell and hurried away.

I didn't have long, and I really didn't want to be one of those people irritating the rest of the audience by sneaking back to their seats after the first play has begun. I especially didn't want to disappoint Zosime after I'd got her here in time for us to watch today's tragedies.

To my relief, Apollonides was right. As I skirted the back of the stage building, I saw Lysicrates chatting with a group of friends, all sat on the front steps of the ancient temple. When I beckoned, he obligingly came to meet me. Better yet, he came alone.

'How's your head?'

'Better than my stomach. Listen, I have a favour to ask.' I drew him close with an arm around his shoulder. Quickly and quietly, I explained why I wanted to know of any actors who were particularly adept at foreign accents.

'You'll have to give me some time to think about that.' He looked at me, wide-eyed with shock. 'Should I ask around?'

'If you must,' I said uneasily. 'But don't let slip why you're asking and don't mention my name. These folk are always one step ahead of us. We need to find some way to outflank them.'

He nodded. 'I'll be careful.'

'Make sure you are. They've already murdered one man and they started a riot in the agora the day before yesterday. Anyone could have been hurt or even killed in that uproar. They didn't care.' I didn't want his blood on my hands.

The sound of the theatre crane got our attention. The stagehands were making their final preparations for the first play's opening scene.

'I'll see you later.' I hurried back to my seat.

I wasn't the last one to arrive, but I cut it painfully close. Zosime's expression was studiously neutral as she and Menkaure made room for me on the bench. I sat quietly, swallowing lingering queasiness and wishing the crowd wasn't so loud.

The family behind us were discussing what they knew of the tragedies in this year's competition.

'Oloros will need something special to beat Myron,' the mother prophesied.

Menkaure leaned forward to talk to me past Zosime. 'Tomorrow's trilogy will be about Tantalus and the curse he bequeathed to Pelops and then to Atreus.'

I'm sure it would be very fine, cannibalism and incest notwithstanding. That's another reason why I've made my peace with being a comic playwright. I'd rather spend months polishing jokes about big red cocks and donkey dung than wading through grim tales of tainted blood.

The noisy conversations all around me hushed as the first actor walked out onto the stage. Theseus in his youth had arrived from Troezen with the sandals and sword he'd found hidden under a rock. These tokens were to prove he was King Aegeus's son, heir to Athens' throne.

Even burdened as I was with wine-sickness and other distractions, Dionysos worked his magic on me. Thanks to the actor's mask and costume, no one saw an ordinary Athenian, a man we might pass in the street or the agora. Great Theseus stood before us, his passion ringing around the theatre in the very shadow of the mighty rock where he had built his citadel.

A chorus of citizens appeared to interrogate him. Who was he? What manner of man? Could they accept him as his father's heir? The audience shuddered as the hero regaled these noble Athenians with tales of the monsters he'd defeated as he fought his way to their city. Each challenge revealed a different facet of his merits.

A shiver ran down my back when Medea appeared on King Aegeus's arm. The chorus recalled how she had claimed sanctuary here. They confided their fears to the audience. It looked as if she was intent on claiming a good deal more.

Maybe so. To me, the witch looked extremely Persian in her dress and mannerisms. Her accent, too. Though I strained my ears for the voice underlying every word, I was forced to conclude whoever wore that mask wasn't the actor we were looking for. This wasn't the fake Ionian from the agora.

Had this trilogy's patron insisted that Oloros put those particular words in Medea's mouth? Who was responsible for the choice of costume and mask? Was it someone keen to stir up more fear and mistrust of anyone from the east? How far did this conspiracy reach?

Or was I getting paranoid? Medea is always an ominous figure and Oloros had hardly invented her origins in distant Colchis, in the furthest eastern reaches of the Black Sea. That has been part of her story since Jason first returned with the Argonauts.

Her attempts to kill Theseus are equally well known, relived here as she connived to send him off to fight the bull of Marathon. His victorious return was loudly cheered by everyone whose fathers and grandfathers had fought the Persians on that same plain.

But Medea wasn't done. We sat tense as she tried to poison Theseus. We breathed sighs of relief when her scheming was uncovered. Defeated, she fled before Aegeus could call her to account. Her parting shot was a warning that she would watch and wait and take her first chance of revenge. Was that merely Oloros reminding us all of the gruesome fate that would befall Jason's children – or some more pointed hint that the Persians still menaced Athens?

My suspicions notwithstanding, it was a very good play. The audience cheered and stamped their feet enthusiastically as the chorus made their exit. Though the family behind us still reckoned tomorrow's trilogy would be better.

Zosime caught my eye and grinned. I could see she was eager for that treat. As I returned her smile, I vowed I'd make sure she saw it.

It seemed the gods were determined to hold me to account today. Nymenios tapped me on the shoulder as I queued for three cups of wine in the interval before the next play. 'Where are you sitting?'

I pointed. 'With Zosime and Menkaure. I'm sorry, we didn't see you when we arrived. Where are you all?'

'Up there.' As he jerked his head, I saw Chairephanes waving, sat with the others. They had a good enough spot, but we had better.

Nymenios had other things on his mind. 'Come on, I've just seen Dexios.'

I stared at him blankly. 'What?'

Then I remembered Epikrates on my doorstep with his tale of woe and undelivered leather. That seemed like half a year ago.

Nymenios had already turned away, expecting me to follow him to wherever he'd seen the tanner. I wanted to argue, but today just the thought of trying to dissuade my brother made my headache three times worse. I sighed and trailed after him.

Dexios was deep in conversation with someone I didn't recognise, both of them sipping wine. As Nymenios strode towards him, he greeted us both with an ingratiating smile.

'Good day to you. Such a pleasure—'

'Where's our leather?' Nymenios demanded.

'Forgive me, I am so embarrassed.' The tanner spread apologetic hands, though his dark eyes were as hard as agate. 'My stock's run low, a temporary situation, I assure you.'

Nymenios was having none of it. 'I want the hides we've paid for or I want our silver back. Otherwise we'll see you in court.'

He included me in that threat with a gesture. I did my best to look like a man who could write a thundering denunciation instead of someone quite likely to be sick on his shoes.

'No, wait, you have to listen!' Dexios abandoned his attempts at charm, fat jowls wobbling like a cock's wattles.

'We have to do nothing of the kind,' snapped Nymenios.

I laid a hand on his forearm and glared at Dexios. 'Make it quick. How have you fallen foul of the temples?'

'I've done nothing!' Dexios protested. 'Ten days ago I paid up for my usual consignment from the Temple of Hephaistos. We shook hands on the deal but the skins never arrived. When I went to ask where they were, they said a cart from my yard had already collected them.'

'Really? Did you send word to the Archons? I will check,' Nymenios warned.

'That very same day!' Dexios's grievance was loud enough to turn heads. 'The temple slaves swear they acted in good faith and the chief priest backs them up. He says they can't be held responsible if I've been robbed by such deception. The magistrates say there's nothing they can do until I find out who collected the hides from the temple.'

The tanner clenched his fists and turned to me. 'Will you help me, when I drag these bastards into court? Write me a speech that'll scald the jury's ears? I'll pay whatever you ask.'

That convinced me he was telling the truth. Dexios always haggles Nymenios down to the last sixteenth of an obol. Now he was inviting me to help myself to his silver. 'Have you any idea who did it?'

'Not yet.' He scowled at the avid onlookers as if he suspected them all. 'Not the priest at least. He was appalled to realise how easily he'd been duped.'

Nymenios surprised me by giving Dexios a curt nod. 'You can have until the end of the month. Supply the leather you promised us or return our silver.' He scanned the avid onlookers' faces and snapped his fingers as he saw someone he recognised. 'Kephalos, will you stand witness for me?'

The man nodded, along with several others who looked familiar from local brotherhood meetings, or the Alopeke district council, or somewhere I'd probably remember if I'd drunk less wine the night before.

'The yard will be back in business within days regardless.' Now Dexios was smiling, visibly relieved. 'With all these sacrifices for the Dionysia, we'll have as many hides as we can handle.'

'Let's hope so.' Nymenios turned to stride away before the tanner could say anything else.

I hurried after my brother. 'At least that's settled. If Dexios can get us the skins, all well and good. If he can't, we'll just do business with Pataikos.'

Nymenios shook his head, looking grim. 'I saw him earlier. He says everyone's bidding against him for those hides from the temple at Acharnai. He says every temple he deals with in the city has had someone pay coin, up front, for all this festival's hides. If Dexios wasn't so busy guzzling free wine, he'd know that for himself.'

I stared at him, astonished. 'Who has that much silver?'

'Nobody knows. The temples aren't telling, presumably to keep the coin coming.' My brother's face hardened. 'As soon as the festival's over, we need to talk to everyone in the leather trades, and the other tanners. We need to find out what's going on before we're all beggared.'

'Then why did you give Dexios until the end of the month?' Now that really confused me, with or without my headache.

'To give him every incentive to find out what the fuck's going on.' Nymenios let slip a hint of desperation. Then he turned on me. Ever since we were kids, if something's bothering him, he finds a way to give someone else grief. 'When are you coming to see Mother? She wants to talk about your play.'

She wasn't at the theatre today. She'd lost her taste for tragedies after burying her husband and losing one of her daughters with a stillborn grandchild, all the while mourning her lost son.

'Soon.' I hesitated. 'I hope so, anyway. You're not the

only ones with troubles. Someone's spreading lies about me.'

I explained, swift and succinct, about the paint on my wall. I didn't particularly want to tell my brother, or have to listen to his advice, but Nymenios was the head of the family. I decided I wanted him forewarned before someone stirring up shit brought home a rumour that I was a Persian sympathiser.

'I'm trying to get to the bottom of it, but that could take me the rest of the festival.'

Nymenios nodded with reluctant understanding. 'So we'll see you if we see you.'

'Say sorry to Mother for me.' Someone else I owed amends.

I barely reached my seat with the cups of wine that I'd promised Zosime and Menkaure before the second play started.

Wracking my brains over who could be wrecking my brothers' business, as well as wondering why someone was stirring up trouble among Athens' allies, was an unwelcome distraction as the drama got underway. Theseus was on board ship, sailing for Crete with a chorus of youths and maidens, all to be sacrificed to the Minotaur. In a nice touch, these were the sons and daughters of the citizens' chorus from the previous play.

Poseidon offered to save him, in return for Theseus installing him as patron god of Athens. To no avail. Theseus stayed loyal to Athena. Poseidon revealed himself as the hero's true father but, once again, Theseus wouldn't be swayed from his duty to King Aegeus and the city.

Duty was the thread running through this play. When Theseus returned in triumph, to relieve the fears the chorus had been sharing with the audience, he brought Ariadne with him. He explained how her help and her ball of yarn meant he'd been able to slay the Minotaur and escape the Labyrinth. But he still left her on the island of Naxos, as the chorus performed a very fine rendition of the Crane Dance. As Theseus heroically explained, yielding to his love for her would fatally split his loyalties. Athens had his allegiance, first and always.

I was out of my seat as soon as the chorus left the dancing floor. I'd caught a glimpse of Lysicrates over by the rehearsal ground.

'I won't be long,' I promised Zosime.

'Make sure you're not or all the cheese will be eaten.' Menkaure was unpacking a lunch basket.

I had to go the long way round, circling the back of the stage building. When I arrived, I searched in vain for Lysicrates. I did see Oloros and he glowered at me. Was he anxious about the tragedy competition or was he part of this conspiracy to turn Athenian hostility eastwards? If he was working with the city's enemies, why would he do such a thing? My head ached. All these questions could drive a man mad.

A moment later, Lysicrates appeared at my side, disgustingly bright-eyed. 'Enjoying the plays?'

'Of course.' I waved that away. 'Well? What have you heard?'

He jerked his head sideways and we walked away from

the bustle. 'You want to find out what Leptines has been doing lately.'

I frowned. 'Do I know him?'

'Played a Phoenician for Phrynichos the year before last. A Spartan for Critias a couple of years ago, and a Macedonian for Oloros before that.' Lysicrates nodded at the tragedian who was still dithering a few paces from the theatre entrance. 'But he hasn't been hired for a play for the last two years and he can't even get a place in a chorus. That's very bad news for a man with his expensive tastes.'

This sounded promising. 'Why isn't he being hired?'

'He's offended too many people, swaggering about, boasting how they couldn't possibly win without him. He's good, but no one's that good.' Lysicrates wrinkled his nose. 'We all know what happens to tall poppies.'

'Anything else make you think he's our man?'

'For a man who's not performing at this festival, and who's had a lean time of it lately, he's got silver in his pockets all of a sudden. He's also spent a lot of time with Strato.' Lysicrates held up a cautionary hand. 'There may be nothing in that. People have been wondering if Leptines is giving up the stage to write.'

He folded his arms. 'The thing is, though, if that's the case, what's he doing with Strato? I can't see Leptines turning to comedy after a lifetime playing tragedy. I can't see him writing anything, to be honest. He isn't one of those actors you always know will take up a pen. He's good with someone else's words, but on his own? A beardless boy could out-argue him.'

'That sounds worth looking into,' I agreed. 'Thank you.'

'Watch your step.' Lysicrates looked at me, serious. 'Strato came around here earlier. He was very keen to make sure everyone knew you were accused of being a Mede sympathiser in the agora a day or so ago. He knew an awful lot about what had happened for someone who wasn't even there. I saw him here in the theatre myself, all that afternoon.'

'I wonder if Pheidestratos is part of this conspiracy.' This sounded even more promising. 'Did he tell Strato to write his play around the notion of sending citizens to settle confiscated lands?'

'Lands confiscated from Ionians as a penalty for not paying their tribute?' Lysicrates speculated.

'You've heard talk about that?' I looked at him.

He nodded. 'There's all manner of wild rumour flying around. No one knows why our allies expected a reassessment this year, but now word's spreading that it won't happen and our honoured guests are far from happy. Some of them swear if that's so, there won't be a single silver owl offered up next Dionysia. Not unless they get a fair hearing, and they want that well before the scheduled reassessment at the next Great Panathenaia. Apparently some men from the Troad are planning to stay in Athens, to air their grievances as soon as the Assembly is back in session. They say they'll make sure that everyone in Attica, from Sounion to Rhamnous to Eleusis, understands their demands for relief are just.'

'That's what they're saying, specifically?' That sounded suspiciously like professional rhetoric to me.

'Word for word,' Lysicrates confirmed.

So we could look forward to more fistfights in the agora.

'Have you any idea where I could find Leptines?' I definitely wanted to see if he had been that man playing an Ionian to whip up a hostile crowd.

'Sorry, I've no clue,' Lysicrates said regretfully. 'But I'll keep on asking. Someone is bound to know where he'll be drinking tonight, especially if they think he'll be paying.'

'Thanks.' I nodded. 'I'll find you after the satyr play.'

Once again, I had to hurry to get back to my seat before the last play started. This time Zosime rebuked me with a frown.

Now King Theseus was a grey-bearded old man. This chorus was the men and women he'd saved from the Minotaur in Crete, grown old alongside him. He was taking a stand against Creon, Prince of Thebes, after Polyneices, son of Oedipus, failed to unseat his usurping brother, Eteocles. King Theseus and the Athenians were horrified when weeping Antigone brought the news that Creon had decreed his own nephew, his sister Jocasta's son, must lie unburied on the plain outside the city, to be devoured by dogs and crows.

No matter what the quarrels of mortals may be, so King Theseus proclaimed, all men must do their duty to the dead and to the gods. He would not let such dishonourable conduct stand. He would march with the Argive army to bury the fallen or die in the attempt. The chorus tried to dissuade him. Surely Athens had suffered enough loss?

King Theseus would not be swayed. Whatever the cost, those who died fighting for what was right must be honoured for their valour. If he fell before the gates of Thebes, he laid the duty of avenging him on the chorus and their sons.

Fortunately for all concerned, after the chorus lamented the tribulations of war and its enduring legacy, King Theseus returned victorious. More than that, he brought blind King Oedipus back with him. Athens would always be a refuge for those who had suffered through no fault of their own, so Theseus prophesied, as long as his bones rested in this citadel.

The chorus reluctantly agreed, ending the play on a muted note as they prayed to divine Athena that the costs of upholding honourable principles wouldn't prove too high for their descendants.

'I wonder why he chose that ending,' mused Menkaure.

The family behind us were far more forthright. Oloros had just lost the competition as far as they were concerned. Tomorrow's play would surely win the prize unless the third trilogy offered something truly ground breaking.

Zosime squeezed my hand. 'I thought that was very good.'

'Philocles.' Menkaure nudged me. 'Is he looking for you? That man you were talking to earlier.'

I saw the Egyptian meant Sarkuk. The Pargasarene was climbing the hillside with long, hasty strides. I realised he was trying to attract my attention with furtive gestures.

I made my way along the benches to meet him on the

dusty path worn into the grass by countless feet. 'What is it?'

'Archilochos,' he said, succinct.

'The scroll seller? The man who convinced Xandyberis the tribute would be reassessed?' I looked down the slope. 'Where?'

Sarkuk nodded. 'There, in the dark blue tunic with the green cloak.'

I studied the knot of men in the theatre's western entrance. 'Going bald, next to the greybeard in the brown cloak with the stick?'

'That's him,' Sarkuk confirmed.

That group of men weren't waiting for the satyr play to restore Dionysian jollity to the day. I felt sure they were about to leave. Would we ever find them again if they did?

I made a quick decision and beckoned to Menkaure. When the Egyptian reached us, I nodded to Sarkuk. 'Introduce yourselves, then find Kadous. Send him after me. Tell Aristarchos what's happened. Tell Zosime I love her and I'm sorry.'

The two men didn't waste time on questions. I headed towards the theatre's exit, my eyes fixed on the balding man in blue.

Chapter Eighteen

The group headed southeast through the city, into the Limnai district. There were four of them, all told. Archilochos was in blue, wearing a green cloak, and even at this distance, I could tell those were expensive, deep-dyed fabrics. He might be losing his hair but what he had left was as precisely trimmed as his beard, so some barber saw his coin on a regular basis. I found it hard to believe selling scrolls in Ionia was profitable enough to pay for all that.

The greybeard in brown beside him was slightly lame and leaning on his walking staff. A younger man who carried himself like a wrestler strode ahead of them. He wore a dun tunic without a cloak, all the better to display his massive shoulders. A slightly built man brought up the rear, swathed in a voluminous cloak that would have made me suspect he was a sneak thief if I'd seen him in the agora.

I hung back as far as I dared, not wanting them to see me following. I might not know who they were, but I had no idea if any of these four would recognise me. Thankfully, they were only walking as fast as the old man with the stick could limp. It didn't seem to occur to them that they might be pursued.

Snatching glances over my shoulder whenever possible, I looked urgently for Kadous. Had Menkaure been able to find him? I hoped I hadn't already been out of sight before the Phrygian had left the theatre. I didn't dare delay in hopes of the slave catching up. Dawdling would guarantee I'd lose track of my quarry.

The men were following the road that would take them out of the city towards the Panathenaic Stadium. I was wondering if that was their goal, though I couldn't imagine why. To my relief, they turned into a side street, but that meant I had a new problem. All the city's lesser thoroughfares were much quieter than usual, thanks to the festival. If I got too close, I would be far too noticeable. On the other hand, if I hung back, I could lose them altogether.

I couldn't risk losing them. I broke into a run to reach the Hermes pillar on the corner where they had turned. My stomach was churning with apprehension. If they went through some gate before I caught sight of them, I'd have no clue which house they were visiting.

Crouching behind the stone pillar, I offered Hermes a fervent breath of thanks. The four men were still walking down this quiet side street. I saw them turn into a narrow lane on the left.

I sprinted after them a second time. My feet were horribly noisy on the gravel between the silent walls, so I slowed to a walk just before the corner. Peering around a wall with agonised care, I was ready to duck back out of sight in an instant. My head ached as I found that my luck had run out. There was no one there.

I counted a handful of houses on either side of the beaten earth. The four men could have gone into any of them. I could hardly start knocking on doors and asking for Archilochos. Our only hope of gaining some advantage was our foes staying unaware that we were tracking them down.

Besides, I'd bet any door slave would have strict orders to deny all knowledge of him. I also reckoned there was every chance that the balding man wasn't even called Archilochos in Athens. If I were rabble-rousing, I'd hardly use my own name.

Tense, I walked down the lane, poised to run if a gate so much as creaked. To my relief, this wasn't a dead end. An alley ran crossways beyond the last houses, behind the blank rear walls of the buildings along the next side street. This wasn't a district of fine, spacious homes like Aristarchos's, nor yet of close-packed dwellings combined with workshops like my brothers'. It was more akin to the lane where I lived, though these houses were markedly bigger than my own.

I studied the ground. There were scuffs here and there and curling gouges where gates hung loose on their hinges, but I couldn't tell how old such marks might be. Without any recent rain, there were no puddles to leave helpful trails of footprints. No voices could be heard detailing some nefarious plan for a passer-by to overhear. The conveniences a comic playwright relies on never seem to happen in real life.

Reaching the end of the lane, I looked to left and right along the alley. There were mouldering piles of rubbish dumped here and there. Clearly this wasn't anyone's route to anywhere else, so there wasn't much chance of anyone reporting their neighbours for dumping refuse over their back wall instead of taking it to the official middens outside the city.

All this exertion had set my head thumping again and the stink made my unhappy stomach churn. I reminded myself that I'd fought more than once in Boeotia on little sleep, less food and a dose of the shits from bad water. Today's hangover hardly compared.

I picked a spot away from the worst of the smell where I could look back towards the gravelled side street. I was mostly hidden by the corner of the end house's wall and I slid down to sit on my heels, the better to stay unnoticed. As soon as I heard voices or saw a gate open, I'd duck still further back, only risking a look when I heard someone walking away. If they decided to head in this direction, I'd just have to make a run for it and find out where this alley went.

Not too much later, a couple of men appeared at the far end of the lane. They'd followed the same route as I had, coming from the main road. I had no way to know if they'd seen me lurking as I hastily withdrew around the corner. I flattened myself against the wall like a lizard, my heart pounding.

I heard a latch rattle. I snatched a glance. The men were going into the third house on the far side of the lane from the corner where I was hiding. Better yet, I got a good look at these new arrivals. I had no idea who one of them was, but I definitely recognised the other.

I couldn't say for certain if this was Leptines but he was definitely the man who'd played the Ionian in the agora. Today he was dressed as an Athenian and either those long Persian locks had been a wig or he'd visited a barber since that performance.

I'd wager good money that's where this so-called Archilochos was hiding and that all these men were yoked together. But I had no way of letting my own allies know without leaving this vantage point. If I did that, I'd have no way of knowing who else might join this treacherous gathering or where any of them might go when they left.

That was assuming that some or all of them were going to leave. I grimaced, and not just at the reek of the refuse. I could end up spending the rest of the evening crouched in this stinking alley while they settled down to a leisurely banquet. That wasn't an inviting prospect when my legs were already beginning to cramp.

I decided to wait a little longer, all the same. If one or other of the men who'd come here left, I would follow. Where they went should tell me something, and then I could go home. On the other hand, if a troupe of dancing girls and flute players arrived, I'd know they were making a night of it and head for Aristarchos's house. He could send someone to make enquiries and discover who owned this house.

The afternoon wore on. Somewhere out towards the main road I heard a swell of voices, laughter and the slap of countless feet. I realised the satyr play must be long done. The day's trilogy had been thoroughly debated over wine and food in the city's taverns and the theatre audience was heading home.

I found a scrap of broken pot in a nearby heap of rubbish and used a stone to scratch a crude map on it to fix this location in my mind. Once I'd done that, I studied the most obvious scrapes and dents on the gate I was watching, to be certain I could describe it so there could be no chance of mistake.

I heard voices several times, though never from the house I was watching. I crouched low, ready to pretend to be tying my sandal if someone came out to dump a bucket of slops. Then I'd stroll away, back towards the main road. I couldn't risk the uproar of being chased away like some thief.

Thanks to Athena, no one appeared and I stayed there, safe enough. The daylight yellowed and I wondered what Zosime and Menkaure were doing. I hoped they had gone home to Alopeke. Hopefully the Pargasarenes would simply go back to the house where Aristarchos had lodged them. Sarkuk and Azamis would want to see Tur after all.

I wondered if Kadous was still hunting fruitlessly for me. I had no idea how long he'd search before he gave up. But if he went home and confessed he couldn't find me, I had no idea what Menkaure and Zosime might do. If they went to tell Nymenios, my whole family would end up frantic.

Dusk deepened. I decided I couldn't stay here. For one thing, it wouldn't be long before someone could sneak out of that gate without me seeing them, hidden by the gathering darkness.

A fiery glow appeared in the house's courtyard. A pine torch. Someone was leaving. I stood up and flexed my feet to ease my legs, stiff from waiting so long.

The gate opened and four men came out. I couldn't tell if they were the four I'd followed here or if one or more were later arrivals. Even with the torch, the night hid the colours of their clothing. Ruddy light gleamed on a balding head though. With any luck, that was Archilochos.

I watched them make for the street that led towards the main road. As they rounded the corner, I followed as quickly as I dared. All the while I watched warily in case that gate opened again. If it did, I'd have to brazen it out, looking straight ahead and walking purposefully past.

Hermes be thanked, I passed his pillar without incident. I could see the torch heading northwards. I smiled, relieved. With the night to hide me, I didn't have to get too close. I only needed to see which direction they took when they reached the junction with the main road.

Cloth flapped, loud in the quiet night. Someone swallowed an oath. Out of the corner of one eye, I glimpsed a fluttering cloak. Men rushed at me from a lane to my left. Masked men, with eyeholes and open mouths eerie black voids against pale paint.

No chorus ever attacks a drama's principals like this though, and I wasn't about to play the defiant hero. Forget declaiming some defiant speech. I took to my heels, as swift as if I wore winged sandals.

Not swift enough. They were young and fit, not battered and bruised from brawling, or sluggish from a hangover. One long-legged runner drew level with me, his grasping fingers reaching for my shoulder. I flung out a fist to knock his forearm away.

Another sprinter appeared on my other side. He carried a long, solid stick. A spear shaft. He rammed its end into the back of my thigh. My knee buckled and I fell hard, landing with all the wind knocked out of me. That meant I was too slow to see the booted foot coming for my guts. At least curling up around that agony meant the next kick intended for my balls only bruised my thigh.

The spear shaft slammed into my shoulder. I yelled with pain and fury but managed not to arch my back and expose my belly again. I rolled away, onto my front. Another kick came for my head. I seized that fucking foot and twisted it hard.

Taken unawares, my assailant fell over. His flailing arm sent the man beside him stumbling. I seized my chance and scrambled to my feet. The man with the spear shaft swung again, aiming for the backs of my knees. This time I saw him first and spun around to avoid the blow. All the while I shouted curses and insults, desperately yelling for help.

It seemed everyone in this neighbourhood was deaf. Was this how Xandyberis had died? Fuck that. I wasn't going down to the Underworld without a fight.

I grabbed for the spear shaft, one hand taking a firm grip between my attacker's hold and my other hand seizing the middle of the wood. One fist pushing, the other pulling, I twisted the long stick like an oar and sent him staggering backwards.

He'd forgotten one of the first things he should have learned in his hoplite training. Never let go of your spear. Now I had a weapon, even if it lacked a metal point. At least the bastard was bright enough to shout a warning to the others.

Burning pain seared my arm. One of these fuckers had a knife, but I couldn't see who it was in this darkness, surrounded by shadows and swirling cloaks. A hand darted forward, holding steel betrayed by a glint of light. I smashed the spear shaft downwards. Not at the blade. Not at the hand that held it. I hadn't forgotten my training. Knowing the man would flinch from my blow, I aimed for his withdrawing arm. The wooden shaft struck solidly with a crack of bone. The man cursed foully, spitting with pain.

A voice bellowed orders from the darkness. 'Rush him! He can't hit you all at once!'

Curse him to Hades, he was right. But as the men surged forward, Kadous yelled from the end of the street. 'Philocles! Is that you?'

'Yes!' I barely got the word out before an assailant tried to silence me with a punch to the face. I was mobbed like an eagle pursued by murderous crows. Without room to use the spear shaft, I let it fall. Reaching for the closest man's mask, I wrenched it askew. That cost me a painful flurry of punches to the ribs and guts but I tightened my belly muscles and endured it. This close, they didn't have the elbow room to hit me as hard as they hoped.

I got a good handful of another wig and yanked it hard. The man yelled, startled, and reeled away, deaf and blind now his disguise was twisted around on his head.

When I'd fought in Boeotia, we'd soon identified the men in our phalanx who'd performed in a chorus, used to singing and dancing wearing theatre masks and wigs. They were far better prepared for an infantry helmet's eyeholes narrowing their field of vision, and the bronze enclosing their heads to muffle their hearing.

'Hey! Shit-for-brains!' A solid thud of wood on flesh followed up the insult. One of the men surrounding me howled and lurched away. Kadous had found the spear shaft that I'd dropped on the ground. I heard it smack into my assailants again.

Two more attackers quickly retreated from this un-expected intervention. That gave me more room to manoeuvre. I hooked my fingers around another mask's upper edge and pulled down hard. Plastered linen cracked in my hands, and the man tore himself free before I could smash his face into my rising knee.

Somebody's agonised yell followed the thwack of an-other bone-cracking blow. That broke the nerve of the rest. Some fled for the main road. Others scarpered back down the alley where they'd been lurking.

One stumbled and went sprawling. As he recovered and raced after the rest, I saw he'd stepped on the fallen knife, losing his footing as the blade slid away under his foot. Wincing as I stooped, I retrieved the weapon. The next person to attack me tonight would end up gutted like a fish.

I had a whole new collection of bruises to add to my battering in the agora. Thankfully, as far as my cautious fingers could tell, the cut on my arm was only a shallow slice. The man with the knife had been too wary, afraid that he'd stab an ally. Of course, the wound could still fester and kill me or claim the limb. I needed to wash it clean with wine as soon as I could.

Kadous was leaning on the spear shaft, breathing hard. 'You weren't easy to find. It's a good thing I heard you yelling.'

'Thank all the gods above and below that you did,' I said fervently. 'I'd have been dead meat before anyone here got off their arses and sent for the Scythians.'

The Phrygian looked at the silent, shuttered houses. 'Shall we go before someone gets up the nerve to come and see who's left alive?'

'Good idea.' Before the festival, I was just another face in a crowd. Now anyone who'd been in the theatre had heard my name, my father's name and my voting affiliation. If someone here recognised me, I didn't want gossip blaming me for a disgraceful fracas disrupting their neighbourhood.

'Who do you suppose they were?' Kadous bent down to pick up a fallen mask.

Several of the attackers had discarded them. That was hardly a surprise. Being caught with such disguises if the Scythians turned up would make it pretty hard to deny their involvement.

'Men who didn't want to be recognised.' I picked up two more masks. 'Much good that'll do them.'

'Oh?' Kadous heard the satisfaction in my voice.

Once we reached the main road, a few houses had lanterns outside their gates to guide revellers home. I paused beneath one and examined the knife. I hadn't been mistaken.

'This is Tur's knife. He lost it in the agora riot. I need to let Aristarchos know.' That was only one of the things I had to tell him.

'Can't it wait till morning?' Kadous looked pointedly at me. 'You should let Zosime know you're not lying murdered in some alley.'

I winced, and not just from my bruises. 'Was she very cross, when I left her at the theatre?'

Kadous shrugged. 'She knows something important is amiss. What'll make her furious is being left in the dark any longer than necessary.'

I looked up and down the road. There was no sign of the men I'd been following. Now that my blood was cooling, heading somewhere safe to nurse my injuries and get a good night's sleep seemed a sensible notion.

Aristarchos couldn't usefully do anything so late in the day, even if I went to his house at once. He could hardly send messengers out to make enquiries or slaves to knock on doors with spurious excuses in the dead of night.

I nodded at Kadous. 'Let's go home. Lend me that stick to lean on.'

Chapter Nineteen

I didn't sleep well. Not because of any row with Zosime, she was too relieved to see me safely home to berate me. Not just because of my second beating in three days. It was realising what lay ahead of me this morning that had me staring at the ceiling in the dead of night. I'd rather face the labours of Heracles.

We sat in a subdued circle to eat our breakfast. Kadous was desperate to explain why he hadn't reached my side any sooner. 'Menkaure had a real struggle to find me.'

'I'm not surprised,' I assured him. 'It really wasn't your fault.'

I'd tell the Egyptian the same, when he woke up. For now, he was still asleep in the end room, staying the night after seeing Zosime home.

She was just as concerned that I knew the Phrygian hadn't let me down. 'My father gave Kadous a good description of those men you'd seen.'

'I don't doubt it.' I squeezed her hand.

'I asked everyone I met outside the theatre,' the slave went on unhappily, 'until I found some people who'd seen that group passing by.'

Unfortunately, once the men I was tailing had turned

off the main road, the trail had gone cold.

Kadous's face reflected his despair. 'All I could do was search every side street for some sign that you'd been there.' He tried to make a joke of it. 'I couldn't face telling Nymenios or Chairephanes that I'd come back without another of their brothers.'

I dutifully did my best to laugh. Zosime sat between us, stony-faced.

'Then I heard the uproar.' Kadous heaved a sigh.

'At least the night was quiet enough for the noise to carry,' I said, bracing.

He shook his head. 'It took me far too much time to find a way to the fight.'

'You got there. That's all that matters.' He'd have to get over this in his own good time. Meanwhile, I had to go and tell Aristarchos what I'd discovered and what I suspected. I really didn't want to, but I couldn't see that I had any other choice. I rose from my stool.

'You're not going into the city until I see how badly you're hurt,' Zosime said curtly. 'And you'll need to soak that rag off otherwise you'll set your arm bleeding again.'

'Of course.' I'd rebuffed her concerns last night, binding up my wound with a scrap of cloth and saying it could wait until morning. 'You were right, as always.' I offered my apology as an olive branch. 'I should have let you put a proper bandage on this.'

The cut on my arm stung evilly when I eased the makeshift dressing off. At least it was still reassuringly superficial in the daylight. Zosime sniffed as she cleaned off clotted blood with sour wine and coated the slice

249

with hyssop lotion. I gritted my teeth and kept quiet as she used a strip of clean linen to bind it up again.

'Stand up. Take off your tunic.'

I did as she asked.

After she had anointed the worst of my bruises and grazes, she explored my ribs with carefully probing fingers. 'Where does it hurt?'

'Ow! There!' I winced. 'Never mind. I'll be fine, soon enough.'

Zosime wasn't going to be comforted. 'A broken bone could have skewered your lung, leaving you to drown in your own blood.'

I tried to change the subject. 'What happened in the theatre, after I left?'

She gave me a long, measuring look. I offered her a hopeful smile. She rolled her eyes, still exasperated, but at least she decided to answer.

'Oloros had satyrs invade Pirithous's wedding feast, rather than centaurs. Theseus reached for the closest weapons, which turned out to be bread rolls, to help the Lapiths drive off Silenos and his mob.'

'It sounds a lot of fun.' More fun than I'd had. Much more fun than I was going to have. But there was nothing to be gained by delaying my first unwelcome task.

'I'm so sorry, my love, but I can't come to the theatre today. There are things—'

'I'll go with my father.' Zosime shrugged.

I wished I could tell if she genuinely understood that I was forced to let her down, or if she had just given up on me after yesterday. I forced another affectionate smile.

'Thank you for being so understanding, sweetheart, and Kadous is going with you both.'

'Master?' He didn't like that.

'I cannot be distracted today by worrying about you left here on your own.' He definitely wasn't staying on watch, in case last night's killers tried again.

'Do what you must.' Zosime gathered up her salves and bandages, leaving me to find a clean tunic and my sandals.

Menkaure came out into the porch, yawning. He nodded at me. 'Good to see you in one piece.'

'Thanks to you sending Kadous,' I told him.

'Barely,' Zosime snorted.

Menkaure and I exchanged a glance, silently agreeing to drop the subject.

I left Zosime to find her father some breakfast while I fetched a barley meal sack from the storeroom. That hid Tur's knife from our curious neighbours, along with the attackers' masks that Kadous and I had retrieved. Once Menkaure had eaten, we all set out. We barely spoke a word until our paths divided inside the city.

'Have a good day.' I kissed Zosime, still trying to convey my apologies. 'I wish I could come with you—'

'Be careful.' She gave me a gentle hug.

I decided to take that for a good omen. 'Believe me, I will,' I promised her.

Such relief was fleeting. As the others headed for the theatre, I went on my way to face my day's second daunting challenge.

★

Mus opened Aristarchos's gate with a broad smile cracking his stern face. 'I am glad to see you safe.'

'Thank you. Is your master at home?' Some treacherous part of me wished he'd say Aristarchos had left for the theatre.

Mus crushed that frail hope with a clap of his massive hands. 'Of course.'

Lydis appeared so quickly that I guessed he'd been waiting for my arrival. 'This way, if you please.'

I followed him through the archway to the inner courtyard. The family accommodation overhead was noisy with activity and an upper shutter slammed on girlish laughter. That made me even more uneasy about what I had come here to do.

'Please take a seat.' Lydis indicated a table beneath a portico surrounded by cushioned stools. 'The master will be with you shortly. Can I fetch you something to eat or to drink?'

'No, thank you.' My mouth was so dry that anything I tried to swallow would choke me.

Aristarchos wasn't long. He looked searchingly at my bruised face before contemplating my bandaged arm. 'How bad's the rest of you?'

I shrugged. 'I'll live.'

He grunted and moved on. 'Sarkuk said you were following this man Archilochos? He's the one who's stirring up trouble in Caria?'

Cowardly, I seized on that. 'Where is Sarkuk? And Azamis?'

'They've gone to see the Polemarch to discuss what's

to be done with Xandyberis's body. The man must be buried or cremated, and soon.' Grimacing at the thought of a five-day-old corpse, Aristarchos took a seat. 'So, what happened to you last night?'

I took a deep breath and related the afternoon and evening's events as steadily as I could.

Aristarchos considered what I told him for a long, silent moment. 'You're sure it was Tur's knife?'

'I have it here.' I took it out of the barley sack. 'It looks exactly the same to me. I'm sure he'll know it for his own. If not, it's still a Carian weapon. Someone wanted Ionians blamed for my death.'

'There can be no doubt that they knew who you were.' He wasn't asking a question.

I nodded, chagrined. 'One of them must have seen me following. Or perhaps someone else in the theatre saw me dogging their trail and sent a message on ahead. Maybe that house has a back gate or someone climbed in over a wall. Who knows? Once they got word that their trap was set, four of them set out to lead me into that ambush.'

I shivered, thanking every god and goddess on Olympos that Kadous had found his way to my side in time. Sometimes real life does enjoy a drama's conveniences.

Aristarchos nodded at the sack. 'What else have you got in there?'

I took out the battered chorus masks and laid them on the table. Flakes crumbling from the coloured plaster littered the stone paving.

'This one is from Strato's play three years ago, *The*

253

Washerwomen. If I remember rightly, this is one of *The Discus Throwers*, from the year before, by Ephialtes. Pheidestratos was that play's paymaster. I can't identify that one but it's a comedy mask as well.' I pointed to the one which I'd mangled by ripping it off an attacker's head.

'*The Discus Throwers* and *The Washerwomen* were both winning plays,' Aristarchos observed. 'Those masks will have been dedicated in a temple. Anyone could have stolen them.'

'True enough.' I wouldn't want to be writing the speech for someone standing before a jury and hoping to condemn such an influential man on this flimsy evidence.

'And you didn't see where those men were headed, before you were attacked.'

Once again, he wasn't asking a question. I nodded confirmation.

'We must find out who owns that house.' Aristarchos turned to his slave sitting quietly on a stool by the arch. 'Lydis—'

I knotted my fingers together to stop my hands shaking. 'We may be able to do that more quickly.'

'What do you mean?' Aristarchos frowned as he heard the tightness in my voice.

I cleared my throat. 'I recognised one of my attackers' voices.'

'Go on.' Aristarchos prompted.

My nerve failed me. 'I'm sure it was one of the young men who were in the procession with your son on the festival eve.'

'Indeed?' He gave me a thoughtful look before turning

to Lydis again. 'Ask Hipparchos to join us.'

Clearly that wasn't a request that his son could refuse.

We sat in tense silence, waiting. After a few moments, I reached out to put the masks back in the sack.

'Leave them,' Aristarchos said curtly.

I folded my hands in my lap and contemplated the Carian knife. 'How is Tur recovering?'

Before Aristarchos could answer, Hipparchos strolled into the courtyard. He looked as though he'd just rolled out of bed, hair tousled and a stray linen thread caught in his beard. He'd dragged on a clean tunic, still belting it as he arrived. His face was flushed and puffy and his eyes were red-veined. Too much wine the night before.

'Father?' He was clearly annoyed at being rousted so early. 'You wanted—'Then he saw the masks on the table and paled.

'So.' Aristarchos was as coldly furious as any marble statue of Zeus the Thunderer. 'You *do* know what this is about.'

'I—' Hipparchos gulped, ashen. I thought he was going to be sick on the pristine paving.

'Philocles was attacked last night, by men wearing these masks. They were intent on killing him. He says he recognised a voice.' Aristarchos's gaze flickered to me, swift as lightning. I saw that he knew that I knew exactly whose voice I had heard.

'He says he remembers this voice from the night before the festival, when we all met in the theatre. Though he cannot, or will not, put a name to the villain.' Aristarchos stared unblinking at his son.

Hipparchos licked dry lips. 'I—'

'Think very carefully before you speak,' Aristarchos continued as though this were any ordinary conversation. 'Lie to me and I will see you exiled. Not just ostracised for ten years, exiled. For the rest of your life.'

Hipparchos was horrified. 'Mother—'

'Your mother will have no say in this,' his father assured him, 'whether I send you to Massilia or to the furthest shores of the Chersonese. She will have no say as to whether I send silver to support you or if I have you thrown onto some distant street to beg for your bread and shelter.'

My father would have been shouting by now, scarlet-faced and with his calloused hands furiously waving. Aristarchos's icy composure was even more terrifying.

'You tried to kill a man. If this comes before the courts you will be stripped of your citizen's rights and exiled. Since I can see the guilt in your eyes, I will save our city and its people such time and trouble. I will also shield your brothers and sisters from the spreading stain of your crime. What do you have to tell me to mitigate your offence, to deserve my mercy?'

To my astonishment, Hipparchos's lip curled in a sneer. 'He can't be certain whose voice he heard and there are no witnesses. It would be my word against his.' A hiss of contempt made it plain what he thought of my social standing.

'There was a witness,' his father countered.

Hipparchos was still defiant. 'A slave?' He looked at me, smug. 'His evidence will have to be tested under torture. When do you want to deliver him up to the public executioner?'

The Furies hound him to Hades. He knew I'd never hand Kadous over to suffer such agonies, just because the law insists that's the only way to prove a slave isn't his owner's mouthpiece.

'How do you know this witness could be a slave?' Aristarchos enquired calmly. 'If you weren't even there?'

He cut his son off with a sharp gesture. 'No, don't lie to me. Not if you want any chance of remaining within this household. Don't threaten Philocles either. No one will lay a hand on him or his slave because this will never come before the courts. I will see justice done as is my right and duty as the head of this family. Your only hope of mercy is to tell me the truth, and all of the truth, here and without delay.'

Hipparchos looked at the masks. I saw his fists clenching. Then he looked at the knife on the table and visibly came to a decision. He moved towards a stool, about to sit down. 'I never sought to kill anyone—'

'You will stand,' ordered Aristarchos. 'Continue.'

'I wasn't carrying the blade,' Hipparchos protested, plaintive.

I struck at that first chink in his arrogance. 'No, but you were carrying a spear shaft.'

I hadn't been going to mention that, to leave Aristarchos with at least the pretence of doubt over Hipparchos's involvement. But the little shit had threatened Kadous.

'I took it off you,' I reminded him. 'Hoplites learn how to do that, as well as to keep hold of their own weapons.'

Evidently no one bothered teaching the cavalry such skills.

'But that much is true.' I turned to Aristarchos. 'I used the spear shaft on the man with the blade. Hard enough to bruise his arm, maybe even break a bone.'

We could all see there was no mark on Hipparchos's arms, bare to the shoulder in his embroidered sleeveless tunic.

The boy looked surprised to think I was showing him some support. I strove to keep my face as impassive as Aristarchos's. He was the one I owed the truth to, not his fool of a son. Though it couldn't hurt to give Hipparchos a reason to be grudgingly grateful to me, to counter any urge to seek revenge, once this was all over.

'So you didn't set out intent on murder. What a relief.' Aristarchos's sarcasm echoed around the courtyard. 'What were you doing and with whom?'

Hipparchos capitulated. 'We went to a tavern after the satyr play. Nikandros came to find us. He said a friend of his had a sister pursued by an unsuitable suitor. The man had taken to lurking in the alleys around their house. A good beating should scare him off, that's what Nikandros said. That's all I was there to do.'

His pleading eyes slid from his father to me and back again. I guessed that was as much of an apology as I was going to get.

'The name of Nikandros's friend?' Aristarchos demanded. 'His father and his voting district?'

'I don't know,' Hipparchos muttered.

He looked shamefaced enough to convince me that was the truth.

'So you simply took Nikandros's word?' Aristarchos shook his head with disgust. 'When you know full well he's dragged you into utter folly more than once, and lied about it afterwards, just to save his own worthless skin?'

I wondered what that was about but it was hardly the moment to ask.

'Whose idea was it to wear masks?' Aristarchos snapped. 'Where did you steal them from?'

'One of the other men brought them.' Now the youth was growing sullen. 'I don't know where he got them.'

'So you're a fool and a brute, but not a would-be murderer nor yet a despoiler of temples,' Aristarchos observed. 'Your mother will be so relieved.'

Hipparchos reddened. 'I can ask Nikandros—'

'No.' Aristarchos forbade that notion. 'You will go nowhere and speak to no one until I have got to the bottom of whatever crimes you have committed. Lydis!' He didn't look at the slave, his gaze still levelled at Hipparchos, as piercing and as menacing as the point of a javelin. 'Make sure that the entire household knows my will on this matter. Tell Mus first of all. Tell him he may accept any letters delivered for Hipparchos but they are to be brought straight to me. No one is to carry any messages for my son, written or repeated.'

'Of course, Master.'

Aristarchos flicked a hand at Hipparchos. 'You may go.'

The boy took a step, then hesitated. 'What . . . ?'

Aristarchos raised an eyebrow. 'What will happen to

259

you now? That will entirely depend on what I discover. Go to your rooms. I don't want to see you until I send for you. If you remember something else that I may need to know, ask to see Lydis and he will bring me word.'

Hipparchos retreated, his head hanging like a whipped dog.

I took a deep breath once the boy had gone. 'I am so sorry—'

Aristarchos silenced me with the same sharp gesture he'd used towards his son as he turned to his slave once again. 'You know as well as I do which young fools he goes drinking with. Draft letters to their fathers from me. Warn them that Nikandros Kerykes has been sucked into some rabble-rousing plot against our Ionian allies. If they don't want to see their sons face charges of stirring up civil strife, they had better rein them in hard and quickly. With my compliments, naturally.'

'And Nikandros Kerykes?' Lydis ventured.

'I will call on his father myself.' Aristarchos's expression was ominous.

'I'm sorry.' Too late, I realised I'd repeated myself.

Aristarchos dismissed Lydis with a flick of his hand. 'Don't apologise to me,' he said when we were alone. 'You've done my family a significant service.'

'Really?' I allowed myself a little sarcasm.

'I don't mean to undervalue your injuries, I can see you're in pain, but let's be grateful that no one died,' Aristarchos said frankly. 'My situation – this whole household's situation – would be far worse if you had been killed. You can't imagine you were the only target here.'

I glanced at the knife. 'I'm sure they were out to implicate Tur.'

'Then I would have had to vouch for him, to insist that he couldn't have left his bed. My slaves would be put to the torture, to swear that the boy was laid up and being cared for, throughout yesterday and last night.' Aristarchos shook his head. 'I could no more allow my household to be abused like that than you would see your man Kadous suffer. So our enemies would be free to whisper and murmur all around the agora. What disgraceful secrets could I possibly be hiding, if I refused to let my slaves testify? What's my real connection with these ungrateful Ionians? If they're not paying the tribute they owe to Athena, whose strongbox is their silver filling?

'As for Hipparchos . . . ' He shook his head again, eyes shadowed. 'I don't suppose he would have been openly accused of your murder, not at first. I imagine someone would have visited me discreetly, to let me know that he'd been involved. Of course, they'd have witnesses to your death. Hades, depending on what they wanted from me, they'd probably have ten men ready to swear that he'd held the knife that killed you.'

He startled me with a growl of wordless fury.

'I don't know what their price would have been to save my son from public trial, exile or execution and my other children from disgrace. Perhaps it would just be my silence while they set Athens and Ionia at each other's throats. Or if they were bold enough, they might have demanded that I do something to promote their cause. You have saved me from those particular dangers.' He brushed plaster flakes from the table onto the paving. 'As for Hipparchos, he was always going to get into serious trouble, sooner or later. All things considered, I'm glad it was sooner and no worse than this. The boy has been spoiled and sheltered all his life. That's as much my fault as his mother's,' he admitted, his voice tight. 'After his brother was killed in Egypt . . .' He closed his eyes.

'I know.' I didn't need him to say any more.

After a moment, Aristarchos regained his composure and looked steadily at me. 'He's run wild ever since he came back to the city, him and his idiot friends. They're so certain that their names and their families' money will shield them from any follies they fall into. But now he has stepped into this swamp, he realises he needs me to drag him clear of it. He's had a glimpse of just how easily he could have sunk and drowned.'

He sighed. 'That's a lesson I was able to teach his brothers before they risked their necks. If Hipparchos has chosen to learn this the hard way, that's between him and Athena. You have nothing to apologise for. If anything, I owe you my thanks.'

'We both owe whoever's behind all this a hard and painful reckoning,' I retorted.

'That is very true,' he agreed.

'But we're no closer to finding them.' I let my exasperation show.

Aristarchos's sigh betrayed his own frustration. 'Perhaps

we'll get some indication when I speak to Megakles Kerykes.'

'Nikandros's father?'

He nodded. 'He won't want his son's involvement in some attempted murder made public, nor several other things that I could let slip about his business dealings.'

I rose cautiously to my feet. Even sitting for a short time meant I'd stiffened up horribly. 'Let me know as soon as you hear anything.'

'Go home,' Aristarchos advised. 'Go to bed and rest until I learn something useful and we can plan our next steps in this campaign.'

That was tempting, but my day's labours weren't over yet. 'I have to go to my brothers' house. I owe my mother a visit. That's not too far, and I can't believe these people are so bold that they'll murder me in broad daylight inside the walls.' Though it was unnerving to feel that my own city's streets weren't safe. 'When I'm ready to leave, someone there can walk back to Alopeke with me.'

He nodded. 'I'll send word when I have news.'

Chapter Twenty

I had several good reasons to head for my brothers' house once I left Aristarchos. The walk home last night had been long and exhausting, even with that spear shaft to lean on. Kadous and I had passed several people who knew one or other of us. They'd all exclaimed with concern over my battered face and dirty clothes. With Rumour so quick on her wings, some busybody or other would have surely decided it was their duty to alarm my mother with lurid exaggeration.

I was right. The slave who opened the gate clapped his hand to his chest. 'Zeus be thanked! You're—'

'Walking, slightly wounded,' I said wryly. 'Maybe a couple of cracked ribs. I assume you'd heard far worse?'

He bit his lip. 'The master is on his way to your house.'

I grimaced. 'When did he leave?'

'Not long ago.' The slave looked expectant.

I nodded. 'Send someone to run and catch him.'

If he found my gate locked and the house deserted, Nymenios would surely fear the worst. Not that learning I wasn't laid out and clutching my obols for Charon's ferry would see me forgiven. Since I wasn't all but dead, he'd be furious that he'd missed today's tragedies.

Still, I reminded myself to look on the bright side. At least I didn't have to go all the way to the theatre and try to persuade him to leave in the interval between two plays.

'I must speak to my mother.' I walked through the courtyard, past the empty work benches. Every knife and tool was neatly racked, ready for work, and a silent reminder of my duty here. Now I no longer had my play to occupy me, I had to help save the family business. I headed for the door to the house. The wide porch was swept clean and tidy. Baskets of fleece would soon clutter up the empty space here, needing to be combed and spun before the yarn could be woven into household essentials. These generous gifts come from Mother's brothers out in Kolonai, and are as much of an annual ritual for our family as the summer festivals are for the city.

Most families have some such ties with the villages out in Attica. Back in my great-grandfather's day, Cleisthenes wisely decreed that each voting tribe in our new democracy should be a triad of city, country and coastal districts, to make sure that everyone's interests were represented. As a result, the men of Alopeke, including my father, were honour-bound to help Kolonai's refugees when Mother and her family fled the Persian advance. Their parents became good friends, and Father was of an age to want a wife while Mother was of an age to be married. The match was made and they were happy together, until our family's worst sorrows a decade ago.

Going inside, I could hear voices in the upper end

room, where Mother and my sisters used to sit and spin with their distaffs and spindles, or weave finer lengths of cloth on smaller looms. I followed the corridor to the corner and went up the stairs.

No one was spinning or weaving today. Mother was clearing out her storage chests while Melina was relaxing on a couch, watching her children as they played amiably on the floor.

'Uncle Philocles!' Nymenios's two little boys came running to the door, their wooden animals abandoned.

Hestaios might only be five but he's as tall as boys a full year older. Kalliphon is catching up fast, for all the two years between them. Without thinking, I stooped low to sweep them up in my arms, one onto each hip. Staggering, I nearly dropped to my knees as I lowered them hastily back down to the floorboards.

'You need to spend more time at the gymnasium,' Melina observed drily.

Mother rushed to embrace me. 'They said you were beaten senseless and left for dead!'

'Careful! I may have a cracked rib.' Though I wouldn't have admitted that much if I'd had any other way of stopping her hugging me painfully hard.

'What happened?' Anxious, she stroked my bruised face with her hard-worn hands.

I glanced at the children. They were staring at me, open-mouthed. Even Amynta's beloved ragdoll was forgotten.

Melina clapped her hands and one of the household's girls appeared. 'Please take the children to their room.'

As I stepped aside to let the slave pass, Hestaios and Kalliphon protested loudly.

'We want to—'

'But Uncle Philocles—'

My niece was already on her way to the door, dolly in hand. Melina smiled. 'Amynta may have a honeycake.'

That goaded the boys into gathering up their toys and begging for the same treat.

'That depends,' Melina interrupted their pleading. 'If you've been good, you may all have a cake this evening. But Amynta still gets one now because she did as she was asked without arguing.'

I tried and failed to hide a smile as the disgruntled boys trailed out after their sister. I recalled my own child-hood, with both parents teaching me and my brothers and sisters that it was in our best interests to co-operate.

Mother examined the bruises on my arms. 'I'll find some salve. Sit down.'

I obediently took a stool and shared a grin with Melina. 'Where's Chairephanes?'

Her smile broadened. 'Gone to the theatre with Pam-philos and his family.'

'Do you think he and Glykera will make a match of it?'

She nodded. 'I hope so. She is a very nice girl.'

I looked at her ruefully. 'I'm so sorry you're missing the plays. It's my fault Nymenios had to go to Alopeke.'

Melina shook her head. 'I wasn't going to the theatre today.'

An unplanned day at home with her feet up? I

wondered if she was pregnant again. It wasn't easy to tell if her waist was thickening under her pleated gown's swathes. It wouldn't be much of a surprise though, Amynta was well past her second birthday. But it wasn't my place to ask.

Mother returned with a tray of cups and a jug of well-watered wine as well as several pots of pungent paste.

'Now,' she commanded. 'What's this all about?'

I related a carefully crafted summary of the past few days. I told no lies, though I did hold back too much distressing detail, and I definitely didn't share this morning's speculations. I didn't want a breath of this floating around the local fountains. I also didn't want Mother knowing how close she'd come to burying another one of her children.

Melina sipped from her cup while Mother pulled up a stool and anointed my bruises and grazes with various concoctions. I tucked up my tunic to allow her to salve the boot print on my thigh. I could tell she wanted me to strip off completely to see what damage had been done to my ribs, but thankfully she wouldn't ask me to do that with my brother's wife there.

The glint in Melina's eye told me she knew it too, so she wasn't going anywhere. I slipped her a grateful wink as Mother tugged my tunic back down to my knees and swapped the pot of ointment for her own cup of wine.

She sat clutching the black-glazed ceramic, thin-lipped with anxiety. Even though she's lived in this city for thirty-five years, Mother has never forgotten the tales her own mother and aunts told her, warning of all the dangers lying in wait for innocents in Athens. Still, her countrified ways are no bad thing. She's as vigilant as a hawk watching over her grandchildren. If Mother lives to see little Amynta married, no one will ever be able to cast doubt on my niece's citizen-born rights by claiming she'd been seen behaving like some foreigner, ignorant of Athenian decorum.

'Can Aristarchos Phytalid put an end to this trouble?' she demanded.

'I believe so,' I said firmly, 'and all the sooner, if we can help.'

'What can we do?' Melina sat up straighter.

Like our father before him, Nymenios had looked for a wife who could manage the family business's accounts and records. Well-born girls might only need to be decorative and to bear handsome children, but a wise man knows women of our class can contribute a great deal more to a household. So Melina's father had the sense to teach his daughters to read, write and reckon as skilfully as his sons.

'That depends on the answers to some questions. As soon as Nymenios gets back, we'll go and see what we can learn.'

'You two are not to go off getting into trouble,' Mother said sharply, as though we were beardless boys heading for a day's larks at the gymnasium.

'We won't,' I promised, just as sincerely as I'd always promised her. Which is to say, I was mentally adding, '*Unless someone else starts it.*'

As a schoolboy I'd learned the trick of turning a

conversation to distract her, and I hadn't lost that knack either. 'So, do you think Chairephanes and Glykera will marry?'

'He'll be a fool not to ask for her,' she said crisply.

'How soon?' I prompted.

Discussing Pamphilos's daughter's merits and pondering the likely timing of the wedding, as well as where the newlyweds might set up home, kept us all happily occupied until I heard the gate opening down below and Nymenios calling for his wife.

I rose to my feet. 'I'd better—'

'Yes, go.' Melina waved me away.

Down in the courtyard, Nymenios looked torn between exasperation at the time he had wasted and shock at the sight of my bruises. 'I thought playwriting was a safe trade.'

'You'd think so, wouldn't you?' I offered him a sincerely apologetic grimace before I told my tale for the third time that morning, though I still didn't mention Hipparchos's involvement.

'I want to see if I can find out which temple those old theatre masks were stolen from. You want to find out who's paying over the odds for the hides from the Dionysia sacrifices. How about we go and ask our questions together? Then I can stand as a citizen witness for whatever you find out, and you can stand witness for me.'

Every temple has its loyal families so, with luck, I'd learn if someone with ties to our existing suspects knew where those particular masks were easily accessible. Or maybe I'd hear that someone who didn't belong had been hanging around just before the masks went missing. Either way, with Athena's blessing, I'd pick up something that would chime with whatever Aristarchos learned. Something to lead us to solid evidence that would ring true in court.

Nymenios scowled. 'I told you. None of the priests are saying who they're selling to.'

I raised a hand. 'The priests who are profiting and being paid to keep their mouths shut will all be at the theatre. Whoever's in the doghouse will be tending the altars today. There's nothing like a little resentment to loosen a man's tongue.'

Nymenios still looked dubious. 'I don't think—'

'Let's start with the Temple of Hephaistos. Remember what Dexios said? The first batch of hides to go missing wasn't bought out from under his nose. That cartload was stolen, so let's see what we can learn. I'm sure I remember seeing some of the masks I'm looking for there.'

'I suppose so,' Nymenios said ungraciously. 'I might as well make some use of the day. As long as we don't get ourselves into trouble.'

'That's what I promised Mother,' I assured him.

'Not unless someone else starts it, you mean,' Nymenios answered, with a glint in his eye. 'I'll let Melina know what we're doing.'

As he headed inside, I stayed in the courtyard. He could run the gauntlet of Mother's interrogation. As the eldest, it was only fair he shouldered such obligations along with enjoying his birthright's privileges. A few moments later, Mother came outside with him, protesting, as I'd known she would.

'At least wait for your brother. Take some of the slaves with you.'

'If we turn up mob-handed, there's bound to be trouble,' Nymenios countered.

'The two of us will just be brothers out for a stroll,' I agreed. 'Why shouldn't we pay our respects at a temple and enjoy a little conversation? Where's the threat in that?'

'Shall I fetch you a mirror?' Mother asked acidly. 'I don't suppose you were threatening anyone last night!'

'All the more reason for me to be extra careful today,' I assured her. 'I couldn't wrestle a wooden duck off Hestaios. Believe me, I won't do anything foolish.'

'I won't let him,' Nymenios said firmly.

Mother glared at the pair of us and stomped off back into the house. Setting out, we exchanged a rueful glance as the slave closed the gate behind us.

'We had better come back safe and sound,' Nymenios said, 'or Mother will find her way down to the Underworld just to box our ears.'

'So will Zosime, and Melina.' I glanced sideways at him as we walked. 'I was surprised to find her at home today. Is she unwell?'

His veiled look told me he knew what I was asking. 'Not unwell, Demeter willing.'

So they weren't going to announce their hopes until there was no hiding the news. I wondered if that would

272

make loss easier to bear, if this early promise didn't bear fruit. I couldn't imagine it would.

While we were making this tour of the temples, I'd seek every god and goddess's favour for them. Though there was little reason to fear for Melina, I told myself firmly. She'd already borne three healthy children, as well as the poor mite born between Hestaios and Kalliphon who didn't see out his first month. I need not dwell on our sister Ianthine's fate.

Though that was easier said than done as we walked towards the agora. Thermopylae aside, there's precious little to admire about Spartans, but that's one thing they do right. Their women who die in childbirth are honoured as the equals of soldiers who've died in battle.

As we approached the market place, I tensed, alert for any hint of trouble. To my relief, there were no rabble-rousing orators whipping up spite against Ionians like foam on a stormy sea. A scattering of visitors admired the monuments. Knots of men who'd found some excuse to escape a house full of visitors sat exchanging commiserations and sipping wine. They were already looking forward to getting back to work.

I took the proper path to the Hephaistion today, instead of scrambling up through the bushes on the hillside. A few men and women were paying their respects to the god, their voices echoing softly around the pillars of the colonnade that surrounds the walls of the inner sanctuary. Then we heard the sharp sound of hammering from the far end. We found a young priest fixing nails to the walls of the porch that shelters the sanctuary door.

There was a stack of lead tablets on the floor. I picked one up and read the words roughly scratched into the soft metal.

I, Nikochoros, alert Hephaistos to the villain who took my cloak in the Grove of Kolonos. If he steals it away, may the fires of the god's forge sear him with fever. If it was taken in error and is returned to me, I will make an offering in thanks.

I wondered if the unknown Nikochoros had indeed been robbed, or was just careless. Either way, I hoped he got his cloak back without paying too much for the privilege. Some of the agora's idlers make a nice profit at the big festivals 'accidentally' gathering up other people's property before taking the spoils to a temple in hopes of getting a finder's fee.

'Thank you,' the young priest prompted me, his hand outstretched. He'd finished hammering in his nails and was ready to hang the curse tablets up for visitors to the sanctuary to read.

Nymenios was scanning the ones already fixed there. He reached up to tap a broad square of lead placed where everyone would see it first. 'Excuse me, what do you know about this?'

I read the summons for divine vengeance.

I, Emphanes, humble servant of mighty Hephaistos, declare the hides taken by deceit from this temple are property of the god, now stolen. Let those who have so vilely betrayed my trust and misused the god's bounty

pay with blood and boundless suffering. But let those
who may have handled these hides in ignorance of this
theft be spared by Hephaistos's grace. May they be blessed
and rewarded if they reveal those guilty of this impiety.

Dexios was right. Emphanes, the priest who'd been tricked, was absolutely furious.

'No one's come forward as yet?' It wasn't just cloak thieves who regularly checked these tablets. The agora idlers who kept their eyes and ears open could earn useful money by supplying information that helped to solve a crime.

Today, the young priest shook his head. 'Maybe after the festival.'

'What a bizarre thing to happen. Forgive my interest,' Nymenios explained as he introduced himself. 'Dexios, the tanner who was cheated, he supplies my business with leather. This sacrilege is causing us all serious trouble.'

'You may rest assured we'll show Hephaistos our gratitude,' I added quickly, 'as soon as he smites the thieves.'

Nymenios shot me a glare but he played along. 'If someone brings you evidence good enough to drag the guilty men into court, we'll split the damages we're paid with the god.'

I saw the young priest hesitate, swapping his hammer from one hand to the other and chewing on a wisp of his straggly beard. The lad knew his duty to encourage offerings to the temple. I could tell he'd also seen things he was eager to share. On the other side of that hypothetical drachma, he knew he wasn't supposed to gossip.

'Dexios is livid,' I prompted, to weight the scales. 'They must have heard him bellowing up on the Acropolis.'

That tipped the balance. 'I know. I was there. I thought he was going to hit Emphanes,' the lad confided.

'Surely not!' I leaned forward like a comedy slave, avid to hear more.

The young priest stepped closer as I'd hoped he would, and so did Nymenios. Unfortunately, the lad only repeated what we'd already learned from Dexios. It seemed Emphanes couldn't have looked more of a fool if he'd been up on stage with a red leather cock in his hand.

Nymenios tried to rein in his exasperation. 'And now there are no hides to be had anywhere. Do you know who's outbidding us all?'

'I've no idea,' the lad said unconvincingly, before he added pointedly, 'though a month or so ago, we were offered half the usual silver for that selfsame cartload.'

I seized on that unsubtle hint. 'For the hides that were stolen? Who offered the god such an insult?'

'Nikandros Kerykes,' the young priest said with sudden venom. 'Swanning about like he was doing us some gracious favour. Emphanes sent him off with his ears ringing.'

I had to swallow a profane exclamation. I'd hoped for answers but this was an unlooked-for blessing. When we got to the bottom of this, I'd be showing Hephaistos my gratitude with my own silver.

'Good to know the prick doesn't always get his own way.' I managed a chuckle. 'I've crossed paths with that arrogant bastard.'

'He didn't care.' The boy's resentment boiled over. 'He sent some bare-knuckle fighter to tell us to take the silver and keep quiet, or we'd lose our teeth or worse. I—' His nerve abruptly failed him and he hastily gathered his tools. 'I must be about my duties.'

As the young priest scurried off, Nymenios looked at me, narrow-eyed. 'What?'

'Just a moment.' I ushered him out of the porch and a little way around the colonnade. 'Wait here.'

I hurried to the far end of the sanctuary where the rear wall offered an alcove for sundry dedications to Hephaistos. My memory hadn't played me false. A handful of masks from Ephialtes's *Discus Throwers* were hung there. A group of friends devoted to Hephaistos must have been in that chorus.

I walked back to my brother. 'What does Nikandros Kerykes want with a cartload of fresh hides?'

'How hard did they hit your head last night?' Nymenios raised a sardonic eyebrow. 'Megakles Kerykes owns three tanneries that I know of, though he only sells his leather to his well-born friends' workshops.'

'I wonder when Nikandros got involved in the family business.' I could certainly see that pustulent little cock deciding to steal what he couldn't buy. When he realised that robbery wouldn't work, long term, I guessed he'd sent some pet henchman to do his dirty work. But suspicions wouldn't get a Kerykes into court.

'Megakles certainly has deep pockets,' Nymenios mused.

'Do you think he's trying to corner the leather market?'

We could speculate but once again, that wasn't proof.

Nymenios's beard jutted belligerently. 'Let's go and see.'

'What do you mean?'

'Megakles has a tannery close outside the walls, just north of the Diochares Gate. Let's go and see if it's busy.'

I was ready to call it a day and take this latest news to Aristarchos, to see what he might make of it, before going home and trying to make peace with Zosime. I kept my mouth shut and nodded instead. I know that set of my brother's jaw. Nymenios had made up his mind to go, with or without me. We started walking.

The young conscripts guarding the Diochares gate barely gave us a glance. I guess they assumed we were rural visitors making our way home ahead of the crowds who would clog these routes over the next few days. There were already knots of travellers on the road outside the city walls, where the buildings and businesses were far more widely spread. I was glad to see them. The two of us on our own would have been far too conspicuous for my peace of mind.

We both turned our heads as we heard trundling wheels on the road behind us. Nymenios dragged me into the shade of an ancient, obstinate olive tree that forced the road into a bend. The wagon rumbled past and I coughed to try and get the stink out of my nose and throat. There's no mistaking the rankness of fresh skins still smeared with blood and shit.

Other trades might be enjoying the festival, but some things couldn't wait. With the high prices paid for these hides, whoever was running Megakles's tannery wouldn't risk them getting flyblown before they were dunked in the yard's soaking pits.

'That cart's from the Temple of Ares. I recognise the priest who's driving it. I also know he told Pataikos that a valued customer has paid in advance for every hide from their sacrifices until the end of the year.' Nymenios broke into a trot, well able to keep pace with the reeking cart.

I followed, but anything beyond a fast walk left me breathless with discomfort. By the time I caught up with my brother, the cart had arrived at its destination. A short distance ahead, a walled yard was surrounded by scrub and turf roughly grazed by goats. As we loitered beside an anonymous warehouse's door, the tannery opened its gates wide to admit the stinking load.

I'd visited Dexios's yard often enough as a boy to know the scene within would be a pungent bustle of activity. First, the skins must be soaked for a day or so. Then slaves would scrape the water-softened hides clean of lingering flesh and fat. More experienced men, slave and free, would tend the pits of lime-wash, waiting for the moment when the skins were ready to be scoured free of hair. Then the hides would be handed over to grim-faced slaves who would trample them for half a day in troughs of stale piss and a few other choice ingredients. Finally, the yard's master would supervise the transfer of each consignment into the tanning vats. Every tanner has his own secret brew concocted from oak bark and selected leaves.

I dragged Nymenios into hiding behind the warehouse's convenient corner.

'What?'

'Hush.' I raised a hand to silence him, before peering cautiously around the rough masonry. Hilarious moves in the right comedy, but this was no laughing matter. Satisfied, but still wary, I withdrew.

'Did you see that man in a brown tunic? Shoulders like a wrestler?' He'd been standing in the gateway as the wagon went in. 'That bastard was in the thick of the fight last night.'

He'd been with the scroll seller Archilochos in the theatre yesterday, too. He'd gone with the three men I followed to that house where the fake Ionian from the riot turned up.

Now Nymenios understood my caution. 'You're sure?'

'Certain,' I said with savage satisfaction. 'Looks like I broke the fucker's arm.'

The wrestler's forearm was heavily bandaged and quite possibly splinted. His injured arm lay across his belly, with that hand thrust through his belt for support.

'Who is he?' wondered Nymenios.

'No idea, but I'm willing to wager he's the one who scared the piss out of that priest. Let's go and tell Aristarchos.' I was getting my second wind.

Chapter Twenty-One

I spoke too soon. By the time we got back to Aristarchos's house, I was flagging badly. Worse, he wasn't there.

'Can you tell us where he's gone?'

I might as well have asked one of the mountains in Mus's homeland. The big slave had clearly been told to keep his mouth shut and so he shook his head, impassive.

'Shall we wait?' Nymenios looked at me, hands spread, uncertain. Ruling the roost in his own home was one thing. Insisting on entry to a well-born man's house was quite another. Some other time, I'd have found this highly amusing.

To my relief, Lydis appeared. 'Ah, it's you, and . . .?'

My brother meekly introduced himself. I would have to tell Chairephanes about that.

'Who were you expecting?' Not us. I could see that much from Lydis's face.

'The Pargasarenes,' the slave said briefly. 'Do you wish to come in and wait for the master? He's gone to call on Megakles Kerykes.'

'Yes, please, and thank you.' I spoke quickly before Nymenios could refuse. Apart from anything else, I really needed to sit down.

Mus stood aside and as Nymenios went ahead, I caught Lydis's elbow. 'Tell me he hasn't gone alone.'

'He took Ambrakis.' The slave smiled briefly as he saw the name meant nothing to me. 'Our torch-bearer.'

'Good.' I was glad to think Aristarchos was escorted by that sturdy slave.

Mus was about to shut the gate when we all heard a shout outside.

'Ho there!' It was Sarkuk, accompanied by Azamis and, more surprisingly, by Tur.

No one would be looking at my bruises if the two of us went out and about together. The boy's nose was horribly swollen and he still couldn't see out of one gaudily bruised eye. The other was blackened now and his split lip looked vilely sore.

The three Carians were accompanied by a handful of Scythians, all armoured in linen and leather and ready with their bows.

Their leader bowed to Azamis. 'We'll bid you good day.'

I recognised Kallinos, who'd come to recover Xandyberis's body. 'Good to see you again. The Polemarch sent you as an escort?'

The tall Scythian nodded. 'The Archons are gravely concerned about these recent disturbances. He didn't want these honoured guests of our city to suffer any further insult.'

'Good to know.' So the city's highest magistrates weren't involved in these attempts to stir up ill-feeling against Ionians. 'Have you learned anything more about Xandyberis's killer?'

It was worth a try but Kallinos shook his head without elaborating.

'Thank you for accompanying us.' Azamis offered the Scythian his hand. 'Good day to you.'

'You must need some refreshment.' Lydis ushered the Pargasarenes in as the armed men marched away. 'I'll see that wine and food is brought to you.'

His glance included Nymenios and me in this invitation, so we followed the three men and the slave to the far side of the courtyard.

As Lydis withdrew, Azamis heaved a heart-rending sigh. His wrinkled face was drawn with grief. Sarkuk cleared his throat and made a visible effort to be polite despite the burden of his own sorrows. 'Good day to you, Philocles. Are you going to introduce your companion?'

'Forgive me.' I was embarrassed by my thoughtlessness. 'This is my brother and the head of our family, Nymenios Hestaiou.'

He shook Sarkuk's hand. 'I wish we were meeting under better circumstances. My condolences on your loss.'

'Thank you.' Sarkuk grimaced. 'We buried him this morning. It was for the best.'

He didn't need to elaborate. We've all seen death. Even kept in a closed room away from birds or insects, Xandyberis's corpse must have been turning putrid. Better by far to shroud the gruesome processes of decay under the kindly earth.

'We will take his bones back, after we've returned for the Great Panathenaia,' Azamis said, resolute.

We nodded our understanding. By the height of summer next year, the grave would hold only a skeleton. Disinterring such remains and sending them home is common enough practice when travellers from some great distance have died unexpectedly in the city.

'Meantime, his shade can keep watch,' Tur snarled, 'to make sure that your Archons deal fairly with us when this cursed levy is reassessed.'

Before anyone could react to that, the young man burst into tears. As he hid his face in his hands, I winced in sympathy. Not just for his grief but at the thought of those racking sobs twisting his swollen face and setting his bruised ribs heaving.

'My grandson . . .' Azamis struggled with his own tears. 'He hoped for the best for so long. When Xandyberis didn't come back to the hostel, he convinced himself that our friend had been seduced by your city's entertainments. After all, a man has his appetites and Xandyberis lost his wife some years ago.'

'He was not easy to like, not until you got to know him.' Sarkuk's bearded chin trembled. 'But he was always an honourable man. He was dedicated to our town's well-being and to preserving the rule of law against tyranny, whether by the Persians or from among our own people.'

'A loyal friend.' Azamis's shoulders sagged. 'A faithful husband and a loving father.'

'A eulogy any man would be proud of.' My own throat tightened.

'Does he leave young children?' Nymenios's question betrayed his own worst fears.

The old Carian shook his head. 'His eldest son is some years older than Tur, well able to shoulder his responsibilities. The eldest girl married a good man, my own sister's grandson. We will all support them.'

As they spoke, I heard a noise above us. Glancing up, I saw a shutter rattle and wondered if there'd been a gust of wind or if someone was listening to our conversation. If so, it could be a slave or one of Aristarchos' family; his wife or one of their daughters. Unless it was one of his sons.

I found myself fervently hoping Hipparchos was eavesdropping. I very much wanted that arrogant shit to see the full extent of Tur's injuries. I wanted him to hear the boy's searing distress at Xandyberis's murder. Let that sheltered and privileged ingrate learn about Xandyberis's family, now left without a father. Let him consider how their little town would suffer, deprived of such a staunch guardian. These were the crimes against gods and men which his friend Nikandros had dragged him into, when he'd drunkenly agreed to have some fun brutally beating a stranger to a pulp.

'We must decide if we send word on ahead, to break the news of his death.' Sarkuk sighed heavily again. 'Or if we should wait and tell his family in person once we arrive home.'

'How long before you travel?' Nymenios asked.

The older Pargasarenes exchanged a glance. Tur was still lost in his own distress.

'If there's no reassessment of the levy, we have no reason to stay.' Sarkuk rubbed the back of his neck wearily.

Azamis looked at me. 'Aristarchos has asked us to remain as his guests until he uncovers who is stirring up such hatred for Ionia. How long do you suppose that will take?'

'Do you suppose he'll be able to do it? I mean no disrespect.' Sarkuk hastily assured Lydis as the slave returned with two girls carrying laden trays. 'But I imagine these malefactors will have covered their tracks quite thoroughly.'

'We have a new scent to follow,' Nymenios began.

'That remains to be seen.' I cautioned him with a stern look before explaining to the Pargasarenes. 'I don't want to raise your hopes, not until Aristarchos hears what we have learned.'

I didn't want to discuss what we'd learned until Aristarchos was here. Distressed as he was, if Tur was recovered enough to see Xandyberis buried, he was capable of rushing out to start hammering on doors and demanding answers. I didn't want the young hothead getting a knife in his throat like his friend.

'Thank you.' I took a cup from Lydis and offered Athena the first sip. Then I drank deep. Aristarchos didn't save his fine wines for rich and powerful friends. Even this household's day-to-day refreshments were better than the finest vintages I could afford.

The tray of food offered morsels of fresh fish and tender venison lightly seared in herbs and oil along with a choice of olives, fresh and pickled vegetables, together with fine wheat bread. Even Tur shook off his misery and ate a little food, though he glowered as he chewed. To ward off any comment about his unmanly tears, I guessed, or because some punch in the agora had loosened a few of his teeth.

Sarkuk surprised us with a sudden bark of laughter. 'Do you remember Xandyberis and that octopus?' he asked his father. 'On Mykonos?'

Azamis shed decades with his grin. 'Of course.'

'What are you talking about?' Tur didn't know this story.

Nymenios and I sat and drank and ate and laughed appreciatively in the right places as the Pargasarenes reminisced about their friend. As they spoke I found myself wishing I'd had the chance to know Xandyberis. He'd assuredly deserved better from Athens than his miserable fate. This city owed his friends justice for his foul murder.

Aristarchos returned as we were picking at the last tidbits and I was wondering if we might summon another jug of wine. As Mus answered the gate and we heard voices, Lydis appeared from the inner courtyard.

'No, don't get up.' Aristarchos strolled across and pulled up a stool. He looked thoughtful.

'I hope we haven't intruded.' Nymenios looked more nervous than I had seen him for a good long while. I introduced him to Aristarchos and went on. 'We've been fitting some more pieces of all this together.'

'Have you, indeed? Thank you.' Aristarchos waited for Lydis to set down a fresh tray of food. A serving girl brought more wine.

287

'Do tell,' he prompted, reaching for bread and salad leaves.

'It seems that Megakles's son, Nikandros, is securing as much leather as he can. My guess is they're trying to profit from outfitting any phalanxes sent east to quell dissent in Ionia.' I'd been thinking about that while I sat here, remembering Father cursing rich men who sent other men's sons to die while they grew richer still trading in timber and metal and linen and everything else that Athens' fleet and army needed.

I explained what we'd seen and learned today, with Nymenios chipping in as his unease faded. Finally I told Aristarchos we'd seen the man with the broken arm at Theophilos's tannery yard.

He turned to his slave. 'Lydis, establish just how many leather workshops and tanneries Megakles owns and whom they trade with.' He looked at me. 'I wonder how Nikandros is financing such extensive purchases?'

That seemed an odd question. 'Using the Kerykes fortune, surely?'

'That's not as substantial as you might think,' Aristarchos said crisply.

'Megakles told you that?'

'Hardly.' Aristarchos smiled, thin-lipped. 'But one hears things around the right dinner tables.'

'What did he have to say? What did you tell him about last night?' I was at a loss to imagine how Aristarchos had started such a conversation.

'I wished to share my concerns that our two young sons had fallen in with bad company,' Aristarchos said gravely. 'It seems they were involved in some brawl, though I informed Megakles that Hipparchos won't tell me the details. I suspect an intrigue over a woman so perhaps I would rather not know.'

As he shook his head with fatherly dismay, Aristarchos's act was so convincing that Apollonides and Menekles would have applauded.

There was an appreciative gleam in Sarkuk's eye. 'What did he say to that?'

'Oh, he was very grateful that I'd come to him.' Aristarchos's sarcasm was as acid as the vinegar on pickled beets. 'Apparently Nikandros admitted to getting into a fight but it seems that he and his friends were provoked by unruly Lydians insulting Apollo Delios and Athena Polias. Can you believe that these villains were swearing they no longer owed the gods their allegiance? More than that, they swore not a bent scrap of silver would be coming from Ionia next year. Naturally these well-born youths took up arms, or at least used their fists, to defend our city's honour.'

'We already know they are telling lies.' Azamis was unsure where this tale was heading.

Aristarchos grinned. 'Megakles doesn't know that I know these stories are bilge water. All he knows is I support the proposition that Athens should look westwards as we seek to profit from Callias's peace. I'm in favour of expanding our colonies in Etruria and other untroubled, uncontested lands. So he was eager to persuade me that Athens must first put down these troubling hints of rebellion in the east, and do so hard and fast, by force of arms if necessary.'

'Did he say that?' I looked at Aristarchos.

He shook his head. 'Not in so many words. Though he has invited me to be his guest at a private banquet to-morrow, to meet those of his friends who have convinced him that looking eastwards promises far better returns than westward ventures for wealthy men with money to invest.'

'Are you going?' I asked, apprehensive.

'It's surely our best chance to see how far this rot has spread among the great and the good,' Aristarchos pointed out.

'I wonder if we can find out who first spread these rumours, and when.' I'd been thinking about that. 'Nikandros wanted to start stockpiling leather before these slanders against the Ionians began circulating.'

'Suggesting Megakles knew someone would create a demand for military equipment which the Kerykes tanneries and workshops could then satisfy?' Aristarchos looked at me, his reservations plain. 'We'll need solid evidence, not merely suspicion, if we want to accuse him in court.'

I nodded, exasperated. 'And whatever might be said at this banquet, it will be your word against theirs without at least one other Athenian citizen witness with no stain on his character.'

Aristarchos set his wine cup on the table and leaned forward, resting his elbows on his knees. 'So how do we get you in, so you can testify in court?'

I sucked my teeth. 'If we don't know who's going to be there, we don't know who might remember me from the theatre.'

Aristarchos leaned back. 'Would you,' he asked cautiously, 'consider shaving off your beard? No one would recognise you then.'

That was undoubtedly true. Like everyone else here, I hadn't gone clean-shaven since I could first boast whiskers. Seeing Aristarchos arrive for an evening of fine dining and wine with a beardless companion, one with his curls dressed with perfumed oil just for good measure, Megakles and his friends would doubtless dismiss me without closer inspection. A rich man's couch companion is often an idler who uses a razor to signify his lack of interest in taking on a citizen's duties, preferring a life of indulgence in the pleasures of the flesh.

It would be Aristarchos they'd be looking at more closely, surprised that he indulged in such dalliance. There's no law against it, but he'd never had a reputation for dissipation. A model Athenian, he was well known for his long and respectable marriage.

I frowned. 'What happens afterwards, once these people know you're their enemy, if they start spreading word that you've taken a younger lover to a dinner? You don't think they'll twist the tale to hint that you're one of those unsavoury types who like to prowl a gymnasium and grope little boys without any hair on their balls? They've already painted me as a Persian's cock warmer,' I reminded him.

I also didn't relish the prospect of staying indoors until my beard grew back to a respectable length, to avoid the startled glances and indelicate curiosity of family, friends and neighbours if I ventured out.

Aristarchos's grimace told us he took my point. 'That is a risk I'm prepared to take. My reputation should be sound enough to withstand it.'

'But if someone does recognise him?' Nymenios demanded. 'They've already tried to kill him once!'

Sarkuk was frowning. 'We know they're watching Philocles. If someone sees him without a beard the very day after this banquet, they'll guess he was Aristarchos's companion. They'll surely try to silence him then, to make certain he can't speak up in court.'

'Could he go pretending to be Aristarchos's slave?' wondered Tur.

'A slave won't be admitted to the drinking and entertainments after the food.' Aristarchos spoke half a breath before I slapped the boy down for his ignorance. 'That'll be when anything incriminating is discussed. Otherwise I could just take Lydis.'

'A slave could still bear witness to who came and went,' the young Carian said stubbornly.

'Enough!' Sarkuk silenced his son. 'Surely admitting he'd been willing to pretend to be a slave would discredit Philocles in the eyes of most jurors?'

'It would,' I confirmed. In fact, it was worse than that. An Athenian seen behaving like a slave, with no regard for his obligations, is swiftly stripped of the citizen privileges he has so clearly shown he disdains.

'Does anyone have any ideas?' Aristarchos asked, exasperated. 'He can hardly go wearing a chorus mask.'

'No,' I said slowly, 'but I don't suppose they'll give the musicians a second glance. I can play the double pipes—'

'Aristarchos can't turn up with his own piper,' Nymenios objected. 'That's not like bringing an amphora of wine as a gift for your host.'

'You would need to arrive with the musicians they've hired,' Aristarchos looked at me with tentative hope.

'If we can find out who they are,' I said slowly. 'I'll bet Hyanthidas would know.'

Aristarchos's grin answered my own. 'Lydis, go and offer my compliments to the Corinthian, and ask him to call here as soon as convenient.'

We had the beginnings of a plan. Hopefully, whatever we found out would shed some light on recent events.

If not, well, at least I'd have an idea for a hero's masquerade to work into a new comedy plot. Though I reminded myself how often such schemes go awry on the stage. It would be no laughing matter for us if this all went wrong.

Chapter Twenty-Two

Hyanthidas proved invaluable. He soon discovered that Megakles had hired Potainos, an Aitolian with a reputation for providing tastefully erotic entertainments. Potainos was perfectly happy to add another pipe player to his ensemble in exchange for a fat purse of silver. That was merely to stop the rest of the troupe asking awkward questions, he assured us. Aristarchos obliged without comment. Potainos wasn't asking any questions and that was well worth paying for.

Though the Aitolian did insist on hearing me play. Then he made me promise I would only wave my double pipes around and mime. His musicians had their good names to consider.

I didn't waste my time feeling insulted. It would be much easier to hear the dinner guests' chatter without my own tootling in my ears. Add to that, even after another night's rest and an undemanding day watching Zoilos's superb final trilogy of tragedies, I was still in no fit state to be taking deep breaths without sharp pains in my ribs. Most importantly, I needed to get in and out of the banquet without anyone recognising me. I hardly wanted to attract undue attention by blowing sour notes.

As the evening arrived, I left Menkaure to escort Zosime home from the theatre. Following Hyanthidas' directions, I found Potainos' courtyard where his troupe of entertainers gathered before setting out for the symposium. Most were women, and I found that frankly disconcerting.

There were eight girls, all told. They stripped off their everyday dresses and painted their faces before draping themselves in indecently flimsy fabrics pinned with gaudy brooches. None of them showed the least concern that I was seeing them naked. As they chattered and laughed I heard accents from every part of Hellas and cities far beyond. That was no surprise. No citizen woman would make her living like this, unless she was left utterly friendless and destitute.

A generously breasted Arkadian reached into her bag for a sponge and a small oil flask shaped like an erect phallus. 'Potainos! Will we be fucking tonight?'

She was so matter-of-fact she could have been asking what was on the menu. Well, in a way, she was.

Potainos was equally business-like. 'Just a bit of cock-teasing and maybe a sticky handful.'

I watched the girl put her sponge and flask back in her bag. I supposed that design of flask was one good way to make certain that particular oil didn't end up in someone's kitchen.

'Just as long as the guests know that,' one of the musicians said dourly. He was a lyre player from Crete. There were two other pipe players and one with a hand drum. They were far more interested in checking their instruments than ogling these undressed beauties.

The lyre player caught my eye. 'We're not there just to play. If anyone gets rough with the girls, you get rough with them. Understand?'

'Understood.' I fervently hoped that Megakles's guests would behave.

Potainos brought me a long grey tunic brocaded with startling red flowers. 'If any of the dinner guests slips you some silver when a girl puts a smile on their face, you give it to me.' He narrowed his eyes at me. 'Are you expecting the usual share?'

'No, thanks all the same. I'm not here to cheat anyone.' Pretending to be a musician was one thing. I drew the line at playing whoremaster.

Potainos clicked his tongue, seeing how I was struggling to secure the pipe halter around my head. 'Let me help you with that.'

Hyanthidas had found me a halter with wider leather bands than usual, to obscure my face all the more. There was an extra strap over the top of the head as well. That helped secure the wig I'd begged from Sosimenes, while we were waiting to hear back from the Corinthian.

I'd trusted the mask maker with the barest essentials of our plan, though not with everything that had led to it. Sosimenes had been happy to help and waved away any thought of payment. He'd said often enough how glad he was that Callias's peace would save his sons from fighting in battles like the bloody clashes of his own nightmares.

Potainos didn't blink when he discovered the false curls hanging down over my eyes. Enough of his girls were enhancing their own tresses with flowing locks shorn from some pauper or slave, or possibly an unwary horse's tail.

The pipe players watched the two of us, amused. Neither of them wore a halter. Only a feeble musician would need such a thing for playing indoors. But, true to Potainos's word, no one asked me any awkward questions.

Once we were done, the Aitolian clapped his hands. 'Right, let's be off!'

The girls hid their tantalising dresses under dowdy cloaks and we headed for Megakles's impressive residence in the Diomea district.

This evening the city had a very different feel. The Dionysia was over, now that Oloros's *Theseid* had won the tragedy competition, though personally I think Zoilos was robbed. The festival's closing rites were concluded and everyone would be up at first light tomorrow, getting back to work.

As we threaded our way through the busy streets, we passed those who hired out their skills or labour heading home for a good night's sleep. Merchants who'd be trading day-long in the agora were intent on the prospect of supper, barely sparing a glance for any passers-by. The wealthy had resumed their own entertainments. We saw another troupe of musicians heading for a private banquet, and Potainos and their leader exchanged a brief wave of acknowledgement.

Once we arrived, we humble hirelings weren't invited into Megakles's private dining room. We weren't wanted until his honoured guests had eaten their fill of exotic delicacies. So we sat in the Kerykes courtyard and watched the rich man's slaves carry out successive tables laden with plundered dishes, empty seashells and well-gnawed bones.

Over in the opposite portico, I saw Ambrakis, Aristarchos's torch-bearer, sitting with a handful of other tall, muscular men. These slaves were waiting to escort their masters home, so woe betide anyone prowling these streets after dark looking for well-dressed victims too drunk to fight back.

Ambrakis was chatting with the other bodyguards and I hoped he might glean some useful information before the night was out. I avoided meeting his gaze though. We didn't want anyone to think we knew each other.

We were offered barley porridge. It was inadequately spiced, according to the lyre player's whispered complaints. I hoped my refusal didn't make me conspicuous, but I didn't want to remove the pipe halter. Thankfully the food wasn't nearly tempting enough to make me regret that. I barely sipped the thin, tasteless wine through the hole in my mouth strap. If I hadn't already had good reason to dislike Megakles, such miserliness would have been enough.

The girls didn't care. The food and drink was free and that made up for any lack of flavour. As they ate, they speculated about the guests in the dining room. Evidently these well-born citizens would pay Potainos generously for the right to fondle and kiss the sort of women they'd sneer at in the streets.

The dessert table was finally removed, bowls smeared

with the remains of fruit in honey and dried grapes revived with aromatic wine. The girls gathered up their instruments; single pipes and light lyres. Two produced juggling balls from somewhere and the Arkadian girl fetched a set of pan pipes from beneath her stool. Standing up, they tugged open the unsewn sides of their dresses to reveal alluring skin from thigh to breast in every shade from barbarian ivory to Nubian ebony.

A slave appeared and handed us all garlands of ivy and laurel. I reached for the bushiest one on offer and dragged it down to my ears. The more thoroughly I was disguised the better. Another slave carried more expensive garlands fragrant with myrtle and herbs on ahead of us to the dining room. A boy followed with perfumed oils and linen napkins so the honoured guests could clean their hands before the entertainment began.

'Good,' one of the girls remarked. 'No chance of peppered tuna sauce getting where it's not wanted.'

As her colleagues giggled, I hoped the pipe halter hid my blushes. The district brotherhood dinners I'm used to are clearly more sedate than these upper-class banquets.

As we were ushered in, the diners were ready to make the first libation of the evening; taking their first and only sip of unmixed wine from the symposium cup that marked the end of the eating and the start of serious drinking.

As Megakles piously entreated the Spirit of Holy Goodness and the cup began to circulate, Potainos gave his musicians the nod. They struck up a hymn of praise and I mimed as the girls sang. They were as good as

Hyanthidas had said and I couldn't blame Potainos for warning off an amateur like me.

As we concluded the hymn, I studied Megakles. A man so well-fleshed could never have gone hungry. His beard barely concealed the slack flab beneath his chin, and his loose, expensively brocaded tunic didn't do as much as he hoped to conceal the rolls of fat cascading from his chest to his belly.

As host, he stood by his couch behind an enormous wine-mixing vessel. It was one of the fanciest styles, with high decorative handles featuring bunches of grapes. A picture of Dionysos lolling on a boat decorated the curved side. The god was eating grapes from the vines that were coiling up through the rigging while hapless sailors leapt into the sea, to be transformed into dolphins.

It stood twice as tall as my forearm is long, but it would have to be that big to keep every cup filled. This was quite a gathering. Not that this was a problem. Megakles's opulent dining room was easily big enough to accommodate all his guests as well as this troupe of entertainers.

'Shall we mix the wine with four measures of water or three?' Megakles asked no one in particular. Slaves stood patiently waiting, one with the amphora of wine and one with the heavy jug of spring water. Several guests offered opinions, all men used to getting their own way.

I reckoned that helped me identify those who wanted to get down to business before everyone got too drunk. One measure of wine to three of water would be too strong, they insisted. One to four was too weak, protested the others. I guessed they were here to be beguiled like Aristarchos.

Megakles raised a commanding hand. 'We will mix five of water with two of wine. No!' He halted the slave about to slosh water into the mixing vessel. 'How cold is that?'

As he held up a cup for a splash of water in order to check its temperature, two of the men who'd differed on mixing the wine united in their objections to pouring the water first and then adding the wine. Others were equally vociferous, insisting it should be done the other way. Blessed Dionysos save us all from such fussiness.

Megakles acknowledged his guests' differing opinions with a courteous nod. 'We will pour the wine first next time and see who can tell the difference. Now,' he continued, finally allowing the studiously blank-faced slaves to tilt the heavy jug and the amphora, 'who will give us the first song?'

Four guests fancied themselves as praise singers and eagerly raised their hands. Megakles decided who should perform first and Potainos dutifully handed over his own lyre. I stood behind the other musicians and tried to look as if I was gazing at the room's fine decor.

It was worth admiring. The walls behind the diners' couches were painted with fine scenes of ships at anchor in some distant island's bays where nymphs frolicked in the surf. Twelve benches were raised up on the broad ledge that ringed the room. Each one comfortably accommodated two men reclining on plenty of cushions. Toss a few of the cushions aside and there would be room for a cuddlesome companion, if this had been an evening when the Arkadian lass would earn her silver by spreading her thighs.

But there was no such expectation tonight. All of the benches were occupied, with no spaces left by the door to welcome latecomers or unexpected arrivals. None of the guests had brought the courtesans so often welcome at such gatherings. This wasn't a night to leaven the masculine atmosphere with feminine wit, or to satisfy wealthy men's tastes for sensual pleasures and sex without the risks of robbery or disease.

There were no younger men with perfumed curls, clean-shaven chins and no interest in public affairs, so I was glad we hadn't pursued that notion to get me in here unrecognised. This was an evening for serious discussion among the great and the good.

Wine circulated and everyone drank a toast to everybody else's good health. The men who thought this was a normal banquet competed to sing their songs. They were passable performers, making it easy for Megakles and his cronies to flatter them. Finally the winner was agreed: a man who I remembered seeing in the theatre's marble seats. He wasn't the only guest I recognised, though I couldn't put names to them all.

The ones I could name convinced me we were in the right place. The man the Pargasarenes knew as Archilochos was reclining in the humblest seat, ingratiating himself with smiles to all and sundry on the other couches. A few places further along I saw the man who'd insulted me and the Carians in the agora.

Megakles waved to Potainos, to indicate that the girls could begin dancing as he mixed another serving of wine. The Arkadian led the others into the middle of the mosaic floor. A gang of craftsman's apprentices must have spent a month sorting those pebbles to match them so precisely by size and shades of cream and grey. Dolphins chased each other's tails in a central medallion and octopuses writhed in the corners of the square frame of identically curling waves.

The girls danced and entertained us with juggling and acrobatics, which gave the banquet guests a good look at their plump breasts and luscious buttocks. I stood behind the other musicians in the space where the doorway interrupted the square of couches. While I faked a tune on my pipes, I listened to the guests' conversations.

Pheidestratos was in the seat of honour beside Megakles, with Strato on the next couch along. The playwright had no interest in assessing the musicians for any professional purposes. He was nodding vigorously and obsequiously every time his comedy's patron spoke to the man between them. Their target's name was Thrasymachos. I knew him from his speeches before the People's Assembly, vehemently contesting Pericles's plans to use Delian League funds to rebuild our ruined city.

Not that Thrasymachos had argued on behalf of our hard-pressed allies. He was utterly opposed to the notion that ordinary citizens should make such decisions. He believed that the people should abide by the choices made for them by the well-born and wealthy. He was soon ready to agree that these ungrateful Ionians needed showing a firm Athenian hand.

I edged closer to the nearest couch on the other side of the doorway. Archilochos, so-called, had his back to me, reclining beside another playwright, Leukippos. He was intent on convincing the tragedian about something, though he didn't seem to be making much progress.

'Enough, Gorgias,' Leukippos objected. 'I'm sure the Ionians are as relieved as we are to see peace agreed, and grateful that Athenian triremes sail their waters to guarantee that tranquillity. I cannot believe that any city or island's assembly will vote against paying the agreed tribute, whatever a few hotheads may say.'

I stepped backwards, well satisfied. Now I had this fake Archilochos's real name, we could ask around the agora about a man called Gorgias, with his description to confirm who we meant, who traded poetry scrolls in Ionia. It wouldn't take us long to learn who his father had been and his voting district. How would his sworn brotherhood react, when they were told he'd been rabble-rousing among our allies, not caring if their sons went to war, so that wealthy men could get richer?

It was clear that this gathering of noble citizens was drooling at the prospect of profits. On the couch beyond Gorgias and Leukippos, the man who'd insulted me and the Carians in the agora was all but promising fat contracts to a man called Metrobios who shared his couch. Metrobios had interests in timber, thanks to his family's contacts in Thessally, and he owned joinery workshops in Athens.

'Hoplite shields, triremes, oars.' The speech maker threw out his lures. 'All needed quickly and in quantity.'

'You think the Council will open the Treasury's strongboxes, Parmenides?' Metrobios countered robustly. 'No, some poor fools will find themselves beggared when they're nominated to supply and outfit a trireme as their service to the city. I don't want to draw the magistrates' gaze when they're looking for wealthy men to shoulder that burden.'

'You can't be asked to provide a trireme if you're already sponsoring a play for next year's Dionysia.' Parmenides gestured at the playwrights in the room. 'We have excellent connections when it comes to the theatre. You don't imagine it's a coincidence that one of our allies wrote a comedy this year, while another served as his patron?'

Metrobios still wasn't impressed. 'Putting on a play hardly comes cheap.'

'But then you need not undertake any public service, even if the magistrates pick you,' Parmenides assured him. 'We'll help you make a case to nominate someone else to take on that obligation. Won't we, Glaukias?'

The man he appealed to was someone else I recognised, and I was sorry to see him here. Glaukias is one of the most sought-after speech writers in the agora. I had no doubt that he could get Metrobios excused such a civic duty, or anything else he asked.

'Is there someone you'd like to do that particular

disservice?' the speech writer asked archly. 'I can make anyone you care to nominate look as rich as Croesus while convincing everyone else that you live modestly within your means.'

'Look to the future,' Parmenides urged. 'Once we see the Ionians condemned as Persian sympathisers, their lands will be ripe for confiscation.'

'And every field and pasture will be given to the poor from Athens' slums,' Metrobios objected.

'Not all.' Parmenides shook his head. 'There will be plenty left for us and our friends, to earn us rents in silver and goods.'

'Not that the magistrates here will have any idea what those rents may be worth,' Glaukias said quickly. 'You need not fear that they'll add it to what they know of your wealth.'

'Far from it,' Parmenides agreed. 'Indeed, your new foreign holdings will offer a refuge for your income from Attica and any property you hold in Athens. Or you can ship your silver to one of our banks in Crete, in the care of someone you trust. No one will be able to point to your strongboxes lodged here in Athens.'

'If anyone asks where your money has gone, you can say you are investing in Ionia, for the sake of future peace,' Glaukias said, mock-piously.

Metrobios still dug in his heels. 'All my money could be lost if the Persians get wind of this unrest and take it seriously. What if they seize their chance to invade Hellenic lands?'

'That won't happen,' Parmenides promised him. 'We

have agreements with satraps all along the coast. They'll convince Artaxerxes that this is a passing storm and he'd be most unwise to try riding its currents.'

It's a good thing I wasn't playing a tune. Hearing such rank treason openly admitted took my breath away.

'When you have holdings of your own in Ionia you'll be well placed to profit from Persian trade,' Glaukias observed slyly.

'You're sure the Medes aren't really our enemy?' Metrobios seemed to be weakening. 'Because my sons will be called up as hoplites if you tip us into a war. We're not all cavalrymen.'

He looked enviously at the well-born around the room. As well as Megakles I recognised men from the Thaulonid and Eteoboutid lineages. Though if I was right, they were both public debtors, named and shamed by the People's Assembly. They would remain stripped of citizen privileges and denied any chance of high office until they paid what they owed to the city. No wonder they were interested in this.

'You need not worry about that.'

Parmenides spoke at the same time as Glaukias.

'There are always ways to make sure that the right men are excused from the muster, when any order to summon the draft goes out to the district brotherhoods.'

'Is that so?' Metrobios raised his cup to summon the slave who was circulating with a jug of wine dipped from the mixing bowl.

It was a good thing I was effectively gagged by the pipe halter and twin reeds in my mouth. Otherwise I could

307

have told this trio what I thought of their treachery. As it was I swallowed my ire and retreated behind the other musicians.

Megakles was preparing a fourth serving of wine. I consoled myself with that well-known saying about drinking at banquets. The first cupful promotes health while the second warms the flesh for pleasure, though none of these men looked interested in fondling the dancers. A third cup promises easy sleep and the wise all agree that's as much as a man should drink.

A fourth serving? That's a sign of hubris, according to popular wisdom. Arrogance. Vainglorious display. Contempt for the gods and humanity alike. Yes, that's what this was. I fervently hoped I would be a witness when Athena punished these men, as they so richly deserved. I spared a moment of silent prayer to humbly offer the goddess my own hands as her tools.

Meantime, I wondered what inducements Aristarchos was being offered, over on the far side of the room. He was sharing a couch with a man of a similar age and confident bearing. Aristarchos already knew him, judging by their easy conversation, readily resumed after they broke off to politely applaud the dancers.

We couldn't talk tonight without arousing suspicion. I'd have to call on him first thing tomorrow.

Chapter Twenty-Three

The following day, I walked Zosime to the pottery work-shop and cut back across the agora to Aristarchos's house. I discovered my noble patron and Lydis were already hard at work. They sat at opposite ends of a long table set up in the inner courtyard. Papyrus covered the polished wood, in single sheets and scrolls. More scroll baskets were lined up on the paving.

Lydis was busy writing, his fingers stained with ink. A sheaf of drying letters awaited the imprint of Aristarchos's seal ring.

'Good morning.' Aristarchos spared me a smile, sorting through a handful of documents. 'What did you learn last night?'

As I related what I'd overheard, Lydis set the half-written letter aside and made notes on a fresh sheet of papyrus. Once I'd finished, I waited for Aristarchos to tell me about his evening but he looked at his slave instead. 'Make the same enquiries about Metrobios and Thrasymachos.'

'What are you asking about?' I was curious.

'This and that.' Aristarchos's grim expression promised no good at all to the men who'd gathered in that dining room. 'Marshalling facts.'

This sounded promising. 'What can I do to help?'

He raised a forefinger to tally his requests. 'Call on your brothers and ask them to make enquiries of other craftsmen, to see who's stockpiling wood or wool, linen or metals, just as Nikandros has been amassing hides and leather. Discreetly, and only approaching men whom they trust.'

'Of course.' I didn't need that warning.

Aristarchos raised a second finger. 'Go to the agora. Take your usual seat in the Painted Colonnade so passers-by can offer you writing commissions. Keep an eye on Glaukias. Take note of anyone who comes to talk to him. If they're strangers, ask around. See if you can learn their names.'

'By all means.' I'd brought my bag of writing materials with me. If Aristarchos hadn't needed me after this conversation, I'd planned on heading for the agora to get back to work like everyone else.

Lydis glanced up, a question in his eyes. Aristarchos acknowledged his slave with a placating gesture.

'You can also save Lydis some walking. Call on your actors. We want to know who Strato and Leukippos have dealings with in the next few days. Ask Hyanthidas to find out if any of our friends from last night are hosting their own banquets, especially Thrasymachos or Metrobios.'

'Anything else?' Though that would keep me pretty busy.

Aristarchos looked even grimmer, if such a thing were possible. 'Think of a way to find proof that these men deliberately set out to stir up unrest in Ionia, with malicious intent. At the moment, we can only prove that they're gluttons keen to gorge on the consequences.'

'Megakles didn't let slip anything useful?' I was disappointed.

'Megakles doesn't know anything much at all, as far as I could tell. He was saying that he's handed over much of the day-to-day running of his business to Nikandros.' Aristarchos's scorn showed what he thought of that. 'Megakles is devoting his leisure time to the arts and to drinking.'

'So Nikandros is at the centre of all this?' I looked at Aristarchos, dubious.

'Seems unlikely, doesn't it?' he agreed.

I had no answer to that. In the silence, we heard the gate open and the low rumble of Mus's voice.

The Pargasarenes entered the courtyard, and I was relieved to see that Tur's face was less swollen today. He could open both his eyes, though his bruises were now nauseating shades of purple.

Sarkuk looked preoccupied. 'Shall we call back later?'

'No, no,' Aristarchos assured him. 'Philocles and I have discussed all we need to.'

I nodded. 'Yes, indeed.'

Aristarchos clapped his hands. 'Seats, please, Mus. So, what have you learned from your fellow Ionians?'

As I helped Mus fetch stools from the opposite side of the courtyard, I heard the Carians detailing the taverns and meeting places where they'd sought out their countrymen while I was busy with wigs and musicians yesterday.

I should ask Menkaure and Kadous to see what they could find out as well, I decided as I waved farewell to Mus. 'I'll see you later.'

Heading for my family's workshop, I was relieved to find Nymenios, Chairephanes and the slaves all busy cutting, decorating and sewing leather. 'You have found some supplies.'

'Not enough to keep us in business for long.' Nymenios looked at me, anxious.

'Aristarchos is doing all he can,' I assured him. 'And you can help.'

As I explained, Chairephanes laid down his tools. 'I'll go and see Pamphilos. He and Kalliphon will know if the city's carpenters are seeing anyone disrupting their business.'

'Tell them to be discreet,' I insisted. 'Only talk to men they trust.'

Chairephanes and I walked out of the gate and along the street together. When he stopped to knock on Pamphilos's doorpost, I headed for Soterides's tavern, down by the Itonian Gate. My luck was in. Apollonides and Lysicrates were sharing a late breakfast of cheese, olives and bread, along with a jug of well-watered amber wine.

'Join us!' Lysicrates beckoned.

'Thanks.' I took a stool at their table. The tavern keeper brought me a cup and I leaned in, elbows on the table. 'How would you two like to do Aristarchos a valuable favour?'

'Do tell,' Apollonides invited.

I outlined our suspicions. I emphasised Parmenides' claims that these plotters could influence the magistrates' decisions over who would be awarded choruses for next year's festivals, or who would be chosen as patrons for the plays. As I anticipated, both actors were outraged.

'We want to know who Strato is friendly with,' I explained, 'and we're interested in anyone sidling up to Leukippos.'

'And if anyone else is sharpening words to slash at passing Ionians?' Lysicrates's eyes were bright.

'Don't risk getting knifed yourself.' I showed my bandaged arm and told them what had so nearly happened to me. Their smiles faded. Satisfied, I got up from my stool. 'Come and tell me what you hear, or leave word at Aristarchos's house. But be careful,' I warned a second time.

'We will, we will.' Apollonides waved me on my way.

It wasn't far to Hyanthidas's lodging. He rented one room of a house shared by an ever-changing array of musicians. He came into the courtyard looking so creased I guessed he'd slept in his tunic. He yawned as he offered to tear me a lump off the barley loaf he was eating.

'No, thanks. I just wanted to let you know that everything went well last night. When do you need that pipe halter back?'

'No hurry.' He shrugged. 'What did you find out?'

I told him and explained that Aristarchos wanted word of any symposium where the plotters might be gathering again.

Hyanthidas nodded. 'I'll keep my ears open.'

'I know this isn't really any concern of Corinth's—' I began.

He silenced me with an upraised hand. 'There are greedy fools there as well. They'll imagine they can pursue their local ambitions if Athens is distracted overseas.'

He wasn't wrong. I remembered the long history of Athens and Corinth competing for influence over Apollo's sanctuary at Delphi, as well as the more recent skirmishing in Aegina and Megara. These fool plotters could start a much wider war and see bloodshed far closer to home than the safely distant killing they intended to provoke.

'Thanks.' Leaving him yawning and eating his barley bread, I headed for the agora.

The market stalls were busy with workaday bustle instead of a festival throng. Traders offered everyday staples, not exotic dainties, and customers were haggling hard, not tempted into self-indulgence.

Men were going in and out of the Council Chamber, most likely those taking their turn as the Council's executive. That particular responsibility is taken in turn by each group of fifty men nominated annually as councillors by every voting tribe. That's only one of the checks and balances that safeguard our democracy.

I found it hard to believe these conspirators really could overcome all such measures and pitch Athens into war. These laws had been instituted precisely to make sure that our city never again fell prey to oligarchy or tyranny, subject to the greedy ambitions of a few. But the men at that banquet had seemed very sure of themselves.

I glanced up at the Acropolis and silently begged gracious Athena to show me how to bring down these bastards who so blatantly scorned our democracy.

Public slaves were taking down some of the white-washed and red-painted boards hanging from plinths and altars. That made plenty of space for new decrees and proposals. Those measures would be put before the popular assembly as soon as the executive committee summoned the full council to approve them.

Normally I wouldn't have thought anything of it. Today I wondered if the plotters had some allies already at work in the Council Chamber, enlisting support for some spiteful rebuke guaranteed to rouse Ionian ire.

The hum of business-like conversations rather than visiting philosophers' bold declamations filled the Painted Colonnade. There were no story-telling historians here today to impress idling festival-goers and garner their appreciative coin. There would be plenty of Athenians wanting something or other written though, prompted by family news or a commercial agreement made during the Dionysia.

I found a space at one end of the colonnade and perched on the topmost step along with the other humble scribblers. That meant I was well able to see inside where the more exalted writers set up folding tables and stools for their clients. Glaukias was in his usual spot, secured by long custom and his exalted reputation.

'Looking for anyone in particular?' Phrynichos put his cushion down beside me.

He often sat on the steps close to Glaukias, I recalled

315

uneasily. That didn't mean he was some conspirator though. All of us lesser scriveners flock to gather crumbs from more famous men's tables, quick to offer our services when some great speech writer spurns an inadequate offer or an insufficient challenge for his finely honed skills.

'Who was that man looking for you before the festival?' Phrynichos asked as he sat. 'That Ionian?'

'He had some mad notion that the Delian League tribute was to be reassessed,' I said casually. 'I told him he was mistaken but he didn't want to hear it. Do you know who recommended me? Who gave him my name?'

Phrynichos considered this for a moment, his face open and honest as far as I could tell. 'He'd been asking about everyone who'd been awarded a chorus. He wanted someone with a solid record of wins before the courts but when he found out how much that would cost him, he started looking for someone good but cheap. He told me your name kept coming up.' He grinned at me.

'I suppose there are worse reputations to have,' I managed to say lightly before changing the subject. 'Where's the historian from Halicarnassus gone?' That gave me an excuse for openly scanning the colonnade's shadows.

'Giving a series of lectures at the Academy.' Phrynichos studied the crowd criss-crossing the agora, alert for any potential customer.

'Who's that with Glaukias?' I wondered casually. 'I'm sure I should know his name.'

Phrynichos glanced over his shoulder, uninterested. 'Stratonides.'

316

'Of course.' I waved a rueful hand at my apparent forgetfulness.

'Good day.' A weary-looking man approached us. 'My son's ship has been lost at sea. We need a verse for his memorial.'

Phrynichos was on his feet first, though he waited politely to see if I wanted to compete for the commission.

I waved him on. 'Go ahead.'

I was more interested in watching Glaukias and Stratonides, because they'd just been joined by Parmenides, the fake orator who'd started the riot here on the first day of the festival. The rest of the morning passed in similar fashion. A handful of notable men stopped to exchange a few words with Glaukias. Each time Parmenides popped up from wherever he was lurking. He escorted the men away, leaning confidentially close. I committed their names to memory with increasing misgivings. This conspiracy seemed to be growing more heads than a hydra.

Meantime, I took on two commissions. A heartfelt eulogy for a beloved grandfather found peacefully dead in his bed. A speech for an indignant farmer from Acharnae ready to argue his case in court. He had been summoned to the city to answer an accusation that he'd fraudulently moved a boundary stone to encroach on a neighbour's more fertile land.

The Acharnaean was so outraged that I was pretty sure he was innocent. As a rule I don't ask, or even try to guess. My job is shaping a client's arguments into their most convincing form. I leave justice to Olympian Zeus.

Around noon the Acharnaean was finally satisfied that

I understood the enormity of his neighbour's offence. I reckoned he had a strong case. He certainly had an impressive list of arguments and witnesses to put forward in his own defence.

We agreed to meet at noon three days hence, when I would show him my draft of his speech. The man departed, hissing under his breath. I was reminded of my mother's ferrets when something irritates them. As I gazed after the Acharnaean, I could almost imagine him lashing a fluffed-up tail, twisting this way and that as he eased his way through the crowd. Ferrets as a comedy chorus was an interesting idea. Sosimenes could make them some fabulous masks. But could I weave enough of a story around that idea to make a play?

I stood up, ostensibly to stretch my legs after sitting down for so long. Twisting, I feigned easing a stiff neck as I watched Parmenides approach Glaukias once again. The writer was turning to the slave who kept him supplied with papyrus and pens as well as fetching wine for new clients. The slave gathered everything together and folded up the table and stools. So Glaukias was leaving. If he intended to return after lunch, he'd have left his slave sitting there. I knew that was his usual custom.

'Time for something to eat,' I announced to the colonnade in general.

Phrynichos waved a vague acknowledgement. He was deep in conversation with a man wanting a bridal hymn for his daughter's wedding.

I sauntered through the agora following Glaukias and Parmenides. Enough other people were going in the same direction for that to be unremarkable. This time though, I was acutely alert for any hint of someone following me. I wasn't going to be caught out a second time.

They went to a discreet tavern in a side street to the north of the agora. It looked like an expensive place, and one with a very select clientele. A solicitous, implacable waiter directed passers-by who showed any interest to a less exclusive drinking den on the corner.

I strode past like a man on his way to an important meeting, his mind on other things. Turning the corner, I ducked back to lurk behind the posts of the drinking den's vine-clad porch. Athena be thanked, I could get a clear view of the table where Glaukias and Parmenides were sitting. A deft slave was setting out a generous lunch for them to share. A few moments later, Nikandros joined them.

'Can I help you?' The drinking den's owner plucked at my elbow.

'Almost certainly,' I assured him. 'I'll be back very soon.'

Leaving the baffled man behind me, I headed for the Kerameikos district, walking as quickly as I could. I'd have preferred to run, but that risked attracting unwanted attention.

The workshop door stood open, with all the potters back at their wheels and the painters at their benches decorating the bowls, vases and wine vessels that had been left to dry out over the festival. Kadous spared me a nod. He was helping the old Thessalian as the man prepared the kiln for the second stage of firing that ensured the vivid contrast between the red characters detailed by the painters and the glossy background that would turn black in the heat.

Menkaure was shaping a mighty pedestal on his wheel. The great vase's bulbous body and smoothly curving neck were already resting on a board, until the pieces could be seamlessly stuck together with clay. He didn't look as if he'd welcome interruption, so I went straight through to the back of the workshop.

Zosime was working on a tall, slender flask, so intent that she didn't notice me approaching. I wished I didn't have to interrupt her. I certainly waited till she'd lifted her brush from the white surface, so I didn't make her smudge the paint. 'Hello.'

She turned, her surprise blossoming into a smile. 'I didn't expect to see you so early.'

'I need your help.' I leaned forward and we shared a kiss.

She looked into my eyes. 'What do you need?'

I'd told Zosime about the symposium when I'd got home last night, and everything Nymenios and I had learned, as well as the growing suspicions we shared with Aristarchos.

'I want to find out if Nikandros Kerykes was involved in killing Xandyberis,' I said grimly.

The conniving bastard hadn't hesitated to join in the attempt to murder me, and now we knew he was neck-deep in this conspiracy, not just a gullible fool like Hipparchos. If we could tie Nikandros to the Carian's murder that was a crime we could haul him before the courts to answer for. Doing that would drag this entire vile conspiracy into the merciless light of day.

'Then we can see his family get justice.' In her hurry to stand, she knocked her workbench. The flask she'd been working on wobbled. As she caught the black glazed base to steady it, I got a better look at the design.

'Is that him?' I couldn't be certain it was Xandyberis, not until she added more colour and the final touches, but the man's profile looked familiar as the figure gave a speech with one arm raised in a rhetorical flourish.

'Azamis and Sarkuk should take something home.' Zosime's eyes were dark with sympathy. 'Until they can fetch his bones for his family to bury next year.'

'That's perfect.' I swallowed a lump in my throat.

She looked sternly at me. 'Perfect will be them taking home word of his killer's arrest and execution.'

I nodded agreement. 'Let's go and do something about that.'

Chapter Twenty-Four

We hurried back to the drinking den and, this time, I asked the bemused tavern keeper for a table. Before he could decide where to seat us, I led Zosime to one with a view of Glaukias and Parmenides, still enjoying their leisurely lunch with Nikandros. I breathed silent thanks to Dionysos for that good fortune. Then I asked the god to keep them all from looking our way, even with the vines around this humble tavern's porch shading us.

A serving girl brought us food and wine and looked on with curiosity as Zosime took pen, ink and papyrus out of my bag of work materials.

'Thank you. That will be all.' I smiled at the girl, hoping that would take any sting out of my dismissal.

Thankfully, no one else was paying us any attention, more interested in eating and getting back to work. In between mouthfuls, Zosime worked swiftly and skilfully, drawing a vivid likeness of Nikandros.

She paused, pen poised as she considered the portrait. Deciding it was finished, she turned to me. 'What do we do now?'

'We wait here for a few moments.' I shaded the side

of my face with one hand, turning my shoulder to the street.

Parmenides and Glaukias had eaten and drunk their fill and risen from their table. They were walking this way, laughing together and chatting. I turned my back to the street, to make sure they didn't see me. The chances of them recognising me were slim but I wasn't taking any risks. My back itched as if I expected an arrow between the shoulder blades.

I looked at Zosime. 'What are they doing?'

She raised her cup of wine to mime taking a drink. 'Going on their way.'

'What about Nikandros?'

'He's still at the table.' Looking over my shoulder, she frowned. 'Someone else has joined him. No,' she corrected herself. 'They're getting up. I think they're going to leave together.'

It was no good. I had to see. As I turned, my blood ran cold. Nikandros's new companion was the brute whose arm I'd broken when he tried to kill me. Before I realised what I was doing, I was halfway to my feet. Zosime rose beside me.

'No.' I laid my hand on her arm to force her back onto her stool.

She looked at me, astonished. 'I need to see him more clearly, if I'm going to draw a decent likeness.'

'No.' I couldn't command her with a husband's authority but by all the gods and goddesses above and below, she was going to listen to me. 'He doesn't know who you are and I won't risk him seeing you with me. That's the man who tried to knife me.' I raised my cut and bandaged arm as evidence.

Something in my voice or face convinced her. She sank down, unwilling but complying. 'What's his name?'

'I don't know.' Frustrated, I stole another glance over my shoulder. The brute was waiting with an impatient scowl while Nikandros chatted to the exclusive tavern's owner. The thin-faced man was bowing obsequiously, clasping the young noble's hands.

'How are we going to find out who he is, if we don't have a picture of him?' Zosime demanded. 'We need to know. Look, they're leaving.'

Hades help me, she was right, and on all counts. I risked turning around, to see Nikandros and the unknown man walking away. They had their backs to us and their heads were close together in conversation. Any moment now I'd lose sight of them in the bustling street as people headed back to their daily labours after their midday break.

'Wait here. Don't move until I come to get you.'

They say fortune favours the bold. I begged the goddess of luck to help me, and any other deity who might be listening. Leaving Zosime at the table and praying that she'd do as I asked, I slipped through the crowds. I only wanted to get close enough to hear something, anything, to give us a hint about the killer. Some scrap of conversation that might tell us where to go to learn more.

As long as they didn't look round, I should be safe. They had no reason to think they were being watched. If they did turn, if I was seen, then I'd take to my heels, as fast as Hermes in his winged sandals. I wouldn't care about people looking. Far from it. I'd want every eye on me. Nikandros and his friend could hardly cut my throat in front of a street full of witnesses.

Whatever they were discussing, Nikandros was getting agitated. His hands waved with increasingly animated gestures. The man with the broken arm walked stolidly beside him, barely answering. Then, all of a sudden, he grabbed Nikandros's tunic and forced the arrogant youth into a narrow side street.

I clenched my fists and sprinted to the corner of the building at the mouth of the alley. I felt sick as I recognised the voice of the man who'd tried to kill me two nights ago.

'If you want any more silver from me, you snivelling little bastard, you'll do what I tell you!'

'Iktinos—' Nikandros choked on a gurgle.

That was so utterly unexpected that I looked around the corner before I realised what I was doing. I caught a glimpse of Nikandros pushed up hard against the wall, the other man's hand around his throat. Even using one arm, this Iktinos was astonishingly strong, powerful enough to lift the young idiot off his feet. Nikandros was on his tiptoes, expensive sandals scrabbling in the dust.

'Do you understand me?' Iktinos shook him like a dog with a rat.

I half expected to hear Nikandros's neck snap. As it was, he gasped some sort of assent.

Satisfied, Iktinos released him. 'Then I'll see you at the Academy, at sunset.'

I'd heard enough. More than enough. I shrank back, my heart pounding. An instant later, I hurried away, trying to put every man and woman on the street between me and that alley. As soon as I reached the sanctuary of the friendly tavern, I shrank onto my stool, cowering behind the wine jug.

'Did they see me? Can you see them?'

Zosime ate an olive, reluctantly amused. 'No, and no.'

I sat up a little straighter and poured myself a cup of wine. My heart was still racing and my mouth was as dry as the deserts of Egypt. The wine quenched my thirst, though I had to fight to calm my shaking hand enough to drink it.

'Well?' Zosime prompted.

'I heard his name.' I managed a smile.

'So?' She looked at me, expectant.

I took a deep breath. 'Now we go home.' I nodded at the portrait she'd sketched, the ink now dry. 'When we've found out what that can tell us, I'll take everything we've learned to Aristarchos.'

Zosime gave me a long, contemplative look. Finally, she nodded. 'Very well.'

We walked back to the pottery first, to collect Kadous. I wasn't leaving Zosime at home on her own, even if I was convinced Nikandros and his murderous friend hadn't seen us. Though, judging by what I'd seen in the alley, their relationship was rather more complicated than well-born paymaster and hired killer. That gave me plenty to think about on the walk back to Alopeke.

As we turned past the Hermes pillar, I straightened my

cloak and my tunic and brushed a hand over my hair.

'You look thoroughly respectable,' Zosime assured me.

Kadous grunted his agreement, walking a few paces behind us just as a biddable slave should, and carrying my scrivener's bag.

As we approached our gate, I turned and held out my hand. Kadous gave me the portrait of Nikandros. Then he and Zosime went to stand on our threshold while I crossed the lane to knock on Mikos's doorpost.

The little slave Alke opened up. She was so surprised to see me that she just stood there, gaping.

'Is your master at home?' I asked formally. 'Please tell him Philocles Hestaiou has urgent business to discuss.'

'Of course.' Her voice rose in a startled squeak as she closed the gate in my face.

I wondered how long I'd have to wait. I glanced at the Hermes pillar and prayed to the god of messengers that Mikos wouldn't just ignore my request and punish Alke for relaying it.

A few moments later, the gate opened and I saw that Mikos's curiosity had got the better of him.

'What do you want?'

'To talk to your wife, in your presence naturally,' I said with measured politeness.

Now Mikos was really puzzled. 'What about?'

'You must recall the dead man left at my gate.' I unrolled the papyrus in my hand. 'We believe this may be one of his killers. I wish to ask your wife if she saw anything that night. Perhaps she can identify this man.'

'I don't want her involved. We don't know who that is.' Mikos didn't even look at the picture I held up. 'I don't want to get mixed up in any trouble.'

That was true enough and I could hardly say it came as any surprise. It was a safe bet that the next time Mikos heard some disturbance out in the lane he'd head for his house's innermost room. He'd be shutting his eyes and sticking his fingers in his ears, while better men than him had their throats cut. I wanted to beat the sweaty coward's face into a bloody ruin.

Instead I took a deep breath, to make certain I could continue speaking in a calm and even tone. 'Then everyone at the next district council meeting will learn how Mikos Theocritou Alopekethen is too craven to play his part in securing justice for a murdered visitor, an honoured ally. That you choose not to serve grey-eyed Athena by seeing this vile insult to our city answered. That you spurn your obligations to the Furies, as they turn their gaze this way, summoned by the dead man's blood. Unless you would rather I told all our neighbours how crucial your help has been to restoring their peace of mind, helping to make sure there are no more local commotions?'

I don't think I quite managed to emulate Aristarchos's cold poise but I reckoned Lysicrates would say I'd performed well enough.

Mikos's lip curled, grudging. As I'd hoped, if honour couldn't make him do the right thing, fear of disgrace among all his friends and associates made him reconsider.

'Give that here.' He stretched out his hand for the papyrus.

'No.' I twitched it out of his reach. 'I need to speak to your wife myself.'

I didn't trust him not to come back and swear that Onesime didn't recognise Nikandros, whatever she might actually say. I also wanted two citizen witnesses to whatever she said. I was sure I could find some threat or reward to compel Mikos to give evidence in court.

'What do you want?' Onesime appeared behind him. Alke must have fetched her mistress. The little slave cowered a few paces away.

Taken by surprise, Mikos stood there dithering. I seized the initiative and raised the portrait so that Onesime could see it.

'Do you recognise this man?'

She pressed a shaking hand to her mouth. 'He was one of those who brought the dead man here. One of the gang who painted your wall.'

'Thank you.'

Mikos interrupted with a weak man's belligerence. 'Be off with you then. You've got what you wanted. Don't bother me about this again.'

I bowed low, mostly to hide my contempt. When I stood up, my face was an expressionless mask. 'You are to be commended, citizen, that your wife understands her duty to Athens so clearly, and that she has taught her slave the same. I trust you will show them your approval.'

I looked Mikos in the eye, unblinking, and hoped that he understood that I'd find some way to make him regret it if we heard Alke's wails as she was beaten this evening, or if Zosime saw Onesime with bruises at the fountain tomorrow.

He muttered something wordless and slammed his gate shut.

I turned to Kadous and Zosime, still standing silently by our own doorposts. 'So now we know for certain.'

I walked across the lane and kissed Zosime before unlocking the gate. 'Don't open up to anyone we don't know.' I handed the key to Kadous.

'Watch your back.' The big Phrygian looked troubled.

'It's broad daylight.' I tried to reassure him. 'The streets are busy, and don't forget, these people have no idea that we're out to foil their plans.'

He glowered at me. 'That hasn't stopped them trying to kill you.'

'True enough.' I could hardly deny it. 'Which is why I'll go and see Aristarchos, and be back here as fast as I can. I swear it.' I glanced at Zosime to include her in this promise.

'Make sure you are.' Her expression was unreadable as she turned and went into our courtyard.

I waited until Kadous bolted the gate before heading back to the city. Passing the Hermes pillar, I asked the god's blessing as I promised myself a day of sitting in the sunshine, going nowhere and doing nothing but reading poetry, once all this was done and dusted.

Passing through the Itonian Gate, I followed the Panathenaic Way through the city. I didn't take the turn that would lead me to Aristarchos's house, continuing through the Kerameikos district and on to the Dipylon

Gate. I hadn't said I was *only* going to Aristarchos' house.

As I followed the road that led to the Academy, I quickened my pace, constantly checking the sun. I had a fair way to go and the daylight was starting to yellow. I absolutely needed to be done with this errand well before sunset.

Reaching the Academy, I skirted the sacred grove of olive trees and ignored the athletics and wrestling grounds, heading for the sanctuary where the healers gathered.

The first doctor who passed me assessed my bruises with an expert eye. 'Can I help you?'

'I'd like to speak to Spintharos, if that's possible,' I asked politely. 'My name is Philocles and I'm here on business for Aristarchos Phytalid.'

That was true enough, even if Aristarchos didn't know it yet. When the brute Iktinos had mentioned the Academy, I'd remembered the name of the doctor whom Lydis had summoned to tend young Tur's broken nose and bruises. Athena willing, he'd have a few more of the answers we needed. Then we might finally have enough pieces to fit together to show everyone the whole picture on this amphora.

'I imagine he'll be able to see you. Wait here.' The doctor waved me towards a modest colonnade where a handful of patients sat morosely on benches.

I took a seat as far away as possible from anyone who looked remotely contagious and hoped that Spintharos would arrive quickly. As soon as a tall, lean-faced man in a blue tunic appeared and started scanning the glum-faced gathering, I stood up.

'Excuse me, I'm Philocles—'

'I know who you are.' An unexpected smile lightened his severe features. 'I enjoyed your play very much.'

'Thank you, I appreciate that.' I allowed myself a moment to bask in that compliment. Then I led him a short distance from the colonnade, far enough not to be overheard. 'Can you tell me anything about a man called Iktinos? Does he train here? Though, please, keep this to yourself. He's—'

'You don't need to warn me about him,' Spintharos said tersely. 'I've treated enough injuries he's caused.'

'Who is he?'

'A wrestler by trade, supposedly in training for the next Nemean Games. I believe Megakles Kerykes pays his expenses.' The doctor didn't hide his scepticism.

'You don't seem convinced,' I prompted.

'He doesn't train like any athlete I've known. He's gone for days at a time and there's rumour he breaks heads and legs for the Kerykeds. Oh, he wrestles here often enough,' the doctor assured me, 'but out of lust for fighting, not to improve his skills for the sport.'

'Is he any good?'

Spintharos snorted. 'He wins, more often than not. He never gives up and he's not satisfied with just winning. He likes to make sure his opponent knows he's beaten. If he can't get the better of his victim with skill, then he'll hurt him. I've seen him force an elbow joint too far, to deliberately tear a muscle, treading on someone's foot before a throw to wrench their ankle into a sprain. Of course, he always claims it was an accident.'

The brute would get thrown out of any pan-Hellenic games with that attitude. 'Is he ever beaten?'

'Occasionally,' Spintharos said judiciously, 'and he hates it. Anyone who does get the better of him on the wrestling ground needs to spend the next month watching his back and to avoid walking alone after dark. More than one of his opponents has been jumped on some deserted street and left there beaten bloody.'

'I can imagine.' I checked the sky again. I definitely didn't want to be on the road late enough to risk meeting Iktinos or Nikandros on their way to their sunset meeting. 'Do you know his father's name, his voting tribe or the district where his family live?'

The doctor frowned. 'I don't believe I do.'

'If you can find out discreetly, please send word to Aristarchos Phytalid. Iktinos may come here to consult you or one of your colleagues. I believe he has a broken arm.'

This time Spintharos's smile was far less charming. 'Quite a few people will be happy to see that.'

'Don't let him see you have any particular interest in him,' I warned.

'Of course not. Now, is there anything else?' He looked me up and down.

'Not today, thanks all the same. I really need to get back to the city.'

'I'll wish you good afternoon.' Spintharos headed back to his patients without further ado.

I hurried back to the Dipylon Gate. Thanks to Athena, Hermes and every other deity from Olympian Zeus

333

down, I didn't see Iktinos or Nikandros.

When I arrived at Aristarchos's house, he and Lydis were still besieged by scrolls. The stacks of papyrus were now reinforced with the first replies to the queries sent out this morning. I pulled up a stool and began to explain what I'd learned. They both set down their pens and listened intently.

I kept my promise to Zosime and went home as soon as we finished discussing the day's news. It wasn't my fault that it was well after dark by the time we'd decided what to do next. At least I arrived safely home with both Mus and Ambrakis escorting me. That went some way to placating her.

Chapter Twenty-Five

I headed for the city at first light. Once I was there, I made a few essential preparations. Then I made my way to Megakles's house in the Diomea district, where he'd held that treacherous symposium. Finding a convenient alley to lurk in, I watched and waited until the first visitors of the day arrived. Megakles had a steady stream of callers. I recognised some faces. Others were unknown to me.

There was no sign of his treasonous bastard of a son. By midmorning I was snatching glances at the Acropolis and wondering if Athena had turned her face against our plan. I tried to swallow my bitter frustration. If the gods willed it, I must accept their judgement. But I'd give them to the end of the day to change their divine minds.

Sometime after noon, Nikandros emerged, scowling. 'Get out of my way, you oaf!'

He shoved the big gate slave aside, which is to say the Kerykes doorkeeper let him pass. The man wasn't as tall as Mus but his shoulders were so wide that he risked getting wedged between those gateposts if he didn't turn sideways to go in and out. That might make a good joke for a play. The right actor would get a big laugh from that doorkeeper's eloquent shrug of contempt once the young master's back was turned.

I followed Nikandros to a nearby tavern, where he paid for a large measure of barely watered wine. He sat at a corner table, moodily searching the street for faces he knew, glowering at the oblivious passers-by.

I could guess why he was in such a foul mood: he had none of his friends to drink with. Hipparchos had been sent to the Phytalid estate in Steiria, escorted by his brother Xenokrates, who knew exactly what the young fool had done. Aristarchos had informed me that provided Hipparchos applied himself to study and prayer they would come back at the start of Thargelion. The Thargelia is a festival of purification and expiation, after all.

If Hipparchos felt hard done by, sent away from Athens for a full two months, I was sure his older brother would remind him how much worse his fate could have been. My own brothers would have rubbed my nose good and hard in such disgrace. For the moment, I was just relieved to know I wouldn't trip over the idiot as I pursued our quarry today.

Seeing Nikandros was getting restless, I walked into the tavern and sat at his table. 'Good day to you.' I waved the wine seller away. There was no chance this side of Hades that I'd share a drink with this shit.

Unsurprisingly, he was outraged. 'What the fuck do you want?'

I smiled. 'If you're expecting to see Euphorion and

336

Andokides, think again. They've been sent to their families' holdings in Attica and won't be back before the Panathenaia.' Their fathers had followed Aristarchos's advice.

'Now.' I leaned forward. 'Shall we discuss what you owe me for painting those false accusations on my house wall?'

'What?' He sounded exactly like his father, astonished that some commoner dared challenge his misdeeds. 'Who says so? You'll never prove it.'

'I have witnesses.' I laid the sheet of papyrus with his portrait on the table and tapped it. 'Witnesses who will swear that they saw this man painting those lies and defaming me to all and sundry who might walk past and see them.'

The arrogant youth gaped like a fish. But he could still flip himself out of this net if I wasn't careful. I waited for him to speak.

Predictably, he chose defiance. 'What of it? Nothing will come of this if we go before the courts.'

I raised a chiding finger. 'Why should I want to drag you into court, if we can come to some other arrangement?'

He looked at me blankly for a long moment. Then his lip curled as he thought he understood me. 'How much?'

I was happy to oblige, and even happier that I hadn't had to explain what I meant. This was going to work far better if he thought he was the one with the upper hand.

'One mina should be sufficient compensation for the employment I've lost thanks to your filthy slurs.'

'One mina?' He was startled into a laugh of contempt. 'You greedy rogue.'

That was good, coming from him. But I knew this demand for money would allay his suspicions. Those who reduce everything to its worth in coin rarely imagine that other men might value different things more highly.

He shook his head. 'I have no such funds.'

'You've got the money to pay the highest prices for all the festival sacrifice hides,' I pointed out. 'Where's all that coin coming from? Or shall I go and ask your father?'

'That's business.' He looked me straight in the eye. 'We raise capital like everyone else, through loans against the harvests from our land holdings. I cannot divert such silver for my personal use.'

His tone was firm, his expression convincing. A tense quirk of his lips betrayed him. This bastard was lying through his teeth about where his money was coming from.

I leaned back, hands on my knees, as if I was about to stand. 'Then I'll see you in court.'

'Half,' he countered quickly. 'Thirty drachma.' Presumably making that clear in case I was too ignorant to calculate such large sums. 'I'll wager that's more than you earn in half a year.'

As it happened it was about what I earned in a really good month, so he was right about one thing: demanding one whole mina really was more extortion than compensation, or it would be, if I really was as mercenary as he imagined.

'One mina,' I said placidly. Now he was haggling I

knew I had him on the hook. 'Or you can take your chances before a jury.'

He stared at me, clearly infuriated and just as obviously trying to work out how to get around this.

I rose to my feet. 'Bring the money to my house just before sunset. Oh, and bring Iktinos,' I added as though that was an afterthought.

'Iktinos?' Abruptly, Nikandros looked wary. 'Why?'

I leaned on the table, looming over him, my voice low and menacing. 'I know he tried to knife me when you and your foolish friends beat me up. I want his oath that he'll stay away from me and my household, and I want you there to witness it. Then if his shadow so much as crosses my path, or he goes anywhere near me or mine, I'll call you both before the courts for attempted murder.'

'All right, all right.' Nikandros recoiled to escape my vehement spittle.

'One mina.' I jabbed a finger in his chest. 'At sunset today.'

I strode away, fighting the urge to look over my shoulder to see what the boy was doing. Hopefully he'd go running straight to Iktinos. That's what we were counting on. But if either of them realised he had been followed, they'd know something was up. We just had to trust to Athena.

Meantime, I had more preparations to make. Various tasks kept me criss-crossing the city for the rest of the day. I was weary and footsore by the time I got home but I didn't mind. Our plan had gone well, so far.

There's a phrase the tragedians play with. I'd even

made a note of the last variation I'd heard, thinking I might be able to turn it into a joke. When the gods wish to bring down a man, first they make him smug. I should have remembered that.

At least Nikandros was prompt. The sun was barely dipping below the roofs of the neighbouring houses when he arrived and hammered on our doorpost. 'Hello within!'

I was relaxing on a bench with a jug of amber wine, or trying to at least. I set down my untasted cup and went to open the gate.

'Good evening.' I stepped back to invite the two men into the courtyard.

'No slave to do your bidding?' Nikandros looked around my modest home with undisguised disdain. 'Is that why you want to steal my money? To buy yourself a man of all work?'

'Has your Phrygian run off?' Iktinos fixed me with an unfriendly stare. Even with that bandaged and splinted arm he looked very dangerous.

I ignored the brute, while making sure that I stayed well out of his reach. 'You don't seem to have brought my money,' I pointed out to Nikandros. A mina is too much silver to carry in a purse tucked inside a tunic.

'Because you're not getting an eighth of an obol,' the wrestler spat. He stepped forward, pushing Nikandros aside. There was no mistaking who was in charge. 'Not until you tell us who your witnesses are. Prove you can make a case against us.'

I took a step away and looked past the brute through our open gate to Mikos's house. Our neighbour's gate stayed stubbornly closed. I did my best to conceal my apprehension, folding my arms with an air of unconcern that I'd copied from Apollonides.

'You want me to tell you who to threaten until they recant their testimony?' I looked at Iktinos.

'You tell us and you might get *some* silver.' He smiled but I didn't believe him. He looked as trustworthy as a rabid dog.

I nodded at Mikos's gate. 'It's our neighbour.'

Iktinos half turned to take a look.

'Our neighbour's wife,' I said quickly. 'You won't get anywhere near her.'

'A wife?' That got me Iktinos's full attention. He stared at me, incredulous. 'She can't be a witness in court.'

'Her husband can,' I insisted. 'On her behalf.'

His smile grew even more predatory. 'We'll see about that.'

'Master?'

Iktinos and Nikandros spun around, both startled to find Kadous behind them. That meant neither of them saw my relief. I'd been waiting to see the Phrygian slip silently through Mikos's gate, with Alke swiftly bolting it behind him. As soon as he appeared, he'd raised a single finger. Good. Now I had the answer to a crucial question.

'Where the fuck did you come from?' Iktinos scowled at Kadous.

The Phrygian pushed our gate closed and stood there, barring their way out.

'Who is this?' Nikandros demanded. 'What's going on?'

Iktinos sneered at Kadous. 'You think I couldn't take you with one hand?'

'You're welcome to try.' The Phrygian flexed his arms to show off his muscles.

'Nikandros.' I cleared my throat. 'Let's discuss the matter of additional compensation for the man you killed. The Carian whose body you left at my gate.'

That's what Kadous' signal meant. Now that Onesime had seen the so-called wrestler in the flesh, she had identified Iktinos as the leader of the men who'd dumped Xandyberis's corpse.

'So who gets to pay up?' I looked from the boy to the brute. 'Who struck the fatal blow?'

'That wasn't my doing!' bleated Nikandros. 'We didn't know he hadn't managed to speak to you. We were only supposed to beat him senseless, to warn you both off.'

'Same as the other night?' I challenged. 'When you dragged Hipparchos into your treason?' I jerked my head at Iktinos. 'You didn't imagine he'd use a knife then, same as he'd done before?'

'Prove it.' The wrestler grinned at me, convinced he was the victor yet again.

'You don't deny it?'

'Why should I?' He shrugged. 'Your witness won't ever make it to court and no one will believe your slave's testimony against an honest citizen called Kerykes. Not even after he's had his fingers crushed to make sure that he's telling the truth. So you can shove your claims for compensation right up your slack, dribbling arse.'

342

A slow smile spread across Nikandros's face. 'That's right. Shove it up your arse.'

'You can't even think up your own insults. How sad. Never mind.' I raised my hands in surrender as the boy took an angry step towards me. 'You may as well play his echo while you can. You're tied together for life, or at least until he decides that it's safest to eliminate any witnesses to his murders. Tell me, have you seen all the others who were with you that night? Are you sure some aren't already lying dead in some ditch?'

'They're fine,' Nikandros retorted.

'Really? Tell me their names,' I invited. 'Let me see that for myself.'

'Shut your mouth.' Iktinos glared at me. 'We're leaving and your slave had better not try to stop us.'

'Let them go,' I told Kadous.

If he'd only opened the gate a little faster, that might have been an end to it all. But the Phrygian took a moment to glower at the smirking pair before turning to raise the latch.

Tur erupted from the storeroom. 'Why did you kill him?' he raged.

Iktinos spun around, ready to fight, broken arm or not. 'Who the fuck are you?'

Sarkuk hurried out to back up his son. 'Friends of the man you murdered.' He was as furious as Tur, though less foolhardy. 'We are respected allies of Athens who can call you before the courts! You will answer with your life now that we've heard you admit your crime!'

343

For the first time, Nikandros looked scared. 'I admit nothing!'

'They're foreigners,' Iktinos said rapidly. 'They're no ones from nowhere and no jury will condemn us just to satisfy them. You're an Athenian citizen.' He took a menacing step towards the Carians. 'Fuck off back to your mountainside and screw your scabby goats!'

Kadous looked at me, wanting to know what to do. If I could have reached Tur, I would have slapped him. Beyond that, I was at a loss.

The plan had been for the Pargasarenes to stay out of sight in the storeroom so they'd hear whatever confession I could trick out of Iktinos and Nikandros. Then they could go to the Polemarch to lay a formal accusation. I'd never intended for them to challenge this murderous pair face to face. At least Azamis showed more sense that his son and his grandson. He was still hanging back in the doorway.

'I'm sure we can come to some accommodation.' Nikandros looked at me, as sickly pale as a man who's been stabbed. 'I can pay compensation. You asked for one mina?'

'Fuck off,' I snarled, 'and take him with you!'

If I could scare the boy off, I could only hope that Iktinos would follow. Though there was the very real danger that the wrestler would snap Nikandros's neck before they reached the Hermes pillar on the corner. He must know the boy would turn against him now he faced the prospect of going to court.

'I don't think so.' Iktinos drew out a knife that he'd

carried concealed in the bandages wrapping his arm. A blade long enough to pierce a man's liver or slash an artery in his neck or leg. A killer's weapon.

I moved, more careful than ever. 'You think you can kill every one of us?'

'I can try.' Iktinos's confidence meant he liked his chances. I didn't blame him. None of us had a knife.

Sarkuk began circling the wrestler, moving in the opposite direction to me. 'You do realise he'll kill you as well?' he said to Nikandros without ever taking his eyes off Iktinos.

'Don't be so foolish.' The boy pressed himself against the wall. It wasn't clear who he was talking to. It didn't matter. No one was listening to him.

'What lies will he tell your father?' Kadous wondered. 'Blame some cloak-snatcher lingering after the festival?'

The Phrygian was staying directly behind the wrestler. Iktinos scowled, shifting from foot to foot as he tried to keep both me and the Carian in view. He knew Kadous was behind him but attacking any one of us meant turning his back on at least two other enemies.

'He'll say Nikandros came here on his own,' I suggested. 'He'll swear he followed the boy to keep him safe, but he tragically arrived too late to save him from these Carians' revenge.'

'He'll probably say Nikandros killed Xandyberis,' Sarkuk observed, 'to put himself beyond suspicion.'

'Just to be on the safe side,' I agreed. 'But there's one thing he's forgotten.'

I raised my voice to be quite sure I was heard. Iktinos

whirled around as the door to my would-be dining room opened.

Kallinos stepped into the courtyard. He was grinning. 'I know this one. Public slaves can testify in Athenian courts without being put to torture.'

Nikandros recognised the Scythian's uniform of linen and leather. He collapsed, sliding down the wall as his knees gave way. Burying his face in his arms, as though that could make all this horror disappear, he wailed like the spoiled child he was.

Iktinos had more backbone, and he knew it was time to flee. Kadous stood between him and the gate. He sprang at the Phrygian, slashing low and wide, seeking to spill my slave's guts on the ground.

Kadous had been in enough knife fights to avoid that fate. He might even have got the knife off the wrestler if he'd been given the chance. I'd seen him do that in the past. Mus and Ambrakis hurried out of the dining room. We'd agreed not to take any chances when it came to bringing Iktinos down.

Only Tur decided to help, and it seems that Caria needs wrestling trainers as much as it lacks teachers of rhetoric. The idiot Pargasarene threw himself onto Iktinos's back, crushing the wrestler's arms to his sides in a ferocious bear hug.

In fairness, if Iktinos hadn't been so experienced in competition as well as brawling, Tur might have succeeded. The Carian was big and strong. But Iktinos simply bent his knees and dropped his shoulder in one swift, smooth move. That lifted Tur clean off his feet and hurled him over Iktinos's head to slam into Kadous.

The two men collapsed, entangled. Blood splashed over them both. Tur was screaming like a sheep savaged by a wolf. I saw Iktinos had thrust his knife right through the boy's forearm, in between the bones. The bastard hadn't just stabbed him. He'd twisted the knife as hard as he could.

Sarkuk ran to his son's aid, ripping off his tunic to staunch the fearsome wound. With all these men in the way, none of us could reach Iktinos. No one could stop the murderer as he dragged the gate open and fled down the lane.

Kallinos considered the carnage unmoved. 'Dados?'

The sleepy-eyed Scythian emerged from the dining room's shadows. He already had an arrow ready. I followed him to the gate, skirting Sarkuk and Tur as Kadous ran for bandages from Zosime's stores.

Ambrakis and Mus pursued the killer but neither man was a sprinter. Iktinos had a good start on them and showed an unexpected turn of speed. He was running for the main road. If he reached the corner, I knew we would lose him. He'd keep on running all the way to Piraeus. He'd be on board the next ship sailing anywhere before anyone could find him.

Dados contemplated the fleeing man for a long moment. Then he drew his bow and loosed his shaft in a single fluid motion.

The arrow took Iktinos in the back, to the left of his spine and just below his shoulder blade. He collapsed by the Hermes pillar, screaming as he writhed in agony. By the time we reached him, his cries were fading and bright red blood frothed on his pallid lips.

'I'd have brought more men if I'd known we'd be carrying another corpse all the way back to the city,' Kallinos remarked.

'I'm sorry to make so much work for you.' I watched Iktinos's struggles for life and breath fade until his eyes glazed in death.

I was content to see the bastard pay the ultimate penalty for his crimes. He would have died sooner or later. He'd been marked for the Furies' vengeance, ever since the Scythians heard his confession. It wasn't as though Megakles would have paid for his defence if Iktinos had been brought to trial before a citizen jury. He wouldn't have let the murderer implicate his son Nikandros. The best the wrestler could have hoped for was an anonymous gift of hemlock to cheat the public executioner, as payment for his silence.

On the other side of that coin, I would much rather he had died later than sooner. Now we had no chance of getting vital answers out of him in return for that cup of hemlock. More than that, without him in the Scythians' custody, there was no case to take to court, to make the conspiracy the talk of the agora. Kallinos had heard Iktinos confess to murdering Xandyberis but Nikandros had denied it. Now that the wrestler was dead, he could shoulder all the blame. The plotters would retreat into the shadows and bide their time before another attempt to profit by dragging Athens into war.

'He's going to drip blood all down my back,' complained Dados. He hauled the dead wrestler up all the same, hoisting him over one shoulder.

I watched them walk away and returned to my house. As I reached the gateway, Kadous was binding up Tur's wounded arm and reassuring Sarkuk.

'It looks worse than it is. He can still use all his fingers. See? Show us, lad.'

Frozen-faced with shock, Tur nevertheless managed to oblige. I winced.

Still huddled in a heap, Nikandros was wailing incoherent entreaties.

'Get up!' Suddenly furious, Azamis seized his black curls. He dragged the boy towards the gate. Enraged, the old man was stronger than he looked. 'Get out!'

Seeing me on the threshold, Nikandros stretched out beseeching hands. 'Please, please, I beg you. Let me make this right. Five minas? For the dead man's family?'

Azamis let him go. Nikandros staggered to his feet. He straightened his tunic, relieved, until he saw the force of the old Carian's loathing.

'You think you can buy your way out of everything?' spat Azamis. 'You think any silver can outweigh your sins?'

Nikandros didn't see the blow coming. I doubt he'd ever been slapped by a parent or a tutor. The old man's fist took him in the side of the jaw. I don't know if it was the punch that knocked him out or smacking his head on the gatepost, but he fell to the ground, utterly senseless.

'Is he dead?' Azamis rubbed his bruised knuckles as I stooped over the sprawled youth.

'No.' Though he had a nasty gash in his scalp where he'd struck the corner of the solid wood. When he woke up, he'd have a vicious bruise. If he woke up, if his skull was still whole.

I heaved a sigh and called out to Kadous. 'Find our guests some good wine while I fetch Zosime.' She'd gone home with Menkaure to his rented rooms when they'd finished work at the pottery. From the moment we'd hatched this plot, I'd been intent on keeping her as far away as possible from Iktinos and Nikandros.

'Mus, Ambrakis.' I beckoned to the slaves. 'We'd better take this garbage back to the city.' The walk should give me time to compose some convincing explanation for the guards on duty at the Itonian gate.

I hated to think what Aristarchos would say when he learned how badly our plans had gone awry. Given the choice, I'd dump Nikandros in a ditch. Let any god or goddess who cared look after him, if they felt the fool boy deserved mercy. But I didn't have a choice. Justice might have been done for Xandyberis, but more innocents would die if the plotters still got their war.

Mus and Ambrakis grabbed Nikandros's wrists and ankles and carried him, limp and with his head lolling, all the way to Athens.

Chapter Twenty-Six

I arrived at Aristarchos's house at noon the following day as requested. Mus opened the gate and Lydis led me through to the inner courtyard. Azamis, Sarkuk and Tur were already sitting there, silently waiting. We'd tried to persuade the boy to stay in bed, but he insisted on being here, his eyes bright with fever as he cradled his bandaged arm.

I didn't speak. We'd all been warned not to make our presence known. We satisfied ourselves with silent nods and brief, grim smiles.

Lydis joined us as one of the household girls brought refreshments. None of us could eat, though the wine was welcome. As we all wordlessly offered a libation, I wondered who the Carians prayed to. I sought Athena's blessing, to help us foil her city's enemies once and for all.

Everyone tensed when we heard the gate open. Mus's voice echoed around the outer courtyard as he announced the visitor to his master.

'Megakles Kerykes.'

'Good day and thank you for coming.'

Aristarchos was sitting in a tall, cushioned chair carefully placed by the archway to make sure we could hear this conversation. The long table, the stools and all the scrolls and letters had been cleared away. The stage was set for a dramatic confrontation.

'Mus, a seat for my guest.'

We heard the sharp clatter of a stool being set down. I strained my ears for any hint that Megakles had brought a slave as an escort or bodyguard. No, there was no business of handing over a cloak, no instructions for some underling to sit out of earshot. Good. Aristarchos had been right. Megakles felt safe enough walking these wealthy streets at midday. Besides, the fat fool was coming here confident that Aristarchos was ready to join him in concealing his son's treason. The fewer witnesses to such duplicity, the better, even slaves.

'I was relieved to get your letter this morning,' Megakles said stiffly. 'To know that you understand how closely our interests align.'

'Forgive me.' Aristarchos didn't sound the least remorseful. 'When I said I wished to discuss resolving the consequences of your son's activities, I should have made myself clear. I wish to see him suitably punished.'

'What?' Megakles was audibly stunned.

'I also wish to explain my contempt for the proposals put to me at your symposium. I remain convinced that Athens should look to the west, to Italy and to Sicily,' Aristarchos continued calmly. 'To build new cities on fresh ground rather than stealing land which our allies have ploughed for generations. I will never help foment mistrust between this city and the Delian League. I will never be part of conniving to wave a false threat of some

Persian menace over everyone's heads. I will never ally with men stirring up strife in Athens in order to fill their own strongboxes.'

'I played no part in that.' The stool's feet screeched on the paving as Megakles lurched to his feet.

'No,' Aristarchos agreed, 'but only because you were wilfully deaf while treason was discussed around your dinner table. Just as you were wilfully blind to whatever your son was doing, and with whom. An honest citizen, any responsible father, would have acted long since to curb his arrogance and greed.'

To give Megakles his due, he rallied quickly. 'I would warn you against rash accusations. You forget I have many friends in this city. Powerful friends.'

Aristarchos was unmoved. 'You may wish to consider how they will react, when they hear what I have to say. The Archons. The Polemarch. The Tribute Commissioners. The Board of Auditors who will assess your fitness if you're ever selected for high office. The men who will ratify your accounts if, by some miracle, you're approved to serve a magistrate's term. The senior men of your own noble lineage when they hear just how your son's treason threatens them all with utmost disgrace.'

'It will just be your word against mine,' Megakles snarled.

'No, it will not,' Aristarchos assured him. 'I can call a witness to the plotting you allowed to flourish under your very own roof.'

That was my cue. I walked through the archway to the outer courtyard. Lydis followed, carrying my stool and retreating as soon as he'd set it down. I took my seat.

Still standing, Megakles stared at me, dumbfounded. He didn't have the faintest idea who I was.

'This is Philocles,' Aristarchos said helpfully. 'He was with the musicians you hired for that symposium you invited me to. He heard everything that was said.'

'One of those Aitolians?' scoffed Megakles. 'His word is no good in Athens. You might just as well put forward the slave who carried your torch.'

'Hardly. I value my slaves. In any case, you are mistaken. Philocles is an Athenian citizen who can call any number of men from his district to vouch for him and his family. Though I'm surprised you don't recognise him,' Aristarchos remarked. 'He wrote the comedy I sponsored for the festival.'

I was pleased to see a flicker of uncertainty on Megakles's face. Nevertheless, he half turned and took a pace as though he was about to leave.

'And of course, your son tried to have him killed,' Aristarchos continued in that same measured tone. 'To add to the first murder we can lay at his door.'

'What?' Megakles turned back. Apprehension coloured his protest. 'Nikandros would do no such thing.'

'You don't know your son very well.' Aristarchos was politely contemptuous. 'Do you know how he was financing his attempt to beggar the city's leather workers so that your tanneries and workshops would profit?'

I followed his prompt. 'He told me he had raised loans against the produce and the property of the farms and the vineyards you own.'

'He did what?' Megakles was aghast.

'Without your knowledge or consent?' Aristarchos pursed his lips. 'That disgraces you both. Or it would, if it were true. In fact, Nikandros was conspiring with a wrestler who claimed the protection of your patronage. We have yet to establish where they got the silver that funded their treason.'

I made sure my face was as calm and assured as my patron's. In fact, we had yet to establish if Nikandros had raised loans using Kerykes land. It would take twenty or thirty days for Aristarchos's men to ride out into Attica and return with any proof either way. But when I'd said I didn't believe it and cited Iktinos's threats to Nikandros, Aristarchos had been convinced.

He was still speaking. 'Philocles was attacked outside the house which you own in Limnai, where Gorgias has been living whenever he returns to Athens. That's where he takes a break from his travels masquerading as a scroll seller called Archilochos. He has gone the length and breadth of Ionia assiduously stirring up resentment and doubt as to the Athenian people's good faith. Do you seriously expect the city's great and good to believe that your son did all this without your knowledge?'

Looking at Megakles's slack jaw and hollow eyes, I was convinced he hadn't known a thing about it, but that wasn't the point.

Voice shaking, he still tried to strike back. 'Accuse my son and you accuse your own, and others besides. You'll make more enemies than me if you drag any of this into court.'

'You think his friends' fathers will rally to you?' Aristarchos raised his voice. 'Lydis!'

The slave reappeared with two letters. He handed them to Megakles. I never did discover what they said but Megakles paled as he read them.

'It's Nikandros who has made powerful enemies for *your* family,' Aristarchos said softly. 'Seeking to take advantage of foolish boys easily led.'

'We'll see about that.' Megakles turned the papyrus sideways as though he was going to tear both sheets in two.

Lydis was too quick, plucking the letters from his hands.

'You honestly think that I'd hand you the originals?' mocked Aristarchos. 'Even if I were so foolish, a letter can always be rewritten.'

Megakles threw up his hands in extravagant fury. 'I cannot believe that you'd condemn your own son. Such cruelty to your family! Such disloyalty to your bloodline!'

'I have three sons still living.' Aristarchos looked at him, as cold and unyielding as marble. 'You have only one.'

I found myself wishing I wrote tragedy. The theatre sees so many Cleons and Agamemnons condemning their nieces and nephews and sons and daughters with foot-stamping denunciations. If I could pen such a brutal judgement delivered with composure as ominous as this, I'd have an entire audience holding their breath.

Megakles looked at the paving, histrionics abandoned. Aristarchos continued serenely.

'Not that I intend to bring such treason to court. I

356

have more than enough evidence to accuse Nikandros of corrupting temple officials, and extorting compliance from others with threats of violence. That's how he secured all the hides from this year Dionysia's sacrifices.'

Lydis had been busy while I'd been trying to trap Iktinos. Aristarchos had always intended to secure a fallback position.

'Tell me,' he invited, 'is he looking to put every other tannery and leather worker out of business or merely to make sure they're obligated to your family? Though I don't suppose it matters. Any jury of honest tradesmen and craftsmen will see a rich man greedy for still more coin, who is willing to ruin men like themselves by destroying their humble livelihoods.'

'There are no laws against securing commercial advantage,' blustered Megakles.

'There are laws against bribery,' Aristarchos pointed out.

'Go ahead then,' Megakles spat. 'Call us before the courts and we'll see who wins. I'll have Glaukias compose my son's defence. Who will you have at your side? This—' he gestured at me, struggling to find some insult bad enough '—comedian?'

Aristarchos's grin reminded me of the crocodile Zosime had drawn for me once. Those lethal creatures were one of the few things she remembered from her childhood in Egypt.

'Strato and Pheidestratos were stupid enough to underestimate Philocles, and they lost.' He waved that away. 'There's no need for you to spend your money on

Glaukias. I have no need to prove anything before a court of law.'

'What?' Now Megakles was thoroughly confused.

Aristarchos raised his voice in a shout. 'Mus!'

The massive slave reappeared. He was carrying a basket so big and so heavy that it was a burden even for him. He tipped the contents onto the paving in the middle of the courtyard. Broken pottery cascaded in all directions. Red dust rose from the slithering, cracking commotion and black chips skittered away from the growing heap.

Mus stooped to pick up one of the shards and handed it to the gaping man. Nikandros's name was scratched through the black glaze, leaving the letters as vividly red as the pottery beneath. All the other pieces said the same.

Megakles looked at Aristarchos, appalled. 'You wouldn't.'

'Oh, I would,' he promised with absolute certainty.

Megakles hurled the potsherd onto the heap. 'It'll be months before someone can call for an ostracism. Not until next year. It'll be two months after that before there can be a vote to nominate anyone.'

'Quite so,' Aristarchos agreed. 'Which gives me plenty of time to secure all the votes I could possibly need to condemn your son. All those tradesmen and craftsmen I mentioned? Athens has what, thirty thousand citizens? Let's say so, for the sake of argument. I'm sure we can persuade six thousand of them to turn out to make sure that he's exiled. They'll have no time for you either, after they've heard about your family's plot to monopolise the leather trade. Then there are your son's cronies' promises to help Metrobios get the same stranglehold on carpenters and joiners.'

Kalliphon and Pamphilos had confirmed that.

'You're putting your trust in artisans?' Megakles sneered. 'The well-born—'

'Let's say a thousand men in Athens are wealthy enough to be called upon to finance festivals and triremes. Maybe fifteen hundred?' Aristarchos leaned forward. 'You think that you can convince them to vote to exile someone else in hopes of saving Nikandros? They're more likely to vote against him, and to make sure their sons and brothers and nephews do the same, once they learn how you and he have hoarded your family silver abroad in order to shirk your share of such obligations to our city.'

Because that's the thing about ostracism, as we'd explained to the Pargasarenes. They'd heard of the custom, obviously, but it turned out they were vague on the detail.

A case for ostracism doesn't have to be argued before a jury. There is no burden of proof. There simply have to be enough votes cast by the People's Assembly, declaring that it's in the city's best interests to send a known troublemaker into exile. Since there are generally a few candidates who've made themselves sufficiently unpopular, a second vote is held to choose which particular man to condemn.

'Athens' citizens, from highest to lowest, won't even have to bring their own potsherds. We'll supply everyone who wants one a token with Nikandros's name on it.' Aristarchos gestured at the heap. 'Though of course they might choose to condemn you instead. No father can truly be innocent of his son's crimes.'

Megakles was sweating now, sickly pale. He couldn't drag his eyes away from the broken pottery. I silently acknowledged that Aristarchos had been right. He'd insisted that uttering this threat wouldn't be enough. We needed to make his son's peril too real for Megakles to ignore.

So Menkaure and Kadous had loaded a handcart with discards and breakages from the alley behind the workshop. We'd been up since dawn sitting alongside Aristarchos's slaves, all laboriously scratching Nikandros's name onto shard after shard after shard. Not that there were six thousand pieces to condemn him here, but we didn't imagine Megakles would count them.

'Of course, someone else may decide to level charges of treason at one or both of you,' Aristarchos mused, 'once they have heard the case for your son's exile. Especially once they've heard these Ionians' evidence.'

That was the Pargasarenes' cue. Tur was the first to appear through the archway, as quick as a hound after a hare. Sarkuk and Azamis followed while Lydis and Mus fetched their stools. Aristarchos welcomed them with a courteous nod.

'Our friends here will investigate Gorgias' rabble-rousing in every town and village he visited calling himself Archilochos. He was there at your son's instigation. If our fellow citizens choose to condemn such treachery before the courts, Nikandros won't be choosing some comfortable city to wait out ten years of exile.'

Aristarchos remorselessly outlined the worse fate that threatened Nikandros.

'He'll be sent to the city's executioner and I don't imagine you'll be permitted to buy him a kindly cup of hemlock. Not when everyone learns that you can afford it because you've conspired to avoid paying what you owe to this city. How do you suppose it will feel, to lie shackled hand and foot to a wooden board, while the strangling collar is tightened? Do you think he'll still be conscious when he's cast out beyond the city walls with the executioner watching over him until he finally dies?'

Megakles looked as if he was about to pass out. He collapsed onto his stool, barely managing not to slide off it and onto the floor. 'He barely clings to life as it is. You accuse him when he lies so grievously injured? When he cannot defend himself?'

'Then what will you do to save him? What will you do for your wife and daughters? If your son is exiled or executed, your death will leave them at the mercy of whichever relatives claim your property is forfeit by Nikandros's disgrace.'

Megakles stared at Aristachos. He tried to speak, only to cough and try again. 'What can I—?'

'Lydis?'

Aristarchos's slave promptly handed Megakles a list of the plotters we'd identified so far.

The desperate man waved the papyrus, whey-faced. 'I can't put a stop to all this! Exiling me or my son won't end it! Even if you called for an ostracism every year, you can only get rid of us one at a time!'

'I need only to cut the head off this snake,' Aristarchos told him with implacable menace. 'That will be example enough. Your son's exile, or your own if he dies, will leave everyone on that list desperate not to be the next man accused. No one will stand by your family once you've been disgraced, not when they realise your crimes implicate them. Far from it. They'll be the first to condemn you, long and loud, to save their own necks from the strangler. They'll be calling on Glaukias and every other writer for hire, paying fistfuls of silver for speeches to explain how grievously the Kerykeds misled them.'

Megakles choked on his despair and buried his face in his hands. Silence filled the courtyard like the threat of a summer storm.

Aristarchos threw him a lifeline. 'You were going to ask me what you can do? Stop aiding this conspiracy. Stop supporting Gorgias. Turn him out of that house in Limnai and withdraw whatever help you've given him abroad. Stop allowing your son's fellow plotters to use your house and hospitality to lure greedy men into their schemes. Stop buying all the hides from the temples and ensure your tanneries deal fairly with the city's leatherworkers.'

Megakles's expression veered from precarious hope to dismay and back again. 'But they will—'

'Nikandros and his conspirators? What will they do?' Aristarchos challenged. 'Run to the Archons and complain that you've thought better of a scheme to undermine this city's peace and stability? That you've repented of your part in a plot to bring down the entire Delian League, for no more honourable goal than making you and your rich friends still richer?

'Point out how much trouble you could make for them, far more than they could ever make for you,' he advised. 'Make sure that they know you've left sealed records of vital evidence with trustworthy allies, to be delivered straight to the Archons, if anything untoward happens to you or your household.

'That's what I have done,' he added, 'in case you get any ideas about sending some wrestlers to beat out my brains in a dark alley, or paying them to silence anyone else.' He gestured at the rest of us.

'I don't ...' Megakles's bemusement convinced me he knew nothing about Iktinos, but he abandoned all protest as pointless.

Aristarchos studied him for a long moment until the fat man hung his head, a guilty blush restoring his florid complexion.

'Most importantly,' Aristarchos continued, 'you will not say a word in opposition when a proposal comes before the People's Assembly next month to make an un-scheduled reassessment of our allies' contributions to the Delian League's treasury. You will convince all the men on that list to stay silent as well. This review will happen at the forthcoming Panathenaia, to ease their burdens before the scheduled reassessment the year after.'

Megakles didn't look up. 'And then?' he asked in a hollow voice.

'Then I will burn the bushel-baskets of evidence that I've gathered,' Aristarchos said calmly. 'Though a denunciation will go to the Archons if anyone here dies a suspicious death, and the records that will prove it most assuredly remain.'

'Will you swear it?' Megakles rubbed a hand over moistly glistening jowls. 'And to leave my son alone, if he lives?'

'On whatever altar and by whichever gods you wish,' Aristarchos promised.

Megakles didn't reply. He lurched to his feet and headed for the courtyard gate. Mus opened it to let him stumble out onto the street.

'Lydis?' Aristarchos's nod sent the slave after the fat man. 'Not that he'd notice a hoplite phalanx in full panoply following him at the moment,' he observed. 'But I think we should know where he goes.'

'Can we be certain that he will yield?' wondered Sarkuk.

I wasn't sure who the Carian was talking to, so stayed quiet. It wasn't as though I had an answer. I had no idea what Megakles would do now.

Aristarchos was more confident. 'I believe he will.'

'And the rest of our enemies?' the Pargasarene persisted.

'Once they learn that we're ready to use ostracism against them?' Aristarchos smiled with thin satisfaction. 'They'll scatter like cockroaches when someone opens a storeroom door. No one will want to be the last to hide, so slow that they get stamped on.'

'Will you truly destroy the evidence?' I hated to think of our hard work going up in flames.

'If he remembers to ask me to swear to it.' Aristarchos

grinned, as mischievous as one of my nephews. 'If I do burn it, what's been discovered once can always be recorded a second time with newly sworn testimony. Lydis has an excellent memory, I can assure you.'

'What are we to say to Xandyberis's family?' Azamis asked quietly.

'Is Nikandros not to answer for that murder, when he's as guilty as the man who wielded the knife?' Sarkuk reached for his father's hand.

For the first time Aristarchos's composure faltered. 'I fear that no good could come of publicly accusing him. He will simply blame Iktinos, and a dead man cannot answer back.'

He heaved a sigh. 'Indeed, an accusation might well do more harm than good. As things stand, I believe this conspiracy will fall apart without Nikandros. Megakles will see to that, if only to save his own skin. But it will be months before the ill feeling that these plotters stirred up finally fades away. If we haul Nikandros into court for this murder, then the city's outraged Ionians will learn that one of their own was foully murdered. Meantime, too many Athenian citizens will feel insulted and unjustly accused for the deeds of a selfish few. The strife that these plotters were hoping for might still boil over, without anyone stoking the fire.'

Tur looked mutinous, cradling his bandaged arm. 'We owe a duty to Tarhunzas—'

'You heard what Megakles said.' I appealed to the older Carians. 'Nikandros lies at the very threshold to the Underworld. Surely we can leave him to the gods and goddesses of the dead? They can pass more certain judgement than any court ordained by men. If he dies, that's divine retribution. If he awakens, his penance is assured, lifelong.'

'I will see to that,' Aristarchos promised.

Sarkuk spoke to his son in their own language, more sorrowful than rebuking.

Tur bit his lip and subsided. Azamis stared up at the sky, blinking rapidly as he fought back tears.

Sarkuk rose and bowed formally to Aristarchos. 'I must thank you, on behalf of Pargasa's council, for all that you have done.'

'I should apologise, on behalf of all honest Athenians, for the troubles that have beset you and yours. There's no recompense I can offer you for the grief of a loss that's beyond mending.' Aristarchos's regret was heartfelt.

I looked up at the cloudless blue sky. There was no crack of thunder, no haunting cry of a wheeling eagle to indicate he'd been heard, but I felt certain that the gods above and below would bear witness to what we'd done here. Now I had one last duty to discharge, at Zosime's insistence.

'Please,' I invited the Carians, 'come back to Alopeke with me. I would like to offer you my household's hospitality today, so that we might all remember each other in happier circumstances before you travel home.'

After their initial surprise, Azamis and Sarkuk agreed. Tur didn't get a say. Aristarchos sent Ambrakis back with us, not as a bodyguard but to carry an amphora of very fine wine.

Zosime and Menkaure were waiting and we celebrated confounding the plotters and a measure of justice for Xandyberis with a long afternoon and evening of good food and companionable drinking as my beloved, her father and the Pargasarenes swapped traveller's tales.

I finally learned that Tarhunzas is the Carians' thunder god, when Menkaure and Sarkuk discussed the temples they'd visited in distant lands and cities. They both assured me that Egypt has monuments to outstrip whatever magnificence Pericles has planned for the Acropolis.

Some day, I decided, I really must travel beyond Boeotia. Even the Carian boy Tur had seen more of the world than me.

Chapter Twenty-Seven

We met in the city cemetery to say our farewells to the Carians. In the field where travellers are buried, Zosime and I watched from a polite distance while Azamis poured oil onto Xandyberis's grave. He used the black-footed white flask that she'd painted for them. It was one of her finest pieces.

Azamis handed the flask to his son and stood with his head bowed. Sarkuk poured his own libation, reciting prayers for the dead in the Carian tongue. Tur stood beside them, still unpleasantly flushed from the fever that had seized him in the days since he was wounded.

That had delayed their planned departure, but now they were due to sail. Spintharos had finally pronounced the wound free from festering and agreed there was no longer any danger of Tur losing his arm to save his life. Zosime and I had sacrificed a cockerel in gratitude to Asclepios this very morning.

'Good day.' Aristarchos arrived at my side, carrying a libation flask of his own. Lydis was a few paces behind him.

'Good morning,' I said quietly, careful not to disturb the Carians' rites.

'Nikandros has woken up.' Aristarchos spoke just as softly. 'His wits don't seem to be addled, or any more so than they were before that knock on the head.'

'Good.' I was glad to hear it. 'Has he admitted to lying about those loans?'

Aristarchos nodded. 'Though he claims to know nothing about the source of Iktinos's silver.'

'I imagine he took care not to know. He wouldn't want inconvenient knowledge getting in the way of his profits.' I didn't hide my contempt.

'I want to know,' Aristarchos said grimly. 'Whoever did this is a heinous enemy and a mortal foe of Athens.'

'We'd be fools to assume this setback will make them give up,' I agreed. 'Perhaps Nikandros can tell us more about Iktinos himself.'

We hadn't been able to find the dead man's family. No one had ever heard him mention which voting tribe or district brotherhood he belonged to. Remembering how he had insisted Nikandros was a citizen without ever claiming such protection for himself, we were starting to wonder if Iktinos was even an Athenian. As to what had happened to any hoard of coin when he died, that remained a mystery.

'You couldn't learn anything from his belt?' Aristarchos prompted.

Hoping for some clue, I'd persuaded the Scythians to let me examine Iktinos's body. His belt was sufficiently unfamiliar that I'd taken it to Epikrates to see if the wizened slave could identify where it was made.

'It's Peloponnesian, though whether it's Corinthian,

Argive or Spartan, Epikrates can't say.' I shrugged. 'And of course, he could have simply bought it in any of those places when he was passing through.'

Aristarchos grunted. 'On his way here, intent on doing Athens harm, with that fat purse he got from someone who wishes our city ill.'

I nodded agreement. 'Where there's one rat, there are ten that you'll never see, ready to plunder and foul your stores.'

'So we must keep an eye out for more vermin.'

'We certainly shall.' I shared Aristarchos's conviction that some enemy of Athens had enlisted Iktinos to seduce Nikandros into treachery, using the boy to plant the seeds of conspiracy in the fertile imaginations of greedy and selfish men.

He went on, low-voiced. 'Kallinos has made his report to the Polemarch. He considers Xandyberis's case closed with Iktinos's death, as we anticipated. He sees no realistic prospect of a conviction, even if someone brought a case against Nikandros. The boy will simply say that he had no reason to think that murder would be done.'

'I'm sure Glaukias would write him some powerful self-justification.' I found I wasn't sorry. I had no wish to stand up in court and try to explain the bloody events in my courtyard. Besides, there had been enough death. Spending half a morning with Iktinos's corpse convinced me of that. I was content to leave Nikandros to face divine justice.

Aristarchos slid me a sideways look. 'Lydis tells me Megakles swears, by Athena and Apollo, that as soon as

Nikandros leaves his sickbed he will spend his days at the Academy, only going to lectures and to the training grounds. When he's not there, he'll be at home busy with further reading and reflection. This will be his offering to repay the gods for saving his foolish life.'

'May his studies prosper.' I spoke more out of respect for Athena than any hope of Nikandros learning lasting wisdom.

'Hipparchos had better prove equally industrious when he returns to the city, though he will be studying at the Lyceum. He should make a better class of friends there,' Aristarchos said acidly, 'whatever his mother may think of their lineage.'

To my surprise, he hesitated. What he said next startled me even more.

'I would be grateful if you'd allow Hipparchos to observe you working on my speeches for the People's Assembly, in favour of the Delian League tribute reassessment. Show him how you use the Carians' evidence as the basis for our case. How you anticipate and counter the arguments you expect will be raised against us.'

'Of course.' I could afford to play tutor while he was paying me so handsomely. Besides, Hipparchos's offences had been in a different league to Nikandros's conspiracy. Aristarchos's son had been arrogant and gullible but if those were ever called crimes, half the young men in Hellas would be driven into exile.

'Thank you.' Aristarchos smiled briefly.

The Carians had retreated from Xandyberis's grave so

Aristarchos went forward to make his own offering and pray to the gods below.

Azamis, Sarkuk and Tur came over to me and Zosime. The old man had been weeping but his faded eyes were at peace. He clutched the oil flask and smiled at Zosime. 'Thank you, dear girl, once again. His family will treasure this gift.'

'It's the least I could do.' She embraced the old man and he kissed her forehead like a grandfather.

I offered my hand to Sarkuk. 'We'll tend his grave at every festival until you return.'

'Until the Panathenaia.' The Pargasarene clasped my forearm like a warrior.

'Commend him to Tarhunzas,' Tur said abruptly. Realising that sounded ungracious, he tried to make amends. 'As well as to Athena and Dionysos. We will entreat Tarhunzas to watch over you and yours, in our gratitude for all you have done.'

'Thank you.' I was willing to accept an unknown god's blessing in this mutual spirit of goodwill.

Aristarchos completed his obsequies for the dead man and joined us. We walked back to the city where Ambrakis and some other slaves waited by the Dipylon Gate with the Carians' baggage. They would escort the three men to Piraeus and see them safely aboard their ship. We said our final goodbyes and watched them set off on their long journey home.

'Shall we find a cup of wine in the agora?' Aristarchos suggested. 'I'd like to hear your ideas for your next play.'

'I've nothing much as yet,' I confessed.

Aristarchos wasn't troubled. 'It's early days. Still, we must make sure that you have enough time to prepare,' he said as we walked down the Sacred Way back towards the heart of the city. 'You want to be ready well before you're called to read for the new year's magistrates. We cannot allow this work on the Ionians' behalf to spoil your chances of being awarded another Dionysia chorus.'

I felt Zosime's fingers entwine with mine. She had no doubt that I would get another chance to compete with a new comedy next year. Aristarchos wouldn't be my paymaster though if I won that honour. No man, however wealthy, could be expected to bear such an obligation for two years in a row. I could only pray that Apollo would send me another such agreeable patron.

As we reached the agora, I gazed up at the Acropolis, at those ancient ruins and the bright new temples replacing them. I wondered what good fortune and unexpected challenges blessed Athena might send me in the months to come.

Meantime, I knew where to get a fine jugful of wine to wash away any lingering sadness after the Pargasarenes' departure. We could sit beneath the plane trees in the agora, discussing ideas for comic plays as we watched the Athenian populace pass by.

I turned to Aristarchos. 'Let me introduce you to a friend of mine called Elpis.'

Acknowledgements

I'll confess to a fair amount of trepidation about embarking on a project like this after decades away from serious academic study. I owe sincere thanks to Tony Keen, for his initial and ongoing encouragement, and for a very useful reading list in the earliest stages of this venture. I am similarly grateful to Edward James, and to Kari Sperring, for reading the first draft with suitably critical rigour, and assuring me that it passed muster as entertainment as well as found the right touch with historical research.

Through the writing and rewriting, I am indebted to Julia and Philip Cresswell for cups of tea and conversation to sustain me before and after visits to the Bodleian, and to the Ashmolean. Their interest and sustained enthusiasm for Philocles's adventures were invaluable throughout the Herculean labour of submissions to agents and editors. I'm similarly grateful to Gill Oliver for her unfailing belief that the book would land on the right desk at the right time, especially on those days when my own stamina was flagging.

Sincere thanks go to Sam Copeland, for putting me in touch with Max Edwards, who is now representing Philocles at Mulcahy Associates. I am hugely grateful to

Max for bringing fresh eyes and excellent suggestions to the final round of revisions, as well as for his indefatigable determination to find the right editor for this book. He's certainly succeeded. Craig Lye at Orion is a pleasure to work with, as well as a consummate professional, and his input has improved this book through each successive phase of editing.

Catching up with thirty years of classical scholarship would have been utterly impossible without the ability to search for, and frequently read, the papers and books most directly relevant to this story via the internet. My thanks to all those academics, institutions and publications who now make their research available online through JSTOR and Academia.edu.

Lastly, but by no means least, thank you to my family, near and far, for all their support.